River Bones

River Bones

Sara Mason Mysteries Book 1

Mary Deal

Titles by Mary Deal

Fiction

The Ka, a paranormal Egyptian suspense
River Bones, the original Sara Mason Mystery
The Howling Cliffs, 1st sequel to River Bones
Legacy of the Tropics, adventure/suspense
Down to The Needle, a thriller

Collections

Off Center in the Attic – Over the Top Stories

Nonfiction

Write It Right – Tips for Authors – The Big Book
Hypno-Scripts: Life-Changing Techniques Using Self-Hypnosis
and Meditation

For Charley Ramirez

Acknowledgements

Many thanks to lifelong Delta friends...

Jim and Glenda Faye Emerson, Courtland, CA

Donna and Bob Nunes, Rio Vista, CA

...who offered valuable insights as we reminisced about our days along the River.

Author photo by *Faces Studio and Salon*, Honolulu, Hawaii

Chapter 1

Blood-red letters filled the top of the news page on the monitor screen...

Serial Killer Victim Identified

Each time Sara Mason went online to read and learn about the Sacramento River Delta, the hometown area she never had a chance to know, her homepage featured headlines about the elusive psychopath. She read the Internet posts with concern and remembered the fear caused by the Zodiac Killer of the 1960s and 1970s. Like with the Zodiac, authorities had no direct clues as to who the killer might be.

Reading the updates always set her nerves on edge. Just after moving into her home she thought she had heard someone walking around her property late at night but could never find a trace of anyone being there. Was she imagining things?

The news went on to disclose...

The graves of two unidentified skeletons did not contain an ID or personal belongings, as was the case with previous burial sites found. Cat bones buried in the graves were the tie-in with previous victims, all found with bones of a small animal.

"A cat," Sara said out loud. Then an intrusive old image came to mind: *A pink dress and a small furry bunny.*

> *Cold case detectives identified one of the two sets of remains as that of Paula Rowe, a convenience store night clerk from Sacramento. She had been missing twelve years.*

Previous reports indicated the victims were placed in the ground with the belongings they had at the time. The killer dug the graves in remote areas near rivers and streams where the ground was soft and damp, promoting decay.

A police profiler indicated the perpetrator presumably lived within the crescent-shaped area where the graves were placed. Remains were found beyond Interstate 80 to the west, Roseville to the north, and east of Rancho Cordova along the American River. Within the crescent extends the entire Sacramento metropolitan area and suburb towns. Most of the victims had been missing for years, some for decades. Considering the graves discovered in recent times did not contain fresh skeletons, it is assumed the killer either left the area or simply quit killing, which law enforcement believe to be unlikely. Now and then, a new name is added to the growing list of missing people, the killer still unknown.

One last item in the Internet article disclosed...

> *Since victims are both male and female, and of differing races, it is difficult to determine a possible motive, except that authorities have an elusive madman on their hands.*

If she was not careful, Sara's imagination could get out of hand. The break-ins were increasing in the barrio where she lived in Puerto Rico for the last three decades. This left her looking over her shoulder and the need to find a safe place to live life grew heavier. Some communities on the island were simply too dangerous, and her neighborhood had become one of them. She needed a place where she felt secure, but never guessed she would find herself clear across the country.

Once deciding to return to live in her hometown area, her first major decision was to look for a house along the river, but not confined to Rio Vista in Solano County where she attended high school. Many people moved into the Delta and built multimillion-dollar mansions along the river. That was not for her.

She slipped into town before Christmas a few months earlier and bought an older house, a present to herself. Wanting to own a Victorian mansion was a lifelong dream that never faded. She found one such place, and to the astonishment of the real estate broker, immediately signed the sales agreement for the full asking price. Upon approval of her offer, she paid cash by way of a wire transfer.

After signing the documents, she overheard the hotshot Sacramento real estate broker boast to someone in another office, "Some wealthy middle-aged blonde woman—a real looker outa' Puerto Rico—just bought that damnable eyesore down along the river." Sara wasn't offended and smiled secretly. She knew she held her age well and knew exactly how she would refurbish the old mansion.

Next, Sara contacted her alma mater, Rio Vista High School, about class reunions. Through high school records, she located Daphine Whelan, her best friend back then. If anyone else remembered her, it was probably as a quiet, bashful girl with stringy blond hair.

"You know what they say about that house," Daphine had warned over the phone.

"The real estate agent filled me in," Sara said. "I don't believe most of it."

Daphine's mood was upbeat, knowing her childhood friend was back in town. But her conversations about the house was somber. "Just be careful, okay? That maniac is still on the loose, and the previous owner of your house is still missing."

Most of the sketchy information about the estate seemed mixed with rumors and gossip. "Daph, the real estate agent filled me in on some of the history of that house. He said that Orson and Esmerelda Talbot were the second owners. They named it *Talbot House*. The original owners built the house in 1928. Since it was only a copy of an original Victorian home, it was unable to be registered with any historical society. The Talbots wished to leave congested city life in the San Francisco Bay Area. Being that 1928 was the year Orson Talbot was born, they interpreted it as an omen to buy. Soon afterward, Mr. Talbot went missing."

"Yes, I've heard the history of that dilapidated Victorian."

"Daph," Sara remembered saying. "Ramshackle or not, I've got my dream house, and nothing will keep me away. Just wait till you see what I do with it."

Daphine's silence through the phone seemed more like a warning.

Though her hands remained at the keyboard, Sara found herself staring at her little sister's photos hanging on the wall covered with old blue floral wallpaper. Little Starla was long dead, but Sara always found a measure of peace just seeing her sister's face. Many times, Sara had placed photos of her youth next to Starla's pictures. Had they been born closer together in years, they could have passed for twins.

"I miss your laughter," Sara said to the close-up of Starla's face. Would Starla's sunny blond hair have stayed that way, as hers had? Would Starla have had the same slender figure, been tall, and offered a chance to do some modeling, as she had? Would the sparkle in her large baby blue eyes have remained too? Or would it have diminished once Starla understood about their parents?

Later, after breaking away from the computer and climbing into bed, Sara became consumed with thoughts of remains being found. The need for caution instilled in her in Puerto Rico had yet to wear off and take its place in distant memory. But for the time being, her sense of self-preservation remained on high alert. The roads were greatly improved since she had lived in the area. The entire Sacramento and Delta regions could be covered by auto in little time. If the perpetrator left Sacramento, he could have gone anywhere. She rolled over and tried to clear her mind and visualize the old house remodeled and decorated. The wind gusted, and the back part of the house creaked. It was a sound with which she had become familiar.

She snuggled down and gave thanks for flannel pajamas, something unnecessary in the Caribbean. Just as she drifted off, she was startled by noises outside. Footsteps. She had heard them before. More like boot steps. On the sidewalk on the north side. Passing right outside her bedroom window!

"Dreaming," she said, half asleep. "Must be dreaming."

She couldn't just lie there if someone was trying to get in. She had been told that homeless people and vandals, at times, got inside. Whoever was out there needed to know the house was now occupied. She threw back the covers and was about to leave her bedroom when she remembered that all the windows were no longer boarded up. With the old heating system not yet working, little to no condensation accumulated on the windowpanes. Nothing to hide anyone inside. If that was not a homeless person seeking shelter—her mind flashed on the serial killer whose whereabouts were unknown—she wasn't about to throw on the lights and expose herself as a captive fish in a goldfish bowl.

"Should have left the windows boarded," she said, whispering to herself. Her bedroom and bath were the only rooms where temporary curtains hung. She listened again but heard nothing else. She dropped to the floor and crept toward the sitting room, watching the windows to see if any shadows moved outside. She felt paranoid and wondered if this was what her neighbors endured in Puerto Rico when intruders broke into their homes. Paranoid or not, it was best to be safe. She watched the windows again.

Nothing moved.

She crept to the dining room doorway, studied the windows, and saw nothing. Passing the fireplace, she made it into the pantry where she waited and listened just off the kitchen.

She heard nothing.

A butcher knife lay in the dish rack where she had left it to dry. She crept low to retrieve it.

More noises... toward the front of the house at the opposite end.

She grabbed the knife, crept back into the pantry, and found a hammer where she had left it when removing old shelving.

If someone were walking around the grounds, she might be able to see them from an upstairs window. She began to climb the dark back staircase between the kitchen and dining room that was once used as the servant's access to the rest of the house. One stair squeaked, and the sound echoed off the walls of the enclosed stairwell.

Sara's heart beat wildly. She held her breath.

Upstairs, she moved quietly from room to room, peeping outside without getting too close to each window. She saw nothing but trees bending against the night sky and heard no sounds other than the wind rushing around the corners and gables of the house.

She felt isolated, sleeping alone in a monstrous four-level, forty-five hundred square foot house, where sounds reverberated off the walls of the empty rooms. Finally, she sat down again on her bed and made sure her cell phone was still on the nightstand. But what good would it do her if she was caught in trouble upstairs and her cell phone was downstairs?

She clutched the phone and argued with herself about calling 911. The noises could simply be her imagination. Still, someone needed to know what was happening.

She hesitated, then punched the code, and waited till someone answered. "Buck, it's me, Sara."

A yawn came through the phone. "It's after midnight, Sara. This old man doesn't stay up working late like you do."

She had stayed briefly with friends Buck and Linette till escrow closed. She sighed. "Buck, I just read more about that psychopath, and now I can't get to sleep. I thought if you guys were still awake, I'd come over and—"

"Don't you dare go outside in the middle of the night!"

"So, you think that psychopath could be in this area?"

"I just want you to be safe. Learn to stay indoors at night when you're alone."

"I-I guess I'm over-reacting."

"You have a weapon?" he asked, through another yawn.

"Yeah," she said, eyeing the knife and hammer lying beside her on the bed. "I'll be okay."

Finally, back in bed, the silence was deafening. How could she even think about letting someone scare her out of her house? To help her relax, as she often did, she thought of innocent little Starla, who loved to sing. Decades earlier, Starla had heard the obscure theme song from the 1960 movie, *Circus of Horrors*, on the radio and felt rapport because of her name. Sara imagined hearing Starla's sweet voice singing, *"... when you feel there is no one to guide you... look for a star."*

Sara shivered, and it wasn't from the old house having no heat. "I hope I can sleep tonight," she said softly. She sighed and glanced at the knife and hammer lying on the nightstand, strategically placed for a quick grab.

Chapter 2

Worrying about the whereabouts of the serial killer caused Sara to lie awake too long. She rose late the next morning, running behind schedule, but finally arriving at her last stop of the day.

Winter debris littered the graves. Sara gathered a fistful of small branches and faded leaves, clutching them so tight the twigs cracked in her hands. She pitched them vengefully against the larger marker.

Three white marble headstones stood side by side in the older, forlorn section of the Elk Grove Cemetery south of Sacramento, unchanged and visible, like her memories. She stared at the inscription on the double-sized stone that said:

MASON
Quincy Everett and Petra Lou.

"Both born the same year and died together. Two of a kind." She grimaced. "I often wonder if you're in heaven… or hell." She stooped down and touched the ground in front of a smaller marker inscribed:

Starla Gay Mason.

"Hi, Sis," she said. "I'm here. It's payback time." She remembered her sister lying in her coffin, her body whole, but ghastly pale.

She always thought of her that way. Whole and sleeping, in her only dress, pink with white bows. At the last minute, Sara had stuffed Starla's favorite toy, a fluffy white rabbit, under her sister's arm.

Sara positioned the arrangement of pink tulips in the built-in vase beside the headstone and waited till the tightness in her throat eased. After moving to Puerto Rico following the deaths of her parents and sister, she imagined her own ashes eventually being strewn in the crystal clear water of the Caribbean Sea. Having returned to her hometown, that plan may change. She always had difficulty thinking of Starla lying in the cold ground. Sara couldn't imagine herself lying beneath the headstone beside Starla, pre-marked for her:

Sara May Mason.

After the purchase of the other two, her headstone was a gift of pity from the marble company; given to a poor family who had nothing and whose only teenage survivor had even less.

She glanced at her parents' marker. "Poor no more," she said. The thought of them depressed her. Sara needed to put the past behind and focus on her exciting new life.

She stared at her sister's name. "I saw him again," she said, smiling and feeling hopeful. She thought about the man she had recently seen on several occasions in a restaurant in Sacramento. The first time, he and his group sat in the booth behind her where she sat alone. His voice was distinct but not boisterous. He spoke of an older brother who had taught him to ride a bicycle and who, long ago, would teach him to ride a motorcycle after the brother returned from Vietnam. The man spoke of his sister as if she were a financial genius. He spoke lovingly of his siblings and parents. Clearly, family meant everything to him. Sara tried not to eavesdrop and felt guilty listening, but his family seemed the kind she could only dream of.

Their group departed ahead of her. As they passed her booth, the man turned and looked her straight in the eyes. He had short dark wavy hair and deep-set brooding eyes like blue-topaz sparklers! Their eyes locked into the kind of stare that made a connection long before words were spoken. He slowed his pace, and his intensity softened. He finally smiled, and his curiously sad expression melted.

Sara had gone back to the restaurant several times and each time saw the man leaving with a couple of other men. Her timing always seemed off. On another occasion, she had walked out of the restaurant just as they walked in.

"Hello there," the man with the blue-topaz eyes had said.

"Hello," Sara said. All she could do was walk away because making an excuse to go back inside seemed contrived.

On yet another of her jaunts to a furniture shop in Sacramento, that same man walked down the street with others. While she sat at the light and wondered how they might meet, he walked into a building on the next block. As she drove past, she saw that the building housed government agencies. She wondered about the man until she realized she was quite taken with him. Or was it his love of family?

"The next time I see him at that restaurant," she said to Starla's headstone, "I'll start the conversation." Sitting at Starla's gravesite allowed her to relax and sort out her thoughts. She had not seen man in the three weeks since. She had to overcome her shyness about meeting men. Some part of her childhood programming still wanted her to believe she didn't measure up. She knew it was wrong to think that way and vowed this was another flawed aspect of her personality that she would overcome. It was never too late to change, and she really did wish to find a new love one day.

Since returning to the Delta, she wondered if anyone would recognize her after thirty years. Would they remember her?

Other than her family's deaths, that were considered just more river drowning, her life back then had been unremarkable.

Another image that stayed with her from her teen years was when the Sheriff had to inform her about the accident. The horrible pictures and images flashed in her mind, fresh as yesterday.

She had stayed home alone to work on a class project. Her parents were late getting home, with Starla. When they drank they were always late. Unbeknownst to her, while she sat doing homework, deputies searched the Sacramento River with grappling hooks just a quarter mile down the levee. They found the old family sedan at the bottom lodged in silt under eighteen feet of water. Her mom and dad, still in their seatbelts, probably drowned easily, having been too intoxicated to know they had inhaled river water instead of air. The divers found scrawny little Starla floating with her eyes wide open in the air pocket inside the top of the car.

"Little Sis," Sara said to the headstone. "You've been my guiding star all these years." She grabbed more twigs and withered leaves and cast them aside without caring, onto her parents' graves. Her fingertips turned red and numb. The gigantic tree nearby was just a sapling when Sara buried her family. She sat cross-legged on the cool grass and stared at Starla's name. Patches of fog slipped in with dusk.

"I learned something else," she said. "We never were poor little white trash girls like they used to call us." She wished she could talk to her sister like they rattled and played when they were young. Memories flooded her mind and jumbled her thoughts.

"Today's Valentine's Day."

Sara remembered that particular holiday as being nothing more than a popularity contest in grammar school to see who would receive the most Valentine cards from classmates. She was lucky to get one or two. Perky little Starla had been deprived of learning how popular she would have been.

"Your name's famous now."

She closed her eyes and then finally opened them. "Mandy died," she said quietly. "But you've been up there watching everything unfold, haven't you?"

Sara felt a chill and huddled inside her jacket. The breeze whipped her hair across her face and wrapped it around her neck. When she looked up, she could no longer see the grave markers in the rows ahead through the oozing white haze.

She remembered the fog of the California Central Valley. The scientific name was Advection Fog. Locals called it tule fog. The condition originated in the San Joaquin Valley. Rains and irrigation would saturate the agricultural area and when a cold mass of winter air invaded the wet valley, moisture in the air thickened and turned into fog. The low-lying blanket of white could cover nearly half of the state for days at a time. In bad years, patchiness in low areas could last well into spring.

Sara gritted her teeth, remembering. Living in Puerto Rico for the last thirty years hadn't dimmed her memories. Tule fog was what surely blinded her drunken father, whose speeding car went flying off the levee road south of the town of Ryde.

She stood, then bent over and scraped more small debris from Starla's grave onto those of her parents. She picked up a spindly dry branch from in front of her own marker and tossed it onto the rest. During a fog, it wouldn't be safe to be on the roads at night. "I'll be back," she said.

With that, she turned to leave and couldn't see her white SUV. She walked carefully in the direction she remembered having parked, arms outstretched to feel her way. A break in the fog came, and she found she had walked past it.

Chapter 3

Sara drove cautiously as she made her way home. When fog blanketed the I-5 in the Central Valley, it could easily cause a multi-car pileup. She strained to see through the windshield and slowed thinking she had found the turn-off. She quickly realized she could have driven into a ditch, and her pulse rose.

"The reflectors," she said, mumbling in frustration. "Where are those…?"

The fog separated momentarily. The faint outline of tombstones in the older, mostly abandoned, Franklin Cemetery came into view in the fading evening light. She breathed easier knowing she had turned onto the correct road.

Several small lights ahead was being cast in different directions as she continued her crawl toward home. Three people with flashlights walked the road, laughing and jumping around on the pavement, inviting havoc into their lives should a speeder come upon them. She stopped to avoid hitting them as they cavorted in her headlights. She could tell they were teens by the way they playfully banged on the hood and peered into her passenger window, yelling like Halloween ghouls. The red flame from one of their cigarettes dragged across the side window. She swerved and accelerated to get past them.

Something vague appeared up ahead.

"Look out!" she said, yelling and stomping on the brakes as a man stepped onto the road a couple feet in front of her. She gave the horn a good long blast. Her SUV spun around, and she felt the front tires drop off the pavement.

An old man's face popped out of the shadows of the fog and headlights and then disappeared again into the gloom. Then a face popped up at the driver's side window, made ghoulish by the haze, with a wide-eyed, open-mouthed, penetrating stare. Sara screamed. Her knee banged the steering wheel when she nearly jumped out of the seat. The face leaned closer.

From out of the darkness, a young male voice yelled, "Hey! Get outta there!"

The old man darted away carrying something with a handle, maybe a hoe or a shovel, as the fog swirled in and erased every trace of him.

Sara remembered the sound of the tires kicking up gravel on the shoulder. "Great! Just great. Now which direction was I headed?"

Someone pounded on the back window. She jumped again. A flashlight beam shone around. It was those teens. One appeared at the driver's side window and knocked. "Hey, you okay?" the boy called out. When she opened the window a crack, he said, "C'mon, we'll get you back on the road." His marijuana breath floated in.

She sighed with relief as the other teens flashed lights and stood along the right shoulder of the pavement. Carefully, the first teen told her how far to back up and then banged on the rear window to tell her to stop, then to pull forward.

When the tires told her that she was back on the pavement, she yelled out the window, "Thank you. I'm grateful."

"Hey," the boy said. His face was a lot less threatening as he came close again. "That's Crazy Ike. He gets off on digging in graveyards."

"And running people off the road," Sara said. "He digs in graveyards?"

"Yeah, he's pretty bizarre," the boy said. The other teens came to stand behind him. "This graveyard's not used much anymore."

"He has a mean dog," the girl said. "A little mangy mutt."

"Oh, yeah," the other boy said as they all leaned in close. "If Crazy Ike sics him on ya, you're supposed to call the cops."

"People go missing out here," the girl said. She shook her head doubtfully. "Never hear from 'em again."

"Nah," the first boy said with a wave of his hand. "That's BS." They stepped away.

"Thanks again," Sara said. She closed the window, waved, and started off, cautiously. Her chest heaved with a long sigh of relief. Perhaps she should have offered the teens a ride, but they were out there, evidently because they wanted to be. She didn't need to be picking up strangers, least of all, any who smoked dope. She continued to strain to see through the fog. "Perfect cover for a serial killer, if you ask me!" she said, realizing her fright was partially caused by the elusive madman newscasts.

The fog came steadily without much clearing between one blanketing haze and the next. Sara had not wanted to be on the roads at dusk at a time like this. She had no experience driving in a fog other than being a passenger in her parent's car. Maneuvering through the blinding white that reflected back the headlights' beams was a frightening experience.

She finally made it onto the narrow winding levee and crept along. She opened the window listening should her tires leave the pavement. She didn't wish to follow her family into the river.

Chapter 4

"A mile and a half to go." She sighed wearily. She hoped never again to be on the narrow, winding levees in such a blinding situation. Her hands were clammy on the steering wheel. River roads weren't equipped with streetlights. "Danged if it isn't dark during a New Moon," she said. Just that one night of the month, even the carefree drove cautiously. Locals who navigated the levees all their lives thought it reckless to hurry along during the dark of the moon.

"The trees," Sara said, straining to see along the levee. "Where are those trees?"

Talbot House was situated about two miles north of Courtland, where Buck and Linette lived.

"Somewhere along here." She leaned forward over the steering wheel. The left side tires suddenly dropped off the pavement and onto the soft shoulder. Screaming, she cut the wheel to swerve back onto the asphalt and realized she had been driving in the oncoming lane. She took a deep breath to calm her pulse and slowly continued to inch her way home. Thinking it was her driveway, she turned the wheel but quickly stopped, before turning too soon. Had she done so, her SUV would have slid or rolled thirty feet down the embankment. She mentally added purchasing driveway lights to her "must buy immediately" list.

"Not exactly the way I wanted to come home again." In her fright, she talked out loud. "Where are those trees?"

As the wind momentarily cleared the fog, the stand of tall eucalyptus trees loomed over her, like foreboding shadows slithering past.

"Another quarter mile."

The imposing image of Talbot House presented itself. Its tall roof spire pointed upward out of the opaque white mist, and dark clouded windows gave an eerie sense. Had she not already seen the house in daylight, she would have been tempted to drive away from the wretched scene and return in the morning. Sara found her driveway just beyond, on the south side of the property, turned, and headed down off the levee. The crunch of gravel under her tires had already become synonymous with being home. She listened, relished the sound, and felt relief. Finally, she pulled into the garage.

The house was built on an elevated earthen pad that sat below the height of the levee but higher than the level of the surrounding fields. It sat back far enough from the levee to showcase an expansive front lawn. She had plans to build a gazebo beside the flagpole under the tall old Pin Oak shade trees. The remainder of the five-acre estate spread south around the garage and east beyond the rear yard. Sara wasn't sure what to do with the empty field. When she described the place to Daphine on the telephone, Daphine had suggested she plant a garden.

"The Delta's loaded with fresh produce," Sara had said. "That's what the Delta's all about." She would plan something else. But first, the rock pile at the back edge by the canal needed to be cleared. The two rusting cattle troughs for holding the salt lick and water would be removed. They were the last evidence of Orson Talbot's use of the property to raise a few heads of beef cattle.

Thoughts of renovating the old house filled Sara with happy anticipation. She burned a lot of incense to rid the place of its stagnant, tired smell. Remodeling was expected to take months, but for her, it couldn't happen fast enough. She liked the name Talbot House and wondered if she should let it stand. What mattered was that she had her river mansion. Having grown up in a rental cottage in shambles, where the roof leaked and the walls groaned with the wind, forced her into dreaming impossible dreams. She clung to those dreams and didn't mind that this house was not an original historic property. She now owned an 1896 Queen Anne Victorian style mansion that deserved a better fate than to stand neglected despite rumors of an alleged resident of the supernatural variety.

"So much for driving in the fog." She intended that time to be her last.

She grabbed the flashlight from the car door pocket and made her way through the empty workshop, situated between the garage and the steps to the back door off the porch and kitchen. It was a good night to stay home. She had plenty of work to do. The company that bought the computer programs she created provided the funds to purchase Talbot House. Now they sent requests to learn her progress on the second half of their deal. She had a year to complete two more programs but might have been crazy for relocating across the country from the Caribbean to remodel a home while completing the contract.

On the steps, the monstrous house with its full basement and attic, and many gables and windows like darkened eyes, loomed above her. She felt dwarfed and wondered if she should have stayed longer with Buck and Linette. Maybe she should have made the Victorian more livable instead of moving in as soon as escrow closed.

After hearing all the rumors about the house, the first thing Sara did before moving in was to re-key the locks. Waking from her first night in the house and hearing questionable noises, the next morning she searched to find what made the intermittent rustling sounds that kept her awake. She stood in the back yard and watched the winter winds whisk dried leaves and twigs up under the eaves. The Delta was rural, with trees and shrubs plentiful. Small branches were easily buoyed along by brisk seasonal wind gusts.

Most of the house noises were repetitive and became familiar. Occasionally, she heard hard thumps in the middle of the night and was unable to find the source. One tree sat too close to the north wall. In its present state of neglected over-growth, the wind might be knocking the branches against a gable, but trees didn't make the sound of footsteps.

Chapter 5

The Asian Festival took place on the first Saturday in March. It would be the first in a string of celebrations throughout the year as Delta residents paid tribute to themselves and their heritage. Sara never had a chance to attend festivities in her younger years, but that was about to change.

Heavy equipment dropped the last concrete roadblock into place where Isleton's Main Street intersected H Street. The sign on the equipment said *Eldon's Crane and Rigging*. Sara smiled and tried to get a look at the operator. She wondered if he might be the same Eldon she knew in school. She could be mingling among former acquaintances and not recognizing them. She wouldn't hide but didn't wish to be seen earlier than planned. She wanted to save what surprise she could for the class reunion. Daphine had said gossiping was the same as it had always been. Out of control. So, word that she had returned might get around anyway.

Seeing old classmates meant a lot. She wanted them to know she had transcended her downtrodden youthful image. She had also grown an inch taller since graduation. Actually, she had nothing to prove. She came back to carry out a life-long dream of owning a Victorian along the Sacramento River. Still, she had a great surprise in store.

Isleton's streets and lanes were narrow and crowded. Tall trees shaded every yard. The closeness enhanced the town's ambiance. Sara found Daphine's house number and parked under the spreading arms of a couple of old maples.

Daphine came outside to greet her and, not wearing a sweater, wrapped her arms around herself in the chill. "Like a lot of homes in this town," she said. "This rental's been refurbished." She seemed self-conscious about her house. Overall, she seemed happy, but hidden in her more revealing moments of conversation was the fact that she struggled to support her lifestyle. Daphine had moved to Isleton after her divorce and rented the house next door to where the movie actor, Pat Morita, grew up. The Morita home melded in on the block with no signs or markers to show that a famous actor once lived there.

"Spring fever's hit me," Sara said.

Daphine's house was full of art canvasses, supplies, and easels too numerous to count. It looked like she had some exceptional pieces of furniture underneath it all. The house was clean, just cluttered. A tiny, crowded corner of the living room, near the window, looked to be where she did her painting.

"Got lots of these in garage sales," Daphine said, motioning to half a dozen easels standing in a corner. "Just when I think I shouldn't buy another, I end up seeing a bargain."

"Surely, you spend most of your time at your store," Sara said, teasing and alluding to the crowded space. They felt instantly comfortable with each other, as before when they were teens. The larger bedroom was glutted with storage articles and didn't invite entry.

"That's my daughter's room."

Daphine nudged her toward the smaller of the two bedrooms, tastefully decorated in pastels of purples and greens. It was the only uncluttered room. In fact, it felt serene and smelled of expensive women's fragrances. "After all these years, you still favor the same color scheme," Sara said.

The tiny house was so full of artist paraphernalia, that Daphine had to move a stack of shrink-wrapped canvasses so they could sit. "There'll be a lot of food up at the fair," Daphine said. Her kitchen didn't look used at all. Soon, she grabbed a video camera and a well-traveled leather tote, which served as both a purse and art supplies bag. During the few times, they had been together, since her return, a drawing tablet always stuck out of Daphine's carryall. When Daphine would see something interesting, she would sketch quickly. It didn't matter where they were. Ideas to paint later, she would say.

They heard the revelry as they walked toward Main Street at the foot of the levee. Sara pulled her jacket close and was thankful she wore comfortable low-heeled boots.

"You that excited?" Daphine asked. "Slow down."

Sara's heart raced. "First-time thrills!" She looked forward to experiencing events she had only heard of when younger.

"More thrilled than when I almost got you a double date for the junior prom?"

"At least now I have something to wear."

They exchanged glances as they walked along, sharing memories and evaluating where they now found themselves in life.

Booths were set up in every available nook and crevasse along the street with the main attractions being in Old Town. Twelve-foot-long grills were filled with various meats cooking. Smoke billowed, and odors teased the senses.

"Let's sample them all," Daphine said, gesturing to some of the booths.

At least one stage was erected on either side of each block. Local talent took turns in the limelight. Bands from Dixon, Sacramento, and Lodi would play. Martial arts masters gave demonstrations and instructed young children. Traditional cultural dances would be performed.

"Mostly, visitors to the area snap up the local arts and crafts," Daphine said. Every store in town did brisk business. Other groups, like the Humane Society, played to the happy attitudes of people in a relaxed frame of mind to find homes for animals.

Sara stooped down to calm a caged dog, a street mutt of a varied mix. It was less than friendly. Dogs with mean temperaments were always the last ones chosen, if ever. She turned to say something to Daphine and found she had wandered off.

A man's large hairy hand eased over her shoulder and into the cage to pct the animal. "Oh!" she said, jumping in fright and falling back on her hands.

The man moved aside. "Didn't mean to scare ya, Missy," he said, smiling strangely. The gangly man's waistband was held too high by suspenders, looking like his pant legs were cut for high water. He wore a knitted dark blue skullcap and seemed out of place among the crowd. He reminded her of old pictures of her long-dead mid-west uncles in worn-out farm clothes shrunken from too much washing. The dog continued to bark. "If people looked after their pets, animals like this one wouldn't have to be put down," he said in an accusatory tone.

He had a point, but the truth was, this dog had been born and deserved a home. The man moved away as Daphine approached.

Later, Sara and Daphine saw him again. He leaned against the corner of a building groping his genitals as a woman walked past. They looked away before he caught them watching.

"I'd say he has a problem," Daphine said under her breath. "And it isn't necessarily on his south end." Daphine hadn't changed much. She had always been straightforward. She could be serious and laughable at the same time. Yet, many of her remarks stretched thin her aura of elegance and sophistication.

They saw the gangly man again in another location down the street. Sara caught him watching them, but he turned away quickly. He didn't participate in any activities, just stood alone watching people and taking long pulls off a cigarette.

After firecrackers exploded and the Chinese dragon parade wound its way out of the area, rolling and thunderous drumbeats sounded.

"Is that what I think it is?" Sara asked.

"C'mon," was all Daphine said as they hurried back toward F Street. People converged on one of the staging areas where a huge banner had just been hung and announced *Taiko Drummers*.

"I always wanted to bang on those," Sara said as the drummers warmed up. The Latin music Sara came to understand in the Caribbean taught her much about rhythms. Taiko drumming was high on her list of things yet to experience.

The lean yet muscular, costumed drummers, including two women, beat out a rhythm as they exploited their instruments and choreography. While Daphine filmed a bit and then sat on the curb and watched, Sara found it difficult to stand still.

After they had the crowd enthused, one of the drummers called out, "Who would like to beat on the drums?"

Sara's arm shot up and she was chosen with others. Daphine positioned herself to film the event. Sara gave it her all and felt entranced.

Afterward, the lead drummer stood in front of her and bowed.

She wanted to scream "*Yes! Thank you!*" but doing so would be disrespectful. She handed the sticks back and bowed in gratitude.

Once off the stage, a young girl stepped up to her and offered her a pair of sunglasses. "They're yours," she said. "They fell off your head."

Sara bent down to give the girl a hug and watched her timidly run away. Then Sara saw the vulgar man standing in the distance watching.

"Over there," Daphine said, gesturing discreetly with her eyes in the opposite direction. "Look. That's Crazy Ike. Stay clear of him. He was investigated for all those murders. Hasn't been cleared as far as I know."

Chapter 6

The March rains hadn't fallen all night. Sara was already up. The sun shone brightly. Tule fog had vanished, but frost laid down a blanket of sparkling white in the very early hours.

While orchard, field crop, and equipment maintenance went on all year, when the weather began to clear in March, more and more farm vehicles glutted the levees.

Sara stayed busy with remodeling plans. No former acquaintances sought her out. After thirty years of being away, a whole new generation of residents had evolved.

Gravel crunched. Someone honked. A curious dream about a man pointing to something dissipated from memory. She had been having that evocative dream off and on for the last several years. She thought the dream would change or vanish after having moved across the country, but it seemed to have followed her. Light footfalls ran up the concrete steps at the side of the house, and someone knocked at the porch off the sitting room.

"Sara? Sara May, you up?"

Sara crossed the sitting room and stepped into the entryway. Through the stained glass window of floral and birds, Daphine's dark hair shone like sheen in the bright morning light.

"Hi, Daph," she said as she opened the porch door. She and Daphine hugged again, like schoolgirls.

Daphine's sharp classic features held the years well. Her sea green eyes still sparkled. She walked in talking and shrugged out of her jacket as it rustled with the sounds of rich, soft leather. Her sweater and brown pleated slacks accentuated her flat stomach and slender figure. Like Daphine, Sara, too, stayed slender from all the outdoor activities she enjoyed in Puerto Rico, and her hair remained sun-streaked.

"I can't believe you bought this creepy old place," Daphine said as her gaze darted about. She slipped back into her jacket. "How you gonna keep this behemoth warm?"

"Lucky for me, the Talbots installed an elaborate heating system. It was the newest thing they did before… All I have to do is bring it up to code."

"Or wear winter clothes indoors."

"You always were a clothes hound.

Daphine stepped back and looked her up and down. "What about you, Miss Designer Jeans." She smiled and got a far-away look in her eyes. "You know what I remembered about us just now?"

"Tell me," Sara said. "Since I've remembered things I haven't thought of for decades."

"Your mom used to collect cast-off clothes to make those country style braided rugs to sell."

"Oh, my goodness!" Sara shook her head. "You remember that family with all those kids?"

"We used to sneak clothes from the rummage bag to give to them before your mom could shred them into strips to braid." She shook her head. "What memories." They stood a moment, studying one another. Finally, Daphine said, "I want to see this place again."

"Bought one big old house." Sara forced a crooked smile. "Had to hire a cleaning team just to remove the build-up of dust and rat droppings."

They stepped into the sitting room. Daphine studied the antiquated fireplace. The room contained few furnishings, an old but comfortable sofa, a chair, and one end table.

"Compliments of the Aldens," Sara said. "To hold me through the renovations."

"Buck and Linette did well with their retirement home."

"With all those antiques and that swimming pool?"

"Buck said he didn't care that some of the neighbors—our own classmates, mind you—gossiped about the way he remodeled that historical place."

"Now it's my turn," Sara said. "And I don't care what people say about what I do to this house either."

Daphine looked up like she expected grand lighting in a house of that design. Capped off wires hung out of the scrollwork in the center of the ceiling where a fixture once hung.

"Missing," Sara said. "Used to be a chandelier in the dining room, this room, and the parlor." She pointed toward the front room of the house.

"Oh, it's the parlor now?" Daphine asked, feigning a hoity-toity attitude and flipping her hand in the air. "I have a living room at my house."

Sara laughed. The empty house gave their voices a hollow quality. "This old castle will look like a showplace when I'm done."

"If you don't end up jumping out of your shorts."

Sara regarded her with a keen eye. "If there's a ghost hanging around, it's about to get evicted." She remembered learning about the voodoo and magic phenomena that permeated the diverse cultures of the Caribbean. Such practices were real, and she had even attended one such event. Sara wasn't afraid of ghosts, but she needed to proceed with caution.

"Remember, they think that's old man Talbot's spirit floating around," Daphine said. "He was never found."

Sara had heard the story more than once. "I'm not about to abandon my dream because of rumors."

"Talbot was much loved," Daphine said. "Did you know that?"

"Heard a few things."

"Anywhere he found a mug and a chair, he sat and talked about Delta politics, coffee grinds, or gold panning. Always with humor." Daphine looked around. "Let me see the house. I looked at it when it was on the market years ago."

"I take it you believe in ghosts."

"Well, I didn't, but a few years ago, I was driving by on a clear night…."

"And?"

Daphine's eyes opened wide. "I saw a light floating around inside here."

"The house was boarded up, wasn't it?"

"Yeah, but that's what made it scary. Dim light filtered through cracks of some of the window boards. No one was supposed to be inside."

Chapter 7

Sara led Daphine through the rooms on the first floor. In the dining room, she said, "This fireplace will be removed."

"Taking it out?"

"Why do I need two fireplaces? We'll be knocking down some walls to showcase these servants' stairs between the kitchen and this room."

"Servant's stairs?"

"You've never heard that term?" Sara rolled her eyes, but proceeded to explain anyway. "In Victorian houses, servants occupied the back bedroom and used these cramped staircases to access the various floors. The homeowners wouldn't think of using this staircase." Sara laughed while Daphine pranced around, shielding her eyes behind a hand, and pretending to be too good to even look at the back staircase.

They peeked into the temporary bedroom on the north side where Sara confined herself, pending renovations. Other than the Alden's loaned twin bed and dresser, she had purchased a new stereo system to enjoy her music. A commercial grade computer and peripheral equipment, also new, filled one end of the room. She needed to complete her obligation of two more games. The new equipment better served her programming. She also wanted to start traveling and could now afford to do plenty of it.

Several years earlier, she realized her only accomplishment was becoming a San Juan tour guide, herding people around to see landmarks. Life had to offer more than that or she would go loony. Her frustration built, at times, to such a frenzy as to render her immobile. Then, out of boredom, she tried her hand at using a computer at an electronics expo. Doing so felt as if a dormant part of her mind exploded into activity.

"Oh, there's little Starla," Daphine said as she stared at the small framed photos that hung near the window. Daphine's expression sobered. She felt the tears rising and slipped out of the room silently.

They continued down the hallway to the front foyer with its traditional black and white flooring squares.

"You leaving these in?" Daphine saw everything through the eyes of an artist.

"Replacing them with more of the same. Every mansion I've seen and liked had these entry tiles."

The large empty parlor sat to the left on the south side of the house along the driveway and also overlooked the front porch, yard, and levee embankment to the west. They climbed the front staircase. "Careful," Sara said. "Some of the spindles are missing. The handrail is weak." Halfway up, a window on the landing provided another view west, and north along the levee to the stand of eucalyptus.

Daphine snooped around like she was a potential buyer. She walked into each of the three bedrooms and into the only lavatory on the second floor, which didn't have a tub or shower.

"I'm claiming half of this linen pantry to enlarge this bathroom," Sara said, measuring back down the hallway several feet. "Got to be able to bathe on this floor too."

They came to the bedroom at the back.

"Victorian homes had bedrooms this large?" Daphine asked.

"Used to be the servant's room. The Talbots doubled the size by extending over the back porch."

"So, the renovated bathroom is for the master bedroom quarters," Daphine said. "The rest of your guests will have to use the downstairs john?"

"Actually, no. I'm dividing that northwest bedroom and installing a third bath."

They climbed the narrow staircase only high enough to push open the attic access so Daphine could peak in. The attic had been cleaned as well, but still looked forlorn. They returned to the first floor via the split staircase into the kitchen with its borrowed table and chairs. The staircase provided access to all four floors, from the basement to the attic access.

"This house is a maze," Daphine said. She never stayed still and sometimes turned circles in the room taking in one continuous view.

Sara smiled, amused at her lifelong friend, who was even more delightful to know. The house was much bigger than Sara had hoped for, but the third owners who purchased from the Talbots decided to unload the tormented mansion, instead of refurbishing.

The smell of fresh coffee filled the air. Clean mugs sat upside-down on a kitchen towel on the old linoleum-covered countertop.

"Seen any ghosts?" Daphine asked, accepting and sipping. "You seem a little rattled this morning."

"I've been visiting Starla." Sara wasn't sure about revealing her recurring dream.

"That spooked you?"

"Not really, I guess."

"Your hands were shaking just now. You eat anything this morning?"

"Hey, I'm fine."

"I don't hear it in your voice." If Daphine was anything, she was as persistent as when she was a teenager.

"Let me show you around the outside," Sara said, heading for the back doorway with her mug.

Sara led the way down the concrete steps to the workshop between the house and garage. Streams of sunlight intermittently broke through the clouds from the east. The air was fresh and smelled of rain. "Talbot added this," she said, pointing to the workshop, which was a little wider than a single-car garage.

"Strange," Daphine said, placing her hands around the warm mug. She turned and studied the direction the Sun would pass. "Men usually build a workshop to catch the south side sun, to get as much daylight as possible, so they can enjoy longer hours at their work or hobby. Should have been built behind the garage."

"The real estate agent said Talbot didn't want to build out into the field," Sara said. The workshop sat adjacent to the garage side. The roof connected over the back steps and porch off the kitchen and nicely covered the walkway. "The house has a full basement. I might tear this shop down."

They walked up the driveway as gravel crunched underfoot. More steps led to the basement entrance underneath the entry where Daphine knocked earlier at the sitting room doorway. Sara opened the lower door. Light filtered in from horizontal windows just above ground level on the opposite side of the building. "No way am I coming down here to do my wash." The large dingy room smelled musty. "I'm setting up the laundry area inside the back porch." The basement contained what was left of the built-in tables and workbenches Talbot installed to process his gold and make jewelry.

"So, seen any ghosts?" Daphine seemed not about to let up.

Sara closed the door, and they headed toward the front yard. "Heard something."

Daphine jumped back and nearly spilled her coffee. "Who? When? Some people have both heard and seen the ghost."

"I thought I heard," Sara said, smiling. "I probably imagined it, since everyone's prepped me for it."

"What did you hear?" Daphine's eyes were intense. She hugged herself.

"Could have sworn I heard someone walking around the property when I first moved in." She rolled her eyes. "Buck says it's my imagination."

"The spookiness won't stop till you leave the place." Underneath it all, Daphine seemed to enjoy the mystery surrounding Talbot House.

"No chance. I'm staying."

In the front yard, Daphine said, "Every old mansion has one of these."

The tip of the flagpole poked up as high as the winterized branches of the tall old Pin Oaks. Stone steps between the trees led up to the mailbox at the top of the levee. Next, they walked around the north side of the house, passing the wrap-around front porch.

"Hey, look at that," Daphine said, pointing at the ground level basement windows.

Sara bent in closer. Pry marks rimmed the window frame. "Someone must have gotten locked out at one time."

"Those look fresh to me," Daphine said. "See the difference in the wood tones?" The artist in Daphine would notice that.

Sara looked again. The window frame was old, weathered and gray, while morning sunlight across the interior of the marks exposed a light brown. "Would be hard to say how old those are," she said. "With the house standing vacant so long, the curious, or the homeless, might try to get in." She motioned for Daphine to follow. "I'm replacing all the windows anyway."

Daphine gasped. "Wait!" She stooped down quickly and ran fingertips across the concrete. "What are these?"

Sara turned to look where Daphine pointed and only recognized the old concrete walkway. "So?"

"Fresh marks," Daphine said. She sat her coffee mug on the walkway beside a mark.

"Marks?" Sara asked, amused. "What marks?"

"I'm not kidding, Sara. Look."

The concrete had been hit with something that formed a fresh scar with a gentle crescent shape that showed whiter concrete underneath the surface. Daphine ran her fingers across the mark again and then found others. "Why here? Why outside these windows with the pry marks?"

Sara bent down. "What do you suppose made those?"

"Clearly, a shovel," Daphine said. "Someone pounded a shovel down in anger when they couldn't get inside. The marks are fresh. Look, here's a chip of concrete that the wind hasn't blown away."

Sara remembered Buck's admonishment and wasn't sure she wanted to hear any more. "Maybe the cleaning people made the marks."

A lawn of weeds struggled to grow around the back, over the house pad and down into the field. Without having had regular care, the ground felt hard-packed and dry underfoot.

"With those marks on the concrete, maybe you really heard someone," Daphine said.

"Ghosts?" Sara asked, playfully reversing her suspicions. "Maybe we should go hear the details straight from Esmerelda Talbot herself. Isn't that when people say the ghost stories began, when her husband went missing?"

"Hey, I'm game," Daphine said, grinning ear to ear. "Let's go visit Mrs. T."

Chapter 8

Sara and Daphine had planned to go to breakfast and then view some new art Daphine wanted to hang in her gallery. Sara hoped to find some paintings of the Delta for her new home, but visiting Esmerelda seemed the more exciting thing to do.

Daphine left her van parked in Locke. On the way, they stopped at a small shop on the levee in Walnut Grove and bought a bouquet of purple tulips. They passed through town on the east side of the river and then crossed over.

"If I remember correctly, this is called the *Miller's Ferry Swing Bridge*—"

"Over Georgiana Slough," Daphine said. "We're on the back side of Andrus Island now."

The morning mists had cleared, but they still needed to have the heat turned on. From atop the levee, they had a three hundred sixty degree view of the horizon, all the way to Mt. Diablo to the southwest. On a clear day, the tallest peaks of the Sierras came into view in the east. In the distance, flocks of migrating birds darkened the sky.

"Won't we be barging in?" Sara asked. "Shouldn't we have called?"

"No need. I've already met her a couple of times. Well, some time ago. She may not remember me."

"Then we should call." Sara reached to pull her cell phone from her waistband.

"Nonsense," Daphine said, touching her and stopping her. "Rumor has it Esmerelda's a lonely old woman who welcomes visitors."

Certainly being in the seventies was not old. "She doesn't get out?"

"Usually real busy with her facility there, but I understand she's slowed down some."

After nearly three miles of winding levee road, a green and white sign along the levee shoulder appeared with the name…

River Hospice

An earthen ramp angled down off the embankment and opened into a parking lot at the back of the main patient facility to the left. A private home and separate parking area stood to the right. Sara stopped in the middle, momentarily surprised by the lush grounds, with farm fields over-wintering in the background beyond a canal.

Tall oaks and elms sheltered white buildings. Trees lined the main walkways. Expansive lawns beyond the main building offered sitting areas with benches or tables and chairs under more shade trees. Winter flowers, like freesia, anemone, and irises put out color spots everywhere.

"Looks like Esmerelda really needed our bouquet," Sara said with a chuckle.

"Well, I don't see any tulips growing," Daphine said.

Several Mexican laborers wearing blue work clothes began wiping morning dew from the furniture.

A house on the right side of the driveway, and painted dark green, stood on numerous crisscrossed two-by-fours and other supports so that the living area was equal to the height of the levee. A squirrel scampered out of the weeds underneath. Many of the houses close to the levees were built up high in case the levees sprung a leak. Even the patient facility was elevated four feet, though the cottages, some of them new, were barely a foot off the ground.

The dark green home had what looked to be a recent add-on deck with outdoor furniture. Trees also sheltered the house and the nearby garage. The smell of coffee invited.

"May I help you, ladies?" a rugged looking man in a white uniform asked as he approached from the main building. Traces of an accent said he was originally European. He ran his fingers through his tousled blond hair. Sunlight illuminated patches of gray at the temples.

Daphine leaned down to see out of Sara's side. She straightened as the man bent down to lean on his arm at the opened window. "We heard Mrs. Talbot welcomes visitors," Daphine said, smiling.

"I'm Sara Mason." She offered her hand.

"Fredrik Verner here," he said with a warm smile, shaking her hand. Then he stuck his face inside and offered his hand past Sara. He seemed European prim and proper, all class and protocol. He noticed the flowers lying across Daphine's lap and smiled out of the corner of his mouth. "You're Daphine. You have one of the galleries in Locke, right?"

Daphine seemed pleased. "Yes, I do," she said modestly.

"I remember you," he said, pulling himself back out of the window though he still leaned. "I tried to buy a painting from you... at least ten years ago."

"Ten years?"

"A surreal, supernatural looking piece. *Fleeing Hell* was the title on it. It was signed 'DEW', and you wouldn't tell me who this 'DEW' person was."

"Not authorized to divulge personal information on the artists," Daphine said. Her eyes twinkled as if she enjoyed the mystery of it. Quality sold most art, to both visitors and locals.

"I tried to find that artist and never could," he said, shrugging. "I still remember that painting." He stepped back and pointed. "Park over there."

They pulled into the driveway behind the house. The garage appeared to be the original structure with sagging eaves and timbers and double doors that manually opened outwards. Only the residence had been remodeled. Fredrik sprinted up the tall flight of stairs as another car pulled out of the parking area on the other side and headed toward the levee. As Sara climbed out of her SUV, she thought she recognized the man in the car but wasn't sure. He was too far away, and she caught only a glimpse of him from behind as his head jerked back quickly, as if he wanted to see something he had missed.

Fredrik was already on the deck as Sara and Daphine climbed the stairs. The door opened, and a woman stepped out as they reached the top. She wore a green Chinese lounging robe and silk pajamas with short-heeled transparent slippers. An impeccably groomed black standard poodle followed behind her. The poodle's coat was the same color as the woman's hair.

"ET, you have guests," Fredrik said.

"ET?" Daphine asked, blurting it out. "You call her ET?"

Esmerelda had a throaty laugh. "Esme, Mrs. T, ET," she said, putting a hand to her chest. "I've been told I'm from another planet." Her voice was lusty with age, but every bit feminine, even sweet. In addition to the bevy of huge diamonds in her wedding ring set, on her right-hand ring finger was a band about half an inch wide, encrusted with fiery gemstones.

"For you," Daphine said, handing her the bouquet. "From us."

"Why, thank you, ladies," Esmerelda said. She seemed deeply moved, paused a moment, then said, "I see you've met my director." She patted Fredrik's shoulder. "He runs the place."

The yaps of puppies came from inside the house.

After introductions, Fredrik excused himself to continue his rounds.

Esmerelda grabbed his arm. "Tell the aides for me, will ya? Don't let old Jonas piss in Tripp's irises again."

Fredrik smiled politely and walked away, accepting the remark like it was all part of the day. He seemed to have sophisticated mannerisms and might have hidden his embarrassment behind the smile.

"Glad to see new faces," Esmerelda said. "A lot of sightseers out these days." She gestured toward the levee road and seemed dismayed. "Not too many come to see us though." She turned and looked out over her property. "This is a place for the old and dying, and I heard that townspeople stay away because of my groundskeeper."

"I've seen him around," Daphine said. "Wears his pants high up under his armpits with his nuts hanging halfway down his leg."

Sara gasped. She and Daphine shared a lot of naughty girl-talk as youngsters. Nothing said went any farther. That's why she trusted Daphine, but being reunited might throw Daphine back into that old naughty habit.

Esmerelda slapped Daphine's shoulder. "I adored you when we first met. Where the hell have you been keeping yourself, girl?"

Sara breathed easier. Daphine really hadn't changed. At times, her ability to slice and dice the conversation knew no restraint.

The pups continued to whine inside the screen door.

The poodle stood poised at Esmerelda's side. "This is my girl, Mimie," Esmerelda said. "Mimie la Jolie." She stroked Mimie's back. Mimie whined low noises of approval and her tail, with a coiffed puff on the end, flicked back and forth in a blur. "Come on in," Esmerelda said.

As she opened the screen door, two very young pit bull puppies ran out; one a deep chocolate brown, the other, coffee with a hint of cream. They wiggled and squiggled and Esmerelda, holding the bouquet, couldn't catch them. Just as they neared the stairs, Sara scooped up the chocolate one. "Get that one, Daph!" She did, and still, the pups wiggled and licked and yapped.

"Feisty little kids," Esmerelda said. "Just two months old and they already know how to recognize a friend."

Chapter 9

Esmerelda's home was over-decorated but adorable. Her antique furnishings told of a woman with taste. Sadly, her life was reduced to a crowded two-bedroom farmhouse with a sun porch to make up for the small living area. It was no comparison to the size and grandeur of Talbot House.

The sideboard in the dining area was loaded with fancy dishes on display stands and a few framed photos. In the front was a wedding photo of Esmerelda and Orson. He was tall and very thin, she, a classic beauty in her youth. On the left was a photo of a younger Orson, maybe a college photo. On the right was a photo of Esmerelda when she, too, was young, though she had changed some with age. Her hair was lighter then. Perhaps she dyed it now to hide her gray. Sara had to smile. Maybe that stylish woman dyed her hair to match her poodle.

"Have you named them?" Sara asked, focusing on the pups again.

"Was hoping to find a home for them," Esmerelda said, motioning for them to sit. She pulled her cell phone off her waistband and turned it off, and then went into the kitchen and returned with the flowers in a vase. "Let their new owners give them names."

"Puppies need names right away." She smiled, somewhat embarrassed. "I studied a little about dogs," she said, trying not to sound braggy. She wanted to have another pet but hadn't made up her mind since she also wished to travel a bit.

"I call them 'Babies' or 'Sweeties'."

Sara checked both pups. The dark brown one was a male, the lighter one female. "What about…?" She pursed her lips.

"What have you got?" Esmerelda asked as she sat down.

"*Choco* for the male, *Latte* for the female."

"Choco… Latte…?" Daphine asked, laughing.

"Magnificent!" Esmerelda said. "Why couldn't I come up with something cute like that?"

After they called the pups by their new names a few times, Choco begged to get into Sara's lap and then resumed licking her face.

"Got them from the same breeding kennels where I got Mimie. Unfortunately, the woman who owns the place said these two were not the picks of the litter."

Choco wouldn't stop licking. "Does it really matter?" Sara asked. She was overjoyed that Choco had taken so well to her. Latte lay on her back in Daphine's lap content to have her stomach rubbed.

"The owner's bitch had a litter larger than they expected, so the lady wanted to get the puppies out into the public eye." She shrugged. "I didn't know pit bulls would be so difficult to place."

"Sounds more like the woman was hoping you'd fall in love with them," Daphine said.

"Well, she was right about that." Esmerelda rolled her eyes. "But three dogs in this little house?" She paused a moment, then said, almost cautiously, "An auto dismantler in Sacramento wants them."

"Why?" Daphine asked defiantly. "He'd just turn them into junkyard dogs."

Sara groaned. She held Choco up in the air as he kicked and squirmed playfully. The conversation came to a lull.

"I wanted to meet you, Esmerelda," Sara finally said. "I'm the person who bought Talbot House. I'll be remodeling."

Esmerelda seemed dismayed and happy at the same time. "You must have read my mind. I was thinking about dropping in to introduce myself."

The ice had been broken. Sara intuitively knew that she liked this woman. "You're welcome anytime. In fact, I hope you visit often."

"I'm glad you're restoring it. I loved that house." Esmerelda looked away like it was painful to discuss something that was once her prized possession. She excused herself and stepped into the kitchen for a few minutes and came back with a tray of tea and wafers with jellies and cheeses.

"You are too kind," Daphine said. She reached to help herself soon as Esmerelda gestured.

"Nonsense. I used to entertain a lot." She got a far-off look in her eyes. "No one to cook for now."

"How about the patients?" Sara asked.

"Too old," Esmerelda said. "They're stomachs are too sensitive for my rich food." She reached down and plopped a cracker into Mimie's mouth. The pups demanded one too. "Sara, girl," she said. "When you get your mansion ready for a housewarming, how about letting me do the cooking?"

"Wha-at?" Sara was surprised at the warm proposal. "I'll have it catered. You'll be my special guest, okay?" From all that she had heard, she already thought of Esmerelda as a grand dowager of the Delta. No way would she allow this woman to labor over her stove.

The conversation switched to Orson Talbot. Sara discreetly watched Esmerelda's facial expressions as she spoke of the past. Her demeanor indicated deep feelings held in check, not just for the loss of her home but also for the fact that her husband disappeared many years back without a trace.

"I know he's gone," she said. "I had to stop his Social Security checks, and his number hasn't been used. He wouldn't stay away. That was our dream house together." She took a deep breath and let it out as she stared at the floor. "I've had him declared dead. It's the only way I could get extra funds to keep our dream alive." She gestured outward toward the facility.

"What do you think happened?" Sara asked.

"They said he must have wandered too far back into the hills and got lost. He was panning for gold to make his jewelry, you know."

Esmerelda said that Orson had raised cattle for income on the acreage behind Talbot House. After a few successful years and subsequent savings, they established River Hospice. Fredrik Verner was a nurse visiting from Sweden and had boarded with them for a month one summer. It was Fredrik who noticed the closest place for the elderly was in Sacramento, thirty miles away from Walnut Grove, and far away from family support. Orson and Esmerelda decided to use much of their retirement pensions and established River Hospice. The existing residence on the property would be their home when they became elderly and needed twenty-four-hour care. Till then, Fredrik moved from Sweden, and they let him live in it while the old farm buildings were being refurbished.

Sara scooted forward in her chair. She wanted to hear more about Orson. "What about bears or mountain lions, maybe vandals? Surely, lots of animals and people wander in the hills above Placerville."

"No blood. No signs of a struggle. Nothing." She sighed. "His truck was still there. Animals probably scattered his bones, wherever he died." She looked straight at Sara and said, "You don't look like a person who spooks easily."

"Nope," Sara said. "Rumor has it, people have seen a ghost lurking in Talbot House."

"It's Orson," Esmerelda said, lightly slapping her knee. "It started a few weeks after he went missing. Right after he disappeared, I used to talk to him all the time—told him I was finishing that workroom he started." Her eyes began tearing. She stood and walked to a window and looked out over the levee. "Orson loved to play with gold. He had a sense of humor too. He paid a bunch of money to bring iron pyrite rocks down from Placer to use in place of gravel for the base of the workshop floor."

"Fool's gold rocks?" Sara asked.

"Exactly," Esmerelda said, wiping her eyes and turning to face them again. She tried to smile. "The rocks were delivered late. Supposed to be delivered during the week so the concrete could be poured before he left to go panning again."

"He went missing late in the year, didn't he?" Daphine asked.

"November '95. Days were getting shorter. Was to be his last trip that year before bad weather set in." Esmerelda put her hand to her forehead like she was trying to remember. She related that the rocks were delivered on the Friday that Orson was scheduled to leave. They spread the dump-load out for the base of the floor and covered it with a tarp over the weekend to keep leaves and debris off until the concrete could be poured the following Monday.

"Then Orson left?" Sara asked.

"Right after we spread the rocks. I stayed at a friend's house in Walnut Grove that weekend, catering her affair," Esmerelda said, smiling warmly. "The concrete for the floor was poured that Monday. Orson was to be away at least two weeks, but he hadn't even called to check on the concrete—or just to talk to me— and that was strange." Her voice caught. "I thought he'd be home when the concrete cured, but he never came back."

"I'm so sorry," Daphine said, reaching over and touching Esmerelda's hand as she sat down. Daphine always exhibited heart-felt empathy for people and events.

"The Placer Sheriff had to go search for him because cellular didn't reach that far back in the hills in those days. If Orson wanted to call me, he'd have to drive into Placerville to use a regular phone."

"It was you who notified the Sheriff?"

"Yes, Orson would have called. He was excited about the shop, and he would have called. He always had to file a panning permit, so they knew exactly where he was to be. They found his campsite but no trace of him." She breathed heavily, having great difficulty retelling the past. "Search party said his full ration of supplies were unused. His truck was locked. He hadn't even unpacked his tent. They believe he got lost soon as he arrived."

"That's scary," Sara said. "Of course, no one had reason to look for him right away, till you called the Sheriff."

"I kept telling him," Esmerelda said as she tapped her temple signifying sending mental messages. "I was finishing that room, and I expected him to come home and see our dreams coming true."

Sara shook her head sadly. "I appreciate you sharing this with us." It brought up emotions she still felt about her own loss.

"After I finished that shop, that's when I began seeing his spirit."

A cold chill ran up Sara's spine. "You can pinpoint it, right to that time?"

Esmerelda smiled bravely but didn't answer, like a person who knew what she was talking about. "C'mon, I'll show you the facility before the trainers arrive for the pups." She disappeared into her bedroom to change and returned carrying a black jacket, wearing sleek black slacks, and a white silk blouse. She truly had great taste. She picked up the tray of edibles and took them into the kitchen and closed the door to keep the animals out till they returned.

"Oh, let's take the babies," Daphine said. "I love them."

"Okay. I'm not supposed to leave these pups alone anyway," Esmerelda said. Pets have a fear of being abandoned. "The aides sometimes take them to visit the patients. It cheers the old folks. Keeps the pups used to being with people too."

Chapter 10

Sara and Daphine carried the pups down the long flight of stairs. They were too small to run up and down on their own. Once at ground level, before the leashes could be attached, the pups scratched and clawed, and both Sara and Daphine dropped them.

"Damned dogs," Esmerelda said, coming up behind and placing a hand on Sara's shoulder. She smirked mysteriously. "They won't get far."

The pups dashed across the lawn and parking lot, yipping and playfully biting one another, tumbling like a ball of energy across the grass. They scampered behind one of the buildings but soon came frantically running back, chased by a man swinging a rake. He was that obscene voyeur who shadowed them at the festival!

Daphine scooped up Latte and Sara chased Choco until she caught him.

The gangly man was covered with dirt and remained at the corner of the main building. He removed the knit cap he wore. Either his head was shaved, or he wore his hair cut close. He didn't say anything, just stood and stared, like the mid-western farmer in the painting, *American Gothic*, by Grant Wood. But this man with the rake looked more sinister than puritan and humble.

"That's Tripp Unwyn, my groundskeeper. Doesn't like the pups. Might tear up his handiwork." Esmerelda motioned in a sweeping gesture over the manicured grounds. The lawns were thick and lush. Each building, large and small, had decorative rocks and flowerbeds beside the walkways to each door.

"He does all this?" Sara asked.

"Mostly by himself. Doesn't want anyone ruining what he's created," she said. "He even finds loads of free dirt when he needs it now and then."

"Free dirt and rocks?" Sara asked. "I thought people charged for everything these days."

"The extra dirt, and those small decorative boulders, he knows where to get everything for free."

"He gives me the willies," Daphine said.

"He's harmless," Esmerelda said. "Old people like him can't retire. No place to go, so they just get grouchy." She attached Latte's green leash.

"People need to see these cuties," Sara said as she attached Choco's red leash. "That's how you'll get them adopted."

"People don't know how to raise this breed," Esmerelda said. "These two have been housebroken, they're papered and all, and they'll stay lovable in the right home."

"If Tripp will stop swinging the rake at them," Sara said.

Pitbull puppies respond to love and will stay gentle if not encouraged to follow their inbred instinct to react with aggression. Esmerelda had supplied much love and seemed to appreciate Sara's knowledge. She motioned them to follow, and they entered the main hospice building through a doorway on the end.

The facility was once an old bunkhouse used by farm laborers decades earlier. A hallway down the middle had been widened. Rooms on each side were partitioned off, each cubicle made smaller to accommodate for more patients. It smelled like a medical facility but not unpleasant.

Esmerelda held a finger to her mouth. Some patients were still sleeping. They peeked into the busy kitchen and then stepped into the sunroom.

"Tripp keeps the grounds manicured," Esmerelda said. "He shames the rest of the workers to compete."

She explained that after Orson went missing, her funds to keep River Hospice functional were running dry. "Orson's gold and his expensive, one-of-a-kind jewelry pieces kept the doors open. The only alternative was to throw the patients out into the fields and close shop." She rolled her eyes upward and shook her head. "I wouldn't want that happening to me when I'm old and sick, and welfare is nearly non-existent." She went on to say that two years after Orson went missing, she reluctantly sold Talbot House without having done much remodeling. "Fredrik had to move in here." She gestured to a larger, nicer doorway near the end of the hallway. "Damned big heart. Never complained. We let him have the three largest rooms."

As they passed Fredrik's door, he stepped into the hallway. "Taking a tour, ladies?" His eyes lit up. "Come in, please." He gestured for Daphine to enter. She stepped backward. "No, come, please." He gestured to Esmerelda who stepped inside. When she did, with Mimie, Sara and Daphine picked up the dogs and followed.

His front room was masculine and tasteful. A floor to ceiling library covered the back wall with his desk and computer in front of the bookcases. The room was a little crowded, but he had a fireplace.

Fredrik nuzzled up to the dogs and got them overly excited. Sara smiled, thinking that at any moment Fredrik might lick them back.

Finally, he asked, "See this space?" He spoke to Daphine as he gestured over the mantle. "This picture is old now. That painting I wanted to buy would have looked stunning up here."

"You still wish to buy it?" Daphine had that twinkle in her eyes. How well Sara remembered the flirtatiousness of her long-time friend.

"Always wanted it. But one day it disappeared from your shop." He sighed. "You must have sold it."

Fredrik's art pieces and figurines were surreal, bordering on grotesque. All seemed to depict souls in death throes.

They exited the building through the rear door. Esmerelda jolted to a stop at the bottom of the short flight of stairs and Sara bumped into her. "I'm so sorry," Sara said, feeling clumsy.

Esmerelda bent down and studied the flowerbeds and poked with a painted fingernail. She scraped dirt aside and brought out something that gleamed through the caked-on soil. "My ring!" She clasped it in her fist and stared wide-eyed off in the distance.

"Mrs. T?" Daphine asked. "How did one of your rings get into the flower beds?"

Esmerelda shook her head and continued to clean the ring. They came to one of the smaller structures. "That's where Tripp lives," she said. It was a tiny duplex, and the head cook lived in the other half. Tripp's clean and highly polished old pickup was parked in the single carport on his side of the structure with an old beat out sedan parked in the carport on the other side. Many gardening tools hung on the exterior wall of the cabin under the carport. Though used, and some were old, they were exceedingly clean and well kept.

Tripp was two doors down at the next bungalow, on his knees at the front door, picking the lock. The employee, who evidently lived there, loudly proclaimed, "I'm sorry. I've never lost my keys before."

Something spooked the pups. They pulled against the leashes and finally went into the flowerbeds and dug around and peed and kicked dirt back over the spots.

Tripp saw them and grabbed up his rake and came running. He was so angry he might have swung at the pups, had they not been scooped up and held. Encircled in Daphine's arms, Latte's expression, the way her lip curled upward, and her stare, seemed to tell Tripp: *Ha-ha! You can't catch me!* Sara, holding Choco, stifled a grin and stepped aside.

Mimie had stayed at Esmerelda's side. A low growl rolled out of her throat.

Tripp's face turned crimson. "Ma'am, I hate animals in my flowers." Infuriated, he carried the rake horizontally and shook it as he paced. He saw that the dirt was disturbed in the flowerbeds and went to rake it.

Esmerelda went to stand beside him. She opened her hand. "Tripp," she said cautiously. "How did this get buried in one of the flower beds?"

"Awk!" Tripp said as he jumped backward.

"I found it at the back door," she said, gesturing toward the patient building. Esmerelda blew dirt from the ring.

"I didn't take it, Mrs. T. Maybe ask Fredrik. That's his private area back there. Honest, Mrs. T, I ain't been in your house." He breathed heavily.

"I'm not accusing you, Tripp," Esmerelda said. "Nor do I think Fredrik would steal. What I'm wondering is how it got into the flowerbeds?"

"Maybe it just fell off your finger."

"Orson made this," she said as she clasped it in her fist and pressed it to her heart. "You're right Tripp. When the weather's cold, my rings can slip right off my fingers."

"Well, I didn't take it," Tripp said, like a little boy who had been scolded. He pouted momentarily, then stooped down and laid his rake on the walkway. With fingertips, he brushed the dirt off the decorative rocks. He blew a breath across them to further clean them. He seemed obsessed with those damned rocks. Finally, he stood and picked up his rake again. "I like things kept nice," he said, all the while his anger seethed. He was definitely one strange human being. If his face got any redder, it would explode. He kept gasping for air.

"C'mon, Tripp," Esmerelda said, starting up the three steps. She needed to diffuse the situation. "Come, sit down." She opened his front door and led him into his living room where she sat on an old couch and pulled him down beside her, like calming an upset boy. He acted just like one. The living room and open kitchen area were spotless. His furniture was decades old, common and over-used, but clean. He kept the old linoleum floors waxed and shiny. Yet, the open doorway to his bedroom at the back revealed an untidy mess. Belongings glutted the room, piled haphazard, surprising and curious, considering the cleanliness of the rest of the place.

Mimie stayed at the doorway. Sara wasn't about to leave Esmerelda alone with that crazy in the mood he was in. She stepped inside while Daphine stayed just outside the doorway for lack of space.

Tripp saw the dog in Sara's arms wiggling to get down. "Get that thing out of here!" He still clutched the rake and shook it at her.

Sara felt herself shaking, but not as hard as Tripp was. She turned to leave and noticed a large shadow box with a glass front hanging on the wall. It contained at least a dozen rocks of various elements, colors, and grades.

"I'm giving the girls a tour of my facility," Esmerelda said as if reminding Tripp who was in charge. "They were appreciating your handiwork around the grounds."

Sara went to stand at the doorway while she and Daphine tried to keep the wiggling puppies calm. "You're exceptional with plants," Sara said.

Tripp kept an eye on the dogs and seemed confused but smiled at the mention of the well-kept grounds. 'I like perty flowers."

"I see you're a rock collector," she said, trying to sound pleased to soften Tripp's mood. "Where do you—?"

"I gotta git back to work." He said stood abruptly, shaking the rake again. "Go on, git!"

Esmerelda stood and patted Tripp's shoulder. "Don't worry about the pups. I'm looking for a home for them."

"Good. Good. I don't want them tearing up my flowers."

"The cooks are baking brownies," Esmerelda said. "Come over after work, Tripp, and get some."

Tripp's rigid posture melted. "Brownies for me?" he asked like a little boy. "Did I do good today, Mrs. T?" He seemed more relaxed, but the gleam in his eyes still gave him away. He looked straight into Sara's eyes. Without blinking, he said, "I don't mind you hanging around, girlie, 'cause you're kinda' perty. But them dogs could ruin everything I done."

Tripp's ingratiating attitude made her skin crawl. She was no girlie. She had gray in her hair and a few wrinkles. What was he trying to prove? She walked away without so much as a smile.

As they walked the property, Esmerelda said, "Tripp told me that long ago he had a rock collection of about 30 samples. He forgot how many. His dad threw them away, so Tripp started collecting again as he did odd-jobs around the valley."

"Well, he hasn't collected that many more, has he?" Sara asked, remembering the shadow box.

"Oh, but he does collect. The rocks at his front steps and over the grounds," Esmerelda said, gesturing to other flower beds. "He collects from wherever he travels."

As they wandered the grounds, making their way back to her house, Esmerelda mentioned the upcoming anniversary for River Hospice to be celebrated near the end of August. She had plans for a public reception to take place just about the time of Fredrik's birthday. "Kill two birds at one time," she said, but her heart wasn't in her words.

Sara had the feeling that money was scarce. Esmerelda would probably never admit such a thing, but having two obligatory parties in one would be less expensive. Esmerelda didn't seem the type to elicit sympathy. Sara totally admired this widow with a gutsy attitude and good old-fashioned pride.

About time to leave, Esmerelda said, "I'm sorry Tripp mistreated you."

"He's got a lot of misplaced anger," Sara said. "Too bad he takes it out on the dogs." Receiving only love was how pit bulls, in particular, tolerated living with another animal or being held by strangers. "I'm sorry they got away from us."

Sara looked over the grounds again. Esmerelda and Orson once shared a heartfelt plan to help the elderly. Esmerelda was trying desperately to live out that dream. One part of her was convinced Orson was dead, while another part of her still hoped he would return. Sadly, Esmerelda, before too many more years passed, would end up a patient in the very facility that she and her husband established. Not much to look forward to alone. Sara felt warmed by Orson and Esmerelda's contribution to the people of the Delta.

She caught a glimpse of Fredrik watching them out of the window at the end doorway of the patient building. He jumped back, as if not wishing to be spotted, and then turned quickly and disappeared. She looked across the lawn toward the canal that separated the property from the adjacent farm fields. Gawky great blue herons foraged in the open fields. Other birds flew in. At the edge of the hospice property, Tripp, bare-handed, shoved a huge boulder aside. For a man in his sixties, he only looked feeble.

"I think his mind's deteriorating," Esmerelda said as she also watched. "These energetic pups make him nervous."

"Maybe it's time to let him go," Daphine said.

"I've thought about it," Esmerelda said. "You know, he and Orson had a big blow out just weeks before Orson left on that trip."

"About what?" Sara asked.

"I wish I knew. He worked for us for so long and was so nice. He might have wanted more pay. We only had enough gold at any one time to accumulate a small supply of jewelry for sale. When low on funds Orson would go up north again. We weren't rich."

"So, Tripp thought you had lots of gold?" Daphine asked.

"I'm not sure what the disagreement was over, but I remember it was bitter," Esmerelda said. "I wish they could have made amends. I think that's what's been bothering Tripp all these years."

Chapter 11

Sara stood at the north end of Main Street in Locke. Built in 1912, the town burned down and was salvaged and rebuilt in 1915. It was the only surviving town in the west built by Chinese agricultural workers. Historically, it was a town of gambling, booze, and opium. As a reminder of its past, the town maintained a gambling museum established for visitors.

Looking down the four single-lane blocks known as Main Street, the two-story buildings were old, their dark wood frames sagging from dry rot. Second floor balconies sagged over the sidewalks. The structures stood in the same condition as far back as she could remember. When some of the buildings were leased out, the shop owners repainted. Some of the sidewalls still held faded patches of soft drink and other product logos from nearly a century earlier. The names of many on the buildings were faint, though discernible. What Sara presently viewed was a rekindled memory. She wished to find that identical scene in an oil painting, the right size, the right wood tones, and hues. She wanted it for Talbot House.

Daphine had left her on her own to ogle. Sara peered into windows of empty storefronts and down damp narrow alleys leading to similarly aged residences adjoining Key Street and Locke Road at the rear of the nearly deserted town. In the middle of Main Street, she stared up at the sign for the gallery. It was made to look old to blend with the surrounding architecture. The name *Virtuoso* and artistic logo were painted in blues, greens, and whites with splashes of red. She paused in front of one large painting showcased in the window to the left of the doorway and then studied the one in the window on the right.

Sara had twice driven past but was too late to catch the store when it was open. Today was the day she would share what Daphine had done with her talent and life since she, too, was left alone. Daphine's parents were buried in the Franklin Cemetery. They were from the town originally, back when Franklin was nothing more than a scattering of farmhouses, one general store, and a tavern. It hadn't changed much from the past. Suddenly a thought came that maybe Crazy Ike could have dug holes in Daphine's parents' graves. She shook her head to dispel the bothersome images.

"Get in here, girl!" Daphine said, calling out from the counter at the rear of the long, narrow store. "Lock that door. I'm not open till ten."

The store backed up to the embankment with the upstairs portion of the building being at the level of the top of the levee entering the town. That made the lower street level floor dark and shadowy. Seductive lighting above certain paintings in the alcoves gave the shop a certain mystique.

Soft jazz music came from a stereo on a shelf behind the counter. Daphine lit an incense cone. It had an aroma much like Sara had smelled at a séance once attended in the Caribbean. Unsuccessfully, she sought to find that particular fragrance for sale in local stores. Leave it to Daphine to locate anything rare.

"You don't practice voodoo in the back room, do you?" Sara asked, teasing and gesturing with her eyes to the closed door behind the counter.

"No, we do that upstairs," Daphine said, laughing. "I've never attended one of those séance things." The way she spoke about anything revealed how much interest she had in the subject. She would have been a great friend to have along in the Caribbean.

On the back wall behind the sales counter hung numerous breathtaking nature paintings of various sizes. Several exquisite portrait paintings behind the counter were of a young Chinese woman with enigmatic eyes. *D. Kuan* had signed them all.

Daphine smiled. Her face glowed. "Beautiful, isn't she?"

"This is Jade?" Sara had lost touch with Daphine over the years. Sara was surprised to learn that her friend had such an exotic looking daughter.

During one of their first conversations after Sara returned, she learned that Daphine had married Kuan Ying, a tall husky classmate, and all-around athlete. His given name translated to *Hawk*. His parents disowned him for marrying a white woman. After Jade was born, his parents insisted she carried a Chinese name. *Kuan Qiong* meant *Jade* and Daphine felt it befitting. Jade had inherited her sea green eyes.

"My in-laws never treated Jade as if she were half-American. To them, she was Chinese. Never mind that half of her genes came from me." Daphine needed to get something out of her system, and Sara let her talk. Once Daphine and Hawk divorced, he began teaching English in China with a group of other American-born Chinese from Sacramento. He spent most of his time in China. Jade used to travel back and forth between college trimesters.

"Used to?"

"She has her Masters in Geology." Daphine didn't sound that elated. "Jade could hire on with the EPA restoring wetlands and protecting levees here in the Delta if she'd just come home."

"She lives full time in China?"

"A consultant for the Yangtze River Dam." Daphine swallowed hard. "Too much influence from her relatives." Daphine turned away pretending to be busy.

Sara began to peruse the art pieces and noticed the style of art seemed vastly different from one side of the shop to the other.

"Not your everyday stuff, eh?" Daphine asked, joining her across the room. "I had to come up with something to exhibit that wouldn't compete with the gallery down the street."

Much of the art in half of the gallery seemed surreal, otherworldly, bordering on the paranormal, with names Sara did not recognize. Other pieces were lighthearted, of fragile looking fairies and angels; another alcove contained a series of small paintings of New Age people traveling through the universe on magic carpets; more pieces at the back were grotesque, of people suffering in the throes of what would be anyone's guess. "Looks like the stuff Fredrik has in his room."

"He scared me when he first came here," Daphine said. "I didn't know him. He started right off talking about people floating between this reality and the next before they died." She shuddered. "Made me wonder if he was that sociopath and got off on watching his victims cross over."

"You have a vivid imagination."

"Well, when he showed interest in Fleeing Hell, I didn't want my painting going to someone who might be a killer." She smirked and didn't seem serious.

"You sold it to someone else?"

"No, I painted it for myself." Daphine tapped her chest. "Turns out Fredrik truly comprehends what his patients talk about and how they feel before they pass on."

"That's interesting, but his appreciation seems limited to this type of art. Doesn't that feel creepy?"

Daphine only shrugged. "Wanna see the painting?"

Chapter 12

The rear door opened to a steep, dimly lit stairwell. Dusty cobwebs canopied overhead. At the top, the doorway leading outside to a rickety, planked walking bridge to the levee road was boarded shut. The windows hadn't been cleaned in ages and could well have been the original glass installed when the town and buildings were rebuilt in 2015 after the fire. The upper floor smelled musty, like an old house attic. It contained a lot of small rooms big enough for a bed, probably never having been changed from the original floor plan. Many rumors flew in the old days, about Locke having several houses of ill repute.

"With Locke's history, I wonder what kind of bawdy tales these cubicles might tell if they could speak," Sara said.

Daphine disappeared through a doorway. Sara followed and watched as she picked through wrapped art leaning together in stand-up bins. She pulled out a large one and gently removed the brown wrapper.

"Oh my!" Sara said after catching her breath. Pain on the face of the haunting image in the picture was clearly evident. Versions of the face in torment rose swiftly up in successive overlays, from a hint of a grave in the lower left corner to the upper right. The facial expression cleared and finally looked at peace as it passed upward into brilliant light.

"That mean you like it?"

"That's exceptional, Daphine." Sara reached to turn the picture more toward the light. "Far better than anything Fredrik has on his walls." She looked closer at the signature. "DEW. For Daphine Ella Whelan, right? Couldn't Fredrik figure that out?"

"He knows me as Daphine Kuan." They both laughed. Daphine studied the painting momentarily. "I'm tired of it now. You like?"

Sara couldn't see herself owning such a painting. "What I want are Delta scenes." She glanced at the many pieces wrapped and stored. "You are so talented. I always envied you. Did you know that?"

"Me? You envied me?"

"You had something special to do with your life. I became an idiot tour guide for snowbirds who came looking for sun."

"But the games, Sara. That took brains."

"Hey, yeah. Computers and me did find one another."

"I meant to ask," Daphine said in her straightforward way. "I know you made a bundle off selling the copyrights." It was only a matter of time till Daphine's bold and playful curiosity prompted her. "How much?"

Sara rolled her eyes. She was tempted to keep the truth something of a mystery for herself. "A little."

"Oh, sure. Just enough to scrimp together and buy a mansion." Sara had never told her about having paid cash for Talbot House.

"Well... a little more." Sara hesitated, and they stared at one another. Daphine had never told secrets and hadn't changed. "Low seven figures," Sara said, clearing her throat.

Daphine caught her breath. Her eyes opened wide. "I'm in the wrong business."

They enjoyed a hearty girlfriend laugh. Still, Sara did not disclose the programs she was presently creating that could bring her yet another windfall. She didn't wish to convey wealth to the locals or even friends. People in the Delta were not that well off. While a few landowners got rich, most Delta residents struggled to eke out a living from working the crop cycles. Sara didn't want to be known as a person who made good and then came home lauding it over others, expecting recognition and special treatment.

She had also endured a difficult lesson from her first business manager in Puerto Rico whom she trusted. He had been a personal friend for years, yet tried to cut in on her profit by demanding a whopping twenty-five percent representing advice contributing to her success. A cease and desist order, and measly buyout of his consulting contract, put an end to his greed and replaced the generous bonus she secretly planned to give. She and she alone came up with the idea for her first two computer games. She alone designed them into existence, having nothing to do with who took phone calls, set up appointments, and kept her books. From now on, Sara would protect herself. She would share neither her ideas nor progress with anyone. Her privacy had nothing to do with how much she loved a best friend.

"I'm not sure what to do with this." Daphine re-wrapped the painting and then stopped short of squeezing it back into the storage slot. She looked at Sara.

Sara stared back. Could Daphine be thinking the same thing she was thinking?

Daphine finally shoved the painting back into the slot. "I've got some new pieces beside the counter that I want you to see before I put them on display."

As they carefully made their way down the staircase, Sara said, "I wouldn't have guessed Fredrik to be that strange. He's wholesome looking, and his mannerisms exhibit a lot of class."

"They did a big write-up in the local paper about him years ago."

As far back as Sara remembered, her dad would say if anyone read the *Delta Gazette* long enough, they would come to better understand life along the river.

They reached the first floor, and Daphine closed the door behind them. Street noises out front said the sleepy town was waking.

"Evidently Fredrik sits at the bedside of each and every one of the patients at the hospice as they're dying. Attentive any hour of the day or night."

A kid riding a bicycle tossed a newspaper that smacked against the door. Daphine went to retrieve it and came back to lay it on the counter.

"He sounds preoccupied with death," Sara said. That alone seemed strange.

"The news article painted him as someone who understood it, and who could put patients at ease in their transition."

"But how could anyone see so much death and not go a little whacko?"

Chapter 13

After perusing the paintings that Daphine had set aside, Sara chose nothing. "Maybe it's not time to buy. I need to get some furniture in there first."

Daphine unwrapped the newspaper and spread it on the countertop and gasped. "Another one," she said, sounding exasperated.

Sara looked over Daphine's shoulder. A photo of men digging in the ground sat center front under the bold headline:

Another Victim of Serial Killer.

"What do you know about this?"

"Don't you listen to the news?" Daphine asked as they continued to read.

> A wetlands ecologist counting birds near Stone Lake South, northeast of Courtland below the Hood-Franklin Road, discovered another human skeleton buried with animal bones.

Sara didn't remember reading anything on the Internet about remains being found that far south of the Sacramento metropolitan area. Her thoughts ran rampant. Her face heated. "Stone Lake South? That's less than two miles behind my house—just over the old railroad grade."

"Some rancher leased the land and lived out there before it was turned over to the Wetlands people." Daphine nudged her. "Look what it says."

Sara paced. She didn't want to read. "Tell me about these... these...,." She waved her hand across the paper. "How many?"

"Says here, this one makes twenty-eight. The first to be found outside of the major Sacramento area."

"So, the idiot didn't go away."

"Serial killers never quit."

"I read about that killer on the Net," Sara said. "Now they find remains out by my place?" It was no wonder people claimed Talbot House was haunted.

"Maybe he relocated to the Delta. Says here the body was found in what used to be a cow pasture." Daphine leaned down placing her elbows on the newspaper, still reading. "Says that as water levels in the lake rose and fell, it must have washed away the hard pack that cows trampled over the body." She straightened up from the paper. "Said this ecologist guy saw the skull sticking up like a dome in the dirt in the field."

"Gruesome!"

"You know these fields have been worked to death," Daphine said. "Most of the Delta from Courtland all the way down to Union Island west of Lathrop sits as low as seventeen feet below sea level."

"We're sinking?"

"No, compacted, maybe. From farming and such." Daphine shrugged. "Not up by your house though." She smirked again like she was making light of the situation. "Yet."

"What's that got to do with these bodies?"

"The soil is wearing away. Says here they think that's how the remains got uncovered." Daphine stared out toward the front windows and shook her head. "They've already reclaimed some of the lowest Delta islands for water storage. Who knows how many more bodies lay in the mud at the bottom of those lakes?"

"So why haven't they caught this person?" Sara dared to look at the article.

"The people who work up killers' profiles," Daphine said. "They say this perpetrator is meticulously clean about his kills. He buries all the belongings with the bodies. Leaves no telltale evidence above ground."

"The killer doesn't bother to hide who the victims are?"

Daphine smiled facetiously. "Oh, yeah, he does. He buries 'em deep." She reached back and turned down the volume of the radio. "One other thing." She pressed a thumb and forefinger against her throat and felt around. "You know this bone in here. The *hyoid* bone?" Daphine would know about that, having studied anatomy in art classes. "They always find it broken. Every one of these people was strangled."

An old pickup passed on the narrow street, and the sound of its muffler rumbled off the buildings.

"That's all they know? No forensic evidence?"

"Absolutely nothing. The only thing they can do is bag any remnants of the victims and take lots of photographs," Daphine said. Evidently, clues were few or non-existent if the cold case detectives hadn't solved any of the murders. Some of the bodies had been in the ground so long, the only items found to help identify the person were their larger bones and teeth and credit cards fragments, maybe jewelry. Bugs had eaten any paper or clothing.

"I hope they take a good look at the rancher who owned that property," Sara said. A serial murder victim found close to her dream home was unsettling. "The profilers can't point a finger at anyone?"

Daphine shrugged. "Someone else owned that property and leased it out. Doesn't point a finger directly at the rancher." She only glanced at the other headlines as she turned pages. "Just when they think they've got someone nailed, there's a new twist, and something else jumps up and bites."

"Sounds like trying to hold a snake still with one hand."

The comment must have stirred Daphine's memory. "They caught a vagrant once," Daphine said. "He was wringing a cat's neck."

"Ugh!" Sara said as she cringed.

"They thought they had their man because he fit the image the profilers once drew up. White, stronger than he looked, maybe a homeless person," she said. "But he proved that he lived in Nevada till after the first skeletons began showing up."

"Maybe he visited here from time to time to do his dirty work. Nevada's not that far." She wondered how much police kept track of suspected perpetrators. "The cat, why would he kill a cat?"

"He was homeless. Said he would cook it over a bonfire and eat it."

"Ha! They ought to take a closer look at that guy too." He lived close enough to travel in and out of the California area with no suspicion. She also thought they should take a look at Fredrik's preoccupation.

Chapter 14

Sara spent sleepless nights with her cell phone attached to its charger, left on, and in plain view on the nightstand. Life in the Delta had changed drastically from what she remembered, and it definitely put a cloud over what she had hoped to accomplish upon returning.

The next day, while the contractor's crew worked, she stood at the upstairs landing looking out the window toward the levee. Though the groundhog had seen its shadow in February, the trees in her front yard showed signs of preparing to usher in spring. Spring, with its offer of renewal, had taken hold of her too. Everything she had recently accomplished kept her thoughts humming. A sensation of freedom came over her like she had never known.

As a teenager, freedom and getting out of the house usually meant sitting in the car to babysit her very active younger sister, while her parents sat in a bar for three or four hours. *Only a few minutes*, they always said. *We'll be right back.* The idle promises haunted her.

That was when she realized how much Starla loved to sing. Starla would stand on her knees in the front seat looking back at her in the rear seat, trying to finish some homework. Starla would pretend to be a star on stage. She would sing and try to dance. Dancing on the ragged upholstered seat was nearly impossible, and she would fall with a grunt. Sara always encouraged Starla to get up and keep trying. To see her sister's eyes sparkle when someone had faith in her made Sara want to give and give to that little girl with all her heart.

Neither was it freedom living without her family after the accident while she finished school. Her first taste of freedom came when she moved to Puerto Rico and didn't speak the language and couldn't get a job. Freedom was being all on her own and doing anything she wished. The bigger the challenge, the better as long as she had Starla's photos for company.

Now, freedom in the Delta meant completely overcoming her fear of driving the levee roads. Also, despite the sleazy watering hole tavern her parents favored having been torn down, she needed to know what it was like to pass a Delta bar or tavern without feeling like screaming.

Freedom was having the time to notice the flocks and myriad species of migrating birds and people on horseback exercising the animals. She wanted to explore the several flooded islands that had been returned to wetlands similar to when the Miwok Indians hunted the area. She longed to get into a boat and slice through the rivers and explore and wondered if she was too old to learn to water ski, something she had never—

"Sara," the contractor said, interrupting her reverie. "I need to explain about this wall down here."

A set of blueprints from the Talbot era was included with the escrow documents. Almost daily, contractors and an architect scurried in and about the building in preparation for the restoration.

"From here to there," the contractor said, describing the wall to come down.

After assuring herself it was a necessary change to make, Sara gave the go ahead.

Sara confined her working hours on the computer to the evenings. The contractor had keys and could enter with his men when she wasn't home during the daytime. The only personal valuable items were in the one room she occupied. Other items of value throughout the house were the original wall sconces, the claw foot bathtub, and all the beveled glass windows and fine woodwork throughout. The final reconstruction plans had yet to be approved by the County. That could take weeks.

Esmerelda called several times since the last body was found at Stone Lake to speculate why the investigators had not released the identity. Then, finally, she said, "I've got to stop kidding myself. Orson may never be found. They stopped looking up there in the Placer hills long ago when the search parties turned up nothing."

That may have been the first time Esmerelda openly faced the truth about her husband. Sara wondered why Esmerelda's former friends hadn't rallied to her support. Esmerelda seemed to have no one with whom to share her hopes and fears. She talked little about people from her days of social functions and parties. That meant those people had, most likely, dropped out of her life, perhaps when she began talking about the ghost.

Sara's cell phone rang. "What's up, Daph?"

"Hey, I wanted to find this information on the Net before I told you about Esmerelda's daughter."

"A daughter? She has a—"

"*Had* a daughter. I didn't want to gossip. Wanted you to read about it."

"Hey, we never kept secrets," Sara said, smiling into the phone. Then she realized what Daphine had said. "What do you mean, 'had'?"

"It explains a little about Esmerelda too. She used to be a nurse."

"So that's why she owns a hospice."

"Yep. Her daughter was a nurse too. Listed as MIA in Vietnam."

Sara felt a great surge of sympathy for Esmerelda. "What made you look for information on the Net?" Sara quickly made her way downstairs to her computer as they talked.

"Heard the story ages ago. Didn't want to tell you right away. Thought you might want to get to know Esmerelda first." Sara could imagine Daphine shrugging her shoulders as she usually did when speaking seriously. "You should read about it for yourself on the Web site."

Sara waited with pen in hand. "What's the URL?"

"I emailed you the link. Some guy, another nurse, came back from the war and said he was with Betty—that's Esmerelda's daughter—when a group of them were captured. They were marched for weeks through the jungle and, one by one got sick and dropped. Betty didn't make it."

Sara remembered the many horror stories that war produced. "And now they can't find the spot where they left her laying, right?"

"Till they do, Betty's an MIA."

After hanging up, Sara booted the computer, clicked on the link, and read. Esmerelda had not one dear person missing, but two. Her stamina and ability to carry on despite compounded tragedy was something Sara understood completely. A missing daughter explained Esmerelda treating both her and Daphine like her own. Esmerelda was old enough, and they young enough, and all three bonded the day they got together.

Then Sara viewed a string of photos of Betty Talbot, some with several people, and a couple of close-ups by herself. Sara's hand began to shake over the keyboard. "That wasn't Esmerelda with light-colored hair," she said out loud. One of the close-ups was the same photo that sat on Esmerelda's sideboard.

Chapter 15

The next day, Sara and the contractor were upstairs discussing changes for the added bathroom that the County Planning Department rejected. As they moved into another room, Sara heard the crunch of gravel and peered out a window overlooking the driveway.

A young Mexican man wearing blue work clothes got out of the light green Jaguar sedan and scampered around to the passenger side. He opened the door and took hold of a hand. Esmerelda had arrived. After opening a rear door, Choco and Latte scampered out yapping. Then out came Mimie. Esmerelda's raven hair blew in the strong wind as she looked back and forth the length of the building and then shook her head. The young Mexican man laughed a lot as he scampered after the pups that led him on a zigzag traipse up the driveway.

By the time Sara hurried outside, Choco and Latte had run, barking and yapping, far out into the backfield as if they were on a mission. Sara ran too. The pups could get lost in the fields. After several stern commands, only then did the pups respond. They stopped but paced like they might keep running toward the ditch. She and the young Mexican caught them and returned to the yard. He ran back to the Jaguar to bring the leashes. Sara found Esmerelda inside the empty workshop. Once inside the shop, Choco and Latte began to whine.

"I miss my husband." Esmerelda dabbed at her eyes. "I always feel closer to him when I think of the plans we had for this place."

"Is this the first time you've been back here?" Sara wanted to hug and comfort Esmerelda, but it seemed that woman always made sure she stood on her own two feet.

"Oh, no. Those last owners were friendly and even asked me to help with their remodeling plans."

"Why didn't they finish?"

"Because of Orson. They saw his ghost. They didn't believe in such things, but the spirit kept bothering them till they got spooked and decided to leave." The house stood empty for nearly five years until Sara bought it, enough time for a few people to say they saw a light floating around inside.

Choco and Latte paced the lengths of their leashes and returned, only to do it again and again.

"What's up, babies?" Esmerelda asked as she bent down to pet them.

Choco sat, barked, and stared up at them and thumped the floor hard with his tail. Latte stood on hind legs as if trying to see out the front window. Then she sniffed along the base of the wall and pawed at the floor, finally laying down and scooting around on her back. Their distinct personalities were clearly evident.

"Maybe they know," Esmerelda said. "I took a deposit on the pups from a young couple in Sacramento."

"You sold them?"

"I hope so. The couple lives in a tiny apartment, but they're building a house in a brand new subdivision. They're paying me to board the dogs now."

Latte whined and rolled over onto her back again and scooted around.

"Let's take them into the house," Sara said. "Maybe they'll calm down inside."

Esmerelda was able to give a lot of additional information to the contractor that Sara would never have known. She enjoyed herself as if she were the one refurbishing. She threw herself into the moment and followed the contractor around, and Sara let her be. The young Mexican, Demetrio, was surprised that Sara spoke Spanish. Still, he refused to enter the house but accepted a soda and a hearty sandwich and chips, which he devoured out on the covered back steps despite the wind and some blowing rain. Finally, he went to sleep in the car.

Over lunch, Sara realized that Esmerelda wore no earrings, necklaces, or bracelets. She always dressed quite nicely, and a woman of her stature and bold personality might wear more jewelry.

"The rest is in the safe deposit in Walnut Grove," Esmerelda said, as if reading Sara's mind. "Most of it, anyway."

"You never show it off?"

"I don't go out much anymore." She was afraid of theft too. She had found some pieces missing. "Don't know if it happened here at Talbot House or at the hospice." She kept most of it in one big jewelry box, but any of it could have been lying throughout the house. "Long after I moved, that's when I noticed some pieces missing."

Surely, she could not have lost more due to slipping off her fingers in the cold. "Only rings?"

"No, as a matter of fact," Esmerelda said. "Orson made a pendant for me. Melted his gold and made one good-sized nugget and set two diamonds in it. One for each of us." She was quiet for a moment as she touched her chest where the pendant might hang. "Imagine that. Melting down raw nuggets to make a nugget pendant. But, it's missing." She held up her right hand. "This is one of Orson's creations." She twirled the sparkling band around her finger.

Sara could only sit and listen to this woman who needed a friend and who desperately needed closure.

"I used to attend a social activity every evening. It's what got me through the time when Orson went missing." She paused and seemed to sink deeper into her memories. "When I realized he wasn't coming back...."

"You need to socialize now. More than ever."

"Well, I have my dogs. Although I think I made a mistake by taking the pups."

The pups were confined mostly indoors because Tripp didn't want them around. Though determined and spry, Esmerelda was elderly and three dogs surely too much responsibility. A serial killer in the area was a frightening scenario, especially for Sara, living alone in such a big empty house. Sara put down roots and meant to stay no matter what threatened. She could surely babysit a couple of puppies occasionally. Pit bulls being seen around her property could be a deterrent, especially for anyone snooping around and making those noises during the night that she had yet to identify. "I can help with the pups." Almost immediately, she realized she should have thought more about it first. "Once in a while," Sara said, hoping it sounded less permanent. "It would give you a break."

A look of relief came over Esmerelda's face. "Wish those kids could take the pups now. Most people don't want pit bulls. You ever had a pet?"

"A Yorkie." Sara remembered that Mandy had been great company, and how empty she felt when her pet of sixteen years died in her sleep on the bed beside her.

"You can't leave pit bulls behind when you need to go out," Esmerelda said. "They're potty trained and all, but this type of dog, in particular, would tear up your house."

Pit bulls should be watched to see how they expressed their inbred nature. Mandy was trained and heeled well and was never on a leash unless necessary. These two feisty pups should always be leashed when outdoors, simply because of pit bull temperaments. Puppies were supposed to be exposed to as many people, places, and things as feasibly possible by the time they are twelve weeks old. Surely, Esmerelda had not been able to do that much despite trainers working with them.

Chapter 16

"One of our patients passed away suddenly," Esmerelda said on the phone a week later. "Her family's begun an investigation."

"A what?" Sara asked. Sadly, people relegated to hospices were expected to die. A hospice was last resort for the incurable.

"They believe she could have lasted a lot longer."

"That's ludicrous."

"They're investigating why she died." Esmerelda's frustrated sigh came through the phone. "We don't just kill people off because they're terminal."

Sara couldn't allow herself to become involved. She could help Esmerelda another way. "Let me keep the pups overnight," she said.

"Could you really do that?" Esmerelda never asked for favors, but she knew an opportunity when it was offered. "Tomorrow's Easter. When you bring the dogs back, plan to have dinner with me."

Driving to Esmerelda's, the spring sunlight dazzled. The pear trees were in blossom and honeybees buzzed. Sara lowered the window. She had not paid much attention to flora and fauna when she was younger, except when the pear trees were in bloom.

Pears, especially Bartlett, was a huge part of the crop market of the Delta. Bartlett trees would keep producing each year until after they were one hundred years old. If too many pears began to grow each season, some would be removed to allow the rest to fully mature. From the look of the flower-laden branches, the thinning phase promised to be a busy one. The fragrance emitted by those delicate white flowers blanketing the orchards completely merged with the air. It brought back memories of long past spring times when she always felt renewed. She kept the window down and sniffed the air again and again as she drove. This was one pleasurable memory she would enjoy forever. She began to feel like she was finally home again and the river didn't seem as threatening.

As she maneuvered along the levee, viewing the expanse of crop fields and orchards, houses loomed intermittently on the horizon, then surged past. Each had its chance to make a statement as to its grandeur or neglect before the blankets of green fields blended together again toward the horizon.

At River Hospice, she backed in toward Esmerelda's garage in order to load the dog carriers. Tripp was out washing his old pickup truck.

"Washes it even if it doesn't need it," Esmerelda said. "Keeps it tuned too. Runs errands for me all over the Delta."

Sara always kept her back seats folded down in anticipation of hauling some new piece of furniture or other large items. As they loaded the SUV, Tripp scurried over to lend a hand.

"Hello there, perty Miss Sara."

He had some nerve. Sara pinched her lips together. His interest made her gag. She turned to face him. "Tripp, my name is Sara. You don't need to tack anything else onto it."

"Oh!" he said as if he thought her too uppity. He gave her a look that sliced through her, and then turned and headed back to his truck.

During the few minutes she and Esmerelda finished preparing the dogs for the ride, Tripp glanced over several times. He shrugged as he swiped soapsuds over the hood and talked to himself and waggled his head from side to side.

"Don't be too hard on him," Esmerelda said. "When a patient dies, it sets everyone on edge."

"Surely you get attached to these old folks. I imagine some are here a long time."

Esmerelda shrugged. "Guess it's a fact of life around here. This is a place to bring the old and terminal." She stared at the ground and then shook her head. "Bless Fredrik. He was with her all night, till she expired around four this morning."

Sara couldn't help asking. "Doesn't seeing so much death affect him?"

"Probably. He's awfully dedicated, but he can get nasty if he gets moody. Not sure how he comes to terms with the loss of life."

Chapter 17

Sara did some of her best thinking as she drove. Fields and orchards had greened, soon to be laden with produce. Farmers geared up for the busiest time of the year. While crops flourished and grew, harvesting equipment was made ready for use from mid-summer till after Halloween.

Migrant workers began settling into the camp houses. Sara remembered decades earlier seeing a family of four, in a rusting old pickup laden with worn-out possessions stopped on the shoulder of the levee. The man and woman peered into the dirty and cracked windows of a ramshackle cabin hanging over the levee on the riverside. They were transient farm workers seeking temporary shelter.

Sara sighed and remembered that some people were worse off in their lives than her family had been living in their shanty. Certainly now, she was better off than anyone she knew. As young as she was back then, she had wanted to help that family but couldn't. Yet, she could afford to help people now.

Linette and Buck Alden's support was undeniable. Sara's belongings, and the new items she recently purchased, remained stored in their laundry room behind the garage and in one of their spare bedrooms.

The Aldens had one son, but he had never lived in their retirement home. Following in his father's footsteps, he joined the Air

Force before Buck retired. Linette and Buck never complained about the company and also gave her keys to the house. True, Buck was supposed to be a distant cousin, but once they sat and talked about it, they guessed that their fathers tacked on the relationship somewhere back in the ancestry just for friendship's sake. Years before, when Sara's family died, Buck's parents took her in for the next couple of years.

She had not been a close friend with Linette when they were younger. She knew Linette from a distance and liked her for her gutsy, daring ways, which was something that Sara lacked. Both Linette and Buck were thin in stature and had stayed that way.

Sara's family lived without much of anything, and no one seemed to care. Moving to Puerto Rico was like being reborn. She took a vacation there and never returned. The Aldens shipped her meager belongings. No one in Puerto Rico knew who she was or anything about her alcoholic parents and she made the most of the fresh start. She earned little money over the decades, but lived comfortably enough, mingling among rich tourists and locals alike, exploring sunny beaches and traveling to other islands of the Caribbean to experience the cultures firsthand. Right after leaving the Delta, she tried to stay in touch with Daphine, but she went away somewhere to college and stopped writing. Buck's mom wrote several letters, and then she passed away, and correspondence ceased as the years kept passing.

Then came Sara's brainstorm that netted her several million dollars. When she held that first big check in her hands, she made up her mind that not one of her closest friends would be left struggling for things important to them while she could afford almost anything for herself.

Life had turned good. Sara's dreams began coming true. That's what motivated her to help her special friends now. She wished to repay Linette and Buck for their kindness, but neither would accept anything, claiming they had almost everything they dreamed of or needed.

Quite by accident, Sara realized a dream of Linette's had not come true. One evening over dinner at the Aldens, their friends Zara and Fred dropped in. The men shared guy stuff at the bar in the family room while the women chatted in the kitchen. Linette happened to mention, "I always wanted to purchase a couple of computers for my store. After classes finish for the day, a lot of kids don't have a place to go."

Libraries in each of the small Delta towns had computers, but not enough for all the kids wandering about. Then, library budgets were cut so drastically, they couldn't stay open long enough each afternoon for many students to benefit.

Linette's store, *The Book Nook*, enjoyed a prime location at the foot of the levee beside a mini-mart and two doors away from the Post Office. The Book Nook sat in sight of the Courtland library that sat back of the open lawns where the old high school used to stand.

"So, if you had one or two computers in your store," Zara said, "it would be another place for the students to access the Internet."

"It would be another way to get kids into the store and interested in books too," Linette said. Her idea did have merit.

That was all Sara needed to hear. Linette's store suffered because all of the Delta towns were small. Clientele was limited. Sales of books about the Delta were always her best sellers and tourists purchased most of those. Teens should read more, and that was a market Linette wanted to expand, to benefit the kids and her store.

Linette would discourage anyone from giving her a gift if she knew about it beforehand. Despite paltry interest rates, Sara's savings and investments were making more money than she could spend. After convincing herself that it wouldn't be too overbearing to do, she drove to Sacramento one day and purchased two state-of-the-art computers, complete with peripheral equipment and programs, and had them delivered to The Book Nook. She also ordered the Internet connection for the store. The timing of the delivery was tricky because Sara wanted to make sure Linette didn't refuse the surprise shipment as possibly being delivered to the wrong address.

Sara parked beside the old Courtland High School auditorium, the only building remaining of the old high school. She watched for the delivery from inside her SUV. Luckily, she remembered to bring water and a snack. She was always dashing off somewhere and forgetting to eat. Life was too good, too busy.

She also brought the day's newspaper and perused the local happenings. Her speed-reading was cut short when she focused on one headline on the second page:

Ike Ames Arrested Again.

"Crazy Ike," she said, as she scanned the article. She looked up to see if anyone had heard when she realized she spoke out loud again.

The article reported:

> *Caretakers found Ike Ames digging in a mound of dirt that covered a fresh grave at Franklin Cemetery. Beside him was a dead dog, verified as being his. Ames's only explanation was that he wanted to give his pet a proper burial.*

> *Authorities dug out the fresh dirt down to the coffin to assure that another victim of the serial killer had not been buried in what would have been a convenient spot. Finding nothing, misdemeanor charges were dropped, and Ames was released on his own recognizance.*

The Book Nook was housed on the ground floor of a historic building listed with the Courtland Historical Society. The weathered boards of the building and remaining panels containing decades-old paint gave it a certain charm. Potted philodendrons hung from the sagging upstairs balcony out front. Potted Gerbera daisies had already burst into colorful bloom. Tall gladiolas grew from the ground at each side of the stoop.

The deliveryman arrived and wheeled his hand truck across the ground-level porch. He brushed aside trailing plant stems that swung in the Delta breeze. After he drove away, Sara went in. Linette's eyes were already red and teary. Linette stood beside the big pile of boxes and clung to the edge of the counter with one hand while the other held a tissue as she blew her nose. "You trying to give me a heart attack, Sara?" She dabbed at her eyes.

The next day, Buck and a carpenter friend partitioned off two cubicles at the back of the store and the equipment was set up. Sara was present a few days later when the plastic sheets shielding the rest of the store from dust were taken down. She even helped sweep up the sawdust. Everything about the store looked new, even though only a few bookcases had been repositioned.

"Maybe I should offer coffee or sodas for people who want to sit a while," Linette said. Only four chairs were present inside the small store, but the business had Linette's personality throughout. "Maybe a couple small tables and chairs out front."

"Maybe you should make sure they buy the books first," Buck said. "The library's back there, you know." He thumbed the direction.

"Oh, one more thing." Sara handed the broom to Linette.

Linette looked at her as if she couldn't take another surprise. "You've done enough."

"Not quite." Sara found her bag and retrieved two copies of each of her computer games and handed them to Linette. "Here's something that'll bring the kids in."

"Yes!" Linette said, grabbing them. "We've been playing these at home ever since you gave us a set."

"Let's make sure we've got juice," Sara said.

They booted both computers and loaded the DVDs. Multi-colored stars burst forth on the screens and then were pulled backwards in a sinking swirl as the game rules appeared.

Linette and Buck clapped. "I'm charging for these," Linette said. "The kids can get free allotted time on the computers for homework, but if they want to play these games—"

"And they will," Sara said.

"Then they can pay a small fee," Linette said, finishing her thought. "It'll pay for the Internet connection."

Sara only smiled, having prepaid the Internet fees for a year in advance. "Oh, one more thing," she said.

"No, no, Sara. I couldn't accept anything else."

Sara laughed. "A favor… for me?" Linette relaxed and seemed eager to hear. "Would you find out what area books about the Delta are best for each of the Delta schools and put together a cost? Not just one of each book per school, but one of each book per classroom. Could you?"

Linette shook her head. "That'll be awfully expensive."

"That's why I'm buying through you." Sara smiled, teased. "You want that big sale or not?"

"For every classroom?" Linette asked, eyes widening in disbelief.

That much business for The Book Nook would ring up a hefty profit they would welcome. Since Buck retired from the military, he became the Courtland Fire Chief. Volunteers staffed several Delta Fire Departments. Buck wasn't getting paid a penny for his full days of work. In some ways, life in the Delta hadn't changed from as far back as Sara could remember.

Chapter 18

The following week, the Aldens held a small reception at the bookstore. A local newsperson attended. Sara stayed away. The Alden's begged her to attend but understood. Linette reported the computers came from a donor who wished to remain anonymous.

When work at Talbot House was at a standstill, Sara took Choco and Latte for walks along the river or through town to generally expose them to the elements and people along the way. They had great fun together, and the pit bulls remained lovable. They were now four months old. Sacramento carpenters had gone on strike. Though it was almost certain the strike would run a short duration, the home of the young couple buying the pups, as well as those in that entire subdivision, sat idle halfway through the framing stage. Sara wondered what might happen if the couple couldn't take the dogs.

The next day, a radio newscaster reported the skeleton found near Stone Lake was confirmed as that of a man, as was first thought. Dental comparisons did not match Orson Talbot's, but they were checking through dental charts of other missing persons. If Orson's dental records were already on file, what took them so long to make the announcement? Sara rushed straight over to Esmerelda's place, knowing that she would have a jumble of hopes and dismay to sort out.

Sara bided her time by taking the dogs twice more during the week and kept them overnight. She didn't want to dwell on missing her Yorkie, but the pups filled a void she couldn't describe. She played with them endlessly out in the field. Like Mandy, both lay at her feet while she worked into the night on her computer. They jumped to attention when she stood to stretch or refresh her drink.

Esmerelda benefited too. A lot of tension had left her face. Once when Sara visited, she said, "I went shopping for the first time in ages." She disappeared into her bedroom and walked out holding up a couple pairs of jeans. That stylish, slightly conservative older woman had bought herself some denim.

Each time Sara picked up the pups, Fredrik watched from the window in the door of the patient building. He seemed protective of Esmerelda but always seemed to try not to be seen. Too often, Tripp walked around the property looking busy, but stood and watched from around a corner somewhere until she left. A couple of times, he tried to wave but stopped short when she pretended not to see him. Then, he would stand and stare or sometimes hang his head like a dejected child.

These two men added to Sara's growing paranoia. She found it difficult to shrug off the negativity, especially since the Delta Gazette published a story about another long-time Delta resident who had died at the hospice a few days earlier.

A week before the much-anticipated Saturday class reunion, Sara began feeling nervous. She had not participated in much during high school. Now she was filled with a sense of wanting people to know that she had something to contribute.

Laying wide-awake one night, the house noises were all but forgotten. She contemplated her scheme. She hadn't been in the Delta for thirty years and now planned an event at the reunion that no one could anticipate. Maybe people might think she was taking over. Had she gone nuts? Had she become that self-absorbed? She left as a shy but curious girl. At least that's the way people described her then. Now her over-confidence might turn people off. "Ha!" she said aloud. She placed her hands behind her head and stared at the ceiling through the dimness. "Do it anyway." This would be a genuine surprise for her classmates, some of whom she had never spoken with during four years of high school. It was also a celebration for everyone to communicate what had happened in his or her life, and she intended to make a statement about hers.

Chapter 19

Sara parked outside the old recreation hall in Rio Vista. It used to sit on the outskirts, but the town had spread around it. She looked about and sighed heavily.

"Don't worry," Daphine said. "You'll find enough old friends."

"It's not that. I was thinking about this dream I keep having."

"You were holding your breath."

"Maybe so." Sara sighed again. She had long ago meant to discuss the dream with Daphine because she trusted her judgment. The dream was beginning to scare her, but now was not the time to reveal it. She looked at herself in a mirror on the sun visor. "It's been years. Do I have a lot of wrinkles?"

"Lighten up," Daphine said, jumping out. "Let's go."

Sara recognized only half of her classmates and smiled politely, reminding herself not to expect that people would rush right up to her.

Groups of friends huddled together with drinks, laughing and sharing memories, and updating one another. No one mingled like Sara assumed they might. They stayed within the same circle of friends that they shared in high school. Occasionally one group joined another, but seldom did they cross those invisible boundaries. That was disappointing. Linette and Buck were at separate ends of the room, already mingling. They had attended Courtland High School but made many friends across the Delta and, of course, like few others, would be invited to a Rio Vista class reunion. Finally, when a few people looked her way, Sara thought she saw envy and disbelief. Maybe they thought she had a total makeover.

The Delta was farming country, with nearly half of all school classes made up of minorities. Only a few were in attendance, and that seemed strange. The Filipino brothers, Luningning and Valeriano Rasay, were present. Neither had ever been bashful, always eager to please. One Hispanic woman stood with friends. Zoki Yoshi, whom Sara learned was now a caterer, wore trendy clothes and his hair remained the same as Sara remembered from their teens. It stuck out in all directions with a cowlick at the right temple. Spiked hair being long in vogue surely saved him the cost of having his hair done.

"Is that Morgana over there in the mini?" Sara asked under her breath. In school, Morgana dressed way more daring than anyone else. Now it looked as if she had taken it to the extreme.

"That skirt is too short for women our age," Daphine said quietly as she looked in the opposite direction.

"I'll bet her only claim to fame is when she bends over," Sara said. She remembered that she had not wanted to get caught up in gossip again. "Oops. We're supposed to be looking at the guys, aren't we?"

Photos of classmates hung on a sidewall. Sara laughed out loud when she found her senior picture. How malnourished she looked, with stringy blond hair and a closed smile that hid already-rotting teeth. How out of proportion Daphine looked with eyeglasses too huge for her slender face.

"Thank goodness some of us got better with age," Daphine said. Sara wondered if everyone understood Daphine's humor.

A separate collage hung nearby. A small caption at the bottom told that these classmates were deceased. A note under the last photo of a girl too young for her heavy makeup stated:

"Missing?" Sara put her hand over her mouth. "Not Iana?" She could only stand and stare until her nerves quieted.

"Iana, the wild woman of Rio," a voice said behind her.

That wasn't Daphine's voice. Sara turned. "Caren Olof?" The wealthiest, snobbiest girl in the class, who carried herself like royalty, was smiling and talking to her?

"Caren York now. Remember me?"

Sara felt a rush of warmth to her face. "Yes, of course. Nice to see you again." It sounded lame. What else could she say to someone who never gave her the time of day?

"Poor Iana," Caren said. "She was so morally loose."

"Maybe she went away and left it all behind."

"More likely, got mixed up with the wrong crowd. Otherwise, she'd have kept in touch with her parents."

"True. She was vocal about everything. They seemed the only people she cherished."

"And you, Sara, you were so quiet, no one ever got to know you."

"I-I didn't know—"

"Listen. I heard about your family way back then. It's been a long time, but I want to say how sorry I am." Caren smiled nervously. "And that you look fabulous despite our years."

Sara managed to get through the conversation. They hugged and then headed to opposite sides of the room. Sara found Daphine and breathlessly said, "I don't believe it. Caren Olof spoke to me. We hugged!"

"People do change," Daphine said. She smiled sardonically. "You know who she married, don't you?"

"She said 'York'." Sara had to think a moment and then she recognized the tall man standing across the room with Caren. "Norwood York? Mr. Justice?"

"You know what he's doing now?" Daphine didn't wait for a reply. "They live in Sacramento. He's soon to become the new Police Commissioner."

Sara gasped. "The very rich Caren Olof didn't marry a wealthy landowner's son? She married a cop?"

Chapter 20

Sara and Daphine slipped into others' conversations. Many talked about the string of murders. With the most recent finding as close as Stone Lake, people were scared again.

"Hiya, Sara," Zoki said quietly as he leaned into the group and rested his chin on her shoulder. Then he turned and punched Daphine's shoulder gently.

"Why isn't anyone dancing?" Sara asked.

Zoki, half a head shorter, swept her out to the dance floor. The tune was slow, and Zoki had learned to waltz. So had she.

Dinner was announced. People sat in their little groups at rows of tables, and Sara wondered if any of them had ever spent much time completely away from everyone who knew them.

After dinner, tables were cleared, and the music blared again. Finally, Sara felt relaxed. A grinning man with beautiful teeth came through the doorway, looked around, and then headed straight toward Daphine. He used a walking stick and had a slight limp. His white hair glowed blue from the indirect lights beaming down over the dance floor.

"Daph," the man said. "Great to see you." They hugged.

He glanced over and then tried to see Sara's nametag. She felt embarrassed that someone was interested, the same embarrassment as when someone paid her attention in school. When she looked again, Daphine was smiling like a caricature for a toothpaste advertisement.

"It's gotta be the hair," the man said.

"Pierce was struck by lightning," Daphine said.

"Went white almost overnight," he said.

"Pierce?" Sara asked, dumbfounded. "Pierce Newton?" In high school, Pierce had black hair, a slightly crooked nose, and a front tooth chipped from a sporting accident. His young face was full and strong, his stature robust and suited to the game of football, which he loved. Now his cheeks were chiseled, his body a bit too lean. In a new way, he was still handsome because nothing had changed those same baby-blue eyes. "Is that you?" she asked. His eyes didn't shine as brightly as she remembered, but she had loved him in high school and wished then for more than friendship. Taking care of alcoholic parents and a precocious preschool sister left no time for friendships. After their deaths, her life was in shambles. She retreated inward, struggling to make it through to graduation.

"Sara," he said. His voice was full and warm.

Daphine couldn't stand still. She had known all along what would happen. She turned quickly and grabbed Zoki's arm and dragged him across the room to talk to someone else.

"So, tell me what happened," Sara said.

"Storm came up fast. I saw lightning hit the ground. Next thing I knew, I woke in the hospital with two weeks of my life gone." He swallowed hard. "They told me I died."

While recovering, he was surprised to see how much his facial hair had grown in two weeks. It, too, had turned snowy, as did his brows, to which he presently added some color, he said, to put some life back into his image.

"So, this is what you've been left with?" She gestured to his cane.

Pierce went on to say that several of his vertebrae had to be fused because of the damage to his spine. He had not been able to work since, at least not at anything physical. The lightning had also connected with the metal in his fillings and shattered his teeth. "Plates," he said, snapping them together.

"I'm so sorry." Sara felt emotional and touched his hand. "I'm glad you made it through that ordeal."

"I've written a few books about my experiences." He squirmed like he didn't want to continue. He was about to say something when the former class President, Herbert Frayne, walked onto the stage.

As the evening progressed, prizes of wine, DVDs, and videos, were awarded for the most absurd reasons: To the person who had lost the most hair, and the person with the biggest potbelly. They measured two guys just to make sure. They gave gifts to the people with the most kids or grandkids, a prize for the person with the youngest child. Sara shuddered. Were her classmates old enough to have grandkids? Evidently, some got an early start, while some were still at it. The gifts went on and on, inciting much hilarity. Then the surprise Sara had planned was announced.

"You remember Sara Mason, don't you?" Herbert asked.

Sara cringed at hearing her name over the microphone. She just wanted friends, not adoration. The room became quiet.

Herbert put a hand up to shield his eyes from the stage lights and searched the audience until he found her and pointed. "Sara's developed a couple of Sci-Fi computer games." He held up a copy of both games. "*Star* and *Black Hole*. She sold the copyrights," he said. "These copies are all that's left of the old label with these names. There's enough for everyone to have one of each copy." He pointed to the side table where Zoki lifted the cover off the stacks of DVDs. "Get your hands on these, everybody. They're sure to become collector's items under these labels." The noise level rose as people jumped from their chairs. After the DVD table was bare, people returned to dancing and mingling. No one sought her out, and for a moment, she felt invisible but wouldn't dwell on it.

Sara wondered why she had never come across any of Pierce's books. But then, her life revolved around the Caribbean, which became her haven, and then computers. Her curiosity had not taken her far outside those areas.

Sara remembered the crush she once had on Pierce. She stared deep into his eyes, but the surge of emotion she thought she might feel at seeing him again did not happen.

Chapter 21

Weeks passed as Sara waited while the County caused delay after delay. Most of the renovations were cosmetic. The major approvals needed to be for rebuilding the bathrooms and removing the dining room fireplace in order to redesign the rear stairwell.

The pace of life in the Delta moved slower, more fixed and sure than that of San Juan, where tourists scrambled to get in all the sights in a week or two before heading home. Now on Delta time, Sara felt the crawl seeping in. Boats lazed along shady banks with people clad for water activities. Endless numbers of fishermen and women moving at a snail's pace drove the point home. Surely, the lackadaisical attitude had gripped the County as well when it came to making decisions. Sara had to return to the drawing board each time her plans were not approved. She heard a rumor that people wanted Talbot House either torn down or completely renovated. Why, then, were her remodeling plans being picked apart room by room?

Both Linette and Daphine employed hired help in their shops. Each year, they trained students who were out of school for the summer.

Sara had time to spare. Good sources to learn about the Delta were the historical articles in the Delta Gazette, tourist brochures, or to surf the Internet. She learned about current activities going on by getting out and enjoying the community.

The three-day *Isleton Crawdad Festival* began that weekend. Each year, some fifty thousand people crowded into town: an area that housed under nine hundred permanent residents. Roads became congested and parking non-existent.

"The largest Cajun festival outside of New Orleans," Daphine said. With sales help in her booth, she was free to roam. "It's best to stay in the street."

"Is there some other place to be?" Sara asked.

"The saloons are jam-packed already. It'll get messy."

Coronation of the Festival King and Queen set the parade in motion. Twenty-two bands were scheduled on the festival's four stages over the weekend, the first already playing. The noise level and vibration were enough to bring the decaying, historic *Tong Building* to test. Tantalizing smells of Cajun cooking permeated the air. They arrived at yet another booth that offered food samples.

"You ever had these?" Daphine asked, salivating as she bit into pan-fried okra on a toothpick.

"What a breakfast." Sara stirred her red rice and beans together in the Styrofoam cup.

"You've traveled around. What's your favorite food?"

Sara picked up a sample of okra. "Anything that doesn't come back up," she said between bites.

They sampled Alligator Tails and Buffalo Skins while wandering about discussing recipes with street cooks. When they happened upon Daphine's acquaintances, quick hellos and mild banter limited socializing. The festival offered too much to miss, so people kept moving.

"I meant to ask," Daphine said. "Did anyone thank you for the DVDs you handed out?

Sara shrugged. "It's not something I expected." In reality, she was drawn to revisit teenage emotions, seeking approval from classmates. The recognition she sought, unrealized in high school, had not happened to any extent at the reunion. It was a wake-up call that said she could be looking in the wrong places for acceptance and relationships.

Live music blared. People tried to talk over the noise. Sound raised a few decibels.

"C'mon, anyone contact you?" Daphine asked, struggling to be heard over the noise.

"I received a couple of thank you cards."

"A couple?" Daphine asked as someone bumped her hard in passing. "Only a couple?"

Most everyone wore a tee shirt bearing the copyrighted Festival logo: *Pinch Tails and Suck Heads*. Many who didn't have a shirt stopped anyone who wore one to ask where they could be purchased.

A strong midday sun sizzled. They finally found a place to sit and watch the crawdad-eating contest.

"I can't imagine putting that many creatures in my stomach at the same time," Sara said, rubbing her belly. They left before the winner was announced.

Later that afternoon, after hours of both roaming and minding Daphine's booth, they decided to leave. "One day is enough sales for me," Daphine said. "The first day is usually the profitable one."

Refuse waste containers overflowed, and crawdad shells filled the gutters and crunched underfoot. Over the weekend, nearly twenty-five thousand pounds of crawdads will be consumed.

The afternoon heat reminded Sara she was no longer a teenager oblivious to three-digit temperatures. "You have any more drink tickets?"

"I'm out."

"I'm parched."

"Hey, you gotta try the fermented crawdad drink."

Sara hesitated. "I'll take a sip of yours."

"It won't come back up. I promise."

Daphine turned away, distracted. "Look over there... by the old Tong building."

Sara strained to see through the crowd. "Why? Is it falling down yet?"

Daphine snickered. "Fredrik, with the Underhills."

"Iana's parents?" The couple was elderly, both looking much too weathered and frail. Not knowing their daughter's whereabouts must surely have taken its toll.

"Fredrik used to be outspoken, saying that not enough was done to find that girl right away."

"Was he involved with her investigation?"

"When Iana first went missing, he was really active in the search. Then, suddenly, he stopped his involvement. Word had it he sensed she was dead. Makes me wonder how he could be so sure."

"That's a hell of a thing to say," Sara said. Still, Fredrik was just too preoccupied with death for her liking.

"Iana's family trusted his help. Been friends ever since."

"Friends? He must enjoy watching people suffer."

Chapter 22

Daphine clued her in on some of Pierce's problems. "He lives off Social Security and Disability benefits."

"Then he doesn't have much."

"He has sporadic income from the books he's written, but I guess that's tapered off."

"How do you know so much about him?"

"His life's no secret. When he was struck, the whole Delta rallied around him."

Sara felt glad to hear that. "But so much personal stuff?"

Daphine hesitated but smiled. "I used to date him. Still see him occasionally, but we're just close friends."

Curious about Pierce, Sara invited him along on one of her trips over the levees and sloughs. She needed to pick him up because he couldn't drive. On the way to Isleton, she caught herself again drifting off in thought. She had been doing a lot of that. When she pulled up in front of the property where Pierce lived, she was brought back to reality.

He lived behind a home in a tiny cottage in the older section of Isleton. Both structures were weathered and run-down. His cottage had no flowers or shrubs around it. The shanty sat on concrete blocks. A wooden plank walkway led from the con-crete side yard of the main house back to his front door. The dry, bare dirt around and underneath the structure probably became soupy mud when it rained. Pierce's parents might have been deceased and could offer no help because, clearly, he was just meeting basic needs.

Stepping inside the doorway, the old floor creaked and bowed. Healthy, green Creeping Charley plants hung in pots above each front window. A gigantic, healthy Boston fern hung above the sink. Sunlight twinkled through a stained glass mandala that hung in the side window near a makeshift desk. A freestanding space heater surely provided the only warmth in cold weather. From the size of the house and the living area, she envisioned a tiny bedroom. Sara couldn't imagine a man living so confined, a tall guy, at that.

"You'd think we had enough water around, right?" Pierce asked, smiling. He gestured to a tall hexagonal aquarium sitting on his coffee table, which was a vintage lug box long ago used in pear picking. Tiny brilliantly colored tropical fish swam about.

His antiquated computer setup was probably slower than one of Linette's garden snails on a vacation.

Pierce wasn't doing much entertaining in those quarters. He had no way of getting around except short-distance walking. He was probably very lonely. She felt great empathy.

"Let's rent a boat," she said. "My dad used to catch tule perch in Snodgrass Slough. Want to go fishing?"

His expression perked up. "Why don't we just rent a boat and explore some waterways this time?" He grabbed a backpack and threw a few things into it.

"Okay," Sara said, reluctant. "But one day soon I'll taste those perch again. You had any?"

"Not recently."

"When Daphine and I were kids, she told me how to cook the ones my dad brought home. I can still hear her words: *'Gut 'em and pan-fry 'em a few minutes on each side. Be careful 'cause they might fall apart.'*"

That was how Daphine's mother prepared them. It sounded easy enough to have a good meal on the table in time for Mom and Dad to skip out and have a drink, while Sara did her homework in the car with Starla before the sun went down.

"Sounds great." Pierce seemed timid, as if he'd never discussed ordinary things with many people.

"I remember the taste," Sara said. "Even picking out the bones was worth it."

Pierce directed her back to Walnut Grove for the boat rental. When she was about to head straight past the Isleton Road drawbridge traveling north on the Andrus Island side of the Sacramento River, he said, "Turn! Turn here."

Sara wanted to avoid driving on the Grand Island side. It meant having to pass the town of Ryde where she used to live. It meant passing the spot where her family drowned. "The way ahead is shorter."

"160's better over there." He was already leaning forward as if he might turn the steering wheel for her. He seemed enthused about being out on an adventure.

A wide farm truck entered the bridge from the other side. The bridge was barely wide enough for two sedans to carefully creep past one another. They waited until the truck exited the bridge and passed them. Pierce waved back at the driver.

"Why can't you drive anymore? What kind of damage did the lightning do?"

"Racked up my nerve impulses. My limbs don't always get the proper signals to do what they're supposed to do. Sometimes one leg gives out." He gestured to the walking stick leaning against the seat between them. "At times, my leg doesn't seem to know what to do." He smiled like he was more amused than bothered by it, and he really didn't sound pathetic. He seemed to have adjusted to his inadequacies and gotten on with life, but now he had difficulty relaxing in his seat. "Look over there!" he said, pointing.

Sara missed what he pointed at when two large birds flew right across the windshield and out over the river. Her pulse raced. "What were those?"

"Peregrine falcons!" he said like a young boy as he turned to watch them in flight. "So much nature, right here where we live. It's hard to believe that the Delta hides murder victims."

Why, out of nowhere, did he bring that up? Goosebumps raced over Sara's skin. Why did he sound so sure that the Delta hid murder victims?

The renovated and grand Ryde Hotel came into view, first as a huge block of pink along the levee, then as a memory in its former dilapidated gray. She was about to drive past the point where her parents' car went over the embankment. With both sweating hands gripping the steering wheel, she held her breath and looked away from the river. Then an idea came to her just as she was about to pass the hotel and the junction of Highway 220, crossing through Grand Island. She had to do it. She turned suddenly onto the 220 downgrade and pulled into the parking lot behind the hotel. Finally, she let out her breath.

Pierce placed his hand on top of hers as she clung tight to the steering wheel. He smiled his approval. "You needed to do this, Sara. You can't avoid this road if you're staying in the Delta."

She stared straight ahead. The art deco hotel was built at the height of the Prohibition Era in 1927. It was fully restored with accommodations and amenities befitting any five-star facility. The hotel had a great amount of reputation connected to it, dating back to the original establishment with its ambiance and charm.

The shanties behind the hotel where Sara once lived had long been torn down. The hotel owners carved out a chunk of the orchard and installed a nine-hole golf course; the teeing off area spread across where her family's rental cottage once stood. Sara sighed and choked back emotion. The soothing expanse of green grass helped prevent hurtful memories from taking over her thoughts.

Chapter 23

As they neared the Walnut Grove bascule bridge, the span was lifted open, and traffic needed to wait for a tall-mast pleasure boat to sail through. When they finally crossed, the ominous loud hum the tires made on the grated steel floor brought another memory that leaped out of her past; a sound all but forgotten, was familiar again.

Pickups and four-by-fours parked on the shoulders of the levee and partially blocked the lanes. That was allowed and expected on the narrow roads, even for tourists. They found a place to squeeze in and climbed out.

"Remember these guys?" Pierce gestured toward a shop.

A large sign in the middle of the storefront said:

Rasay Bros.
Bait & Tackle
Breakfast & Boats

"This shop used to belong to...." Sara was about trail off into one of her memories when her cell phone rang.

Esmerelda wanted to know if Sara could take the pups for the evening. She had decided to visit friends she hadn't seen for a while. Sara couldn't say no. They arranged that Sara would pick up the pups around five and return them around eleven since Sara would be going to Sacramento early the next morning. Sara really didn't mind having to make the late trip. The tule fog had vanished with the cool weather. Esmerelda would enjoy an evening out, and Choco and Latte would soon have a permanent home.

Inside the store, at a long counter along the side of the room, a row of men and women dressed in fishing gear hurried through breakfasts of linguica and eggs. Two Filipino grandmothers behind the counter kept coffee cups filled. A small room at the back, with stairs leading down to the ground, contained a refrigerator and looked to be where bait was processed and stored.

Valeriano and Luningning were excited to see them. "You like breakfast?" Val asked.

They had already eaten and passed on breakfast. They decided to rent an outboard boat. Sara insisted on seeing Snodgrass Slough.

"You're still thinking about those perch." Pierce's smile was infectious.

"You like fish?" Val asked.

"Not this time," Pierce said. "Just exploring today."

The Delta Cross Channel gate was open only during certain hours of the day. Sara had never been on the water and Pierce hadn't been in decades. Neither would know their way around.

"I go with you," Luni said. Then, "Ay, sus!" He tapped his forehead. "I have to finish one boat." He was in the middle of someone's boat repair and needed to get it done. Sara was sure they wouldn't need help, but accepted Val's offer to act as a guide on their first trip.

Val and Luni rented and sold boats they acquired and repaired. The same with outboard motors. They operated the only bait shop in Walnut Grove, the next closest shop being at Steamboat Slough, across the Steamboat Slough Bridge on Sutter Island. With the insurgence of people seeking a quiet life among the islands and wetlands, both shops stayed busy almost year-around.

The Rasay brothers kept their boats at a dock directly below the levee. Val chose a 16-foot aluminum boat with an old fifty horsepower *Evinrude* outboard motor. They were on the water in a matter of minutes and passing under the big silver gate of the Cross Channel. Sara couldn't help but smile.

She and Pierce sat toward the front to balance the weight in the boat. They wore thin windbreakers against the spring wind and life vests. Pierce brought his binoculars and kept the glasses to his eyes excitedly calling out the views.

Resorts had sprung up all over the Delta, any place where facilities could be built. Any place accessible by both road and water was a prime location. Houseboats had become a leisurely way to experience the waterways.

"Over there," Pierce said above the sound of the motor. "In that cove."

When Pierce pointed, Val slowed the boat. Sara remembered reading in the brochures that certain areas contained *no wake* laws. That meant boaters were not allowed to travel so fast that their boats left wakes that might disturb those at anchor. Another boat sped by towing two skiers, evidently not knowing the rules or simply ignoring them.

Sara accepted the binoculars. "Water campers?" she asked, talking above the sound of the old motor.

"*Gunkholing,*" Pierce said. "It's called gunkholing. People drop anchor in a quiet cove and spend vacations on their boats. Sometimes the entire summer." He accepted the binoculars back.

Sara turned to view the shoreline and saw more than an occasional bird pecking at the ground or chasing something through the underbrush. Rats, perhaps. Mallards and Grebes were plentiful, the Grebes being great divers that could stay underwater for a long time. In fact, the birds were numerous; she could look in any direction and see many and varied species.

Val eased the boat close along the shore to enable them to better see. He took extra care to avoid sandbars or gravel bars. Winter currents easily filled the bottoms of all channels, and many had to be dredged regularly. Just as they floated past a gravel bar, Sara saw something and looked again.

A long bone.

She nudged Pierce for the glasses, but he was so taken with bird watching he didn't respond. She couldn't help staring at it as they passed.

Their time on the water proved educational and relaxing. Pierce benefited most. When it was time to turn around and head back, Val allowed Pierce to have a turn at steering the outboard motor. Then she took a turn and loved it. She remembered the gravel bar and watched for it. When she sighted it again, she began to ease toward it. Val placed a hand on top of hers on the steering arm and helped guide the boat. They edged as close as possible. Sara wanted a good look at that bone. Val slowed the motor to idle and slowly floated with the current. They looked over the side at the long bone lying half buried and sticking up out of the gravel.

"Aw!" Val said, waving a hand. "River bones."

"River bones?" Again, Sara's stomach felt queasy. Was she so impressionable that river bones would make her feel uneasy?

"Sometimes animals drown," Val said. "People throw rubbish from the boats." He shrugged and took over the steering. "Part of the river flow."

After the boating excursion, Sara drove straight to Esmerelda's taking Pierce along. Pierce seemed overjoyed at finding a friend who wasn't ashamed to be seen with him and his disabilities. His demeanor couldn't hide his elation. Being back in the Delta made Sara realize how much she had missed. She smiled at Pierce. Surely, he felt similar, enjoying things previously out of reach.

When they pulled in below Esmerelda's house, she was outside talking to Fredrik. As Sara introduced the men, Fredrik offered his hand and stared into Pierce's eyes as if searching for something.

"I'm sorry we've never met," Fredrik said finally. "I've always wanted to talk to you about your near-death experience." He relaxed and stood with his hands on his hips. "I've read all your books."

Fredrik was just too preoccupied with death. Sara began to load the dog carriers while they talked. Two Mexican workers passed nearby. Demetrio must have told them that she spoke Spanish, or that she had not forgotten him at lunchtime when he drove Esmeralda over for a visit. The men greeted her with an enthusiastic "*Hola, Senora Mason!*"

Sara waved and noticed Tripp standing outside the end of the patient building across the drive. He simply stood, watching, glaring. Then Sara figured it out. Tripp previously made feeble advances to her. He was always around when she came for the dogs. Now he was seeing her with Pierce. That, and her friendliness with the laborers might be why he fidgeted and pounded the railing lightly as he clenched and unclenched his fist.

Chapter 24

Sara and Pierce stopped for Chinese takeout. They found a wide turnout along the river, sat on the tailgate of her SUV, and ate while birds flew overhead and boats cruised by. She broke open a couple of cans of dog food that Esmerelda supplied and emptied them onto the thick roadside grass. Sara gave the pups water from her Styrofoam cup and when they begged, most of the meat from her chicken chop suey. Before heading home, Sara walked the dogs along a grassy ledge that jutted out along the water.

When she and the dogs returned, Pierce pulled two books out of his backpack. "Here," he said. "Since you expressed interest, I want you to have these."

The first book was titled *True Light*. The cover had a silhouette of a head and shoulders lighted from the inside outward. The other, *Journey Beyond*, showed an ethereal person rising up into the heavens. An attention-grabbing yellow strip across the upper right corner of both books said *Translated into 20 Languages*.

"Hey, you wrote these," Sara said after quickly perusing the back cover blurbs. "They describe your death experience, right?"

"Yep. I've written two others, the first two, but I don't have extras."

Between Esmerelda and Daphine, she learned that Pierce lay in the emergency room for some time covered with a sheet. He later revived in the hospital basement morgue, frightened by three sheet-covered corpses laying in a row beside him. The staff was unaware when he revived. An orderly said that when he delivered the last body from a non-related car accident, Pierce was still totally covered. The estimate was that Pierce had been dead at least an hour.

Though slow on the stairs, Pierce received a grand tour of Talbot House and the property. They stood for a time in the upstairs front hall, talking about the changes Sara would make. A magnificent pink-orange sunset illuminated the sky through the branches of the trees and beyond the river.

The conversation with Pierce was enjoyable and humorous. He seemed glad to be active and took an interest in anything that came his way. One thing was certain he had extreme intelligence.

"So, tell me about this recurring dream you once mentioned," he said.

Could her plans to move back to the Delta have triggered the recurring dream with a man pointing downward? She hesitated, wishing to dismiss discussion of it at the moment. Since the dream began in Puerto Rico before her decision to relocate and the man in the dream was older, no connection existed to Pierce. Still, she needed to understand what haunted her sleep. Finally, realizing she should talk to someone, and who better than Pierce with his brilliant mind, she gave in. "For years, I've seen this older guy. I see his eyes and his hand, pointing at something. It's not frightening, but I don't know why he comes to me."

"If the dream is recurring with more frequency," he said. "Draw him. Can you do that?" Pierce seemed rational and honest. "If he's harmless, bring him to life."

Pierce's energy had waned. He took it slow on the split staircase at the back, and they entered the kitchen. By then, it was well after dark. Choco and Latte were free to explore in the empty house. Instead, Latte lay at Pierce's feet as he dropped himself into a chair. Choco went to the kitchen door at the pantry, alert, as if waiting for someone.

"You drink?" Sara asked. "I make a seven-juice tropical punch. I'm told it's to die for." She rolled her eyes as she opened the refrigerator and withdrew a plastic pitcher. "One of the workmen left some Vodka—"

"No thanks on the alcohol," Pierce said. "Gotta be careful what I put into my stomach. Better weaken the acidity in that juice too." He pulled a small leather pouch from his backpack and dumped out a number of pills onto the tabletop. After choosing at least half a dozen in various sizes and colors, he put the rest back into the pouch. He looked up suddenly and smiled. "I'm not a druggie. All these medicines keep me alive. It's been like this ever since that lightning zapped me. Better get them into my stomach before all my dinner's digested."

A sensitized digestive system was something else he had to contend with. Sara kept large bottles of mineral water handy and pulled out a half-full liter. "We can water it down," she said with a sly smile. "It is a little late in the day for juice, but you gotta try it anyway, okay?"

"Do you mind drinking from mugs? They're all I've unpacked so far."

"I don't mind at all."

They carried the mugs, water bottle, and juice pitcher into the sitting room.

"Gonna take a lot of furniture to fill this place," Pierce said.

Sara smiled as she played with Choco, knowing decorating the big house would be fun. But that energetic dog could wear her out. By the time she looked up, Pierce had filled their mugs with the blended juice.

"A toast to new life and pleasant surprises," he said, holding his mug high.

Sara toasted. The pups finally lay at their feet and stayed quiet, it seemed, as long as they were near someone. Their personalities were changing.

The night winds howled around the gables. After they visited a while, Sara began to feel exceedingly tired. She glanced at her watch. It wasn't yet ten o'clock, and she still had to kill an hour before driving the dogs back to Esmerelda's and take Pierce to Isleton.

She polished off her drink though watering it down gave it a less appealing taste.

Pierce savored his. "Great mix. Strangely bitter, though, maybe salty."

Chapter 25

Sara woke on her bed feeling the top of her head about to blow. The lights in the house were on. It was still nighttime. After she lay a while thinking she was still in a dream state, from somewhere came the memory of things she had to do. The last thing she remembered was looking at her watch.

The house was totally quiet. Had she done her errands and come home that exhausted? She still wore the same clothing. She lifted her head and promptly passed out. When she came to, the room still spun. She lifted her arm to look at her watch, but the arm dropped back to her chest with a thud. When she swung her legs off the bed and tried to stand, she collapsed to the floor. Her pulse pounded at her temples. Anxiety ran rampant through her nervous system. The acute pain of the headache was like none other. She tried to stand again, pausing in a kneeling position beside the bed, barely able to move and when she did, her muscles screamed out. Something was dreadfully wrong. Her lips were numb, and her hands tingled. She tried to stand again and felt drunk, but neither she nor Pierce drank alcohol.

Surely, the juice and water hadn't made her sick. Maybe it was the take-out food. She couldn't remember taking Pierce home. Or the dogs. She clutched the top of her head. Maybe she should call Esmerelda. She glanced at the wristwatch on her arm that lay limp on the bed. She had difficulty focusing but realized it was just after three o'clock in the morning!

Pierce.

She felt hung over. The pain in her head assaulted her senses, worse than the morning after the first and only time she drank Puerto Rican rum.

Pierce.

Pierce mixed and poured the water and juice they drank. She had no previous ill effects from either the pitcher of juice or the bottled water.

Pierce.

Could he have drugged her? Did he have a second little pouch of knock-out drugs in his backpack?

Her mind remained groggy, her limbs weak.

Why would Pierce drug her? She remembered being in the sitting room but woke lying on her bed. Had he tried something sexual with her, knowing that if she resisted, he wasn't strong enough to pull it off? So he drugged her?

The lights were still on. Had he simply left afterwards?

"Choco," she said. "Latte." How feeble her voice sounded.

She heard nothing and remembered the dogs had eaten some of her take-out. Maybe the food was bad, really bad, and they were affected too.

The first thing she needed to do was determine what had happened.

She was fully clothed and knew how her body would feel if she had been violated and dressed again. She had been married eight years and experienced three miscarriages. She was no stranger to sex. She knew the smell of sex and what her body would feel like afterwards. She had not been molested. She dragged herself up and then collapsed to sit on her bed again and fell backwards as her head banged hard against the wall.

Why would Pierce drug her and then leave? Where were the dogs?

The house was eerily quiet. She tried to stand again and could only do so by holding onto the corner of her desk. Before going anywhere, she had to sit on the floor or risk passing out yet again. After great effort, she crossed the hall and then held to the doorjamb at the sitting room entry and peeked in. Pierce was not there, but his cane lay on the floor. Their mugs sat on the end table, as did the juice and water containers. The lights were still on in the dining room and kitchen.

Not knowing what might have happened, but feeling great fear, Sara wanted to arm herself. She made it back to her bed and sat again as she looked around for a weapon. The only thing available was a flashlight.

In Victorian style houses, the kitchen and pantry are considered nothing more than utility rooms and kept fairly secluded from the rest of the living area. In fact, until she could rebuild it, access to the kitchen was through the pantry. Sara needed to pass through the sitting room, cross the dining room, and then go through the pantry. It seemed miles away. She used the wall for support and was thankful the massive sliding pocket doors between the sitting and dining rooms were open. She wouldn't have had the strength to budge them. She nearly collapsed before reaching the fireplace in the dining room. She clung to the mantle and could barely feel her rubbery legs.

Finally, she made it into the pantry. She peered cautiously into the kitchen and through the legs of the table and chairs and saw Pierce lying on the kitchen floor.

"Pierce!" She clung to the door jam and dropped the flashlight as the noise echoed.

He didn't move.

"Choco! Latte!"

No dogs.

Sara's knees gave out. Goosebumps traipsed over her body. The vertigo intensified. She needed to get to the phone and crawled all the way back to the sitting room before realizing her cell phone was still attached to the waistband of her jeans. She fumbled weakly and finally punched in 911.

"We might have been drugged," she said, trying to explain to the 911 Dispatcher. She listened to the questioning and then responded. "We ate five hours before I last looked at my watch. If it was food poisoning, we should have been sick long before then." A few more words and then she closed the phone. She should be near the side entrance when a deputy arrived. Something didn't add up. If they had been drugged, someone had gotten into the house before they returned earlier that evening. Sara clutched the flashlight as she crawled into the vestibule at the side door. It was another New Moon night and pitch black out. She stretched upward using the flashlight against the switch to turn on the outside light and then collapsed into a heap.

Sara stared at her phone and finally checked her messages. Three came from Esmerelda. The last one ended with her saying, "I know the dogs are in good hands. I'll talk to you in the morning." So why hadn't Sara heard her phone ring all those times?

In minutes, gravel crunched. Sara forced herself to stand so the deputy could see her in the window. The woman officer, wearing an authoritative dark blue uniform, pulled flimsy latex gloves from her pocket and put them on as she sprinted up the side steps two at a time. Sara fumbled her way and unlocked and opened the outer door as a blast of cool air greeted her. The deputy followed her back inside.

"Deputy Conroy," she said, not offering her hand. "Johanna Conroy." She glanced around like an animal keen to prey, her attention directed toward the darker portions of the house. "Where's Pierce?"

Sara pointed toward the kitchen.

More gravel crunched. Another dark blue uniform arrived. Somewhere from the back of her mind, Sara remembered that the deputies that attended her parent's drowning wore olive green trousers and light green shirts. She felt confused.

The other deputy, whose name tag said Isidoro, also pulled on gloves and took Sara's arm and helped her walk and to sit at the kitchen table. She doubled over and hugged herself. She needed to go to the bathroom but wouldn't be able to make it there by herself.

Pierce lay sprawled on his back in front of the door to the rear porch.

Johanna pressed two fingers against the side of his throat. "Ambulance will be here any second."

Isidoro went to his car and returned with a camera and began taking photos.

"Don't touch anything," Johanna said. She was a husky, strong woman who looked and acted more like a man and had a deep yet gentle voice. She kept glancing in all directions. "Sorry, we gotta do this." She pointed at what she wanted Isidoro to photograph.

Isidoro glared at her. "Just let me do my job, okay?"

Johanna ignored him and twice cocked her head and listened as if she had heard noises elsewhere in the house.

"Can you excuse me?" Sara asked, trying to stand. "I've got to go the bathroom."

"No, don't do that," Johanna said quickly.

"I have to."

"Wait. If you've been drugged, the proof is right there in your bladder." She pointed to Sara's lower torso. "Sorry, you can't go yet."

A siren wailed, drawing closer. More gravel crunched. The ambulance arrived and killed its sirens and lights as it edged down off the levee.

"A stretcher won't make it through that pantry," Johanna said. She opened the porch door between Pierce's legs.

The EMTs rushed in and dropped trauma kits and bent over Pierce. One looked closely at his face. "Hey, we know this guy," he said.

One felt Pierce's limbs, probably for breaks, since he evidently fell. The medic attached a neck brace. The other found Pierce's medical alert bracelet, and then sought medical advice on his radio. They started an IV. When they could move him, they brought the stretcher into the kitchen. Isidoro helped the EMTs lift Pierce's tall body.

"I'm sorry," Sara said, struggling to leave the room. "I have to go."

"Can't you hold until you get to the hospital?" Johanna asked.

Sara was about to burst and struggled to stand. "Sorry... sorry...."

The medics retrieved a sterile cup from their trauma kit and handed it to her.

"In this?" Sara asked, feeling ashamed.

"I'll have to go with you," Johanna said.

"Into the bathroom?" Sara nearly screeched.

"I'm the only person who can vouch that that's your urine," Johanna said. "And that you didn't tamper with it in there." She waited for a response, but Sara didn't know what to say. Was she being considered a suspect? "Or one of them can go with you." Johanna nodded toward the medics.

They were both men. Sara waved them off and groped her way along the wall. Johanna helped her walk, but Sara's legs gave out in the hallway.

"Easy, there," Johanna said, grabbing her arm and breaking her fall. Sara sat on the hardwood floor, stunned, trying not to wet herself. Johanna stooped down and waited. "This doesn't look like food poisoning to me."

Johanna helped her into the bathroom and seemed more understanding, even a little embarrassed. She stood at the doorway looking out and cocked her head every time she heard a noise.

Once outside in the thick morning drizzle, the medics shoved Pierce into the ambulance. Johanna handed over Sara's urine cup. They placed it into the brown paper bag and left.

After the ambulance pulled out of the driveway and sped north toward Sacramento, Buck arrived in his old pickup. "Heard about this on my scanner," he said.

"This isn't something a Fire Chief responds to," Johanna said.

"Hi, Jo," Buck said. "Sara's my cousin." He wrapped his arm around her shoulders, and she fell against him.

"No kidding," Joanna said, distracted. She glanced in all directions again, and then came real close and said in a quiet voice, "You may have to leave." She kept looking around. She stopped talking every time she thought she heard a sound.

"Leave?" Buck asked.

"Take her into your truck," Johanna said. "Turn it toward the levee and keep the engine running." She unsnapped the cover of her holster. "If someone's still in this big old house, Isidoro and I are gonna flush him. If someone other than us comes out the door, you two get the hell outa' here."

Isidoro popped the snap on his holster, and he and Johanna talked in hand signals as they re-entered the house.

Chapter 26

Buck pounded a fist on the button to lock all the doors. They sat in the truck with the motor idling. Occasionally, Buck turned on the wipers to clear the windshield of morning drizzle so they could see out. At least they were warm inside the cab, and Sara was beginning to get her bearings. Surely, if she and Pierce had contracted food poisoning, she would have vomited long ago, but she had not felt nauseous.

Someone hit the breaker box, and all the lights in the house came on. That should have motivated anyone hiding to flee. Lights in several rooms flickered or went out, a sign of old wiring or bulbs. Flashlight beams shone in every alcove in the attic. Then they scoured the second floor nooks and closets and came down to the first. Soon, Johanna exited the house while Isidoro must have entered the basement via the interior kitchen staircase. He came out through the side basement door. Johanna walked the back yard and around to the north side of the house, soon appearing beside the front porch flashing her light beam toward the levee. Returning to the entry side of the house, she flashed the light at the side door lock and looked at it closely. After that, she walked back to the kitchen door and flashed her light at that knob and, again, bent down and inspected it.

Isidoro signaled that they could exit the truck and went back inside to turn the lights off. Out in the night air, Sara's headache began easing.

"Your locks have been picked," Johanna said. "Some fresh, deep scratches." She holstered her pistol and snapped the holster cover closed and peeled off the gloves.

"The locksmith probably did that," Sara said. "I had all the locks re-keyed before I moved in." She thought a moment. Maybe now was the time to mention it. "You know, I might have heard someone walking around the house during the night."

"Last night?" Johanna asked. Her eyes had a way of coming to attention.

"No, from the first night I spent here. I looked for footprints around the property but found nothing. And there are concrete walkways all around anyway."

"How often?" Isidoro asked, stepping closer. He removed his gloves and threw both his and Johanna's onto the floor inside his car.

"Half a dozen times maybe."

"And you're just getting around to reporting it?" Johanna asked.

"I thought it was my imagination."

"And you still stay in this big place by yourself?" Isidoro turned and looked the house over.

Almost certainly now, someone had walked around the house. She really did hear footsteps. She knew the sounds. When she lived in Ryde as a teenager, oftentimes transients would walk between the cottages on their way to the levee. But why would that be happening at Talbot House? A transient would have no reason to climb down off the levee and traipse around the house, only to return to the levee to continue on. Goose-bumps ran down her arms. She hugged herself.

Johanna went to use her car radio, and Sara caught the end of the conversation. Johanna reported that this might be a case of someone having drugged both her and Pierce. She climbed out of the patrol car again. "Detectives are coming to take a look."

"The dogs," Sara said as she began to think more clearly. "Where are the dogs?"

Xavier looked at her suspiciously.

Johanna turned on her heel. "What dogs?"

"I almost forgot," Sara said, massaging the throbbing at the top of her head. "The dogs are missing."

"What dogs?" Johanna asked again. "How big?"

"About six months."

Sara's phone rang. Johanna and Xavier listened and took occasional notes while Sara explained the situation yet another time to the person on the phone.

Johanna's expression softened after hearing Sara tell the story again.

Finally, Sara was able to hang up. "That was the woman who owns the dogs."

"Maybe they just got loose," Johanna said.

"Sure," Xavier said, seeming to disbelieve. "Through a locked door?" Clearly, he harbored some dislike of Johanna.

Johanna ignored him. She shoved the notebook into her shirt pocket and stuck the pen over her ear and looked around. "Let's see if we can find those pups."

Chapter 27

"Let's make sure they didn't get killed on the levee," Sara said. She still had difficulty walking, but the dogs were more important at that moment.

All four went to the wide front yard. Isidoro flashed his light underneath the wrap-around porch. He stood and looked out past the garage before joining them heading toward the embankment.

The old rope on the flagpole made slapping sounds as the wind rapped it against the pole. Sara meant to remove the rope. It was yet another thing that would be replaced when renovations began.

Buck went to tie down the rope. He directed his flashlight beam upward. "Whoa!" he said, jumping back a couple of feet. "That can't be." He walked away shaking his head and motioned for them to stay away. "You won't believe this."

Johanna had already walked to the pole. "What is it?" She flashed her light upward.

Sara went, too, and looked up.

High at the top of the flagpole near the tree branches, the shape of a dog strung up by its neck swung heavily back and forth.

"Damn," Johanna said, stepping away.

It was still a bit dark. Sara tried to focus. "Wait," she said. She took Johanna's light and stepped right under the swinging animal and studied it. "That's not a dog."

"Like hell, it ain't," Buck said.

"Not one of my dogs. Wrong color."

Buck fumbled with the rope until he got it free and began to lower the dog. Once it was halfway down, they realized it was only a stuffed animal.

"Someone's definitely giving you a warning, Sara," Isidoro said as he approached.

"Gotta be a real sicko loose around here," Sara said, grimacing. "So where are the pups?"

Isidoro pulled another pair of gloves from inside his jacket, put them on, and took the rope from Buck. "Let me handle this. It could be evidence." He gently brought it down. "So much for doubting there's a prowler." He secured the rope taut so the toy wouldn't move much. "This could have hairs on it. Prints somewhere. Forensics, you know." Droplets of moisture glistened on the fur. The weight of the stuffed animal soaked with dew sagged and pulled against the noose around its neck. He went to get his camera again.

Johanna hurried to her car and returned gloved and with a brown paper evidence bag.

"Pierce and I stood up there yesterday evening and watched the sunset," Sara said, directing their attention to the upstairs window. "We'd have noticed this."

"Then sometime after you two were knocked out," Isidoro said. "Someone strung this up."

"They are toying with the wrong person!" Sara felt some strength returning, if only from anger. She headed toward the steps that went up to the levee between the trees.

Buck followed her. "I didn't see anything on the road when I got here." The morning brightened. He went completely over the levee to search along the riverbank. Buck's voice floated from the other side of the levee. He returned dragging a scruffy old man by the neck of his jacket. He carried a shovel in the other hand.

"What the hell…?" Johanna asked.

Buck dragged the man down the stone steps and into the yard. "Found Crazy Ike sitting down the embankment."

"I ain't done nothin'," he said, whining. His eyes were wide with fright. "Just on my way home and stopped to rest."

"Damned if he doesn't always show up at night," Johanna said.

"And with his shovel?" Isidoro asked. "What are you doing this far down the river this time of night?"

"I'm lookin' for my new dog. My new dog done run away."

"Ran away?" Isidoro asked. "Or you buried him some place?"

Crazy Ike tipped his head to the side and looked confused. "I ain't buried my new dog yet."

Then Sara remembered and told the deputies about the shovel marks in the concrete and the pried windows. Isidoro took hold of Crazy Ike's frail arm and dragged him along as they hurried to the north side of the house.

Johanna placed Ike's shovel edge on top of each mark left in the concrete. The marks were from a full-sized shovel with a wider arc. Ike's shovel was much smaller and angular and just about all a frail man like him could handle.

Johanna looked at Isidoro, shrugged, and said under her breath, "Ike's nuttier than a squirrel's breakfast, but he didn't do this." Her frustration reflected the feelings of everyone in the Delta. They needed to put an end to the mayhem created by the psychopath, and this was one more opportunity that slipped away.

"We know where to find him," Isidoro said.

They gave Ike back his shovel and sent him on his way. He used his shovel like a crutch to help him climb the rough-hewn steps back up to the levee. Evidently, the deputies didn't see him as being connected with much of anything except his mysterious diggings.

"A person can act loony to hide what really goes on," Buck said.

The deputies merely looked at one another and then headed back to the other side of the house.

A sleek pale green sedan crunched gravel and parked behind Buck's truck. Fredrik drove. Esmerelda, dressed rugged in denim, boots, sweater and a jacket, was half out of the Jaguar by the time it stopped.

They renewed acquaintances and briefly brought Esmerelda up to date as she hugged Buck and then shook hands with the deputies. Deltans pretty much knew each other.

"If the dogs are around," Esmerelda said, "Mimie will find them."

"Is she friendly?" Isidoro asked.

"Leashes," Sara said. "We need the leashes from the kitchen."

Buck started toward the door. Johanna grabbed his arm. "Sorry. The house is off limits for now."

"We'd better have the leashes with these dogs," Sara said, not knowing how they might react if frightened.

"Why?" Isidoro asked. "What kind of dogs are these?"

"Pit bulls."

"I'll get the leashes," he said, turning on his heel.

"Behind the kitchen door," she said, calling after him.

Mimie whined pathetically and lifted her feet up and down as if ready to go. Esmerelda grabbed Mimie's collar and held it taut to keep her at attention. "Better get Mimie's leash, too, if we're going far," she said as she pointed into the back seat. Fredrik leaned in to retrieve it.

Isidoro came out of the house. "No leashes in there."

"On hooks, behind the kitchen door," Sara said. "Inside the porch."

"No leashes in the kitchen or on the porch."

Sara remembered hanging the leases when she took them off the pups. Whoever drugged her and Pierce must have taken the leashes with the dogs. It sickened her to think what might have happened to lovable Choco and Latte.

Fredrik spoke after having remained quiet all along. "I guess Pierce got the worst of it."

His stare made Sara feel uneasy. "How do you know that?"

"His life's an open book. He wrote about it," Fredrik said. "With all the medications he has to take, anything unusual could cause an adverse reaction. Wouldn't take much to do him in."

Sara needed to get away from Fredrik's curious glare. His eyes weren't as friendly as when she first saw him. "Let's walk the field," she said to the others. "We need to find the dogs."

Buck took Mimie's leash. Mimie strained hard against it, pulling Buck forward with her.

Most of the land in the Delta was composed of rich peat dirt, filled with settled organic matter from flooding. This rock-strewn area along the levee for half a mile or so couldn't be farmed. The cattle Orson raised didn't mind and packed the earth while laying down trails.

They spread out to cross the field, careful not to trip on rocks hidden by tall weeds. The rising sun elongated shadows and made dew glisten.

"Well, there's no footprints out here," Johanna yelled to Isidoro. "Not since the dew laid down anyway."

Fredrik accompanied Esmerelda, who insisted she had to help. For her age, she maneuvered the rough ground as if used to working in the fields.

Sara listened. If the dogs were around, they might yap. She heard nothing.

They plodded across the wide field being careful not to turn their ankles on the rocks. A canal ran across the back marking the edge of Sara's five acres. Several mallards took flight from the canal bank on the northeast corner. Mimie began to bark and pulled Buck toward the old water trough and salt lick area at the southeast corner. Everyone followed Buck toward the pile of rocks about four feet high and twenty feet long, the rock pile Sara intended to have removed.

Mimie lunged and pulled the leash out of Buck's hand. He took off after her. They converged and immediately heard the pups whining. Mimie barked. The pups came out from behind the rock pile. They wore their leashes, dragging them along. Their faces and legs were sopping wet, and they shivered. They had been drinking water in the canal. When Sara tried to grab Latte, both dogs ducked back behind the rocks.

Isidoro went around the pile from the left and Buck went around the right. Buck slipped in the wet soil and almost fell into the canal. "Damn it!" he said. He came up with mud all over him. Mimie stood barking. The pups managed to climb up the back of the rock pile, coming over the top to the ground to stand in front of Mimie.

The dogs no longer seemed like pups. They were developing the gaunt, intimidating features common to pit bulls. Their present actions proved their maturing personalities.

Strangely, Latte rolled over and scooted around on her back and came up even muddier. Choco barked, just stood and barked.

Esmerelda and Fredrik arrived last. Esmerelda bent down to attend to the pups and screamed in surprise. Her knees buckled and Fredrik had to hold her up. He and Johanna helped Esmerelda to a sitting place on the rock pile. She could only point.

Sara bent over to see what might be wrong. Latte scooted on her back again. Choco sat, stared up at her, and beat his tail on the ground. As Sara reached for the pups, she saw a large white stone among some bigger rocks. Unlike the other rocks, it was fairly smooth. Choco stood and wagged his tail again. He began to paw the ground.

"There," Esmerelda said, pointing toward Choco's feet.

Sara knelt down to see what caused Esmerelda to nearly faint and came face-to-face with a human skull.

Chapter 28

The skull lay at the edge of the rock pile, half-covered with small stones and dirt. The nose area and below had collapsed and filled with soil.

Choco again pawed the ground and barked.

Sara bent again to pull him aside. "Oh!" she said, jumping back. Two long bones lay impacted in the soil beneath his feet. Choco sniffed and looked up at her again.

Isidoro saw the bones too. "Everybody back," he said and immediately began snapping photos.

Johanna bent down to take a look and then straightened and reached for her radio. "We'd better get the spade brigade out here."

Everyone needed to vacate the area in order to preserve what little evidence may have worked its way to the surface. As Esmerelda turned to leave, she said, "Thank heaven. That's not my Orson. He went missing in Placerville."

The pups pranced and nipped at Mimie's heels and played, dragging their leashes, all the way back to the yard. They had enough sense to avoid danger until they heard friendly voices and Mimie's bark, or detected her scent in the air. It was strange that two pit bulls, a breed that had aggression genetically inbred, had not chosen to attack the person who tried to take them. Or, maybe they had and scared him off.

Johanna approached with another brown bag and wearing gloves again. "I'll take those leashes," she said before anyone could touch them. "Might give us some prints." She also knew how to approach a pit bull and offered the back of her hand in a non-threatening way for them to sniff. When they did, she began to pet them. "Tell me which dog is which."

Sara pointed and gave their names. Choco and Latte sat patiently watching Johanna's every move as she first claimed Choco's leash and placed it into a bag and scribbled: Choco - Red. Then the other in another bag: Latte - Green.

Cool dampness permeated the early morning. They sat in the cars to await the detectives. Buck retrieved some old rags from his truck and dried his clothes as much as possible, then wiped down the pups as they shivered. He fashioned a couple of lengths of rope as leashes and finally put the dogs into his truck to dry and warm up.

Fredrik zippered his jacket and stood outside, displaying less interest in the dogs than he had at the hospice.

Two detectives arrived. They questioned each person separately and then asked each to wait in the cars again. The longer they waited, the more the cold morning air added discomfort.

Johanna sat in the patrol car writing her report. She received a call, but Sara couldn't make out the chatter. Johanna kept nodding. A couple times, she glanced in their direction. Her expression was one that said they had some answers. When she finished the conversation, she jumped out of her car and ran into the house. In a moment she came outside and headed straight toward the Jaguar. "Sara," she said, motioning that she should come out of the car. "Can I talk to you?"

"Is it Pierce?" Sara asked, jumping out. "How's Pierce?"

"First, let me say this," Johanna said when they were out of earshot of the others. "It was Rohypnol."

"What is that?"

"You don't know about Rohypnol?" She looked over at Fredrik and stopped talking when it seemed that he might join them.

"Tell me."

Johanna motioned that they move farther away from the others. "It's the date rape drug. Your urine sample was full of it. Word outa' the hospital lab indicates tests spiked big time on the chromatograph."

"What about Pierce?"

"They tested his blood and got a hint of it. Ended up using a catheter to get his urine."

"So, how is he?"

Johanna shook her head. "In a coma."

Sara choked back tears. Buck had been watching and came over and wrapped his arms around her shoulders.

"Tell me something," Johanna said, shifting into an investigative mode. "That stuff you two drank? Anything different about it?"

"It's my own punch mixture, a concoction I learned in the Caribbean. We mixed it with mineral water." Sara paused, remembering. "Wait a minute. Mixing it with water made it a little bland for me, but Pierce said it tasted a little salty."

Johanna dropped her arms to her sides and rolled her eyes like she knew with certainty what had happened. "What about the color?"

"What about it? It was seven juices mixed."

"Someone's got an old stash of dope then," Johanna said. "Stuff on the streets these days turns liquids blue."

"I'd have noticed."

"Detectives are confiscating everything out of your fridge." Johanna nodded back toward the house. "And the bottles and mugs you two had drinks from."

Sara mustered her concentration. "We ate Chinese food too. The containers are in the garbage can in the workshop."

"Rohypnol is usually mixed with fluids."

"Okay, so it wasn't the take-out. I fed some to the dogs, even gave them a drink of the bottled water we bought." Someone had to know about the use of drugs and how much dosage to give. "That idiot could have killed us," Sara said.

"Maybe that's what the person tried to do," Johanna said. "Only the dogs got the best of him."

Isidoro came out of the house with his camera, many sealed brown bags, and Pierce's backpack and cane. Johanna told him about the food containers in the workshop garbage can, and he retrieved them for examination anyway. She turned over the bagged stuffed animal and leashes to him as well.

"They're getting lots of prints," Isidoro said. He turned to Sara. "You'll have to come to Headquarters and leave a set so we can rule yours out."

"Oh, great," she said. "My contractor and his workers have been all over the house."

"No workers here for a while," Johanna said. "You'll have to vacate the premises till the investigation is finished."

"Cold case detectives will be investigating that skeleton at the back too," Isidoro said, nodding toward the end of the field.

Johanna shifted her stance as she made notes. "This whole area is now a crime scene." She motioned from the house to the field. "Although, it may be two separate crimes we're dealing with."

Johanna accompanied Sara back inside the house to pack her bag. She would stay with Buck and Linette again. She looked at her computer and sighed heavily. She was well into her new project and beginning to finally make headway with it. She grabbed her backup DVDs and decided to purchase a laptop. As she left the house, she wondered how she would be able to stay there by herself once the investigations were completed. The cold case murders, that haunting dream, and the noises around the house; now an attempt on hers and Pierce's life—with someone having gotten inside—told her it wouldn't be safe to stay at home alone anymore.

Buck had to go home and change, then go to work. Sara located Daphine working early at her store and asked her to make the trip to Sacramento with her. Daphine was so concerned she dropped everything and ran for her car, asking myriad questions on the phone along the way.

The pups refused to get into the car so that Esmerelda could take them home. Finally, Fredrik yanked the ropes to drag the pups closer. They pulled against the ropes, resisting, warily watching Fredrik. Then carefully, one by one, he picked them up and dropped them on the floor at the back seat as if begrudging soiling his hands. That seemed normal for a man of Fredrik's stature with dirty dogs. However, throughout the events of the morning, Fredrik exhibited a certain mysterious frustration and Choco and Latte had stayed clear of him.

Chapter 29

Isidoro met Sara at the hospital and found a desk to finish writing his report. He waited while the ER doctor examined her. After the exam, he said, "You can ride with me to Headquarters." He sounded insistent.

"Am I a suspect?" Sara asked. It was the second time she felt they might be seeing her that way.

"Not that I know of." He smiled as if realizing his gesture of friendship had been too aggressive.

"Then Daphine can drive me."

During the trip to be fingerprinted, and then driving back to the hospital with Daphine to check on Pierce, Sara said, "This can't be happening to me."

"Sounds more like one of our wild stories when we were kids," Daphine said.

They found Pierce in a private room adjacent to the Intensive Care Unit. The charge nurse was reluctant to give information to non-family members.

"We are his family," Sara said, hoping to get away with the pretense.

"We're perfectly aware of his background. He's been a patient too many times." Then the nurse's voice softened. "I will tell you this. With the condition he was left in after the lightning incident, anything might take him, just like that." She snapped her fingers softly. "I'd be saying prayers for this poor soul."

When they entered the room, the first thing they noticed was that Pierce's face was sunken.

"They took out his teeth." Still, Sara had to smile.

"What's that about?" Daphine asked.

Sara flashed a perfect exaggerated smile.

Daphine looked at her teeth and squinted. "You got your teeth crowned," she said softly. "Your dentist did a great job."

Sara flashed another silly smile and waited. Finally, she said, "Me, too."

The lights went on in Daphine's eyes. She kept her voice low but asked, "You? You wear falsies?"

Sara clicked her teeth together. "All of them," she said, and then smiled again.

They went to sit on opposite sides of Pierce's bed and watched the monitors. Daphine's mood changed, she had tears in her eyes. She slipped a hand around one of Pierce's hands. Even if Pierce was just a friend, as Daphine claimed, Sara saw the pain in her eyes.

She studied Daphine and remembered that once, as young teens, she came to visit, and they walked out into a field and talked and kicked at clods of dirt. They found fresh road kill, a jackrabbit, and Daphine dug a hole in the dirt with her bare hands and pushed the rabbit into it with a stick and dragged dirt over it with her shoe. To her, it needed a proper burial. Now, here was Daphine, taking Pierce's ills upon herself. It was a long time coming, but Sara finally understood the meaning of Daphine's reaction and the ancient burial ceremony.

Through the years, Sara lived with a feeling of isolation and loneliness. She attributed it to being far from home and shrugged it off because home in the Delta was full of sad memories. The new life she made for herself in the Caribbean was good enough without having to be perfect.

Sara looked again and saw that Daphine had placed both hands around Pierce's hand. A sweeping feeling of helplessness came over Sara. She reached for Pierce's other hand and held it, and finally realized she was capable of caring for someone else instead of shying away. She closed her eyes and bowed her head.

Chapter 30

Later that evening, Sara remembered something that jolted her upright in bed. *The long bone that stood up out of the gravel bar in Snodgrass Slough.*

Now she wouldn't sleep. She climbed out of bed.

The long bones that the pups found. They were the same type of bone, human femurs with rounded heads at the hip ends.

Linette, who had been up late working on her bookkeeping, must have seen her light and knocked.

When Sara finished telling her about the bones, Linette said, "You'd better tell Johanna so they can take a look."

Two days later, Sara and Valeriano were in one boat leading the way. Johanna, working overtime that morning, accompanied deputies in another boat. One deputy had suited up to dive.

The deputies eased their craft alongside. Sara held a float between the boats to keep them from jostling together.

"The gravel bar stuck up out of the water," Val said. He kept the boat moving slowly, to find the find exact spot. Twice they found gravel near the riverbank. Twice, the deputy dove and found nothing.

"We may never find it," Johanna said. "The currents wash things in and then washes them out."

"You sure you saw a human bone?" the deputy in the boat with Johanna asked.

"It looked just like the femurs found on my property."

By then, they had attracted a flotilla of on-lookers. Though in full uniform, Johanna still flashed her badge and motioned with a sweep of her arm for them to keep their distance.

Val guessed at another location. The deputies eased close along at the base of the levee in hopes the bone might have lodged somewhere in the tangled growth of tree roots and low-lying shrubs. Johanna scanned through binoculars. If one bone had been there, maybe they would find other parts of a skeleton.

"This is pointless," Johanna said after they had been out a couple of hours. She motioned that they call off the search.

Snodgrass Slough wound and twisted and even split off north of Locke. Eventually, one leg emptied into the Delta Cross Channel, which joined the Sacramento River. If the bone washed into the river, it might never be seen again.

"By the way," Johanna said as they stood on the dock waiting to hoist out the deputies' boat. "No prints on those leashes."

"Not even mine?" Sara asked.

"A lot of smudges. Covered with grime too. The dogs had been into that muddy canal."

The next morning, after having a confusing vivid dream of finding more bones, Sara borrowed Buck's truck and made a special trip to Sacramento to purchase a handgun.

"What's that one the deputies use these days?" she asked.

"That's a Sig Sauer semi-automatic," the store owner said. "Too much gun for you. You can't get approved to own one anyway." He selected a gun out of the glass counter. "Here, try this one."

The gun was so small that it could be nearly hidden inside her palm. She didn't need to blow off her own fingers if she had to use it. She needed to feel secure with a weapon she might need to fire. "What about that one?" She pointed inside the showcase.

The storekeeper glanced at her and back to the gun. He raised his eyebrows and then brought out the pistol. "A .38 Smith and Wesson. Used to be called the Police Special. They've since moved on to those semi-automatics."

If the Smith and Wesson had been good enough for the police, it was good enough for her protection.

"There's a ten-day waiting period," the storekeeper said.

Surely, he didn't think she would kill someone in the heat of passion. "I understand that," she said. "Training. Where can I get some training?"

* * *

An early summer turned the Delta into a cooker. Heat waves wriggled up from pavements and turned the roads into mirages. Patches of asphalt melted into sticky tar. Ski boats, cabin cruisers, and fishing boats glutted the waterways. Boaters who enjoyed gunkholing in secluded coves found themselves in crowded waterway subdivisions as more and more boats sidled in for anchorage. A steady stream of yachts sailed back and forth between the San Francisco Bay area and Sacramento. Drawbridges continually raised and lowered for tall masts, causing lines of cars and crop hauling trucks to wait on the levees. Vehicles overheated.

Preparations for the July 4th celebrations were readied. Neighborhood fireworks started early. Smoke and the odor of gunpowder drifted thick in the air.

Daphine arrived early at the Alden's house to stay with Sara. The Aldens planned to attend the fireworks extravaganza.

"Wish we could just stay home and watch the fun," Linette said, gesturing toward their big screen TV. She and Buck were involved in community affairs and obligated to attend a few functions.

Sara and Daphine chose not to celebrate. The Fourth of July was all about independence, and Pierce, whom they loved, lay trapped in a body that wouldn't respond.

Chapter 31

"Did your battery go dead?" Buck asked the next day as he tapped his head. "Why the heck did you bring that thing here?"

"Eew!" Linette said. "Buck didn't even carry a gun when he was in the Air Force."

Buck took her into the master bedroom and opened the bottom drawer of a chest inside the walk-in closet. "That thing stays in here till you take it home." He grabbed an old tee shirt and threw it over the holstered gun and box of bullets.

* * *

So far, Sara had dodged the reporters. The Delta Gazette and all the Sacramento papers ran continual coverage of the unearthing of the remains on her property. The Bay Area newspapers also carried stories.

Sara's vehicle was finally approved for release from her garage. She would not be allowed access to her property except to remove the SUV.

As she and Buck approached Talbot House, cars and trucks were parked along both sides of the levee. People with binoculars watched investigators, and forensic anthropologists worked the backfield. Pear picking season would begin in about a week, and the glut of parked cars left little room for trucks and other equipment to pass through as farmers scampered to prepare for the crop-picking season.

Yellow banner had been hung between two wooden sawhorses that blocked the top of the driveway and warned:

Sheriff's Line Do Not Cross.

A guard sauntered nearby. "Just don't cross the yellow line," he said as he shifted the toothpick in his mouth.

Buck parked across the top of the driveway, and they walked down to the garage.

A strip of yellow hung from one of the trees near the driveway ramp to the corner of the house, and south to the front corner of the workshop.

Migrant birds landed in the fields. Sara and Buck peered around the side of the garage. Several pheasants pecked at the ground. Others called from a distance. Overhead, riding the thermals with aerodynamic grace, cranes trumpeted. Below them, crime scene investigators dug, measured, photographed, and packaged their findings.

"Look over there," Buck said, showing elation. "Canada geese." A true Deltan, nature thrilled him.

The flock flew low over the men and landed in the adjacent field near a low spot that held water.

The investigators worked alongside a forensic team and their equipment. "Look, a backhoe," Sara said.

"Some of those rocks are huge," Buck said.

The smaller rocks were being removed by hand. More bodies may be buried in or under the rock pile. They wouldn't want to disturb anything by mechanically hoisting the rocks till they were sure.

TV news crews had shown up. When someone caught sight of them beside the garage, one of the camera crews turned and headed back across the field.

"Let's get out of here," Buck said. He swung her garage door open.

She hurried to climb into her SUV and noticed a table with coffee urns and food set up in the workshop.

Two days later, Sara found herself passing time in Daphine's shop before she opened for the morning. All of Daphine's art on the back wall, except the paintings of Jade, had been changed. "You rotate your pieces frequently?" she asked.

"Yeah," Daphine said, smiling in a smug sort of way. "I sell my pieces to people while they stand at the counter. They can't help but see them."

"Not to mention your art is better than anything else in the store," Sara said.

"Different styles. We all have different styles." She busied herself but called out from the far corner. "Fredrik came by the other day."

Hearing that aroused Sara's suspicions about who the killer might be. "What for?"

Daphine returned to the counter. "What for? He came to see me."

As far as Sara was concerned, Fredrik was not in good standing. He could be coming around to casually glean information concerning the investigation. Sara feared for Daphine's safety if, in fact, Fredrik had something to hide. "You going to see him?"

"Went out."

"You've already been on a date?"

"Yep. He's an interesting guy."

"But, Daph." Sara ran her fingers nervously through her hair. "No one knows who the killer is."

"Will you stop?"

"Daph, I've had a chance to see another side of Fredrik's demeanor, with the dogs."

"You're too suspicious. He really came to see if I still had my painting."

"And you went to dinner?" Sara couldn't help being suspicious of everyone. "Daph, Esmerelda's ring was buried in the flower bed right outside Fredrik's door."

"No, it wasn't. It was outside the back door of the patient facility." Daphine threw a glance that said to leave it alone. She opened the newspaper on the countertop and, again, they found themselves bent over it.

> *The skeleton found at the back of the Talbot Estate is tied to other cases of victims being buried with personal belongings carried at the time of death. The remains were identified as a missing fifteen-year-old girl named Laura Baines from Elk Grove. She was involved with an older man at the time of her disappearance.*
>
> *The girl had been missing twenty years. Her older companion would now be sixty-eight years old and is, once again, being sought for questioning. Though he couldn't be tied to other murders, he had been in the Sacramento area when many of the victims went missing. He has long since left the state.*

Sara leaned closer over Daphine's shoulder. "Did more people go missing after he left?" Sara asked.

Daphine straightened and thought a moment. "Considering that the Sacramento bodies were missing for shorter periods than this one, the answer is yes."

"I said it before. This is totally gruesome!"

"Not what you moved home to be a part of, right?"

Sara continued to read.

Only the girl's skull, femurs, and fragments of the largest bones were found. The weight of cattle trampling over her remains crushed the rest as it lay beneath the surface. The hyoid bone from the throat was not located.

The girl's mother identified silver jewelry buried with the skeleton, and provided police with photos of her daughter wearing it. Her mother also said that the girl had a cocker spaniel, also missing. A dog's partial skull and teeth were found under the human remains, making it likely that the teenager and her spaniel met the same end as other victims.

"Do you know what they did last night?" Sara asked.

Daphine kept reading. "What?"

"They flew over my property with equipment that identifies hot spots, disturbed areas in the ground, like more graves."

"Even after years of cattle packing that soil?"

"They made passes back and forth, probably all the way out to Stone Lake."

The end of the newspaper article said:

A new scenario is developing. The Baines girl was missing longer than other skeletal remains identified to date. It was originally thought the killer worked the northern periphery of the greater Sacramento area. The remains recently found at Stone Lake South, and now this burial north of Courtland, were of people missing longer than any others. It is likely the killer used the Delta area to bury some of his earliest victims.

Chapter 32

Sara and Daphine visited Pierce each day. When they arrived, the charge nurse explained that they would have a long wait. Scientists from the university, who monitored his health since the lightning strike, were running more tests.

They went to the hospital coffee shop for breakfast. "Wonder if Morgana's been to see him," Sara said.

Morgana was known to spread jealous rumors in high school, saying that she would end up with Pierce. But Pierce could attract any girl he wanted with his looks and personality.

"Pierce eventually moved to Sacramento and got a Master's degree in agriculture," Daphine said. "Married a girl he met in college."

"So, where's his wife now?"

"Divorced him." Daphine sounded sarcastic. "Probably soon as she knew he couldn't have sex again."

Pierce's life was forever changed. "Has Morgana shown him any attention since?"

"Oh, no. Morgana's a high-maintenance kinda' gal. Likes to be seen with guys she thinks are perfect." Daphine smiled as if pleased. "He never liked her anyway."

Pierce needed all the support he could get. His condition worsened. A week passed, and he remained unconscious.

The next morning, Sara's cell phone rang. Daphine was in a panic. "You know what they've done?" She screamed and breathed hard into the phone.

"Daph! Calm down. What's happened?"

Background noise came through Daphine's end. She was outdoors. "They tore his house down!" Her voice jabbed like a knife through the phone.

"What are you talking about?"

"Pierce's house. The cops took everything!" She sounded out of breath. "They suspect he tried to kill you!"

Sara rushed over and found a parking space down the block from Pierce's house. She ran toward the main house and looked to the rear corner where Pierce's cottage stood in shambles. The floor sagged, caved in at the middle. A wall had collapsed. The roof had come loose from the rest of the house and hung lopsided. A crumpled corner rested on the ground. Bits of shattered glass lay scattered.

Daphine came outside from the main house followed by an elderly Chinese woman. "I sue! I sue!" The woman's cackle could pierce an eardrum. "They take my house, they pay me!"

Daphine pulled back and cringed at the sound of the woman's vocal power. "This is Mrs. Zheng, Pierce's landlady."

Mrs. Zheng wore traditional Chinese clothes and bright-embroidered turquoise slippers.

Sara didn't need to ask what happened.

"They bring search warrant," Mrs. Zheng said, animated. "All men go inside. Six men. Floor collapse!" She had been crying and started again, withdrawing a tissue from her pocket. "That my income. Income gone. I need income—pay my bills."

Daphine put her arm around Mrs. Zheng as they walked toward the cottage. Pierce's belongings, or what was left, had fallen toward the middle of the collapsed floor. The glass aquarium lay shattered. Dead fish lay stuck to the wood, their brilliant colors now muted. The plants in the now pane-less, lopsided windows hung wilted.

"Are they coming back?" Sara asked.

"Mrs. Zheng says she saw them leave with Pierce's computer and some records and other stuff they bagged up."

"They say sorry about house. They go report to housing authority. Say I shouldn't have tenant because my house not suitable for living."

What a pathetic mess. Pierce had nothing to come home to. "Can we salvage anything after the yellow tape comes down?" Sara asked.

"They no come back," Mrs. Zheng said. "They tell me tear house down now. That my income. They take my income!"

Still, Sara had second thoughts. "Let me find out what I can first."

She wouldn't have to wait long. In the Delta, like no place else, news had a way of spreading. She could remember her mom and dad saying it had always been that way. While word-of-mouth was a great way of keeping one's neighbors informed, it also meant information got distorted.

On her way to the Alden's, she picked up a newspaper but found no news about Pierce.

"Seems Pierce is a suspect," Buck said later. "They've even questioned us about him." He paused, looked at the floor, and then eyed her curiously.

"The rumor mill has it the authorities believe he tried to do you in," Linette said. "They're keeping it hush-hush till they can question Pierce."

"That's why they grilled me?" Sara asked. A detective had called days earlier, making it appear like casual conversation. Sara sensed him asking leading questions. "I was sure they wanted to learn about more than just his condition."

"They think he was taking the dogs out to kill them. Then he meant to get you."

"Aw, c'mon! And cart me away with him driving my van?"

Buck only shrugged. "That's the word going around. The dogs got away from him," he said. "Pierce must have mistakenly drunk some of the Rohypnol he slipped you. That's why the dogs got away, and he ended up on the floor."

"No way. He's no killer."

"They're looking at every possible angle," Linette said. "They need to find that maniac."

"Pierce kill people? Break a hyoid bone? He's too weak."

"Don't forget," Linette said. "He may have gone outside with the dogs without needing his cane and then come back in. His cane was found back in your sitting room, wasn't it?"

"What about the stuffed animal on the flagpole?" Sara asked. "If he was knocked out—"

"He could have put that up there after you went unconscious," Buck said. "Coulda' had it in his backpack all along."

"So, they think he's faking his illness?"

"Not necessarily," Buck said. "But Rohypnol would make it easier to get his hands around your throat."

"I don't believe a word of it!"

The Sheriff's yellow tape had been up at Pierce's house for two days. Since the investigators had taken it down their work must be finished. That afternoon, Sara drove to Isleton again, intending to see what she could salvage. She found Mrs. Zheng and several Chinese men removing items out of the shack. The roof and walls had been braced with two-by-fours. One man hammered, driving nails to put the cottage back together.

"I keep," Mrs. Zheng said of Pierce's belongings. She was calmer, even saddened. "I keep for Pierce, but maybe he die."

Sara was deeply troubled and refused to believe that Pierce could harm anyone. Still, she wondered exactly when Pierce's life had changed, and did it coincide with the start of the long list of missing people?

Chapter 33

Unexpectedly, the County approved all the renovations requested at Talbot House. However, the crime scene investigators had not released her property, so work could still not proceed. Sara worried about living at Talbot House again. She wouldn't be alone during the daytime with construction laborers crawling over the place. But before she spent another solitary hour in that house at night, she decided to install a state-of-the-art burglar alarm system.

She detested feeling threatened. If Pierce were the serial killer and arrested, she would be safe. In her heart, she knew he was innocent. With news spreading as fast as it did in the Delta, locals would know when they completed the investigation at Talbot House. It would be a perfect cover-up for the real killer to come back and find her alone.

Sara didn't want to wear out her welcome with Buck and Linette. The next morning, she located two houses for rent.

One was an old single-story farmhouse off Hwy160 on Grand Island near Steamboat Slough. While the farmhouse was the larger of the two, it sat back at the end of a gravel road in the middle of a cornfield. Her intuition told her she shouldn't be isolated.

The other rental was in *Clampett Tract*, also on the west side of the river, but in the heart of Walnut Grove. Older homes with manicured lawns and tall trees sat side by side in the small Tract, the area surrounded by newer expensive homes as more people moved into town and the town expanded. The kitchen and dining areas were up front, and it had three small bedrooms, one separate from the others, with a wide hallway from the living room continuing through to the back yard. Ample sunlight fell into the rear yard. Shrubs were overgrown but could be pruned. A gate inside a trellis laden with honeysuckle and busy honeybees connected to the neighbor's property at the rear.

Sara saw herself living there throughout the renovations at Talbot House. Still, something didn't feel right.

Her cell phone rang.

"Hey," Johanna said. "Isidoro wanted to ask you something."

"Have him call me."

"I know what he wants. It's those rocks on your property. Can he have 'em?"

"Sure, why not?" Sara said as she shrugged. "Eventually, I'll clear that whole field."

"How much would you get for 'em?"

"Why would he want rocks that covered some poor victim all those years?"

"Tell me the truth," Johanna said. "That house isn't really haunted, is it?"

"Sorry," Sara said. "There really is a ghost." Sara wasn't sure but meant to tease Johanna a bit.

"I was afraid you'd say that." Johanna was quiet momentarily. "Well, Isidoro wants those rocks. He does landscaping work when he's off duty. How much would you get for 'em?"

Maybe Isidoro's customers didn't need to know where the rocks had been. "He can haul them away for free. Have him call me first."

Isidoro called the next day.

"I need someone to take charge of my landscaping," Sara said. "If you're interested, get back to me when you can, and I'll tell you what to include on the back lot."

Sara mulled over plans for the Clampett Tract house after leasing it. Finally, she headed over to give Esmerelda a few hours reprieve from the pups.

Tripp sauntered over when they were loading the carriers. "Can I help you with that, Miss Sara?" he asked. He removed the knit cap he always wore and knotted it in his hands. His bald and shaved head was pasty white, unlike his hands and face, which were darkly tanned. For once, he didn't seem offensive, but Sara saw through his disguise. He was still hitting on her by being as nice as he could be.

"How are you, Tripp?" She could at least be polite.

"Top o' the world. Things just go your way when you least expect it." He acted like he had news or a joke and was bursting to tell. The sparkle in his eyes danced. He was giddy as he bent down and tried to be friendly with the pups. They growled in short bursts and kept their distance and stared warily at him. Tripp seemed embarrassed. After the way he treated them, what did he expect? He continued to fidget in his strange way.

"Give the pups a chance. They'll come around," Esmerelda said. She stepped over beside Tripp and patted his shoulder as he remained crouched, trying to get the dogs to come to him. Esmerelda could be such a mother hen.

Fredrik arrived driving Esmerelda's Jaguar. He stopped when he saw them with the dogs. Stopped and stared. When they pulled the dogs aside, he drove into the garage. He gave a small wave of a hand as he walked toward the patient building, seeming too distracted to be friendly. When Sara looked again, he stood inside the door staring back, then turned quickly, and disappeared inside the building.

The next day, Daphine came to have a look at the Clampett Tract house. Sara went out to the sidewalk to meet her. It looked like she had something in the van to unload.

"I got Mrs. Zheng to let me have Pierce's belongings," Daphine said. "What's left of them anyway."

"Where will you keep them? Your own house is small."

Daphine's house was barely big enough for her art paraphernalia. "I'll make room," she said.

Some plans came together in wondrous ways. "You can leave them here," Sara said. "The house is empty."

Daphine handed her one large painting covered in standard brown art wrapper. "I couldn't help myself," she said, pulling out two smaller ones, also wrapped. She kicked the door shut. "You might need something on your walls."

Through decades of absence, their friendship had endured, and they still thought alike. Once inside, Daphine unwrapped the larger painting first. Likenesses of Choco and Latte stared back from the canvas.

"Oh, my!" Sara covered her mouth as she examined the art. "This is overwhelming." She really loved the dogs.

"Check the other two."

Sara ripped at the wrappers. The two smaller canvasses were of Choco and Latte separately. "You've captured their individual temperaments."

Choco stood at attention, his tail high, and an eager testy look in his eyes. Latte lay with her front paws out and her head cocked, as if listening with her eyes and ears.

As they hung the paintings, Sara mustered her courage. "I need your help, Daph."

"Name it."

"You know that strange dream I mentioned?"

"You still having that?"

"If we work together, could you draw what I'm seeing?" All her life, Sara withheld asking for favors.

"You mean like the police do it? You tell me what you see, and I change it around till we get it right?"

"Can you do that?" Sara was elated. Of course, Daphine wouldn't laugh at her.

Sara described her nocturnal visitor. Daphine sketched as they talked. Then they headed to Sacramento to visit Pierce.

As they pulled into the hospital parking lot, Sara's cell phone rang.

"Sara," Johanna said though the phone. "I have some bad news."

"Isidoro changed his mind?" Sara closed the car door. "Hey, that's okay."

"It's not Isidoro. It's Pierce."

Sara waived to get Daphine's attention, and she came around the SUV to also listen. "What about Pierce?" She and Daphine leaned ear to ear.

"Sara," Johanna said. Her hesitation on the other end of the conversation said she was having trouble getting the words out. "They just called me. Pierce's vitals are failing. He may be dying."

Chapter 34

Sara and Daphine raced to the fourth floor of the hospital. A police officer sat near the doorway and eyed them. She and Daphine were unable to enter Pierce's room. At least a dozen people in hospital smocks crowded his bedside. Some stared at the floor, maybe praying. Others watched his face.

"I can't see him," Sara said as she bobbed around trying to see through the crowd. Fluorescent lines on the monitor screens were flat except for an occasional blip. A woman with a notepad stepped back and shook her head as she wrote. Sara caught a glimpse of Pierce before the group closed in around him. His eyes were sunken. Both arms lay limp at his sides. The covers were up over his chest and tucked. Nothing more. His face held that vacant look of death that Sara knew so well: *Starla without a smile. Mom and Dad looking sober.*

The charge nurse came out of the room. Seeing who they were, she said, "Pray that he makes it."

"When did he start failing?" Daphine asked.

"About thirty minutes ago. We've asked others to leave, but you two can stay in the hallway. Just be quiet." She left and returned to the room with some records, which she shared with two of the doctors.

While Daphine sat in a chair outside the doorway, Sara paced. The officer pretended not to show interest but eyed them suspiciously.

Pierce never hurt anyone. He certainly did not drug her. He was patient and kind. How dare they claim he could be a mass murderer? He didn't have much of a life left but was making the most of what had been dealt him.

Sara went to sit. "I don't understand. Who are all of those people ogling him?"

"Haven't you read those books he gave you?"

"Not yet."

"You know he died after that lightning strike, right?"

"He told me that."

"Sara, Pierce has been touched by a power you and I may never know in this lifetime." Daphine's eyes were full of sadness, yet acceptance. "He gave scientists permission to monitor him since he was struck."

"And now they want to be around when he finally kicks off?" It seemed ludicrous. "Why can't they just let him go if that's what's to be?"

"Do you think he should just die?" Daphine asked.

Sara stood and paced again. "I only want peace for him. That's what we should hope for."

Daphine leaned her head back against the wall and closed her eyes. Sara continued to pace. Her mind raced and wouldn't let her sit. They were waiting, like the scientists. It felt ghoulish. Waiting to see if Pierce would die. More than an hour dragged by, interrupted by that ominous occasional bleep that called back everyone's attention. After a long while, the bleeping came no more. Sara tried again to see. Pierce hadn't changed, he hadn't moved. He was gaunt, pale as death. A doctor put his hand lightly onto Pierce's chest, and soon turned to the rest and shook his head. Someone started crying.

Daphine bumped into Sara at the doorway. "He's gone," Sara said.

It took a few minutes for people to clear the room. Sara and Daphine stood stunned as people pushed past them. Several of those in attendance remained in the room, writing the details. Another pulled the sheet up over Pierce's face. Sara and Daphine stood hugging one another while Daphine wept and Sara couldn't get her breath. Neither could move. Neither wanted to leave their cherished friend. A simple flat gurney was brought to the doorway, most likely the one to take Pierce's body to the hospital morgue.

At least thirty minutes had passed when, suddenly, the few inside the room began talking in soft excited tones and then they turned up the volume on the monitors. Turned it up loud.

Sara and Daphine pushed into the doorway. In the quiet pandemonium, no one blocked them when they crowded in at the foot of the bed. A nurse ripped the sheet off Pierce's face.

Someone on the PA system made one frantic announcement after another, calling personnel to Pierce's room. Others arrived and again glutted the tiny space.

With seemingly great effort, Pierce opened his eyes and struggled to keep them open. A nurse threw back Pierce's covers and watched as his chest rose and fell and faltered, sending lines on the monitors askew. The fluorescent flat line was again a pulse, thready, then stabilizing, finally peaking high and almost regular. His breathing deepened. He looked to be doing nothing more than waking from sleep.

Pierce was headline news in every newspaper. After tests were made, they learned he couldn't stomach solid food. He had lost much weight. Any other maladies would be noted as he progressed.

Everything about Pierce's phenomenal experience was rehashed in the newspapers, from the initial lightning incident forward. Comments were tempered. They dared not print total disbelief for fear of discrediting reputable doctors. Many had monitored Pierce for years, some from across the country, several from Europe.

Relegated to one of the inner pages of a Sacramento newspaper was an article about a man arrested years earlier in San Jose...

> *... suspected in one of that city's cold cases. He worked as a street sweeper until being fired after it was learned he had a history of window peeping. Back then, the partially decomposed body of a woman wrapped in a sheet of plastic was found buried in a rocky wooded area outside of San Jose.*
>
> *The meager forensic evidence could link no one to the crime, except that the window peeper knew the woman. No footprints were found, due to the thick layers of dead leaves and heavy rains. The body had been in the ground about a month by the time the grizzly find was unearthed after area flooding washed away the leaves and topsoil. The full skeleton was intact, with the hyoid bone clearly snapped. The case bore striking similarities to the Sacramento cold cases because the remains lay in soft soil near a stream. The difference was that none of the Sacramento area victims had been wrapped in anything and the San Jose burial contained no animal remains. It was ruled a copycat murder.*

Surely, Pierce had an alibi for the periods when each of the missing persons disappeared. He didn't have a car and could only hobble around with a cane. But then, his maladies could only be pretense, as some now claimed.

Pierce continued to thrive. He was moved to a private room near the coronary care unit as a precaution. Twice, they detected an irregular heartbeat. Nothing more as time passed. The IVs would supply nourishment to bring his weight up, and he needed to regain use of his legs.

"Sara," Pierce said some days later. "I couldn't tell the cops anything. I don't know how I got into the kitchen."

"We were drugged."

"They think I'm responsible."

"You don't know that."

"But I do. It didn't take much to interpret the officer's questions. He's definitely hoping I'm their man." Pierce seemed truly hurt by the implication. "You don't think I did this, do you, Sara?"

"No, Pierce. Something else... something scary is happening."

"They want me to take a polygraph." He shrugged. "Oh yes, I called my landlady to let her know I'd be returning."

Sara knew what that meant. Surely, Mrs. Zheng dumped the news on him. "I'm sorry you had to find out that way."

"She told me my rare fish are all dead. And my plants." His lips thinned, then quivered. Surely, the fish were the closest living things that gave him pleasure and that he could easily take care of.

"I'm so sorry," was all Sara could say.

Pierce's mood fluctuated. He seemed to be able to force himself out of despondency when it occurred. "I'm really surprised. The investigators accepted responsibility for the damage to the property. They'll settle with Mrs. Zheng."

"Did they mention what you're supposed to do without a home?"

He shrugged. "Lots of cheap rental places around. At least people know who I am. I'll find something, but I need to get out of here first."

"They owe you something too."

"Maybe. I've already contacted my attorney." In typical Pierce Newton style, he remained upbeat about his grave situation. "Need to find my own mansion."

"Just get your strength back. Daph and I will help you find a place."

"Okay, but it needs to be close to a medical facility. Nothing like Esmerelda's hospice though. I'm not ready to die."

Chapter 35

The mercury continued to climb. Deltans sweltered. Crops across the Central Valley were being picked or harvested and emptied fields plowed or burned off. Trucks sent up billowing clouds of dust on parched field roads as they made their way to the highways with burgeoning loads. Wavy heat danced from the ground and pavements. Strings of trucks moved along like train cars, end to end on the Interstate on their way to canneries in nearby Stockton to the south and Sacramento to the north. Diesel fumes hung in pockets in the air.

Each year, the last Sunday in July is reserved for the raucous *Courtland Pear Fair*. The city park, where the old high school once stood, filled with rows of tented booths. A makeshift grandstand and stage were erected. Tall shade trees dotted the park-like setting.

"This booth is mine," Daphine said as they walked around in the early morning. She closed her shop when festivals took place because her booth attracted more people than the few who would come to the store.

"What's that stuff?" Sara asked of the curious objects in the other half of the booth.

"Junk chimes. A man from Placerville, originally from Walnut Grove, makes them out of metal objects he finds in antique stores." She rattled one and smiled. "He gets a ton of business. I always try to share his booth."

Dozens of bicyclers rode down from Sacramento. Later, an old farmer wearing coveralls and a faded short-sleeved shirt entered two giant pears in a contest and won, each pear being larger than a baby's head.

"People do dress for the weather," Sara said.

"Ha! I didn't know the Delta showed so much cleavage," Daphine said.

The parade began at noon. Buck rode the fire engine with other firefighters to lead off. Local children waved to the crowd from atop two more trucks.

"Grand Marshall," Sara said, reading the sign on the car that followed the fire trucks.

One of Buck's friends chauffeured the Pear Fair Queen and Princesses in Linette's 1966 Ford Mustang convertible.

"Completely restored," Daphine said. "Right down to the white ragtop, the Midnight Turquoise, and the Pony interior. Linette's real proud of that car."

Daphine stayed in her booth. Sara wandered around chatting with sellers and then cut through the crowd to visit Linette at The Book Nook.

Later, Daphine had taken over the entire booth. Sara spotted Fredrik watching from a distance. The next time she looked, he had disappeared. Sara had secretly dubbed him the *elusive ogler*. What could be his purpose of always watching but never saying hello, and then mysteriously disappearing, like he hadn't meant to be seen in the first place; like a window peeper getting his thrills out in the open.

"The junk chimes sold out," Daphine said. "The guy walked away with a fat wallet."

"Let me help with that." Sara grabbed hold of one side of the wooden stand that contained cubbyholes filled with rolled paper prints. "Why didn't Fredrik lift this for you?"

"Was he here?" Daphine asked, looking around briefly.

"He just stands and stares," Sara said. "I'm sorry, Daph, but he's the one who gives me the willies. Some hidden current must run through his mind."

Daphine sighed as if she couldn't be bothered. "Twenty thousand people should pass through here today." She made two trips to her vehicle to bring back more framed artwork.

The festivities continued. Johanna was over by the Humane Society cages. Sara decided to say hello. Johanna was asking a woman, "What kind of dogs are missing?"

"Just two stray bitches," the woman said. "Both spayed and given shots. We'd hoped to recover our costs through a donation for the animals."

A little boy said, "Officer, Crazy Ike and a woman played with the dogs. They had 'em out of the cages."

Around mid-afternoon, after saying her goodbyes, Sara headed toward her SUV parked at the base of the levee. Tripp stood with his foot on her bumper, talking to another man. When he saw her, he said, "Sara, I didn't know you were here."

What was he up to, and why lie? How could he not know she was there, when he had his foot firmly planted on her bumper?

Sara headed north to Talbot House to retrieve her mail before heading back to the Alden's to get some work done while it was quiet. She couldn't get Pierce out of her mind. Who would pay his hospital bill?

It really was payback time for her. She determined to help people in need since good fortune endowed her with the means to do whatever she wished. She could help old Mrs. Zheng restore Pierce's rental. When she realized that Mrs. Zheng's helpers had simply thrown that shack back together, she decided it was no place for Pierce to live. Sara sighed and spoke to herself out loud, "You can't save the world, girl."

On Monday, she telephoned the hospital administration offices. "Pierce's care is paid by a trust that was established decades ago," the voice said. "To study death survivors. Pierce will never have to pay another doctor bill."

Since childhood, Sara had been consumed by feelings of inadequacy, coupled with a need to prove her worthiness. Her inability to do anything about it through the years was handicapped by a small income. Plus, in her younger years, she yearned for fun and to cast off past disappointments. Accumulating wealth had not entered her thoughts back then. Now, in her mature years, and wishing to be of service, she had another brainstorm. She stood and then paced. "It took having money to make me think of it," she said.

The idea wouldn't take all her earnings. In fact, others would fund her plan because what she had in mind, a charitable foundation, would benefit others. She would get the paperwork started immediately.

Chapter 36

Concentrating again on making the Clampett Tract house livable, she hurried to get it furnished. The first priority was getting all the appliances in, connected, and computer lines installed. She had formulated another use for the house, told no one, and meant to pull it off. But again, caution nudged from the pit of her stomach.

She surfed the Internet and found copies of Pierce's first two publications in used bookstores in Sacramento and purchased them during one of her jaunts. Daphine called numerous times to discuss details about the dream drawing. While her intrusions were necessary, evenings were spent in seclusion at the Alden's place while Sara learned about a fascinating man who had died and been revived. Now twice.

At the Clampett Tract house one morning, while Sara waited for furniture to be delivered, Daphine showed up.

"Got more stuff for you," she said as they stood out on the sidewalk. The back of her van contained more than a dozen wrapped pieces of art.

"What are you up to?" Sara asked.

"I want to help you decorate." She gestured toward her van. "Something for your walls."

Sara remained quiet. Her taste for art was personal. She hadn't seen a lot of Daphine's work and wished she could have a choice.

Inside, Daphine unwrapped the pieces. "This is Grand Island Ranch."

Much to Sara's relief, that painting would be her favorite without seeing the rest. Rows of blossoming pear trees stood in an orchard, with hazy pink hues of sunrise in the background. One tree branch in the foreground protruded, loaded with delicate white blossoms. Stamens of white filaments with deep pink anthers almost leaped off the canvas. "I can almost smell them," she said, placing a hand over her heart, closing her eyes, and breathing deeply.

More of the artwork was just as superb. She shouldn't have doubted Daphine's creativity.

"Okay, you weren't here during the time our area became a stop-off along the Pacific Flyway," Daphine said. She continued to unwrap. "So, I have these since you're enamored with our feathered friends."

Sara expected to see masculine-looking close-ups of bird heads, which definitely wasn't her style. Instead, a triptych showed green-backed herons and white-faced ibis in flight over yachts dotting the Sacramento River below. In the distance lay the Rio Vista drawbridge and rolling Montezuma Hills.

It was another lesson not to second-guess Daphine's intuition, but to allow the surprises to unfold.

Daphine's eyes flashed and said something special was about to be revealed. "Remember, you told me about those two Peregrine Falcons you and Pierce saw?" She didn't wait and pulled the wrapper away from another painting.

Sara gasped. "You painted this?" She studied the perfect composition. "Of course, you did."

The horizontal rectangular painting called attention to two Peregrine Falcons in flight, the perspective from above them, with wetlands below, Mt. Diablo and departing clouds in the background.

"Did it a few years ago."

"I know exactly where to hang that one."

Sara loved them all and wouldn't have said anything to hurt her cherished friend if she didn't. Daphine's ability to capture her subjects and make a statement through her talent was indeed rare. "How much?" she asked.

"Just keep them until you get tired of them. Then we can hang new ones." Daphine looked around, and her expression changed to puzzlement. "I must have left one in the van." She dashed outside. Sara held the door open while Daphine carried in a tall rectangular piece. "Stand over there." Daphine pointed across the room. Her eyes were full of excitement. "Go on."

Sara backed up. Daphine purposely removed the wrapper slowly and teasing, kept checking to assure she was building suspense. Finally, she tossed the loosened wrapper aside.

Sara was stunned. She closed her eyes tight and then opened them again while her mouth hung agape. "That's him! How did you... so soon... that's him!"

The framed pastel drawing, though scant, brought her attention to the upper left corner of the drawing where the eyes and temples of a middle-aged man looked back. The depiction was similar in style to the eyes in Leonardo da Vinci's *Self-Portrait*. The dream figure's lower left arm and hand, positioned midway down the composition where it should be on a person standing up, pointed downward.

"That's exactly what I've seen, over and over in my dreams."

"You like it?" It was sepia and shadowy grays to emphasize the spooky mood of the dream.

The overall portrayal was that of a man shrouded in fog, with clarity intensified in the eyes and hand trying to communicate a location or object. The depiction invoked intense apprehension and incited the feelings Sara felt each time she had the dream.

"You nailed it, Daph, right down to his crow's feet." She felt as if the man had stepped out of her dream and into the room. She went to hug her cherished friend. "Thank you," she said, barely able to whisper. She turned and ran her fingertips over the glass, wishing to sense the man's vital energies.

Daphine leaned the art against the wall and stepped back. "I'm sorry. I can't stay to help you hang these. I brought a bunch of hangers and nails though, if that'll help."

Sara's cell phone rang early the next morning.

"Sara," Johanna said in her usual conclusive way. "The investigators just released Talbot House."

Sara jumped with glee. "Thank you," she said, gushing into the phone.

"Listen," Johanna said. "If you're moving back in, consider having someone stay with you at night. Know what I mean?"

"I hear you."

"And don't eat or drink anything you haven't cracked the seal on yourself at that moment." She took a breath. "At least till we find out who doped you two. Okay?"

Patio furniture and a barbeque arrived at the Clampett Tract home the following afternoon. Later, after making the beds, the house finally looked ready for occupants. Sara struggled with her fears, trying to decide what was best for her.

She telephoned the news of the release to the contractor.

"We can begin next Monday then," he said.

"Great. I'd better get my computer out of there before the dust starts flying."

Sara punched her cell phone to end the call and stared out the window. Neighborhood children skateboarded past in the street. Though she seldom saw people mingling and talking out on the sidewalks, the old neighborhood felt safe. Why then was there a continual nudge from the pit of her stomach?

Then she realized that moving her computer and living in Walnut Grove meant an inability to manage the reconstruction of Talbot House. She envisioned working on her computer projects while the crews worked in other parts of the structure. The plan was to oversee their progress and still get her electronic work done.

Sara threw up her hands. Finally, she knew what had been gnawing at her ever since she signed the lease agreement. Part of her plan was to move into the Clampett Tract house, a temporary stay due to feeling guilty about imposing on the Aldens. It meant yet another move before returning to Talbot House. She detested moving her clothes and boxes of belongings, and especially her computer equipment, more than necessary. Finally, she realized the real reason was to get away from being alone at Talbot House because of the frightening activities taking place.

She need not worry. She owned a gun and knew how to fire it, and she would if need be. The alarm system would be installed. With the investigation by the Sheriff's Department and the cold case detectives being so recent, anyone looking to do harm would be scared off. She had succumbed to circumstances dictating how she lived.

"Not on your life!" she said, not caring that she was the only person who needed to hear the words. Yet she still intended to carry out the rest of her plan.

Chapter 37

The hospital released Pierce the next day. Sara went to retrieve him and brought him a gift. Pierce opened the end of the package and out slid a new walking stick. His expression was humorously solemn. He lifted the stick high as he raised both arms in the air, like a conjurer about to cast a spell. The edges of his hospital gown flapped out like a magician's cloak. It was good that his gown opened at the back.

Sara drove as Pierce pulled on his seatbelt and leaned eagerly toward the windshield. They headed south through Freeport, the *Gateway to the Delta*. Tall leafy trees lined Hwy 160 that hugged the foot of the levee. A long row of weathered, wooden single-story buildings lined the road. "Slow down," he said, pointing ahead. "Just… about here."

Sara pulled up in front of the *Coffee Oasis*. "Yeah, we can do this," she said as her stomach growled.

"You know who owns this?" Pierce asked. He didn't wait for an answer. He was already slipping his weak body out of the SUV.

The front door stood open inside. The flimsy screen door lazily slapped shut behind them as they entered. Inside the cafe, patrons consisted of two women couples with one couple holding hands under the table. Johanna walked in through the back door wearing men's work clothes. Now Sara understood. Johanna acted masculine that morning at Talbot House when she arrived in uniform.

Johanna saw them and came straight over to hug Pierce for a good long while. "They turn you loose on the world again?"

"Yeah," he said, smiling out of the corner of his mouth. "I'm a real terror."

"I guess we shouldn't be here since Pierce is considered a suspect," Sara said.

Johanna shrugged. "Hey, I can't control who walks through the door."

"So, this is your second job?" Sara asked.

"Sorta," Johanna said. "Xena and I own it." She gestured to one of the women behind the counter. "This is where you can find me when I'm not in uniform."

"You still haven't changed that name," Pierce said, flopping into a chair at one of the tables.

Three men sauntered in and ordered coffee and a load of pastries-to-go, but talked more about bait and tackle.

"Probably won't," Johanna said. She turned a chair backward and straddled it and waited until the men left. Then she turned to Sara and snickered. "My lover and I wanted to name this place *Les Beans*, but, Ha! They'd have my badge."

Sara and Pierce polished off a delicious home-style breakfast. Pierce's stomach seemed to have recovered nicely. A constant stream of coffee drinking farmers, fisherman, and women kept the place in motion to the tune of the screen door squeaks and slaps. Two deputies made a quick trip in and out for their usual. One seemed to recognize Pierce. He glanced from Pierce to Johanna and back to Pierce again. He said nothing, but his eyes contained a look of suspicion that all law officers get.

"The other deputies support you?" Sara asked.

"All except Xavier." Johanna jumped up to make a couple of fresh pots and then returned. "How are the dogs?"

"Those pups," Sara said. "I hope we've found them a good home."

"You looking to get rid of 'em?" Johanna asked.

"Esmerelda may have found a home. We're hoping to keep them together."

Pierce couldn't resist a wedge of pear pie. "Yeah, but one pit bull is a handful," he said between bites. "Try handling two."

Chapter 38

During the drive home, Sara hedged. "I've found you a place to live, but I need to show you something first." They pulled into the driveway in Clampett Tract. "C'mon, wave that wand and fly yourself indoors."

"Cute house," Pierce said. "But why are we here?"

She felt pleased with her deception and smiled. "This is where you'll be staying."

"You found me a room in someone's house?" Emotion showed on his face and changed from surprise and gratefulness to denial and then curiosity.

Sara pretended distraction. "Sort of. Let me show you around."

Of the two tiny rooms on the right, Sara had set up the front bedroom as a fully equipped office. Behind that was a sparsely furnished bedroom containing a queen bed and a small dresser and that was about all the room might hold. They just peeped in.

The master bedroom was across the hallway beyond the only bathroom. The master bedroom contained a king-sized bed and an armoire.

"I don't need to see someone else's room." Pierce hesitated at the doorway. "And I don't feel right about living with strangers."

Sara pushed him into the room. "This is your room."

"What?" Pierce nearly stumbled, trying not to enter.

Sara held to her charade. "The lady of the house is pretty busy. She's letting you have the bigger bedroom because you're going to be around more than her."

Questions flashed across his face. Finally, he turned around, crossed the hall, and peeked again into the office. He eyed the elaborate computer system and then smiled wistfully. "Guess mine's still being held. I need to write about what just happened to me."

"What about your book manuscripts, all the stuff on your computer?"

"That's all I had on it. Manuscripts. My publisher has them both on DVD and in a Cloud."

"So use this computer." Sara tried to stay behind him so that he couldn't read her face.

"I wouldn't want to be responsible for a stranger's equipment. It looks brand new. Any chance you'll let me come over and use yours till mine's returned?" Still, he entered the room and then turned and saw the painting of the Peregrine Falcons. "I love this! This homeowner has pretty special taste." Then he re-membered something and nearly fell, trying to hobble back into the living room. "That's Choco and Latte." He pointed with the cane. "What are they...?" He collapsed onto the sofa as his eyes darted back and forth studying each painting, putting pieces of the puzzle together. "Okay, so this is Daphine's art, right? But she doesn't live here."

"Yep and nope."

He rose and went to stand and stare a good long time at the sepia and gray rendition. "This is what you dream."

"Yep."

Pierce looked weak and braced himself with a hand against the wall. Sara felt sorry that she had overwhelmed him. "Maybe you'd better lie down a while."

Back in the master bedroom, Pierce touched the armoire and ran his hand down the wood grain. It wasn't a real expensive piece of furniture, but it was handsome and made for a man.

Sara accidentally glanced in the direction of the closet where Pierce's clothes hung, cleaned and readied by Daphine herself. Boxes of his salvaged personal items sat inside on the floor. On to something, he limped his way to the second bedroom and looked into the closet and found it empty. "Okay, who lives here?"

Sara smiled. "You do, Pierce."

"But who else?"

Sara could no longer keep from smiling. "I had planned to stay here till my house was done, but I changed my mind."

The truth hit Pierce all at once. "I can't," he said, turning away. He tried to speak and couldn't. Overcome, he waved her away, and hobbled up the hallway again, nearly stumbling by the office door. Surely, he couldn't remain on his feet much longer.

Sara pulled out the chair from in front of the computer desk, but still he wouldn't sit. "You're the only one who lives here, Pierce. The investigators have released Talbot House. I'm going straight back home from the Aldens soon as the alarm system is in."

"You think that'll keep you safe?"

She had already considered the possibilities, and no one would change her mind now. "This is your new computer, Pierce. My gift to you for your gift to humankind."

He finally understood. "I-I can't—"

"Oh, yes, you can." She wouldn't let him talk himself out of accepting. "You're too valuable in this important research not to be able to hold up your end of the deal."

He looked weak and said nothing. She offered the chair again. He fell into it and turned away, stifling tears.

"You'd better lie down."

He stood and reached for her. "Sara, you've got the purest heart."

"I'm just living the way I think is right." This was one of the ways she would pay back her good fortune. After a lifetime of just getting by, she had so much, and Pierce deserved to have his life turn around.

"May I hug you?"

"Why would you want to do that?" she asked, making a feeble attempt to tease. Then she saw that he was serious. She had never hugged people and always felt they might somehow learn of the misery she held inside.

"Because you don't have the ability to harm a living soul."

Sara didn't know what to do next. It was true. She would never cause harm, and she was closer now to being the person she knew she was. If anyone would recognize the real her, it would be Pierce. Deep down, that might be what she needed from another human being. To be understood. Now she could have it, an opportunity to grasp. She began to tremble and felt utterly awkward but also felt as though she might throw herself into his arms. She bit her lip and managed a smile. "How do we do this?"

He smiled mischievously and slowly reached for her hand. "Like this." His expression sobered.

"I'm not sure I can do this." She tried to pull away.

Pierce held tight and wouldn't let her back away. He leaned his walking stick against the desk and reached for her other hand and pulled her close enough to place her hands behind his neck; his, tenuously around her back.

Sara felt a rush of emotion and empathy as they melted together in a full-body hug. Him caring at that moment forced Sara to face her loneliness. After a moment Pierce reached up and gently took her hands and brought them down between them.

Sara's head spun with the intensity of mixed emotions. It wasn't a falling in love kind of feeling they were experiencing. It was about two people with nothing to hide and learning how great it was to know that neither harbored ill will of any kind. Except for her, maybe. Sara sensed a need to learn forgiveness. Feeling embarrassed by this self-realization, she needed to get away to think and would save the rest of the surprise for another time.

Chapter 39

Pierce's health remained in a state of flux. The research doctors again found a live-in nurse they felt would be right for his anomalies. The energetic, middle-aged woman quickly settled into the Clampett Tract house.

The nurse cooked and cleaned constantly because Pierce slept a lot. The woman could not be idle, except when she gobbled up books faster than saying cover-to-cover. She did the yard work too. She was a wonder woman who spread the word around the subdivision that she could take on another part-time patient as long as she could remain close to Pierce.

Sara was thankful someone was available for her cherished friend. She purposely stayed away, frequently taking Choco and Latte to give Esmerelda some relief. Two more of the patients at River Hospice passed away within days of each other and Esmerelda was too busy to care for the dogs.

"I wanted the owner to take them back," Esmerelda said during one of their conversations. "The woman said it would be detrimental for the pups to change hands so much." The young couple that planned to eventually take the dogs still paid boarding fees. That was some consolation.

Due to Sara's frequent visits to check on progress at Talbot House, Choco and Latte became accustomed to the crews working there. The pups became their mascots.

Sara cornered the electrical foreman. "When will the alarm system be in?"

"You'd better talk to the general," he said. "He's got us moving walls and replacing most of the wiring. Can't just hang new before the old stuff comes out."

* * *

After Sara slept a few hours each night, she would rise to work on her computer. Two o'clock in the morning was when her creativity woke her, like an alarm. She stayed as quiet as possible in order not to disturb Linette and Buck. She was afraid her extended stay would wear thin the bonds of friendship.

Just as dawn broke the next morning, she tiptoed to the bathroom so she wouldn't wake anyone. Buck snored loudly from the master bedroom. A light shone under the closed door to the den. Sara couldn't help herself and tapped lightly and waited.

Linette cracked the door, and they stood staring at one another. She wore pajamas and had a pencil stuck over her ear.

"I was up working," Sara said.

Linette snickered behind her hand. "I've seen your light almost every night. We have the same habits."

"You mean you were…?" Linette's laptop was running. Business documents lay spread across the desk.

"Is everyone okay?" Buck asked as he yawned coming up the hallway. He wore only his pajama bottoms. Sara almost laughed. Buck always wore various caps with some sort of Courtland logo on them. Considering that he once said he never bared his body in a bathing suit, as skinny as he was, Sara was sure she was one of the few people who got to see him half-naked. She stifled a smile, wanting to remind that he had forgotten to put on a cap.

"I guess it's not too early for some of Sara's juice," Linette said.

At least now she knew that her presence was not a disruption in their lives. How patient and kind these people were. How blessed she was. Still, she longed to be back at Talbot House. She needed the use of her commercial grade PC instead of the laptop, which lacked the capacity to fully build the types of programs she created.

* * *

On one of her early morning trips to retrieve mail at Talbot House, Sara heard a siren and, in the rearview mirror, saw the flashing lights of a patrol car approaching fast. She eased onto the soft shoulder to let it pass. The speed of the patrol car kicked up dust and rocks as it cut across the shoulders as if trying to straighten bends in the road. It was Johanna, tight-lipped and determined looking, keeping her sight riveted on the narrow winding pavement.

When Sara arrived at her property, barely enough room remained to park. New yellow Sheriff's banner secured the area from the back door to the side of the garage. Johanna walked slowly, studying the ground as she unraveled more of the tape, all the way from the south side of the garage to the levee where she attached an end to some shrubs on the driveway ramp.

Sara parked on the levee and hurried downhill toward a group of contractors. "What now?" she asked. The fact that yellow banner was, once again, being strung meant she would be kept out of her home even longer. She felt like screaming.

Some of the construction workers eyed her curiously, signifying something bad had again happened.

Isidoro showed up and then two detectives, leaving their vehicles on the narrow shoulders of the levee. Isidoro set out orange cones to alert traffic.

Johanna came up behind and tapped her shoulder. Sara nearly jumped out of her shoes.

"Sorry," Johanna said, taking a step backward and holding up both hands. "Sorry." She looked toward the garage. "Sara, I told you. Someone's trying to send you a message."

"Why? What now?"

Johanna saw Isidoro with others peering and pointing at the ground on the other side of the yellow tape. "Watch where you step," she said, barking the order and pointing.

"Come see this," Johanna said. The deputy led her into the garage. They peered out the back windows, which were shoulder height. Just below the wall, other deputies began putting down yellow, tented markers.

Sara pressed her forehead against the glass, angled her gaze downward and, repulsed, jumped backward. "Who the hell does this guy think he is?" Below the window lay a hole in the ground the size of a grave. She could only imagine for whom.

Johanna pointed. "See that?"

Sara looked again, this time rising on tiptoes to better see immediately downward. She was stunned by what she had missed. "Who does he think he is?" she asked again, screaming. A dead cat almost the color of the soil lay at the bottom of the excavation.

"He didn't intend to do you in though. At least not last night."

"Is that a joke?"

"No, look. The hole's only a foot deep."

The excavation was only the depth of a shovel scoop. "The graves already found were a lot deeper than that," Sara said.

"This may not be the serial killer's work," Johanna said. "There's no evidence that any of his victims were stalked before they went missing."

"This could be someone else?"

"A copycat sicko, maybe, who likes to taunt."

"How could anyone get away with digging here?"

"Look, it's behind the garage." Johanna motioned side to side. "Hidden from the levee. There's no one on three sides for miles."

Large footprints, clearly marked, rimmed the hole. The detectives continued to number them off. One officer got down on his knees and stood several markers in the hollow beside the cat.

"He's toying with the wrong person!" Sara said through clenched teeth.

"Oh, I don't think this guy's playing. He's definitely got plans for you."

Sara turned and walked all the way to the mailbox up on the levee and retrieved her mail. She sat in her SUV and watched as people scurried. Some of the construction workers were sent home. After she calmed, she walked downhill again.

"A couple of the guys and I are gonna keep working," the contractor said. "Whoever it was didn't get into your house. We've been leaving our tools laying loose in there overnight, and nothing's missing."

Johanna had joined the conversation. "It isn't tools this one's after. How did you guys find that hole back there anyway?"

The contractor seemed embarrassed. "We made a mistake of tearing out both of the bathrooms at the same time," he said, thumbing back toward the house. "One of the men went into the field to relieve himself." His expression soured. He walked away shaking his head.

"We gotta wait for our lab guys," Johanna said. "They'll take castings of those strange boot prints."

"Strange?" Sara asked. "How so?"

"Far as I can tell," she said, studying the ground. "Looks like someone wore boots way too big, maybe to cover their actual foot size. Only the heel and mid-foot left a good mark on the ground. Some toe marks are way out front."

"I would think it would be hard to walk in over-sized boots," Sara recalled that Daphine always had great shoes. Among the items, she gave to that large family in need, were shoes, something that Sara was always in need of too. Daphine let her decide if she wanted to keep any before donating them. Daphine wore a size larger, but Sara had shoes to grow into.

"Sara, you okay?" Johanna asked.

"Uh, yeah," she said, shaking her head to dispel yet another forlorn memory. "The boot marks. What about those? I know a little something about shoes that don't fit."

"Looks like they did get some good toe marks in the overturned dirt. Whoever the boots belong to, they had some monster feet." Johanna seemed relaxed doing her job, relaxed and overly friendly. Maybe that was her nature.

Johanna freely talking about evidence might be one of the things Isidoro didn't like about her. "I didn't know you're allowed to give out the kinds of information that you do."

"You the one wearing the boots?" Johanna asked, glancing down at Sara's feet. After a moment, she said, "I think I'd like to find out if ol' Crazy Ike has more than one shovel."

Buck, the Fire Chief, got wind of everything and disclosed more in private that evening. The area behind her garage would be thoroughly examined, and every detail photographed. Molds were made of the footprints and the marks left by the perpetrator's shovel in the damp packed earth. The dirt would be sifted for hairs, clothing fibers, anything. That cat in the open grave indicated the elusive psychopath was still very much active if this wasn't yet another copy cat crime. "Stay away from your property if the crews aren't around," Buck said. "Someone means to do you."

Chapter 40

Late August brought a heat wave, and the *California State Fair* in Sacramento. Sara would wait until the next year to attend. She was just too busy, and the Delta offered way too many distracting activities to fit into her schedule.

Hordes of kids ambled about, getting in last minute water skiing and river sports before school began. Wet bathing suits and stringy, dripping hair was the norm. So were calloused feet, from walking barefoot throughout the summer.

The rivers and streams remained glutted with watercraft. Skiers sometimes couldn't make a good run without being knocked down by someone else's wake. It was the height of the tourist season. Visitors and locals alike wore shorts and tees or as little as possible. Those who didn't would stay mostly indoors. Sara traded the humid heat of the Caribbean for the dry heat of the Delta. She was a sun worshipper any place it chose to beat down. She hadn't lost what she considered a permanent tan. Her hair remained sun-streaked.

Esmerelda's River Hospice anniversary celebration would happen on Saturday. Dignitaries from Delta towns across the valley would honor the grand lady with their presence.

While Esmerelda directed last minute preparations that Saturday morning, Sara and Daphine passed time inside Esmerelda's house with Mimie and the pups. Daphine stared out the window a lot, always with her back turned, being too quiet. She seemed preoccupied and then suddenly blurted, "I'm giving Fredrik the painting for his birthday."

Sara caught herself before saying something she might regret. Gifts and generosity were okay, but just because Daphine dated Fredrik a few times didn't seem reason enough. "The one he tried to buy?" Sara asked, knowing her response was lame.

Daphine must have sensed her feelings. "Sara, you've got the wrong impression of him. He was born with the skills to help people in their last days." She took a breath, looked away, and seemed disappointed.

Back when Sara first saw the painting, she had the idea to split the cost with Daphine and give it to Fredrik. Now knowing the maniac on the loose could be a local person made her feel uneasy about doing so.

Just as they left the house with the dogs to look for Esmerelda, a man wearing a colorful Hawaiian Aloha shirt walked toward the parked cars and climbed into one. He backed up and then drove past them, turning to Sara expressing both surprise and utter dismay.

"Someone you know?" Daphine asked.

"Strange," she said as her heart beat wildly. "Saw him a few times in Sacramento. That must have been him driving away the first time we came to see Esmerelda." Sara remembered his blue-topaz eyes. What could he be doing at the hospice? Excitement rippled through her nervous system. "It's still early. Maybe he'll come back."

"You got eyes for this guy?" Daphine asked, again smiling, on to something.

"I wouldn't mind meeting a nice guy."

"One who wears tasteful Aloha shirts?"

Pierce came along for the festivities. He needed to mingle, meet more people. He wouldn't climb the stairs into Esmerelda's house. They found him socializing indoors in the sunroom in the patient facility. Fredrik leaned into the conversation as if needing to glean all he could from what Pierce might say. Soon a staff member appeared and needed Fredrik's attention, much to his hesitancy and dismay.

After the visitors toured the grounds, lunch was served. Guests dined under a large tent or under some of the shade trees at picnic tables. Several large electric fans were strategically placed but did little to ward off the heat. Many people carried paper fans marked *River Hospice*.

"Someone said that Tripp arranged all the decorative floral," Sara said. "Did you know that?"

"He always works with Esmerelda's caterer," Daphine said. "Says they're his flowers. Won't let anyone pick 'em."

The lavishly decorated serving table displayed bouquets and baskets of fruits and blooms. Green stalks with lush leaves lay between the serving dishes. Each eating table contained a centerpiece of a floral basket. Esmerelda trained and brought out the best in her employees, including Tripp. The caterer and not her, however, prepared and served the meal.

They found Esmerelda exiting a patient's room.

"I need your opinion," Daphine said.

"How so?" Esmerelda asked.

"I want to give Fredrik the painting he once saw in my shop."

"Not the one he talked about years ago?" Esmerelda asked. "And talks about again, now that you two have renewed friendships?"

"The one and only," Daphine said nervously. Uncertainty did not fit her personality. "Only, I don't know what you've got planned for his birthday as part of this celebration."

"I usually give him a round trip ticket to Sweden to see his family."

"You do?" Sara asked. Her guilt about being overly generous eased somewhat.

"Not this year, though," Esmerelda said. She had that sparkle in her eyes that said she kept a secret.

"Spill it," Daphine said.

"I've had a little help from his family," Esmerelda said. "I've managed to bring his mom and dad and sister here. Should be arriving momentarily." She glanced toward the end doorway of the facility.

"Oh, my goodness. In that case, my giving him something in front of all these people is not apropos."

Esmerelda laughed. "Your giving him something is quite all right. But I wonder about that art." She still smiled. "I've never seen your painting, but the way he describes it, it sounds a little frightful. Not sure how the guests will take it if you present it out on the podium."

"You're right," Daphine said. "When can we get him aside for a moment?"

"Probably right now, if you like. The guests are eating. Speeches will start soon as his family arrives and have their meal."

Daphine went to retrieve the painting. In Fredrik's room, he pulled at his shirtsleeves and checked his collar, leaving the neck of his shirt open. Esmerelda's rules about a dress code were lax. It was just too hot. Yet, Fredrik dressed to impress, or maybe, he was thankful to wear something other than a white smock on his birthday, and expensive clothes at that. His eyes gleamed when he saw the masculine gift-wrappings. He knew he was about to receive one of Daphine's art pieces. "I'm already thrilled," he said, accepting the gift.

He knew by feeling the wrapper to position the face outwards before he tore off the cover. Esmerelda's eyes opened wide when she saw the painting. "Oh, dear!" she said, but held her composure, not to spoil Fredrik's enjoyment of something only he could love.

Fredrik balanced the framed canvas upright on the floor in front of himself, as if hesitating to turn it around to see. When he did, he almost let go of it. "I'm speechless," he said. He immediately walked to the fireplace, lifted the old painting down, and hung Fleeing Hell. "Now my collection is complete." His enjoyment was genuine. He hugged Daphine. "Just don't go painting any more irresistible scenes. I don't have any more space." Then his look became sullen. Wish my family could have come. Can't imagine why their plans changed at the last minute."

"I'm sure you'll have a chance to get things straight with them, "Esmerelda said, hiding her smile from Fredrik.

If Daphine wanted to get closer to this man, she had just made a giant leap. When she and Sara were alone again, Sara whispered behind her hand, "You want to get married again, Daph?"

"Not sure. Too much like starting over."

"But why not? Everyone's into recycling." Sara ducked before Daphine's slap connected with her shoulder.

Fredrik's family arrived. He nearly fainted at seeing them climb out of the car. Once everyone met and got his or her elation and tears under control, Daphine spent time socializing with the sister. It appeared his parents were enthralled with her too. Fredrik introduced Pierce and must have disclosed some of Pierce's history. Fredrik's family huddled in conversation with Daphine and Pierce as if their group were the only people present. The crowd of more than a hundred attendees finally settled down. Sara cornered Esmerelda, which was something she had been trying to do for a while. "Who was that man wearing the Aloha shirt?"

"Why, that's Huxley Keane," Esmerelda said, seeming distracted. "From Halsey, Oregon. Old money. World traveler. He's off to Asia again, before their winter sets in."

That meant Sara would not see him again for weeks, maybe months. She felt a bit of disappointment. "He goes to Asia a lot?"

"He's with a group. Looking for his brother, an MIA in Vietnam."

The idea struck like lightning. Esmerelda would know of such a group. Maybe Huxley was helping Esmerelda search for her daughter too. They would be searching for any war remains. Sara wanted to ask questions, find out more about Betty, but Esmerelda never once volunteered anything about her daughter. Sara decided not to intrude but said, "That's a huge undertaking," She again hoped her remarks didn't sound nonchalant. She wished she could master the art of small talk.

"It's quite hectic, I'm sure," Esmerelda said. "I wish he could meet someone to make his life more pleasurable."

"He's single?" Sara asked, and then realized her response was too quick, too exaggerated and eager.

Fredrik came up behind and took Esmerelda's elbow. "Speeches are about to begin," he said.

As she allowed herself to be dragged away, Esmerelda looked back over her shoulders with a curious sparkle in her eyes that Sara couldn't interpret at that moment. Sara felt like she might collapse. Huxley was single, and that thought made her heart beat wildly. Until she regained her composure, she watched Esmerelda being congenial with her guests. Watching her joyfully interact was like seeing a rainbow with its vibrant colors, soon she realized there was a double rainbow, even a hint of a third.

The dogs began whining. Sara went to find Daphine. "I'm taking the pups overnight to get them out of Esmerelda's hair."

"Good luck keeping them at the Alden's."

"I'll stay in Walnut Grove. Fredrik can take you home, can't he?"

"Hey, maybe we can ride in ET's Jag," Daphine said, animated and dancing around.

Sara backed her SUV in to load the pet carriers. Tripp suddenly appeared from behind the garage. His long-sleeved white shirt and jeans were clean and pressed. Sara wondered why he wore long sleeves considering the hot sticky climate of the day.

"Can I help you, Miss Sara?"

Chills ran down Sara's spine. She felt repulsed. What could Tripp be doing back there in that narrow space between the garage and the tall evergreen hedge? It would be only a few steps back to his cabin if he urgently had to pee. She had no choice but to be cordial. "Thank you," she said, allowing Tripp to lift the large containers.

"Been meaning to ask," he said. "You'll be needing someone to tend your yards. I could use some extra work, and... and I already know the property."

The least he could do was look hopeful. His ulterior motive showed through his all-too-congenial demeanor. She needed to think of some way to get the point across nicely that she had no interest in seeing him on a personal basis. With his menacing stare, saying the wrong thing just might set him off again.

Pierce hobbled over in the nick of time, not walking too badly, but ready to leave. "You grow some of the heartiest flowers I've ever seen," he said to Tripp as he offered his hand.

Tripp did not offer his hand in return and nearly fell backward over himself trying to leave. Was he that jealous? Sara wondered what he might do if he knew someone else had captured her heart.

Chapter 41

"Is nothing sacred anymore?" Sara asked.

"'Course they'd print it," Daphine said. She hung a new painting on the shop wall and then repositioned the lighting. "People knew that cat's neck would be wrung."

Sara couldn't remember ever having the habit of buying newspapers. Now it seemed she scanned them daily. One article reported that a farmer named Fletcher Grable wore size sixteen boots. "How did they find that out?"

"Probably from other farmers who'd like to see him lose his land."

"They wouldn't do that, would they? Doesn't he own large patches out on Ryer Island?"

"Patches, yes, here and there from the Howard Landing Ferry back to Miner Slough."

"And the bigger landowners want to buy off his small fields?"

"Yeah, and because of that, he's sometimes offensive, but he's never hurt anyone."

"With size sixteen shoes, he must be one big guy."

"You mean with hands strong enough to snap a hyoid?" Daphine asked. "Says here the police interviewed him."

"Read that already," Sara said. "He gave a worn out pair of wading boots to a church rummage sale. Someone at the church remembers them because they were so big." She continued to read quietly.

> *It was the church's practice to allow shoppers to fill a large grocery bag with as much as could be stuffed into it. Each bagful cost a dollar. Anyone could have purchased the boots. Fletcher Grable was not considered a suspect.*

A small article at the bottom of the page said:

> *Twenty-seven-year-old John Glosser from Fair Oaks, a suburb of Sacramento, was declared missing yesterday. His family did not notify authorities for several days because Glosser fished along the American River and sometimes camped out over weekends. Once found, his campsite showed no signs of foul play. Authorities believe he might have fallen into the raging currents of the American River and been washed away. Rescuers continue to search downstream.*

* * *

Pierce released his live-in nurse. He spent the Labor Day weekend visiting backyard picnics around Clampett Tract. Daphine spent time at her shop neurotically rotating art pieces. Esmerelda's time was taken with two new patients requiring admission and logistics.

Sara remained sequestered at the Alden's working on the computer. Unable to get the man out of her mind, she clicked into the MIA Web site where she first learned about Betty Talbot. She ran a search for Huxley Keane.

"Got him!" she said, coming up out of her chair. His name popped up highlighted beside a photo of him with his brother in younger years. Sara read nonstop, totally unaware how much time had passed. Her suspicions had been confirmed.

Huxley's brother was a member of the same group of prisoners that included Betty Talbot. They died in the jungle in Vietnam. Since the war ended, Huxley devoted his life to searching for his brother's remains. Surely, he was helping Esmerelda as well. He had written numerous articles and updates on the problems encountered, including governmental and geographic extremes. His efforts attracted the support of influential people.

Sara forced herself back to work. The two computer programs she started just after returning to the Delta were nearly finished. She returned to Talbot House during the daytime to upload the programs into the larger computer to verify they were actually what she was wanted to produce. The buyers of the programs would, indeed, be surprised. Her marketing manager had practically sealed the deal with the company that purchased her first two games. If they didn't like the new ones, Sara's obligation to them was not binding. Another company waited impatiently to have a crack at the huge revenue potential that could be realized during the wake of *Star* and *Black Hole*.

Though the carpenters' strike was long over, many smaller companies had been forced out of business. Unemployed skilled workers looking to make a buck were plentiful. Sara's contractor chose to use Delta employees first. With the availability of laborers, finally, work progressed rapidly. Walls were moved or new ones built to accommodate three bathrooms, and for the upgrading of electrical wiring and plumbing. Larger closets were installed, unfortunately claiming some space in each bedroom. The interior of Talbot House was a mess, a situation only she appreciated. Out on the front lawn, the rebar and concrete footings for the gazebo stood curing in the hot sun.

That afternoon, Sara shopped for imported foods from a deli in Sacramento. Finally returning, as she neared the Clampett

Tract house, the green Jaguar had backed out. It turned and parked at the curb while Sara pulled into the driveway.

Esmerelda climbed out from behind the wheel. "Well, I can still drive," she said, calling out across the yard.

"I wish I knew you were coming," Sara said. "You could've come to Talbot House to see the progress."

Esmerelda opened the passenger door, and Mimie jumped out, her fluffy tail all a-blur.

"Where are the pups?"

"In Sacramento." Esmerelda flicked her eyebrows and looked disappointed.

"That couple's house can't be anywhere near finished."

"I convinced them to take the pups before they got too old." Esmerelda shrugged, again showing disappointment. "Besides, Fredrik's family is staying at least another month, and I'm up to my ears."

"Are the pups adjusting?"

"They're being kept at the girl's parents' home since the kids are still in their apartment."

"That doesn't sound too bad."

"I shouldn't have pushed," Esmerelda said. "The parents don't know the first thing about pit bulls. They're letting them run loose in the backyard. Their neighbors have already called the police to complain about the barking."

"These dogs were supposed to be exposed to people," Sara said doubtfully. "Guess they're meeting their share."

"I'll be glad when Fredrik gets back. His absence has forced me back to work." She joked, being absurd.

"Hope he's able to show his family a good time."

"Ha! You know what they're doing? First, they went up to pan for gold. And get this. His parents are my age. They're sturdy Swedes, you know? They spent a few days tubing down the American River."

"That's pretty rigorous."

"They love it, even camped out on the riverbank for a week. They really enjoy roughing it."

"The American River?" Sara asked. "Why would anyone camp out there with the investigation of that missing Fair Oaks man still going on?" Sara held the front door open as Esmerelda and Mimie entered. "We have a lot to catch up on."

"How's it working out with Pierce?"

"The nurse started him walking a lot before he let her go. He's more robust now."

"It's this house, thanks to you, Sara. I understand from Daphine that he needed the change."

"He started a new book, about this recent experience." Nothing is wrong with the man's mind.

Esmerelda glanced around quickly and would have walked herself through the house to take a peek, but Mimie began to bark louder than normal. That was not at all like Mimie.

Sara looked out the open doorway, thinking someone may be coming up the sidewalk, but saw no one. Mimie continued to dance around and bark at the wall.

"Shush, la Jolie!" Esmerelda said, taking hold of Mimie's collar and making her sit. Then Esmerelda looked straight up at the dream drawing and froze. "Where did you get that?" she asked, screeching as her chest rose and fell as she gasped. "How did you know?"

Mimie continued to bark.

"Know what?"

"How do you know what Orson looked like?" Esmerelda moved closer and touched the glass covering the eye area. Her hand trembled.

"That's not Orson," Sara said. "I told Daphine about the dream I was having. I told you about that. Daphine came up with this sketch. As much as I see in the dream, that is. I'm surprised that Daphine could—"

"It's Orson! Those are my husband's eyes, I tell you. Right down to the star at the corner of that eye." She pointed. "Right there."

"What are you talking about?" Sara remembered the photo on Esmerelda's sideboard. Orson had seemed very thin.

"Those droopy eyes, and high forehead. A bushy shock of hair protruding at each temple." Esmerelda caught her breath and couldn't stop looking at the drawing. "As Orson aged, his face filled out, and he got real wrinkled around his eyes. Had those bags underneath there too." She fumbled around inside her purse, then stopped and pointed to the corner of an eye in the drawing. "The star."

"They're just age lines that I see in my dream. I'm sure Daph wouldn't draw your husband just to satisfy my curiosity about the dream."

Esmerelda finally found the wallet in her bag and produced a photo of her husband. "See there," she said, pointing to the corner of Orson's eye. "Now look at your drawing."

Sara rocked back on her heels when she realized Daphine's drawing contained eyes identical to the photo Esmerelda held. The crow's feet contained the same cross lines forming a starburst.

Coins fell from the wallet as Esmerelda nearly lost her grip. Her eyes went wild again. "That's him! What's he pointing at?"

"I honestly don't know. That's all I ever see."

"My Orson was left-handed. He's pointing with his left hand. That's my husband."

"I don't understand," Sara said. But strange occurrences only served to encourage her interest. "I've been seeing this man in my dreams since... since—"

"When?"

She shook her head and thought a moment. "Since I went to a voodoo ceremony in Jamaica for Christmas. 1995, I think it was."

"Oh!" Esmerelda said. She groped her way to the sofa and sat down and covered her mouth with her hand as tears fell. Finally, she said, "Orson went missing in November of 1995. I told you that, remember?"

Chapter 42

A splendid Indian summer permeated the Delta, and that meant good working days for the contractors before the weather chilled. It was the middle of September, and the workers had made phenomenal progress.

Sara peeked into the room that served as her bedroom-office during the intermittent periods she lived at Talbot House. A canvas drop cloth covered the floor. Her electronic equipment remained securely covered with blankets and plastic sheeting.

Starla's photos had been removed from the wall and lay face down on the tarp covering the bed. "Oh, yes! No yellows for me," Sara said as she realized the walls were already painted. The color was a shade of soft white that reflected hints of lavender, blue, and pink. Then she realized that her computer desk and furnishings had been moved away from the wall.

The contractor poked his head in. "I have crews with different skills working at full capacity on every inch of this house." He kicked back the edge of the drop cloth exposing hardwood floors beautifully restored.

After joyfully thanking him and shaking his hand, she asked, "You finished only this room?"

"I figured we'd better finish off this room since you'd be coming back soon. The floor crew is up in your attic right now. Big job up there." They walked from room to room through sawdust, loose boards, and scattered tools. "We had to tear out more walls to facilitate bringing the plumbing and wiring up to code. That heating system too."

"What are you saying? The wiring… my alarm system is in?"

"Up and running. But the walls—"

"Never mind the walls. You build 'em. I'm moving back."

Two days later, Sara drove toward Talbot House with a load of her possessions. Buck followed in his pickup filled with storage boxes. Another friend in a flatbed truck, with a tied down load of the few pieces of new furniture she recently purchased, brought up the rear of the caravan. They carried the few possessions that presently meant everything to her. She gave away almost all of her belongings before leaving Puerto Rico. What was left of it would be stored under a tarp in the basement.

Buck climbed out of his truck, stretched, and looked up at the massive structure, encased in scaffolding. "I still don't think this is—"

"No maniac off his hinges," Sara said, cutting him off, "and no ghost will scare me away now."

"That idiot who means to harm you might have all of his hinges loose," Buck said.

Sara watched as exterior walls of the upper floors were stripped of shingles that clattered to the ground and sent up clouds of dust. The shingles would be replaced. On the outside, the house would look like the replica that it was.

"Fletcher Grable, the guy with the big boots," Buck said. "He once owned that farmland out at Stone Lake South, where remains were found. He also just happened to know that Rowe woman who worked in a convenience store—whose remains they recently IDed."

"No kidding. What else does the rumor mill say?"

"He sold the property at a steal to a bargain hunter. Why would he do that?"

"How well did he know Paula Rowe?"

"Grable can't remember where he was when she went missing. Too long ago."

"Sounds like they need to investigate him." The information also sounded as vague as any other clues the rumor mill kept alive.

"Sara, no one really knows who, that is, you can't be alone—"

"Hey, check out the new glass." She had heard enough. The new burglar alarm would assure her safety.

"You're replacing all the windows too?" Buck asked.

"Actually, the glass was fine," Sara said. "But the wood frames were dry-rotted."

Buck helped carry the last of the smaller boxes into her workspace. After poking through the house and talking to some of the workers, most of whom he knew, Sara heard the crunch of gravel as his tires climbed to the levee.

She closed the office door as activities and noise of the workers continued. After hanging her clothes in the closet and filling the dresser drawers, she opened the last shoebox and stared at the Smith and Wesson. "What has life come to?" she asked, mumbling. She glanced around the room, deciding to store it in the top drawer of her dresser. Inside the drawer, the butt sticking out of the polished leather holster, surrounded by delicate lace underwear, was something she would expect to see on a James Bond poster. She grimaced and pushed the gun beneath the underclothes.

What if she had to retrieve it quickly? If ever a case presented itself where she needed to grab it in a hurry, it being buttoned down inside the holster would be a detriment. She removed the gun from the holster, loaded it, and laid it, again, on the top of the clothes. She stepped back and then rushed toward the dresser, enacting how she might grasp it quickly. Satisfied, she covered the holster and box of bullets with her half-slips and the pistol with her lace panties. Now she felt ready for anything.

Chapter 43

Tearing down the workshop became too big of an issue. Sara walked the area with a woman demolitions expert, pleased that more women everywhere had the opportunity to do any kind of work they so desired. More and more women now worked on Talbot House.

"All the exterior work needs to be finished before the weather turns cold," she said to the muscular young woman in a hard hat. "Including getting rid of this." She gestured toward the workshop.

"What would look good in its place," the woman said, "would be a covered arbor between the garage and the house."

The woman echoed some of Sara's earlier thoughts about the space. She nodded in agreement. "A broad trellis covered with lavender wisteria would make a nice gateway to the rest of the grounds."

"I used to know the Talbots," one of the workmen standing nearby said. "My wife and I bought our wedding bands from him. Got to know them both." He shook his head and stared at the ground. "Was sad, what happened."

"If you knew them, then you know it will break Esmerelda's heart to see the workshop go," Sara said. She just didn't need it, but Esmerelda's feelings were important enough to consider. "I've agonized over it for days." She decided that any memory of Orson Talbot was in the basement, the only place he worked on his jewelry. The workshop was his idea, but he had never had a chance to use it. He hadn't even built it. Esmerelda felt closest to her husband in the workshop, but if the man in Sara's dreams was really Orson, and if he was the spirit haunting the house, then he wasn't associating himself with the workshop. "I've made my decision," she said, throwing up both hands. "Tear it down."

Precious days passed while securing the necessary permit. Then, demolitions specialists scrambled across the breezeway roof disconnecting it from the house. The workshop walls came down fast. As much as could be salvaged would be donated to Shelter, a charity group that acquired usable materials to distribute throughout the California Central Valley. They built homes for those in need. As with the house itself, as fast as any material from the demolition came available, it was loaded onto a truck. Even the weather-beaten windows were donated.

The next day a backhoe arrived from Eldon's Crane and Rigging. It had turned out that Eldon was the same Eldon with whom she went to school, and Sara wished to support those whom she knew.

No alternative existed to salvage or transport the concrete pad. The front loader bucket of the backhoe was used to haul a heavy boulder-sized rock from the backfield. The rock was lifted high as possible and dropped onto the concrete floor in several places, rendering the pad full of spider cracks. One by one, the pieces were moved to a growing rubbish pile in the field beside the garage. As the concrete was lifted, sunlight gleamed off the exposed fool's gold rocks that Orson playfully laid down.

"I would have liked him," Sara said to the worker who knew the Talbots. She felt more than a twinge of sadness. "I'm glad Esmerelda chose to stay away."

Sara went to retrieve one of the rocks and turned it over in her hands as it sparkled. A sense of deep sadness for this missing man, who surely had a laudable sense of humor, crept over her. She seemed connected in ways she only now began to understand.

"Pile all the pyrite over there," Sara said, yelling to the backhoe operator and pointing to an open area. To the others standing nearby, she said, "If a guy name Isidoro shows up, let him have it all." Isidoro would need more than a pickup for that load.

The grader dug deep and lifted a scoop from near where the front wall once stood. The woman demolitionist went to pick up stray rocks dropped from the backhoe load. She bent down and then jumped back quickly. "Stop!" she said, yelling, her feminine voice barely audible over the sound of the equipment. She shouted and waved her arms and stooped down again and threw a couple more rocks aside, then straightened, shaking her head. "Hey!" she yelled to the foreman. She motioned for him to come quickly and then pointed to the area at her feet. She turned and motioned with a finger swipe across her throat for the backhoe operator to kill the engine.

The contractor bent down and pulled at the edge of a dirty polythene sheet. Pieces of the black plastic flaked off in his hands. He straightened and his hand went to his forehead in a gesture that Sara read as disbelief. He turned and motioned. "Get back, everyone," he said, yelling. He shook his head and kept motioning for everyone to clear the area. "We're done here for a while."

"Done?" Sara asked as she moved closer to see. The grader had torn the sheet of plastic and disturbed what it was wrapped around. Uncovered were remnants of bug-eaten clothing, a human skull, and other bones.

Chapter 44

Sara's cell phone rang and took her attention from the gruesome scene.

"You'll never guess what just happened," Esmerelda said through the phone.

Sara could barely hear above the excited voices of the others and the backhoe that segregated chunks of concrete off the rubbish pile for the detectives who were sure to appear again. "And I've got something to tell—"

"I just can't believe this," Esmerelda said. "That young couple brought the pups back."

Sara quickly switched her focus. "But why?" She walked out into the field to get away from the voices of the others so Esmerelda might not hear what was happening.

"Someone found an ordinance prohibiting pit bulls and rottweilers in that neighborhood in Sacramento. The kids' parents were going to take the dogs to the Humane Society."

"No, not to a shelter," Sara said. "Who knows what their fate might have been if they had!"

"The pups are changed already. They pace a lot and don't like being indoors." Esmerelda sighed heavily through the phone.

Sara didn't have the heart to tell her at that moment about the newly discovered remains. The killer took advantage of finding a convenient site. Another skeleton showing up on the property the Talbots owned suggested that the perpetrator was aware of Orson and Esmerelda's habits and schedules.

"I'm glad you have the dogs back," Sara said.

"How so?"

Esmerelda had good protection with pit bulls. Sara had to think a moment. "I didn't like them being passed around," she said finally.

"So, what were you about to tell me?"

"I'm coming over," Sara said. "Be there soon."

As she walked to her SUV, she stopped the contractor. "I want new top of the line locks installed on all exterior doors," she said. "Deadbolts too."

* * *

Sara was glad that Fredrik returned from vacation because Esmerelda didn't need to be bothered with hospice detail. Fredrik was out in the parking lot and seemed totally preoccupied. He looked right through her and didn't even wave. His stare penetrated as if he were preoccupied with something he didn't wish to share. So, what had he been up to?

News of the skeletal remains rattled Esmerelda's nerves.

"That's all they know right now," Sara said. "Another body wrapped in plastic."

"Did you see it?"

"Just the plastic and some bones sticking up."

"That killer had to know that neither of us were home that weekend."

"But wait. This doesn't look like the work of the same person," Sara said. "Remember, the serial killer buried near streams and rivers, and he didn't wrap his victims."

"To think we've all lived with that body right there." Esmerelda paced, kept her hand flat against her heart.

Choco had a new habit. He growled. It came out more in a huff, a short burst like coughing. He seemed angry. Latte simply lay with her head between her front paws, but jumped to her feet every time she heard a noise.

Esmerelda's cell phone rang, and though the conversation was brief and about the dogs, her expression hinted at more discouraging news. She tapped her phone to end the call. "It was that couple," she said, acting as if she didn't know what to do next. "They said that when they got back to Sacramento, they received news that their escrow fell through."

"Wha-at?"

"They won't be taking Choco and Latte. They'll stop paying for their care."

Choco and Latte heard their names spoken and both sets of ears perked.

"Just a little more time," Sara said. "Please. I promise. We'll place them."

"I doubt their owner would take them back. She's got two more litters on the way." Esmerelda chewed on her lip and seemed cornered. "Those new pups are already spoken for when born. These two are considered old now."

"I wonder what being away has done to their training."

"Well, take a look," Esmerelda said as Choco paced. Then she smiled suddenly. "Oh, I know what to do. I'll keep the dogs to guard my property. That killer is still out there. Demetrio likes the pups so he can manage them." Esmerelda just solved her problem.

"Yes, that's a great idea. I can help Demetrio learn how."

All the tenseness drained out of Esmerelda's face. "Why, yes. You could teach him well in Spanish."

"What about Tripp?"

"You know, I'm tired of hearing that old man whine. If he doesn't like the pups, he can go flower someone else's yard. The Mexican laborers would appreciate the work." Esmerelda seemed to be letting off a little steam. It was odd behavior. She never spoke ill of anyone.

Sara saw more yellow tape during her time at Talbot House than during the rest of her life combined, and this was her property. She invited two of the regular workmen to bunk down in the house each night. House rules were established: No drugs or parties, and keep the beer drinking under control.

One of them, Beni Noa, had been sleeping in his truck, expressed deep gratitude. His full Hawaiian name was *Benimakemae Nahenahenoa*. He sported a busted nose and a couple of scars across his face from who knows what. His looks caused others to steal fearful glances. He had colorful Polynesian tattoos emblazoned on his shoulders, legs, and arms. Other workers carried small digital cell phones on their construction belts. Beni's phone seemed older because it was much larger. He might have carried it only for the sake of appearances among his peers.

Pete Carswell was just an ordinary fun-loving American hulk. His hands and fingers had grown thick and strong from a lifetime of swinging a hammer. Sara now looked at every man's hands wondering if they were strong enough to snap a hyoid bone.

Sara felt safer, but the men's laughter drifted downstairs well into the night distracting her from work. Beni liked to talk story. That's what they called it in Hawaii. He told so many tales that a person didn't need to go to Hawaii to know the place. Other times, he played the ukulele and Sara drifted to sleep hearing him sing Hawaiian ballads in falsetto.

Until the investigators finished work and removed the yellow tape, she was allowed to park in the driveway. She could come and go from the house through the sitting room or front doorways. The many construction vehicles had to park on the shoulder of the levee.

Ever since purchasing the .38 Police Special, she occasionally lifted her underwear and peered at the gun in the drawer. Now she wondered if she was being overly cautious. Having two men around, or anyone, for that matter, offered a lot of security. She had to stop looking at that weapon just to feel safe.

Working in her office two days later, Sara heard gravel crunch and glanced toward the sitting room doorway. Johanna bounded up the side steps and knocked. Her expression was grim. Seeing the construction workers, she let herself in. "I figured you'd better be around when they break the news," she said.

"What news?" Sara asked. "To whom?"

"The media already has the story. Esmerelda will need all the support she can get."

"What about Esmerelda?" Sara asked. What news would be so stunning as to make that pillar of strength need support?

Johanna paused momentarily. Surely what she had to reveal was not good. "The body," she said after swallowing hard. "In the workshop floor?" She looked away and sighed. She turned back and ran her fingers through her short hair. "It's Orson Talbot."

Sara screamed.

The laborers restoring the fireplace floor stood. They were alert to everything that had happened on the property. "The dental records, right?" one woman asked after a moment of silence among them.

"It's the first set they did a comparison with," Johanna said as she paced. "I'm so sorry." She continued to run fingers through her hair and shake her head. "Sara, you need to go be with Esmerelda. Detectives from Sacramento are already on the way." She glanced at her watch. "Could be there in about half an hour."

"He went missing in Placerville," Sara said. "How could he—"

"They don't know," Johanna said. "They've got to talk to Esmerelda before they can connect the dots."

Sara yanked her cell phone off her waistband and punched the number two. She hurried to retrieve her purse and car keys. Daphine's gallery voice mail kicked in. "Daph," she said. "Meet me at Esmerelda's. It's an emergency. Please hurry." Sara punched the number three, and heard Daphine's home voice mail and left the same message as she ran out the door.

Chapter 45

Sara drove as quickly as she dared. She worried if she should be the one to break the news. As she parked, Daphine pulled in beside her.

"What's happened?" Daphine asked, hurrying around the rear of her van. "Your messages were frantic." Since childhood, she and Sara had shared thoughts without speaking. Daphine stared at her a moment, then her expression sobered. "No!" she said.

"Yes."

A nondescript, white four-door sedan equipped with official-looking spotlights on both sides of the windshield turned down the embankment. A man and a woman climbed out.

Daphine ran toward the patient facility. "I'll get Fredrik."

Before anyone climbed the stairs, Sara introduced herself to the two young detectives, Vance and de Giorgio, and told them who she was. Esmerelda must have seen or heard the commotion and stepped out onto her sun porch.

Once indoors, Choco and Latte jumped to attention. Esmerelda lifted a hand, and they quieted. Sara felt tears erupting. The pups and Mimie, and the hospice represented how much love and patience overflowed from Esmerelda's big heart. She did not deserve the news she was about to receive.

Esmerelda saw her trying to hide her emotions even though Sara turned away momentarily. Esmerelda refused to sit. Questions showed in her eyes, maybe the answers too. She called Mimie close, and both simply stood proudly. Mimie couldn't stay still though. She leaped toward the window and began to howl. It was strange seeing a poodle act like that, howling, like a death wail. Choco and Latte joined in. Sara tried to calm them all but ended up taking Choco and Latte out to the sun porch and fastening their leashes to a post.

Det. Vance put her arm around Esmerelda's shoulders. After they broke the news, Esmerelda collapsed just as Fredrik rushed in. The detectives caught her and laid her on the sofa. Fredrik worked to revive her while Mimie paced and whined.

Someone appeared at the door. The man put his hands up to block the sun as he tried to peer through the screen. "*Por favor*, I take the dogs?" he asked. Sara rushed outside and spoke to Demetrio in Spanish and sent him on his way with Choco and Latte and a promise that he would not say anything to other employees. Not that she had told him anything.

Daphine, too, had jumped to help and came out of the kitchen with several bottles of cold water and drinking glasses on a TV tray.

Esmerelda opened her eyes. Mimie licked her face. Det. Vance helped Esmerelda to sit up. She weakly pointed to the floor, and Mimie obeyed and curled up. Esmerelda didn't say anything but looked to them for answers. Daphine handed her a glass. Esmerelda's hand shook so severely that she needed help to get the water to her mouth. Det. de Giorgio stepped back while Fredrik sat down and listened to Esmerelda's heart and checked her vitals.

"It's finally over," Esmerelda said softly.

"At least now, you know," Det. de Giorgio said. "Now we need to learn how, why."

The detectives sat and opened briefcases and prepared to take notes. Det. de Giorgio put on a pair of glasses that slipped down his nose.

"Please," Sara said. "We can stay, can't we?"

"Of course," Esmerelda said.

"That should be okay," Det. de Giorgio said. He turned to Esmerelda. "We need to search your memory of that weekend."

Daphine poured water for everyone. "Did they find a cat or dog?" she asked.

"No animal," Det. Vance said. "He was wrapped in plastic. No other items."

"Sounds similar to that case in San Jose," Fredrik said.

Sara glanced quickly at Fredrik and then stared at the floor momentarily. Events of the past months made her overly suspicious. It was curious how the Fair Oaks man went missing along the American River at the same time Fredrik just happened to be camping there too.

"You know about that?" Det. Vance asked, sounding all too cool.

"Doesn't everyone?" Fredrik asked.

"The San Jose victim was found wrapped in plastic, without animal remains," Daphine said. "Now Orson's found the same way."

"Was the plastic the same type in both cases?" Fredrik asked.

"Don't know yet," Det. Vance said.

Sara had a hunch that Det. Vance was not about to give out information. Her job was to collect the facts. Det. Vance's nonchalance to Fredrik's questions said she'd like to interrogate him as well.

"We need to ask you some questions, Mrs. Talbot," Det. de Giorgio said. "Do you feel up to it?"

Somewhere between Sara watching the reactions of everyone in the room, especially Fredrik, Esmerelda had regained some strength. "First of all, call me Esmerelda," she said. "I'll always be Orson's wife, but call me Esmerelda."

"We've been through this cold case file many times over the years," Det. Vance said. "Somewhere, somehow, we'll find the missing link."

"You've studied these cases?" Fredrik asked. "What about Orson's hyoid bone?"

"Yes, what about his throat?" Esmerelda asked.

Det. Vance looked up from her papers. "Yes," she said in response to Fredrik's first question. "Broken," she said of Orson's hyoid bone.

Esmerelda's tears spilled over. "So, ask your questions." Her lips tightened momentarily. "We've got to find this madman."

Det. de Giorgio leaned forward. "Walk us through that weekend. Maybe you can remember something you haven't already told everyone." He paused momentarily. "You were staying at your friend's house to cater her party."

"Yes," Fredrik said. "Her name was Margot."

The detectives seemed irritated that Fredrik answered for Esmerelda. Maybe he tried to do what he could to help, but it made him more of an intrusion.

Sara and Daphine pulled up chairs from the dining table.

Esmerelda smoothed things over. "That's right," she said, taking Fredrik's hand. "I wasn't at the house that weekend. The delivery of rocks was late—was due on a Wednesday, the 10th—"

"That would be the 10th of November 1995, right?" Det. Vance asked.

Someone knocked. When Sara answered the door, Fredrik was being called away. He started for the door but hesitated, like he might refuse to go. Esmerelda assured him she was okay. He left looking like a banished child who needed to be present to cover for himself.

Esmerelda tried to stand, and Det. de Giorgio helped her. She went into the dining area, opened a cabinet, and brought back a fist-sized rock with both rough and smooth facets that shined like gold. It was a sample of the very rocks Orson hurried to spread in the hole he dug for the flooring and then covered with a tarp. "He left for Placerville right after, so he could get up there before dark. She handed the rock to Det. Vance.

"He dug a hole?" Det. Vance asked, turning the rock over in her hand and then passing it to Det. de Giorgio.

"For the foundation," Esmerelda said. She seemed awkward, having to explain her dead husband's wit about using fool's gold rocks instead of the usual river rock for the subflooring.

"Why the tarp?" Det. de Giorgio asked.

"To keep the animals and blowing debris off the rock bed," she said. "It's windy that time of year."

Though they said they had scoured the cold case files, these detectives seemed not well versed in all aspects of the Talbot case.

"There was no reason for me to be home that weekend," Esmerelda said. "Orson would be gone for two weeks, maybe three, while the concrete cured." She had returned home late Sunday evening. On Monday, the concrete truck arrived before she was out of bed. It had already backed into place to pour.

"If I remember correctly," Det. Vance said. "Your employees' alibis all checked out."

"We had a lot of different people come and go. A couple of drifters, too, needed a few days wages before moving on," Esmerelda said, shaking her head. "We didn't know a lot of them personally, but we treated them fairly."

How could Esmerelda or Orson not have treated anyone well? It was the only way Esmerelda knew how to be. So who would harm a person like Orson?

"Both Tripp and Fredrik had alibis too," Det. de Giorgio said.

They did. As usual, Fredrik spent all weekend at the hospice doing his job. Dozens of people vouched for him.

"Tripp's been our yard man for many years," Esmerelda said. "During the week before Orson left, Tripp cleared a lot of rocks out of the field in the back. He and a laborer are the ones who piled all those rocks back at the corner where they found that girl's skeleton."

"Do you know where Tripp spent his weekend?" Det. de Giorgio asked as he made notes.

"Back then, Tripp lived with two other men down in Benicia."

"That's what I read," Det. Vance said. "They said the three of them spent the weekend in a drunken stupor. Said Tripp was dead tired from lifting rocks."

"Benicia's a long drive up from the southern end of the Delta. Tripp had to commute every day," Esmerelda said. "He continually made a fuss about not liking to drive long distances."

"He lives here now, doesn't he?" Det. Vance asked.

"One of his roommates died from a heart attack. The other one moved away," Esmerelda said. "So I had Tripp move here. He's devoted to his work. Made this property look more like an estate than a place of death."

Public records said that Orson's vehicle and belongings were found untouched at his campsite in Placerville. With his body found back in Courtland, someone got to him and drove him back.

"The perpetrator had to know you wouldn't be home," Det. de Giorgio said.

"Everyone in town knew us," Esmerelda said. "Knew that no one would be at the house that weekend."

"Was there an investigation of Orson's acquaintances up in Placerville?" Sara asked, jumping into the conversation.

"Believe it or not," Det. Vance said. "We still have problems with claim jumpers up in those hills. What was believed, till now, was that another person could have thought Orson was encroaching on his panning area and killed him. Didn't have to be anyone he knew. But that doesn't seem logical now."

Esmerelda shook her head sadly. "Never met acquaintances he knew in Placerville."

"Since your husband's hyoid bone was broken," Det. Vance said. "It does tie somewhat to victims already found."

Chapter 46

By mid-October, the *Rio Vista Bass Derby*, one of the three largest Delta festivals, came and went. Neither Sara nor Daphine attended. Sara had no real desire to spend much time in Rio Vista. During her school years, the yellow bus picked her up at her front door in Ryde. She attended classes and nothing else, no after-school activities and no visiting because the homebound bus left immediately after classes.

"I get to Rio for a showing now and again," Daphine said over lunch in Locke one afternoon. "When I opened my shop here instead of Rio, I lost contact with my friends. Rio's a different county, a different world."

Later, they stood in Sara's front yard under the shade trees. After nearly four months of having multiple construction crews crawling inside and out at Talbot House, plus the legal investigations and delays, the refurbishing was nearly finished.

The white hexagonal gazebo included steps on the two front and back sections of its six sides. "I wanted this large enough so that several of us can enjoy a meal here," Sara said.

"Could be used as a bandstand for social functions," Daphine said.

Sara reveled in the satisfaction of a dream come true. For just a moment, she visualized herself and a man dancing between the columns; a man with blue-topaz eyes, who occupied all her embellished fantasies.

"Earth to Sara," Daphine said.

Sara felt her face flush. "The house should be finished in about two weeks."

Daphine's grin was playfully mocking. "That's if they don't find another body, right?"

Sara motioned upwards. "Needed to put on a new roof too. Once they removed the fireplace and chimney, they found a lot of dry rot."

"A little more than you bargained for?"

Sara grimaced. "Cost-wise, yes."

A new roof, sea-green upper floor singles, fresh paint, and all new windows completed the exterior work. From the outside, the house looked new. They walked around the structure to view the finished changes.

On the north side, Daphine frowned and stepped closer to inspect the newly installed basement windows. "Oh-oh," she said, stooping down. "Not again."

Sara leaned closer. One of the new windows contained pry marks, perhaps made by a screwdriver or chisel. "Darned construction guys," she said. "Sometimes they rush too much to do the job right."

"The construction people wouldn't be that careless, would they?"

Sara remembered and then gasped. "These pry marks are in the same place as they were on the old window."

"Yeah, someone tried to get in. I told you that back then and… and now, here's more marks on your new window."

"Well, they didn't get in because my alarm system didn't go off," Sara said. "Johanna thinks someone's after me."

"She's got that right!"

"Patrol cars pass on the levee a lot more frequently now. Sometimes they park up at the eucalyptus trees, writing reports, I guess."

"Maybe sleeping."

They walked completely around the house and then stepped into the basement. The newly sanded concrete floors, and the walls now drywalled and painted, made the tired old workspace bright and cheerful. They stepped around the pile of Sara's belongings.

"You put the washer and dryer down here after all."

"Couldn't wait for the back porch to be finished," Sara said.

"You should still put the appliances up there like you planned," Daphine said. "It's more convenient."

With the remodeled staircase off the kitchen, all an intruder had to do was get into the basement, maybe through a pried window, and they would have access to the entire house. She had to remember to set the alarm when alone or away.

They entered the house through the back porch door. The new kitchen cabinets and flooring were outstanding. A lovely light pinkish-greenish Italian marble covered the countertops. Complementary ceramic tile covered the floor.

Daphine took it all in, running her fingertips over the marble. "Of course it's imported," she said.

Farther in, the redesigned stairway flowed down between the kitchen and dining room. What was once a servants' shadowy passageway was now a showcase of elegance. The pantry would no longer be used as a passage to the kitchen. Sawdust, wood, and tools still littered the floor toward the front of the house.

After a tour of the upstairs, Daphine stood on the back staircase and looked upward. "Used to be a separate hole for attic access. Are you telling me we can now use this new staircase and walk all the way into the attic, as easy as climbing to the next floor up?"

Once inside the attic, Sara said. "Finished off these walls too. If I've got the space, I'll make use of it."

"Wow!" Daphine said. "Just look at the north light that pours in." Too soon, as always, Daphine had to run. "I'm totally envious," she said, starting the engine. "Wish I could remodel that rental I'm in. I'm sure I could increase the living space."

Sara went looking for the foreman and found him at the front staircase.

"My guys just wouldn't do that," he said as they made their way to the north side. After seeing the marks, he shook his head. "No reason for my guys to open a window that way."

Sara immediately called Johanna at her cafe. "Whoever it was musta' gave up when they saw your alarm box mounted up there under the eaves," Johanna said. "You'd better keep those two workers living there."

That night, Sara examined the gun in her dresser drawer. She hoped never to use it. She anticipated having a lot of people walk through the house once the remodeling was done, causing doubts about her hiding place. She pushed the pistol deeper beneath the underclothes, hoping her private dresser drawers would not be opened.

Chapter 47

"You brought me good luck," Pierce said over breakfast at Clampett Tract. "I'm getting an advance on my new book."

"So soon?" She passed a bite of dry toast to the dogs. She had kept them overnight again. "I thought publishers were like a government bureaucracy, only worse."

Choco and Latte were big now, though they wouldn't be a year old until the beginning of December. The color of their coats matured and glowed, and they were beautiful animals. They paced a lot and were always hungry. They hadn't changed their demeanor toward her or anyone else that Sara could tell. Still, they were a handful.

"I have a track record with my publisher." Pierce chewed quickly and swallowed. "I can pay you back finally."

"I didn't expect to be paid."

"It's me, Sara. I need to."

"I can't let you. I just finished two more computer games. Pierce, I'm doing fabulous."

Her next two games were directed more for younger children: *Slim, the Slammer*, a baseball game, and *Rubber Band Man*, a silly but challenging exercise with what can be done with rubber bands in addition to seeing how far they can be shot through the air. Both were developed to promote acute hand-eye coordination in youngsters.

"I want to pay you for this house, the computer—"

"I'll tear up your check." She appreciated Pierce needing to feel in charge of his life, surely as she needed to take charge of hers. "Spend your money, but not with me. Start an IRA. Stuff your mattress. We're not getting any younger, you know?"

"I need to start paying the rent."

"I paid it. A year in advance."

"Sara!"

"Pay the utilities then. Pay the gardeners." The couple that maintained lawns at several Clampett Tract homes had also been tending Pierce's yard. Sara flapped her hand, not wanting to be bothered with such things.

"Sara, I don't know how to take you. Haven't you ever needed to do something for yourself and...?" He stopped, thought a moment, then looked up and flashed a sparkling grin. "That was a silly question."

After breakfast, they sat in the living room. Pierce could not keep his eyes off the dream drawing.

"Ever since we found Orson under the workshop," Sara said. "I haven't had that dream again."

"Still have the ghost?"

"Never saw one," she said, being silly. "I keep hearing bumps though."

"What about the footsteps?"

"Not since I have an alarm and two live-ins."

"Still, you need to be cautious. Whoever tried to get us will think of another way to do it."

"You think the person was out to get you too?"

"No prowlers here. It's Talbot House and whoever's in it."

She didn't dare tell him about the new pry marks. Nor would she mention her pistol. What she needed was to spend the day with a friend and not worry or think of her problems. "Let's go for a ride," she said.

"You haven't learned enough about the Delta, I see."

They passed the Walnut Grove Bridge heading southwest around Big Bend. "I notice the seasons more since I've returned."

"We were unobserving kids back then," he said, looking out over the tops of trees. "Pear and apple pickings are finished."

Driving on the Grand Island levee, pear trees that were now mere skeletons would be pruned before the next growing season began. Laborers would bundle up against the cold and drizzle and thin out branches on thousands of acres of trees, one tree at a time.

"I read where they flood the fields after harvesting the corn and wheat," she said.

"Depends on the island. Thousands of acres become a habitat for wintering birds."

Rather than burning or disking, flooding the fields was an effective and less-expensive way of breaking down crop stubble. Water broke down what the birds didn't ingest. It further reduced salt in the ground. The mix of decaying plants and bird manure enriched the soil.

Nearing Ryde, Sara looked at the river. No matter the season, rushing or lazing along, the river was a mesmerizing memory. Water continually lapped; the sunny side of the waves reflecting a silver hue on the greenish, silty surface.

Suddenly, she veered off the levee into the parking lot behind the Ryde Hotel. "Let's have coffee," she said.

He was getting around better, but past experience had taught him to rely on his walking stick. She met him at the tailgate. "Have you walked on the spot where your shack used to stand?" he asked.

"No, just being this close and seeing it covered with fairway grass is enough."

Choco and Latte couldn't be left alone, especially not left inside a hot vehicle, or any vehicle, while Sara and Pierce went inside. Pierce suggested they get a table out on the terrace behind the hotel. There the dogs could remain with them.

"When the dogs stay overnight at Talbot House, do they sense anything spooky?"

"You know? Sometimes they seem to bark at the air," Sara said. "But you know something? They are pretty mature now. If an intruder tried to break in, I'll bet they'd take the person's leg off."

Chapter 48

Pierce's birthday was a week away. Sara wanted to buy him a new aquarium. She decided to drop by the house that afternoon to find out, without giving away her plan, if he still had any interest in one. While in Walnut Grove, she stopped at the Post Office to mail copies of the two new DVD games to the copyright office in Washington, and two copies of each to her marketing manager.

Later, at Pierce's house, he said "Da-dah!" He gestured in an animated fashion to the sideboard in the dining area as she entered. He had purchased an aquarium, hexagonal, like the one destroyed. "Got a steal of a deal on the Internet. He thumbed toward the back yard. "Kid back there through the gate had too many tenants in his tank." Tiny colorful fish flitted around their new home. Truly, living with friendly neighbors was something that Pierce appreciated.

Her surprises for him would end. He acted overjoyed being able to do something for himself. Maybe she would just take him to dinner, to one of those gourmet restaurants in Sacramento. He seldom went to Sacramento, with the exception of health emergencies.

In an instant, Sara felt a sense of release. She worried too much over Pierce, and he was functioning well again. Now her attention could focus on forming the foundation she thought of a few weeks back. It was another of her ideas that quickly took on a life of its own. She needed all her stamina and wits about her because the purpose of the new organization was so important, so dire. It might be her largest undertaking, and she intended to breathe life into it.

Her cell phone rang. As she answered, she stepped out onto the back terrace to find that Pierce had something cooking in the covered barbeque.

"Listen," Esmerelda said on the phone as the dogs barked in the background. "Do you realize that in all the time we've known each other, you've only stayed for dinner once?"

"You do love to entertain, don't you?"

Esmerelda hushed the dogs. "Yep. You have any plans for this evening?" She didn't wait for a reply. "Come as you are. We'll eat about five. I can make my evening rounds afterwards," she said. "The weather's turning chilly and I have a feeling this is one of the last good days for a meal outdoors."

The smell of Pierce's dinner searing on the grill nagged at her stomach. Sara realized she was back at an old habit of skipping meals when busy. She and Daphine were fast becoming known as the two toothpicks among their slowly widening circle of acquaintances. Sara felt ravenous. "I'll be there," she said.

"Good. We'll barbeque on the deck. I thought I'd invite your sister too." Her tone was meant to cajole.

It took a second to understand that Esmerelda meant Daphine. "A little after four then. Is that okay?"

* * *

"Let's get out of the kitchen before we finish off the salad," Daphine said, pinching a last bite of lettuce.

Esmerelda fed the dogs to avoid having them beg at the table. Not that that would stop Choco. Spirited waltzes, *Danses Viennoises*, directed by Michael Dittrich, played through the speakers, both inside and outside on the deck. Esmerelda knew how to set a mood. Sara had made a quick stop at the grocers on the way over. Now she poured together her tropical juice concoction, a substitute cocktail in the evening hours. "Thanks for doing that," Esmerelda said. "None of us drink much alcohol anymore."

Sara stood before the kitchen window pouring the glassfuls when she caught a glimpse of a sedan approaching on the levee and then turn onto the down ramp into the hospice property. By the time she carried the tray of frosty glasses out to the deck, she came face to face with Huxley Keane bounding up the stairs.

The dogs jumped to all fours, noses sniffed, and tails wagged. Sara's heart fluttered wildly. At last, they would meet!

He wore an aloha shirt opened at the throat, exposing a bit of dark chest hair and a tan. His beige slacks and sports jacket flaunted expensive silk. The next time Esmerelda said come as you are, Sara would at least put on heels.

"Hello again," he said, looking straight into her eyes. He dropped a decorative paper bag with oriental writing on it onto the tabletop. "May I?" He took the tray from her hands. He seemed overly gentlemanly, wanting to serve the drinks, or else he had intended it that way so they could make direct eye contact again.

If that were the case, he needn't worry. Sara had wanted to contact him somehow, to talk about the foundation. With her heart fluttering the way it was, she needed to reign in her impulses to talk business appropriately.

"Hux, you're back," Esmerelda said. Her tone and staged expression was a dead giveaway. Esmerelda's scheming brought them together. Sara had hoped for such a coincidental meeting. It was anything but. She guessed that Esmerelda must have learned that Huxley was back from Asia. That was the reason for the sudden dinner invitation. Sara's heartbeat fluttered nearly out of control.

Huxley retrieved the bag from the tabletop before Choco, paws on the edge and nose rooting around, knocked it off. He offered it to Esmerelda. "For you, Esme," he said, kissing her cheek.

Sara's felt she might hallucinate, wanting him to kiss her cheek, her lips. She looked away quickly and hoped her emotions weren't showing. Daphine stood aside with a big-eyed Aha! grin slathered over her face.

Deep sadness still permeated Esmerelda's actions. It was expected. For the moment, she participated in activities only to keep her mind occupied. Huxley's gift seemed to be a healing experience for her. She pulled out the inner bag that showed small cakes neatly stacked in a clear plastic container. She stumbled over the pronunciation.

"*Manjyu*," Huxley said. "From Japan."

"It's the best gift you can bring a hostess," Daphine said, looking over Esmerelda's shoulder. "In the oriental tradition, of course."

"Tell me about these," Esmerelda said.

Huxley looked perplexed and then remembered something. He pulled a sheet of paper out of the outer bag. "I knew you'd want this. It's the recipes for both the dough and the *anko*, you know, the sweet bean filling."

Esmerelda, the gourmet cook, was overjoyed at having a new recipe to try.

Huxley's cell phone rang. After listening a moment, he asked into the phone, "Can you call me in the morning?" Before sitting down to dinner, he checked to make sure his cell phone was turned off.

* * *

Daphine excused herself for leaving so soon after dinner. She flashed one last devilish look. Sara discreetly shook her fist in return.

As dusk approached, Sara stared vacantly out the kitchen window. She had cleaned the table and sink, to hide her nervousness. Esmerelda put the plates and utensils into the dishwasher. Huxley lingered over his last bit of juice out on the deck. He checked his phone messages but didn't make any calls.

"He's the busiest ever," Esmerelda said. "Gets calls from all over the world."

Huxley attempted to get re-acquainted with the dogs, now older, with changed personalities. Mimie lay on her cushion in the corner of the deck, which meant she was accustomed to him being around. Huxley bent down to play. Choco sniffed Huxley's face and ears and even his hair. Huxley just laughed. Latte sniffed his hands and arms, even his loafers. It was most curious to watch.

"If you'll excuse me," Esmerelda said once they were outside again. "I've got to make my rounds."

The music continued. Soon as Esmerelda disappeared, unexpectedly, Huxley took her hand and looked into her eyes. His face was full of expectation. She stopped breathing. His touch surprised her. It was a wondrous spontaneous feeling. She relaxed her hand in his. They stood transfixed, looking into each other's eyes.

The music changed as if on cue. Huxley pulled her to him, and they began to waltz. Didn't ask. Didn't wait. Just took it upon himself to sweep her across the deck... in sneakers.

The melody enticed dancers to embrace. He pulled her close, and she couldn't resist.

Don't be taken for granted! Sara mentally told herself. *Don't let him get away either.* All she did since looking into his eyes that first time was fantasize about him and her in the most sensual of situations.

They melted together and danced as one. Huxley respectfully held to the dance posture so nothing cheap would enter into it. They were two people attracted to one another, and at that moment, surely heat rose from them like the waves that sizzled up from the hot summer pavements.

Chapter 49

A week before Halloween, work finished at Talbot House. One area, the front staircase, awaited materials. Some of the banister posts that had been replaced didn't quite match the existing ones. Sara decided to have them all replaced by the same manufacturer. The old handrail was left in place, although the contractor strung a heavy rope down the staircase for safety. Still missing, as well, were the lighting fixtures for the three rooms downstairs. Sara located an antique chandelier shop in West Sacramento and hoped to soon remedy that problem. Too, driveway lights were not installed. At the last moment, Sara decided that an unwary motorist driving in the fog could mistake them for a car's oncoming headlights, causing them to swerve and possibly run off the levee. She settled for ordinary red ground reflectors that would work just as effectively in a thick blur.

The two construction workers reluctantly moved out. Sara hired a cleaning crew to give all four floors a once over. The house carried an inviting new smell, new wood, and new finishes, exactly to her demanding specifications.

Huxley arrived from Sacramento, his home when not in Oregon. He lived in a condo when in California on business. The MIA search group with which Huxley was involved was based in San Francisco, but he spent a lot of time in Sacramento at the capitol and in Washington, D.C. with politicians and lobbyists.

"At last," Sara said as she gave Huxley a tour. "I can call this house my own."

"You're definitely doing the right thing with your plans for the property."

She admired him secretly, with a whole lot of love and hope. So what if he was four years her junior. The chemistry between them was undeniable, and it had a lot more to do with compatible wants from life than mere physical attraction. Surprisingly, both she and Huxley found it easy to keep their personal desires separate from their work. That determination seemed to seal the unspoken truth of their mutual respect and admiration, though at times, working together did tempt them both toward personal conversations. That glorious physical ever-present tension bonded them closer to taking the next step that surely, they each mulled over since saying their first hellos.

They were finishing an excruciatingly busy ten days, one in which Sara learned just how much this man was respected, giving his life over to the search for MIAs. Her foundation was as important to her as his mission was to him.

Huxley's many contacts would help with activities that Sara planned for her foundation. If her plans were to fall into place, one last meeting was required before filing documents with the IRS and the State of California.

They went to visit Esmerelda. Demetrio took all three dogs for a run. Huxley took one call after another and finally turned off his cell phone.

Sara, Daphine, Esmerelda, and Huxley sat around a circular table in the vacant sunroom inside the hospice facility. Daphine brought along a large drawing pad and stood it on an easel beside her chair. The kitchen staff served coffee and small bowls of fruit slices.

Daphine slipped Sara a newspaper clipping under the table. While Esmerelda and Huxley enjoyed light chatter before settling down, Sara read the article titled:

Missing Dogs Found Dead

The two dogs stolen from the Humane Society at the recent Pear Fair were found with their skulls crushed. Two boys out frog hunting found them in a ditch on the south end of Sutter Island. The dogs were presumably transported, or they wandered across the Sacramento River on the Paintersville Bridge near Courtland before being killed.

> *An old shovel was found near the carcasses, and subsequently identified as the weapon used to kill them. The shovel was traced to Ike Ames. Upon questioning, a Sheriff's deputy verified that Ames had, weeks earlier, reported his shovel stolen.*

Sara's growing suspicions jumped into the fray. The rest of the article suggested a connection between two slaughtered animals and a shovel, used to dig graves. In making their suggestions, what they weren't saying was that the killing could be a sign that the psychopath was active again and his modus operandi was crumbling. He might be losing his grip on what little was left of his sanity. "This has got to stop," she said.

"What is it?" Esmerelda asked.

Sara had not meant to disrupt her own meeting, but the article brought back jitters. News of the serial killer had died down and she, perhaps erroneously, felt safe again in her secured home. "Maybe you should see this," she said, passing the article to Esmerelda. Sara stood and walked to the window looking out over the grounds. She sensed Huxley watching her, and that made her feel giddy. How long it had been since she felt that way. When she returned to the table, he had just finished reading the news clipping.

"We must stay alert," he said. "Including you in that big empty house, Sara. Maybe those construction guys should have stayed with you a bit longer." Huxley's words almost came out as an order. Evidently, his concern did not include jealousy.

"I'll keep the dogs more often," she said.

He turned to Daphine. "You have good neighbors there in Isleton?"

"Nosey as all get-out," she said. "There's always a pair of eyes peeking out from behind the curtains somewhere."

To get the meeting back on track, Sara called their attention and then said, "Our mission is straightforward. The foundation provides funding for families of missing people throughout the state, and the country, to help them continue searching for loved ones. Priority is on cold cases no longer being actively investigated."

"I'm working on getting start-up funding," Huxley said, breaking the silence as each digested the magnitude of the undertaking. "They could match what Sara donated to start the foundation." After the foundation has proven itself, more funds could be solicited from grants, government agencies, and other charitable sources.

Esmerelda thrilled at hearing about Sara's latest project. She simply sat, nodding, absorbing the information. "What about the officers and such?" she asked curiously. She took a bite of an apple wedge.

"Okay, I'll Chair the Board," Sara said. "And sign the checks. You know." She paused and glanced around, watching reactions of the others. She had high hopes for their group, but others should join only if meeting the goals and standards established. "Daphine has consented to become our Secretary, keeper of records and vital advisor. She is the contact person when no one else can be reached—with the stipulation that if the work becomes too much, well, she has her own business to attend. We'd find someone else."

"Thanks for that," Daphine said.

"But we need a couple more members," Sara said. "Executive Director and—"

"How about Fredrik?" Esmerelda asked. "He's followed the Underhill case and others from the beginning. He remains friendly with the Underhill family. He certainly knows how to handle death and closure."

Sara cringed. She had thought little about inviting Fredrik, until they caught the serial killer, or at least until she could rule him out as a suspect. His preoccupation with death didn't seem normal. "He may be a bit too busy," she said in a friendly manner, hoping to hear no further mention.

"I wish there was an organization like this years ago when…." Esmerelda sighed wistfully and stared out the window.

Huxley noticed Esmerelda's discomfort and picked up the discussion. "So far," he said. "We've found two detectives who've consented to join as board members. One is retiring from service and can devote as much time as needed. The work will be right up her alley. The other is a few years away from retiring. Both are well connected in circles and groups we need to count on."

"How did you find them?" Daphine asked.

"Our friend, Johanna," Huxley said. "She recommended them. Sara and I liked both officers when we interviewed them."

"Huxley will be an advisor," Sara said.

"You'll need a lawyer," Esmerelda said.

"Haven't found one," Sara said, shrugging.

"What about mine?" Esmerelda asked. "I've used her for years."

"Now there's an idea," Daphine said. "Do you think she might?"

"Well, let's analyze what works in our favor. She and I think alike. She heads a couple of charity groups."

"Sounds too busy already," Daphine said. "But let's hope she'll be interested."

"One major position remains," Sara said. "That of Executive Director of the board and member in charge of operations. Day-to-day stuff, you know."

Esmerelda looked out the window. "Day-to-day stuff, huh?" she asked, though she didn't say anything more. That was a good sign.

Sara held her breath and looked Esmerelda straight in the eyes when she returned her attention to the meeting. "I want you for that position," she said hopefully. "You have quiet clout, and the public adores you. As do we."

"Oh, please," Esmerelda said, smiling and waving her off, but she knew it was true. She had worked long and hard for peer respect. When she and Orson opened the hospice, the community rallied round and validated her leadership.

"Say you'll join us," Daphine said.

"I don't type anymore," Esmerelda said, joking.

They laughed heartily, then hushed, mindful of being inside a hospice full of very ill patients.

"No typing," Huxley said. "But lots of PR."

"You don't think I'm too old, do you?" Esmerelda asked.

They laughed and caught themselves being loud again.

"I think, given a chance," Daphine said. "You'd work circles around us."

"Well," she said in an openly joking manner. "I was hoping to be included."

Peals of laughter rang out. Fredrik stuck his head inside the doorway squelching the giddiness.

"By the way, what's the name of this foundation?" Esmerelda asked.

"That's the reason it would be right for you to be Executive Director," Sara said.

Daphine stood and rolled back the cover of the artist tablet waiting on the easel.

Esmerelda's jaw dropped. She reached for the tablet and pulled it to her as she tried to focus through bleary eyes. "Orson," she said. "My Orson."

The drawing was of a man's hands holding a pan as he panned for gold. Shiny nuggets reflecting sunlight filled the bottom half, settled under a bit of water. The composition was in tasteful blues and muted whites. The large golden letters OTF shone on the bottom arc of the pan rim. Around the upper arc was the name,

Orson Talbot Foundation.

Chapter 50

Esmerelda insisted they accompany her to the garage storage area when the meeting ended. She pointed to one door, and Huxley opened it wide to let in the sunlight. He pulled the string to the overhead light. Esmerelda pulled back the edge of a dusty tarp and called their attention to three large aging cardboard boxes sitting on a shelf. She fanned away dust. "Hux," she said, coughing some. "Can you bring one of those down without getting grimy?"

Tripp appeared out of nowhere, carrying a hoe. "Can I help?" he asked, propping the hoe outside the doorway.

"Sure," Huxley said. "Grab an end."

As they shifted the box to the floor something inside tinkled.

"Careful now," Esmerelda said. "Tripp, open that, would you?"

"Sure, Mrs. T," he said, producing a pocketknife. He slit the strapping tape on each end and down the middle with as much energy as Zorro carving his initial.

Esmerelda opened the flaps. "Well, I haven't seen your finished house yet, Sara, but these should fit nicely."

In her peripheral vision, Sara noticed Tripp watching her every move. She ignored him and peered into the box. Inside lay an antique chandelier with most of its decorative crystal ornaments individually wrapped. "You're giving these to… what are… where did…?"

"They were in the house when Orson and I bought it," Esmerelda said, with a mischievous grin. "I stole them when I had to sell the place."

"You said 'they,'" Sara said. "You took all three?"

Esmerelda motioned to the other two boxes on the shelf and then came to stand beside her and wrapped an arm around her shoulder. "They're yours, girl."

"This is your lucky day," Daphine said, sounding truly envious. Expressing in that way was something new from her.

Tripp sauntered away. Daphine had to flee again. Anytime she was away from her shop meant lost business.

They stood at the bottom of Esmerelda's stairs saying their goodbyes. Sara had one last offer she needed to make before leaving. She waited for the proper moment, and then asked, "Esmerelda, would you consider moving back to Talbot House?"

Esmerelda looked stunned. She glanced at Huxley, and back again. "No," she said shaking her head and sounding definite. "My life is not at that house anymore."

"I thought you might like to get away from all these stairs," Sara said, half joking.

Huxley remained quiet. He always seemed content watching people's interactions.

"That house has no stairs?" Esmerelda asked, cocking her head and looking at her sideways.

"You could have the downstairs bedroom and bath. Have the run of the house, more space."

Esmerelda stared at her another moment and then shook her head again. "No, my life is here. This was our dream, Orson's and mine." She pointed out across her property. "See those two newer cabins back in the corner behind Tripp's cottage?"

"What about them?" Sara asked.

"I've already had thoughts about combining them into one bigger house," Esmerelda said. "That's how I'll get away from these stairs." She shook her head again. "My life is here." She took Sara's hands. "But I love you for thinking of my welfare." They hugged. Esmerelda swiped at tears as she pulled away.

* * *

On the way back to Talbot House in the SUV, Sara glanced at Huxley as she drove. His demeanor was quiet and severe. "Hey, I'm not psychic," she said.

"Uh, yeah," he said. "Maybe something you should know." He paused again. "The reason I'm here instead of returning home after my last trip. We found a soldier's remains in Nam."

Sara gasped. "Someone who was with your brother and Betty?"

"I see you know about Betty."

"Daphine told me. Esmerelda's never mentioned it. I figure it's too painful for her, so I never bring it up."

"That's wise of you." Again, he went into quiet thought. "Forensic dogs," he said finally, and nodded thoughtfully. "A retired Colonel—part of our group—he and I went straight to Southern California to break the news to the family."

"How could you be certain so soon?"

"Dog tags, an engraved wedding band, two teeth," Huxley said. "One of the veterans in our group knew the approximate area the soldier dropped. We just couldn't find the remains without the dog."

"After so many years?" Sara asked. "A dog sniffed it out after decades?"

"They're also doing DNA tests, but those dogs are magnificent creatures," Huxley said. "They're known as Human Remains Detection Dogs. Officials have used them to find the boundaries of forlorn graveyards."

"They can pick up scents that old?"

The seat belts prevented Huxley from fully turning to face her. "These HRD dogs have been trained not to pick up fresh human scents," he said. "They're trained in detecting ancient remains, like in cold cases. When trained properly, they can detect a residual scent from a tiny fragment of human bone buried for hundreds of years. The animal making the current discovery was trained to detect certain metals, like the dog tags."

"Maybe now you'll find more of those missing."

"We hope," Huxley said. "A lot of the people in our group are getting too old to make the trip, facing days riding in a *Humvee* or walking difficult pathways through the jungle. We need to complete our searches or expand the group with younger volunteers."

Sara reflected on the message of closure Huxley might have brought back to the MIA's relatives. "Both joy and sorrow for that family," she said. She glanced at Huxley again. His expression was one of hope.

"I decided to swing by here on my way home, so I could tell Esme."

"How did she take it?"

"Very good, actually. She knows Betty's gone, but finding one MIA keeps her hope alive."

"And just maybe we can help."

Huxley reached over and touched her shoulder. "I'll miss you. I'll be leaving soon. I need to see my family."

His hand remained on her shoulder, yet she felt great disappointment. She dreaded the day he would leave.

* * *

The following Monday, Sara rushed to get out of the house and to Sacramento. She ended up arriving too early before the government offices opened for the day. Just after ten o'clock, she finished filing the foundation's documents and felt a rush of elation. She wished Huxley could have been with her. At least, she could involve him through her thoughts. Not a day had gone by since she first looked into his wondrous eyes that she did not think of him in some way. She hung around town browsing furniture stores, but her heart wasn't in shopping. She would meet Huxley for dinner. He would catch a flight home around noon on Tuesday.

Sara drove into a newer condo complex just off Highway 50, found the right unit and knocked on the door. Huxley opened it, and she stepped inside while he retrieved a jacket. The condo belonged to one of the veterans and seemed inviting and comfortable. Times had changed. Here she was picking up her date. She contemplated the evolving roles.

"I know a great Chinese restaurant," he said. "They even have those old-fashioned booths and curtains for doors."

Surprisingly, chopsticks weren't that difficult to master. Maybe it was their mood. His casual conversation was light and teasing. Sara hadn't felt so good in years.

"Take a bite of this," he said, offering Lo Mein noodles on his chopsticks.

Sara knew it was impolite to eat off another person's plate. Etiquette classes she took during her twenties impressed dos and don'ts when defining acceptable behavior. She ate what was offered when very young because her family was so poor. They didn't know if they would have anything to eat the next day. Sara's first impulse was not to open her mouth. With Huxley, she let her guard down and leaned toward him. Huxley muffled a gasp as she parted her lips.

After a few seconds of silence and settling down, he said, "OTF has a good start now."

"Thanks to you," she said, savoring the unique flavor of the Lo Mein. "I honestly couldn't have moved this along as quickly without your knowledge."

"The process won't take long," Huxley said as he picked up a platter, served a portion to her, and then scraped the rest of the noodles onto his plate.

Waiting for documents was not a good position to be in with state agencies in Sacramento. "Hope it doesn't take as long as some of the house permits," she said.

"I'll see if there's anything my contacts can do to give it a shove."

They had seen each other every day for more than a week. "May I see you when I return?" he asked.

Sara wanted to know him better, sooner. She had spent copious amounts of time mentally conjuring experiences with him. Doing so made her feel alive again. It had been difficult to keep her feelings subdued, and her mind focused on the business at hand. She might have left him with the impression that she was a prude, or just not interested in a close relationship. Truth was, she harbored thoughts about what it would be like to know Huxley intimately. Over recent years, she repressed thoughts of having a man in her life. Now here she was, unable to stop thinking romantically about Huxley. Her runaway fantasies contained only him. Yet, some old childhood programming kept her from revealing even a hint of her innermost feelings.

"When will you return?"

"A few weeks. I really miss my family. They're everything to me." Huxley had a son and a daughter, both grown and married. They worked the family ranch in Oregon.

"In the Coburg Ridge foothills, in the shadow of Indian Head peak."

"I have no idea where that is."

"My sister and brother-in-law run the operation. The rest of the family work for them."

"Your farm, what goes on there?"

"Cattle, sheep, a few crops, even some marketable timber." He took a sip of water. "My sister—she's older than me—wanted to get into Christmas trees. What a great entrepreneur she turned out to be. Filled up most of the idle acreage, and our bank accounts."

Huxley's face lit up when he spoke of family. He presented photos from his wallet, like a proud parent. "My parents are still living," he said. "If you can call having nurses twenty-four-seven any kind of a life."

"I'm so sorry," Sara said.

"I was ten years old, my brother twenty-one, when he went missing in Nam." Emotion flooded Huxley's face. "I need to bring my brother home," he said, choking up. His lips tightened. "Before Mom and Dad pass away."

Chapter 51

Huxley asked if he could drive on the way back to his condo. "I like playing the male role once in a while," he said with a teasing smile.

"You paid for dinner," she said, acting as though he had taken away one of her privileges.

They had grown up in an era of the double standard but adjusted well to societal changes, could even joke about their roles. Joke, like they had done all through dinner, talked about so many subjects, with a lot of humor that turned into magnetic teasing, with personal comments and gentle touching. She burned with desire she didn't think she was capable of feeling again. She felt young, frivolous, and daring.

It was great to see the tension drain out of Huxley's face as the evening wore on. When they arrived at his condo and parked beside his sedan, he grabbed her keys from the ignition and jumped out, coming around to her side to open her door. Chivalry went right along with the fun of the evening.

"You are so gallant, sir," she said affectedly, taking his hand and sliding out.

He steered her toward the front door. "How about a nightcap?"

Sara found herself inside and toasting with a mug of decaf before she had time to contemplate what she was doing.

He retrieved the car keys from his pocket and dropped them into her opened purse. He leaned slightly across the counter and intensely studied her. "You're the one," he said, nodding thoughtfully. "You're the one."

She loved being with Huxley and didn't want the evening to end, but that was inevitable. "I really must go," she said, coming to her senses.

"I was hoping not to hear that," he said, coming around the end of the counter and reaching for her.

Suddenly, she was in Huxley's arms. Past resolves melted in the heat of true passion. "I should go," she said, hearing desire on her own breath. Huxley kissed her, gently at first and when she could no longer restrain herself, he must have sensed it. His kiss became insistent, until she wrapped her arms around his neck and returned his affection, heartbeat for heartbeat. Then she tried to move away. "Huxley, we—" His mouth came hard against hers. His hands were all over her back, her hips, pulling hers toward him until she felt his desire. She wanted more. She wanted him to touch her bare skin. She wanted to touch the hair that swirled over his chest and feel it against her naked breasts.

Huxley unbuttoned her blouse and she slipped out of it as they walked into the bedroom. She felt both scared and reckless, beyond stopping. He unfastened the button above the zipper of her slacks, and she stepped out of them and out of her heels. He removed his shirt, exposing a magnificent muscular chest with hair that went all the way down to....

Huxley ripped back the bed covers, and in one swoop, picked her up, positioned his knee on the bed, and laid her down. His physical strength surprised her. He turned his back to her and removed his trousers. He was shy about himself. Huxley was shy! He came to bed in his undershorts and pulled up the covers and kissed her longingly. He ran his hands over her yearning body as if wanting to have every inch of her at once.

His fingertips explored. Her bra fell aside, and she squirmed out of her panties as she lay facing him. His fingertips touched her everywhere, without hesitation, followed by his lips. Huxley seemed love-starved.

It was a long time since Sara had been with a man and she felt awkward. She was just as starved. She could now live out the fantasies she conjured about this man. She kissed his chest, dragged her tongue slowly across his nipples, and ran her fingertips any place that made his breath quicken. Together, they went beyond their fantasies.

Each time he heard her breath falter he intensified the pleasure. At times he watched her expression. Surely, she had grimaced in sheer ecstasy and had a fleeting moment of embarrassment at being watched. But Huxley wouldn't allow that for long.

He kicked away the covers and positioned himself farther down the mattress. Sara thought she would surely pass out from the intensity of his probing tongue. When words escaped her throat as nothing more than guttural sounds, he began to bite.

"Hux, no!" she said, though the words seemed barely discernible.

He continued to bite, just hard enough so that she felt stimulated beyond belief. She had wanted him and was getting her wish. "Love me," she said, begging, because she could take no more foreplay. She needed penetration, hard and fast. She needed to be taken, but he continued the pleasure with his tongue.

Finally, he climbed on top. "Hard, Hux," she said. But her voice came out on faltering breaths. She dug her fingertips into his hips and pulled him toward her.

Huxley took her. The way she needed. The way he needed. A feeble scream escaped her throat. Hearing him moan his pleasure enhanced her enjoyment. He held back nothing and didn't stop his forceful thrusts until she was satisfied. Even then, he continued until his orgasm overtook him and he moaned loudly with each spasm. Then he collapsed onto the sheets beside her.

She lay quiet while her breath and heart rate calmed, too awed to move or speak. He drifted off fast, but strangely, kept hold of her wrist and wouldn't let go.

* * *

Sara bolted awake as if someone had shot a gun off in the room. Fear erupted from a deep crevasse in her mind.

What if the serial killer was not from the Sacramento area, not from California at all?

She tried to keep her anxiety and fright under control.

What if he was someone who came into the state regularly and then left?

She had to get a grip on her thoughts, but they kept coming.

Maybe that was why the serial killer had never been caught. He was from out of state. A perfect cover.

Why was she having these thoughts this night?

What the hell am I doing in bed with a guy I know so little about?

She began to tremble.

How convenient to have legitimate business here, then turn off his cell phone, do his killing, and skip out.

Sometime during the night, he loosened the grip on her wrist. How strong he seemed. Overpowering. Why had he tried to detain her?

Huxley's knowledge of war tactics would help hide his crimes.

She tried to reason it out. Why would someone like Huxley turn into a killer? Because he lost his brother and his mind snapped? That was the only reason she could come up with because she knew not much else about him. She trembled fiercely. She had to get out of bed before he woke.

Don't even shower!

Sara eased out of bed, grabbed her clothes, and stood in the darkened bathroom and dressed. When she came out into the bedroom, Huxley wore only his slacks and blocked the bedroom doorway. "What are you doing?" he asked, still sleepy. He dragged a hand over his face.

Sara was scared. Her libido and loneliness had swept away all caution. "I shouldn't be here," she said. "Too soon. This shouldn't have... too soon."

"Is that a reason to leave?"

"Please," she said, motioning for him to step aside. "Let me go."

He still blocked the doorway. "I'm not letting you get away now."

His words filled her with dread. Her heart continued to pound, and her pulse throbbed up the side of her neck. She looked for a weapon and saw only the oversized lamp on the dresser across the room. She did not wish to anger him and managed a tighter grip on her purse, which was all she had if she needed to bash him. He took a step toward her, and she stepped back. "Look, I'm leaving, okay?"

Huxley stared at her for a moment with a look of confusion, then disappointment, and anger. He spun around and went directly to the front door. She followed. He held it open and made no effort to detain her. "Strange," he said. "I hadn't pegged you as a one-nighter."

His words cut deep. Still, Sara eased by him and out the door and never looked back.

Chapter 52

Sara drove like a reckless teenager. She almost missed her turn onto the Hood-Franklin Road to head west again, and it wasn't due to any fog. She passed the Franklin Cemetery, and her mind flashed on Crazy Ike. Ike Ames was just a little off center in the attic, but was not schizoid, and had no record of doing much harm.

Who did Huxley think he was? He had asked to drive in order to keep her car keys, to allow him time to con and cajole her into going indoors.

You're the one, he had said. "The one what? His next victim?" She gritted her teeth. "I don't think so!"

The morning sun hadn't yet shown but began to lighten the sky from below the horizon. Sara crested the levee at Hood, finding a measure of peace in dawn breaking over the Sacramento River. Seeing the river water under a waning moon reminded that she needed a shower. Wash that man right off, and scrub away the false sense of romance and bliss.

She skidded to a stop in her the gravel driveway, not bothering to park in the garage. She headed straight to her bedroom for a change of clothes. She yanked clothes from hangers and turned to the dresser for fresh underwear, finding the top drawer half open. She never left drawers open but must have left it that way during her morning rush.

"How did I allow my excitement over a man make me forget things?" she asked, mumbling.

Sara pulled the drawer farther out. She picked through her underclothes and then closed the drawer. As she turned to head toward the bathroom, she stopped cold. She turned back, pulled the drawer open, stuck her hand inside, and felt around.

Gone!

Her pistol was gone! The bullets all gone! Someone had been inside her house. She trembled violently. She tried to remember if she had moved it.

"Of course not."

Her hand went immediately to her cell phone. She thumped the code for the Aldens.

"Hello," the voice croaked into the phone.

"Buck?"

"Huh?" he asked, sounding like he was fumbling with seeing the clock on the nightstand. "Sara? It's not even sun-up."

"Buck," she said. "My pistol. It's gone. The bullets, the holster—"

He gasped through the phone, and she heard him come awake. "What? When? Tell me."

"I spent the night with a friend in Sacramento. I've just arrived home, and the dresser drawer was open and—"

"Sara, get the hell out!"

"What?"

"Someone could still be in there. Leave!"

"Okay."

"Get out!" he said again. "Get the hell out! Head over here… and don't hang up."

Goosebumps erupted over her body. She went swiftly but quietly to the back door, aware of every little noise in the house, expecting someone to come at her at any moment. She made it out the back porch door and heard the lock click. Perhaps out of habit, she quickly reached behind her and made sure the screen door caught and held.

"I'm in my car," she said. She imagined a face popping up like a ghoul at the driver's side window. Worse than when Crazy Ike popped up that night in the fog. She slammed her fist on the buttons that locked the doors and frantically started the engine.

"Drive, Sara, drive!" Buck said. "Someone could still be in there."

Sara's heart raced, sharp and urgent, like the roll of a marching drummer. Her tires threw gravel. She crested the levee driving too fast while trying to manipulate the steering wheel with one hand. She dropped the cell phone. "Buck?" she yelled toward the phone on the floor. "Can you hear me? I dropped my phone."

His voice was distant but still came through. She bent down to retrieve the phone as the SUV wobbled side to side and ran off the asphalt onto the gravel along the shoulder of the road. That time, the sound of gravel was a warning, and she sat upright and got herself back onto the paved road before running into the river. In a moment, she said, "Okay, I'm on the levee. I'm away."

"I'm heading in your direction. You head toward our house," Buck said. His voice shook, sounding like he was struggling with something, maybe getting dressed. "I wanna meet you on the levee road, so I'll know you're safe."

"Okay," she said. She continued to tremble.

"I'm gonna hang up, gonna call Johanna. Keep coming this way."

After closing her phone and tucking it between her thighs, she gasped as a thought surfaced. "Oh, no!" she said, tears starting. She swiped her eyes. Someone had been inside her house, and it wasn't Huxley. "Oh, no!" she said again. The stalker threatening her life was clearly not Huxley. "What have I done?" she asked, screaming.

She found a wide turnout on the shoulder, stomped her brakes, and slid to a stop. She punched in the numbers of Huxley's cell phone. "Please, Huxley…." His voice mail kicked in. That meant he was still sleeping. She turned off the phone and angrily threw it onto the pile of clothing on the passenger seat. She accelerated and spun around, heading back to Sacramento. As she passed Talbot House and glanced over, she understood that she had left the lights on but locked the doors, yet the back porch door stood wide open, and the screen door swung with the breeze.

Chapter 53

Time seemed to stretch forever until Sara drove into the condominium complex and parked in front of Huxley's unit. She raced up and rang the bell. No one came. She rang again, and he still didn't answer. Huxley could be peeking out from behind the curtain and deciding he wanted nothing more to do with her. She turned to leave and realized the sedan that had been parked in Huxley's space was gone. He had already left, probably in anger, right after she fled.

It seemed all Sara did lately was flee. She checked into the first decent motel she came to and took a shower. She had to try and wash away all the confusion. While standing in the shower, she wept. Wept for hurting Huxley, for losing the most decent man she had met in decades. Wept for being scared ever since moving into Talbot House. Wept for having thoughts of selling off her dream home. Wept for dreams that never came true. Wept.

When she was out of the shower and dressed, she turned on her cell phone again. Several frantic messages waited from both Buck and Johanna. She called Buck.

"Where the hell are you?" he asked. "We got deputies out looking."

"Oh, Buck," she said, trying not to cry again. "I've just made one of the biggest mistakes of my life." She told him as much as she dared. She pulled off a wad of toilet tissue and blew her nose.

"Sara…," Buck said slowly. He always started out that way when he felt sympathetic. "We need to sort this out."

"I know," she said, thankful for his patience.

"You need to call Johanna right away. Call the Sheriff's office. They'll patch you through."

She called. "It's me, Sara." Her voice wavered.

Johanna was silent a moment, maybe biting her tongue. "Where are you?"

"I had to get away," Sara said, hoping that was enough of an answer. "I'm on my way back to the Delta."

It sounded as though Johanna put her hand over the mouth-piece. Her muffled voice yelled orders, "Hey, Isidoro. Call off that search. I've got Sara here." The tone of her voice indicated she was deep into her investigative mode. "Well, we didn't find any evidence of wires being cut," she said. "So why didn't you have your brand-new alarm system turned on?"

Sara gasped. "I-I must have forgotten," she said, embarrassed to admit it. "I was in such a hurry to get to Sacramento—"

"I guess you've just had one good lesson in why you installed that thing."

"I'm not used to living in a lock-down."

"Ha!" Johanna said. It sounded like a laugh, but she wasn't being friendly. "You'd better get used to it."

"I know. You can bet I won't forget a second time." Papers rattled through the phone. Sara visualized Johanna sitting in her car for the umpteenth time outside Talbot House, writing a report. "Do I have to wait for my house to be released again?"

"Yeah, I've already got investigators coming out to lift prints." She almost chuckled. "This is getting to be such a habit it's wearing grooves in my brain."

"You think Talbot House is jinxed?"

"Oh, don't start thinking that way. You'd better be concentrating on how you're gonna keep yourself safe," Johanna said. "Let me tell you something." She paused as if needing to put her thoughts together. "I have a feeling that with those bodies discovered in the fields, then Talbot showing up underneath the workshop, and... and with those two slaughtered dogs, the killer is running scared. He's taking risks because you're somehow in his way."

"So, I can't go home again?"

"I'm tempted to keep everyone away from this property," Johanna said. "But then this sicko would stalk you someplace else, and we gotta be able to keep track of both of you."

She gasped. "So now I'm a guinea pig?"

"It may be there's something on this property that attracts him. Maybe it's not you."

"Well, I need to live somewhere."

"Should be okay tomorrow, as long as you set that dang alarm. I'll call you," Johanna said. "But do yourself a favor. Don't come back until you find someone big and strong to live with. Got that?"

"I'll find someone."

"By the way, you need to bring your gun permit, sales receipt, and other papers to Headquarters."

"I guess Buck can go with me to the house."

"Yeah, anyway, I got something else I wanna run by you later."

"You can't tell me now?"

"Guess so." Sara imagined Johanna shrugging in her animated way. "I believe I've found a home for them two pit bulls."

That was great news for a change. "Where? With whom?"

"I've already discussed this with my people, just talked it over, though. If you're still looking to place 'em, would you consider donating them to our K-9 Unit?"

"Wow, why didn't I think of that?" Suddenly, her emotions shifted into high gear.

"There's no money in the budget to buy purebreds," Johanna said. "So you'd have to donate 'em. But pit bulls make mighty fine search animals."

"They'd have jobs."

"And a great home. Believe me—"

"You don't have to convince me," Sara said. "I should have offered them. That's the best life the pups could have."

"You'll do it?"

Sara wanted to confirm right away but couldn't. "Esmerelda will need to talk it over with their owner first."

"Can you bring the papers for your gun this afternoon? My shift starts again at three if I can get home and get some sleep," Johanna said. "You can talk to the Lieutenant that heads up the K-9 Unit. You'll be armed with better information, and you can talk to Esmerelda afterwards."

* * *

The good news for Choco and Latte should have kept her emotions buoyant. Instead, Sara's mood went into a tailspin. She fled to the Elk Grove Cemetery to visit with Starla. Her thoughts were so jumbled that she forgot to bring flowers. She sat in front of the headstone and lost track of time. Tears rolled down her face. When they dried and her emotions settled, she kissed her fingertips, touched them lovingly to Starla's name, and left.

* * *

She stopped for breakfast in a new place to avoid meeting anyone who might know her. It didn't matter anyway. She wore dark glasses to hide her weepy, red eyes. The meal helped restore her emotional equilibrium.

Later, intending only to pass by Talbot House until someone could accompany her inside, she slowed to a crawl. Investigators were just coming out with their fingerprinting kits. She pulled into her driveway.

"I live here. Can I go in," she yelled as she jumped out of her SUV.

The two men with badges stared a moment. "You have ID?" one asked.

Sara produced her driver's license. "One of the deputies needs my gun permit." She removed her dark glasses showing swollen eyes that couldn't possibly resemble the license photo.

One officer checked her information and handed it back. "Okay, let's go."

Her hands picked up the black fingerprint graphite they used on the doorknob. Every doorknob would probably have the black powder on it again. Black graphite edged her computer table. She found the papers she needed. More powder covered her dresser drawer front and knobs and along the top edge. She felt exposed knowing that surely, they had seen inside her lingerie drawer.

"I hope you took care not to let any of this get into my equipment."

"Yes, ma'am," he said. "We're always careful."

Sara sighed, felt helpless. She decided to impose on Pierce again and grabbed more clothes off the hangers.

"Gonna be a big expense filling this place with furniture," the deputy said. "Nice job you did, though. Like new, through and through."

Of course, they had been through her house, like Johanna and Isidoro did previously and probably did again today, accompanied by these officers. They had walked the house from top to bottom to secure the place. They were getting better acquainted with her house than she was. On the way out, she set the alarm.

* * *

Three trips to Sacramento within twenty-four hours set a record for her. Sara shook her head.

Johanna alerted Headquarters that Sara would be showing up; otherwise, she would be prevented from passing through the tight security.

Sara handed the gun documents to Johanna, who said, "You can see the Lieutenant before he leaves for the day."

Lt. Quill doodled on a scratch pad. "You'll first need to bring the dogs in for evaluation," he said. He watched her curiously. Why was it cops' eyes were so piercing and inquisitive? "Could take the better part of the day. Would you like to set aside some time?"

Sara found Johanna again, about ready to head out. "I'll be bringing the dogs next Wednesday."

"Great," Johanna said. "Stay safe on Halloween."

Chapter 54

Pierce seemed motivated with his book project. It reminded Sara of her own stamina. What they had in common bonded trust in one another. She had no qualms about explaining what had happened.

He listened and expressed a great deal of compassion. "Relationships are difficult," he said. "Because they're influenced by both past and present experiences."

That definitely was an understatement. "Had I met Huxley under the sole condition of learning he was involved with MIAs, there would have been nothing to interfere."

"Talbot House is getting to you?"

"I was determined to make it my future."

"Then don't give up."

"I can't. I just can't. I've got to find someone to move in with me." Who would want to? The reputation of the property was frightful and worsening by the day.

Pierce left her and returned to work on his project.

Sara mulled over the fact that she had always been shy. She needed desperately to hear Huxley's voice so she could make things right. Putting her hesitations aside, she dialed Huxley's number. The call clicked into his voice mail. Feeling both disappointed and relieved, she hung up without leaving a message.

He would eventually see the call he missed from her. Surely, he would call back.

As the hours passed, Sara fought frustration and the urge to get away from it all by cleaning house. Her cell phone rang, and her heart began to pound, but the number on the screen showed the call being from Daphine.

"What are we doing for Pierce's birthday?" Daphine asked. "I always close my shop on Halloween. Too much hell-raising out and about."

Sara longed for diversion and to try to forget the hassles if only a short while. *Do something fun. Laugh a little*, kept playing in her mind. "Wow, I've got a great idea. You available the whole weekend?"

* * *

She had much difficulty getting Pierce to consent to her plans. He finally relented when she offered her laptop for the weekend. The mountainous drive was longer and more arduous than Sara anticipated. Pierce took a nap in the back seat. Daphine sketched scenes she glimpsed out the window. Something troubled Daphine that she hadn't shared. As long as she didn't completely shut them out, Sara let her be. Creating art brought her peace.

They checked in at *Caesars Tahoe* in Reno. The hotel had already discounted the accommodations, charging off-season rates, but for the first time in her life, Sara didn't need coupons and favors to afford things.

Sara opened the door and let them walk in first. She didn't know what to expect either, but it would be no ordinary hotel room.

"A suite?" Daphine asked as they stepped inside.

"The king gets the king bedroom," Sara said. Then she pointed to the opposite bedroom. "We'll take the twin-queens."

"A queen's fine with me," Daphine said, turning circles in the spacious living room. "Look at the size of this place." The living room alone, with its sweeping view, was larger than Daphine's entire house.

At dinner that evening, Daphine and Pierce opted to try new foods. Sara stared at her plate but had no appetite. She checked her cell phone periodically to make sure it was on, but Huxley hadn't called, and she couldn't bring herself to call him again. It was surely the end between them. She had hurt him deeply. Now that her foundation was nearly established, there would be no reason their paths ever crossed again.

"I have a surprise to tell you two," Pierce said. "I'm buying the Clampett Tract house."

Sara and Daphine erupted in surprise. Dining room patrons looked toward the commotion.

"How'd you manage that?" Daphine asked, lowering her voice.

"The owner came around," he said. "Said she was planning to put the house on the market. I asked her how she and I might work out a deal."

"And?" Sara asked.

Pierce finished chewing and swallowed. "Well, you have the rent paid one year in advance," he said. "But I—"

"In advance?" Daphine asked, blurting it out. Again, people looked in their direction. She covered her mouth momentarily, and then spoke softly. "You paid a whole years' rent in advance?"

Sara didn't know what to say. No one needed to know, and she had only told Pierce when she had to. The look on Daphine's face was one of disbelief, maybe defeat. Something was wrong.

"The deal the owner offered was that once your year is up, I could keep renting," Pierce said. "That way, the second year, I'll have my book advance and royalties to put toward the down payment. She's willing to accept my one year of rent as part of it."

"A lease-option," Sara said.

"Yeah, so it won't be mine for another two years." He shrugged and took another bite of food.

Sara knew what to do about that. She was good at solving other people's problems better than her own. "Two years?" she asked. "No chance. A year from now."

"How'd you figure?" Pierce asked. He had stopped eating again, eager to hear. "You've already paid—"

"That's right, Pierce," Sara said. "I can end my lease in your favor."

"How do you know so much?" Daphine asked in exasperation.

Sara couldn't explain it. She just knew. "I'll contact the owner and turn my lease over to you. You've got eight or nine months left. That'll count toward your one year. You pay rent for a few more months beyond that, and you'll have that house a year from now."

Pierce swallowed hard, and not from anything he ate. It seemed he didn't know what to do with his hands. He dropped his knife and fork to his plate, put his hands beneath the table, and hunched forward. "I can't do that. You've done way too much for me."

"Well, if you don't want the help," Sara said, teasing. "Then I'll break my lease and get my money back. You can make your own arrangements."

Pierce sighed and rolled his eyes. He managed a frown as he shook his head. No more was said.

After dinner, trying to cheer up, Sara said, "C'mon, let's play."

"Tell me I won't lose all my money," Pierce said.

"It's fun," Daphine said. "C'mon, Pierce, I'll show you." But she herself hadn't so much as stuffed a single dollar bill into any machine.

Sara wandered off to find a place to sit and spotted a vacant back row of seats in the Keno area. She checked her cell phone again and rotated through the few unanswered calls. She had to stop doing that. He wouldn't call. She turned the phone off and sat quietly, feeling numb.

After a while, a man stopped in the aisle beside her seat. "Sara," he said.

She knew that accent before looking up to see who it was. "Val, what are you doing here?" She stood.

He gestured to the seats up front. "My family."

Most of the seats were filled with Filipinos. A few stood at the Keno Bar buying tickets or cashing in. "Which ones are your relatives?"

"All," he said and then chuckled. "We come twice a year."

"You win anything?"

"No," he said. His smile faded. "Luni has the fever. I come to make sure he don't lost our house."

Sara smiled discreetly, remembering old Mrs. Cheng's broken dialogue and now hearing Val speak. He hadn't learned how to conjugate verbs. Broken English was prevalent throughout the Delta. "That's pretty sad, Val. You can't keep him away?"

"My family likes to play too. Two Filipinos we know won big on this game. They live like royalty in the Philippines now."

Daphine joined them, deciding not to gamble, saying she wasn't in the mood. Fun-loving Daphine couldn't squeeze out a few bills?

They waited too long to make a dinner reservation and scoured the entire facility, but no dining tables were available on October 30th, Pierce's birthday. They settled to celebrate on the 31st.

Just as they sat for dinner, someone recognized Pierce, and the acknowledgment threw him into near shock. The woman had recently seen his photo in the newspapers. That was the end of a quiet birthday celebration. Word spread and before they knew it, people came to the table to ask for Pierce's autograph.

He signed show tickets, slips of paper, and even a few gambling chips. "This is so weird," he said.

Then along came the house photographer, taking pictures when people asked to have a photo with a guy who had died and revived.

Sara leaned over and quietly said, "Not the private birthday party I had planned, but happy birthday, Pierce."

"That's okay, Sara," he said behind his hand. "I've never been a part of anything like this." He autographed someone's business card and then leaned back in the padded booth and spread his arms in both directions. "We look like Hollywood types. This is a great birthday."

Chapter 55

After the long drive home, Sara's energy was spent. For the first time in a long time, she slept the night through. Pierce spent the wee hours on the computer.

Sara drove into Walnut Grove Tuesday morning looking for a new place to have breakfast. She passed the Rasay brothers' store. Construction workers were tearing down the storefront facade, perhaps remodeling. Someone in the Rasay family must have at one time hit it big at Keno.

Just as she passed, she glimpsed a construction worker with tattoos. She knew those markings. Sara found a place to turn around. She could just as well enjoy breakfast at the counter alongside people in coveralls. They were the essence of the Delta. She still needed to find her place among them, despite an invisible expectation that dictated how a rich woman in the valley was supposed to act.

"Hi, Beni," she said as she reached the front door. "You doing okay?"

He shrugged. "Tearing 'em down, putting 'em up." He never complained.

* * *

That evening Sara picked up the dogs and kept them overnight at Clampett Tract. She left for Sacramento before the morning traffic rush. She held vague childhood memories of Sacramento being far away, with lots of flat open farm fields between the Delta and the Capitol. Urban sprawl had taken over years before and claimed the fields.

The animal training area was located in the rear of the Sheriff's Headquarters buildings. To have access to that area, a person needed to pass through the main facility.

Sara was shown through. She and the two pit bulls encountered yet another security checkpoint out back. Steel gates opened into the dogs' training area. Other dogs barked. Choco and Latte pulled against their leashes. Ears went up, noses twitched, and tails dropped, stiff with caution. Beyond the holding kennels stood another fence surrounding a large nearly empty grassy field. Two officers suited in bite-proof gear and a German Shepard in training greeted her.

"They won't test well with you around," an officer said. "Give us until about four this afternoon."

Sara remained in Sacramento, purchasing small pieces of furniture and putting delivery on hold. That afternoon, when she returned to retrieve Choco and Latte, an officer directed her to the Lieutenant's office. Sara found him playfully fending off the dogs and laughing. Both dogs crowded in front of him, with front paws on his thighs, licking his face like a couple of bears vying for the greater portion of a honeycomb.

"Choco," Sara said. "Latte." That was all that was necessary.

Lt. Quill stood and straightened his clothes. "I'll set up a delivery date. These two can begin with the next training session."

Sara couldn't put her finger on it, but the Lieutenant again eyed her suspiciously, as if testing her somehow. Johanna must have briefed him about the events happening on her property. She shrugged it off. "Can I watch them train? Maybe, once in a while?"

Lt. Quill stared at her with a look of sympathy. "That's not wise. If they see you, they may fall back into their congenial habits. Could undo everything they're learning," he said. "If you'd like, I can take your phone number and give you progress reports."

Sara instinctively glanced at his hand. No wedding ring, and in great shape for his age. Hazel eyes. Had to have nice eyes. Huxley had the best. The Lieutenant looked great in his uniform, a picture of strength. Huxley was strong. She wondered what this officer would look like in street clothes. Huxley looked great with no clothes on at all. She stared at the floor and cleared her wandering thoughts before looking up. "I'm sure I can let go for their well-being," she said.

"You probably won't be able to see them till after they're fully trained."

"What will they be taught to do?"

"Cadaver dogs. Our tests point to these dogs having keen noses."

"Sniffers." She beamed her approval. Huxley and his group had used.... "I'm glad they won't be trained to be vicious in their work."

"Sorry, though. You won't be allowed personal time with them afterwards either. They'll have a new master to obey. But there is some good news."

"Great, let's hear it."

"These two pups," the Lieutenant said. He reached down a scratched both their backs. "They can keep your cute names and maybe, just maybe, they'll be able to stay together."

"Oh, yes, please."

"A lady who owned a forensic dog we usually used, well, her canine just passed away. I think she'll take both of these."

"I thought they'd belong to the Sheriff's Department."

"They will," he said. "But this woman traveled the country with her dog contracting work with other law enforcement. An officer can't do that. Plus, we don't have that much work locally to keep cadaver dogs active."

Sara nodded. The news was a great relief. "Knowing these dogs the way I do, they'll be happier if they can stay together." As she accepted their leashes from the Lieutenant, he moved too close, and his hand brushed hers in a most innocent but suggestive manner.

"Think it over," he said. "If you're too attached, think about what you're giving up."

"I'll do what's best for the dogs." As she headed for the door with Choco and Latte in tow, she felt the Lieutenant's eyes following her.

"Don't forget," he said. "I could keep you posted if you'd like to leave your phone number."

Chapter 56

The way out was to backtrack through the main building. The dogs got a lot of stares from other deputies who turned and curiously watched them walk by. Sara kept them short-leashed and navigated the aisles between the desks. She caught sight of Johanna checking and then holstering her pistol. She headed in Johanna's direction.

Choco gave a low growl and pulled hard. Someone must have carried the scent of another dog. Choco growled again. A quick, light backward and sideways kick that tapped Choco in the rib cage startled him. "S-s-st!" Sara said, looking down into Choco's eyes. He sat quickly, stared back, and maintained eye contact. They held to the stare till Choco's tail stopped moving. Then they proceeded on as Choco remembered his obedience training.

"Hey," Johanna said as she petted both dogs. They eagerly sat at her feet as if waiting for a treat. "You gonna do it?" She sat down and continued to play with them as they panted and drooled on her uniform sleeve.

Snapshots of both women and men hung on the wall in the row between Johanna's desk and those of other deputies. Names and dates accompanied each picture. Sara guessed they were photos of missing people, which sometimes hung in law enforcement offices as reminders never to forget. Too many photos lined the wall. Several spaces were empty, possibly representing photos removed after victims were identified. Orson could have been up there. It was a sobering thought.

"Yeah, but I don't know how I'll tell Esmerelda," Sara said. "She's more attached than I am and won't admit it."

"Truth is, we'd really like these dogs."

"Say, Johanna, is there any way you can check out this guy for me? If you can't, I'll understand." She laid a piece of paper on the desktop on which she had neatly spelled out Beni's full name.

Johanna glanced at it. "Huh? What kind of language is that?"

"Hawaiian. It's Beni Noa," Sara said. "Do you know him?"

"That's his real name?"

"He was one of the construction guys who boarded in my house. I'd like to get him back, but only one guy in the house this time? I'd trust him again, Johanna, but I'd like him checked out."

"What can I tell you?" she asked. "Works construction, Volunteer Courtland Firefighter."

"He's a firefighter?" So that's what the extra phone was that he carried on his hip. Bigger than a cell phone. It was his radio. "He never took time off from working on my house."

"Haven't been any fires down there this summer," she said. "He's a pretty upstanding citizen, helped the locals down there on a couple of lost kid searches."

"Are you saying he's okay to let back in and be alone with?"

"I don't know what to tell you, Sara. If I say he's okay and he turns out to be the person we're looking for, well, I don't wanna be the one to put you in harm's way."

"Okay, I'm glad you could tell me that much."

"He doesn't have a rap sheet that I know of."

"Can you find out more? Please?"

"No promises," Johanna said and stood. "Here, let me show these cuties around real quick before I leave." She grabbed up the leashes and walked the dogs to the far end of the room. Deputies crowded around, and everyone made a fuss over two unpretentiously lovable pit bulls that sniffed everywhere and especially embarrassed the burly guys.

Sara glanced across Johanna's desk and what she saw sent a charge through her nervous system. Glossy photos lay in a haphazard pile. On top was an area shot with the back end of her house on the left, the garage on the right, and in the middle, the workshop floor area of her property.

Sara couldn't stifle her curiosity and helped herself to the photos and thumbed through them. Some were labeled with Orson's name and showed his remains lying in a morgue bag after being dug up from the workshop. Many more were taken of Orson, including the hole he laid in, the fool's gold rocks, and the plastic wrapped around him, with other shots of his rotted clothing. Another photo different from the rest, marked as from the Coroner's office, showed a small, broken, horseshoe-shaped bone. More photos showed remains of victims at other sites, along with the bones of animals. Then more shots of the empty graves after the bones were removed. Each scene had been photographed down to its most minuscule detail, with more Coroners' photos of small broken bones. Hyoid bones. Snapped in two. Sara felt sick to her stomach.

She continued looking at the photos. A few showed only skulls, femurs, or pelvis bone fragments, and some vertebrae. The scenes disgusting her, but she couldn't stop examining them even as her hands shook. Some photos contained only minute fragments of bone lying in the dirt. She laid out a photo of each victim in a row, then a scene of the grave in which each had lain. She studied them closely. Her heart beat wildly. Her hands trembled almost violently when she realized all the burials had something in common. If investigators could have known what she had seen months before, they would have solved the crimes by now.

"They couldn't have known," she said, mumbling, lost in thought. "The missing link is not in these pictures. Only I know where it is!"

Sara brought her elbows to the desktop and held her head as she hunched over the photos, absorbed, compelled to be certain of what she had discovered.

She asked herself if she was making too much of nothing, simply because her home and property were involved. Was she acting in desperation, trying to play heroine to bring some kind of closure? Was she trying to compensate her ego after losing Huxley? Question after question, the answer was no. The proof right in front of her was something only she and the killer knew.

"I'm right!" she said, jumping up quickly. To make sure, she looked at all the photos again, becoming more excited and yet scared. "I'm right!" she said again, only this time louder. She couldn't stop shaking and held to the edge of the desk "We've got to stop him!"

"Hey, Sara, what's up?" Johanna asked, coming back with the pups. "You missing them already?"

Sara turned to Johanna. "I know," she said.

"Know what?" Johanna asked. Then she saw the photos spread out. "Hey, you shouldn't be…." She cocked her head as she shifted into her investigative mode. "What do you know?"

Sara gestured to the photos. "Johanna," she said quietly. "I know who the killer is."

Chapter 57

The circumstantial evidence Sara disclosed proved insufficient to obtain an indictment. They needed to validate her clues. The suspect didn't have so much as a speeding ticket, let alone a rap sheet. They put electronic sensors on the man's vehicle, tailed him, and tapped his telephone for more than a week. He did nothing suspicious. Almost as last resort, law enforcement requested Sara's participation in a full sting operation.

"You're the perfect candidate," a Lieutenant had said. "You'll be covered every step of the way."

Sara spent many hours at Sheriff's Headquarters attending numerous orientation meetings to assure that she understood what was involved. She would be allowed to back out at any time if she felt she couldn't pull it off. Law enforcement could as well cancel the whole operation if they thought the risk to her too great.

Sara wasn't experienced at pretension. Now she had to discipline her mind not to make a slip of the tongue during conversations. They said it would be a long shot, but agreed she might be the only person to get him to talk freely. They warned that she could end up in a very dangerous situation.

Her intuition goaded. *Don't think about it. Just do it. This guy must be stopped.* Her intuition was usually always right.

Sara and Esmerelda walked through Talbot House so that Esmerelda could finally view the extensive makeover.

"You haven't tried to move back in?"

"I'm staying at Pierce's till I get my furniture. I'm so tired of the sleeping around like I've had to do."

Esmerelda's head bobbed again and again in approval of the renovations. She walked through the enlarged master suite and viewed the new dressing room leading to the private bathroom. "I love what you've done here," she said. Then her expression changed "You said the Sheriff's Department would take the dogs. When will that be?" Her voice had a ring of relief in it and a wish that it might be soon.

"Not till the next training session. Weeks, maybe months."

Sara's thoughts focused on the sting. She hoped Esmerelda couldn't read anxiety in her manner. The detectives would fit her with a wire. A surveillance van would be near the house. Johanna had said their state-of-the-art equipment picked up transmissions up to a mile away. Sara wanted the van closer than that. A dozen or so officers would surround the house though remain out of sight. But where, considering the empty fields all around? Sara couldn't allow her courage to wane. The psychopath had taken many lives, ruined others, and disrupted hers. They caused enduring pain for Esmerelda in cutting Orson's life short. Sara felt a lot of anger and had to be careful not to let Esmerelda see her hands shake.

"You mean maybe not till after the holidays?" Esmerelda's smile had faded. Surely, she was tired of the dogs.

"I'll take the pups more often. Give you a break. With the house done, I have more free time."

"And you love them, don't you?" she asked. Then she smiled again. "Let's go shopping. You need furniture so you can get those boxes out of the basement."

* * *

The following Monday Sara stopped on the levee to retrieve her mail before heading back to Clampett Tract. She sat in her SUV, crosswise atop the driveway ramp, and opened two large white envelopes. The foundation documents from both the State and the Internal Revenue Service stamped approved and filed, had arrived. She held them in her hands and felt muted elation. Great disappointment in herself over Huxley, and the extremely dangerous liaison planned with law enforcement took the excitement out of the foundation's approval.

Esmerelda needed to get out of her house and completely away from the hospice more often. Demetrio could take care of the dogs. Sara convinced her to come help mail out the foundation's invitations.

"I had planned to set the party for January," Sara said. "But let's move it back to December." She studied her calendar. "You available on the eleventh?"

Esmerelda produced her appointment book and studied it. "Can't see why not. We'll have a Christmas party." She puckered her lips, onto something.

"Don't even think about it," Sara said. "You're not slaving in the kitchen for my party. Period."

"Can't I help?"

"I've already hired a caterer named Zoki Yoshi—"

"Zoki? I know Zoki. We can exchange some recipes."

"He's a former classmate. Great guy."

Sara, with Huxley's help during that one glorious all-too-short period, created the invitations on her publishing software. Now Sara kept her emotions to herself as she changed the date to December 11th. "One more thing," she said. "Do you think it's okay to say 'casual attire'?"

"Say 'Attire: Tastefully casual'." Esmerelda flashed a ridiculous grin. "Then, as hostess, you dress up."

"I hope the eleventh is not too short a notice for everyone," she said.

"It's a month away. Should be okay." Esmerelda began folding the fine-milled stationery.

Sara excused herself. She was about to break into tears. She envisioned Huxley sharing this with her. They were a great team and had raced through the intricate organizational set-up. Rewards such as this should have been theirs together.

Once she got a grip on her emotions, she came back into the room. She and Huxley deeply loved and respected Esmerelda. Esmerelda had not mentioned Huxley, so it was likely he had not contacted her. As much as Sara could put together from previous conversations, he only called her when he came to town or to report activities of his Asia trips. Huxley wouldn't be the type to cry on anyone's shoulder. Their interval together had been too short and ended in such a harsh manner. Time would wash away the memory, maybe. Sara gritted her teeth and helped stuff the envelopes to get them ready for mailing.

"You'll finish the addresses the acceptable way, won't you?" Esmerelda asked.

"Write them longhand? Yep, tonight."

That would be done at Pierce's house. Johanna had yet to get back to her with information about Beni Noa, whom Sara learned had been crashing between one friend's house and another. Until she heard, or at least after the sting that would prove she was right in naming the suspect, Sara would not so much as drive down off the levee at Talbot House alone.

Chapter 58

Sara backed in toward Esmerelda's garage and opened her tailgate. Esmerelda saw her and crossed the driveway from the patient building with Mimie on her heels. "I can take the dogs over the weekend," Sara said.

"Oh, thank goodness," Esmerelda said. "Tomorrow's Thanksgiving Eve and there's so much to do. Some of the patient's families will be eating dinner here."

"The dogs won't be here much longer," Sara said. "What if the Sheriff calls and wants them while I have them? Should I bring them back so you can say goodbye?"

"No, you take them. I'll just give them big hugs each time you pick them up," Esmerelda said. "Give them as much love as I can before they're gone." She looked around. "Where is Demetrio?"

Tripp, as usual, appeared out of nowhere and startled them both. Even Esmerelda seemed mildly irritated at him always showing up like that. "Can I help with them cages?" Taking over, he loaded the pet carriers.

"Thank you, Tripp," Sara said.

Demetrio came jogging with Choco and Latte on leashes. "You take dogs today?"

Choco and Latte didn't seem to know whom to lick first, but they didn't go to Tripp.

Esmerelda was in a playful mood and squatted down in the gravel and teased the dogs and loved them and let them lick her cheeks, though protecting her mascara. Now nearly full-sized the dogs didn't need to jump to reach her face. "I'll miss you two cuties when you're gone, but you'll have a great life." There was no end to Esmerelda's love for animals, friends, or patients.

Demetrio produced a camera from his pocket. "I take pictures in the field. You like picture with dogs?"

Esmerelda was thrilled. "Why didn't I think to do that?" She remained kneeling and posed with Choco and Latte and pulled Mimie in close. "C'mon, Sara," she said. "Tripp?"

Tripp gave a wave of refusal and moved out of range.

After the photo session, which included a couple of shots of smiling Demetrio between Choco and Latte, Demetrio waved and ran off.

"How's your house coming along?" Tripp asked. The question seemed strange of Tripp to ask. Why the sudden interest in her house?

Sara snapped her fingers and pointed toward the cages, and the dogs obediently jumped in. "My house is finished," she said nicely. She turned to Esmerelda. "I received some of my furniture, but they dumped it into the first floor rooms. I'll have to wrangle the mattress and stuff to get it upstairs."

"Get some help," Esmerelda said. "How about some of your construction workers?"

"That might work," Sara said. "But who would work on Thanksgiving Eve? I need it done right away. How about Fredrik? When we saw his rooms, I noticed he has a great flair for decorating."

"Fredrik lift furniture?" Esmerelda asked, nearly laughing. "The only things he lifts are patients."

"I can lift," Tripp said as he stepped closer and wrung his hands. "I'll work anytime."

"Why not Tripp?" Esmerelda asked quickly. She patted his shoulder. "He's as strong as an ox."

Though she hesitated, Sara said, "You know, Tripp? I hired a landscaper to draw plans for the rear acreage. I've got some great computer drawings. Would you like to look at those at the same time and give me your opinion about flowers and hedges?"

"Oh, I don't know nothing about computers," he said. "But I could tell you about flowers."

"You could tell me which type plants would look best in certain areas. Could you do that?"

Tripp looked up as if searching for an answer in the sky. After a moment, he said "I s'pose that's a great plan. Yeah, fits together right nice."

"Great," Sara said. "I've got a full evening tomorrow, so we'll only have about an hour to get things done. Can you come around six?" She waited while Tripp thought it over. "I'll have something for you to drink and a bite—"

Tripp again looked up at the sky as if waiting for answers to be revealed. Then he smiled suddenly. "Six o'clock on Thanksgiving Eve, huh? I can be there," he said, nodding. "Six o'clock."

"Great," Sara said.

"Yeah, we can take care of things." He snapped his fingers. "Just like that."

Chapter 59

On the way home with the dogs, Sara's cell phone rang.

"Jade's here!" Daphine said. "Just showed up at the door."

"That's wonderful."

"She's taking me to Lake Tahoe for the four-day weekend. We're packing right now. She's so changed. We're playing catch up—taking lots of pictures—"

"Daph," Sara said. "Daph, catch your breath. Enjoy your wonderful Thanksgiving. I'll meet Jade when you return."

Sara attributed Jade's timing to serendipity. She didn't want Daphine anywhere near Talbot House until after the ordeal with the Sheriff's Department. In fact, Sara confided in no one, not even Buck and Linette, about the dangerous liaison underway. She wasn't worried about Pierce. He had no way of getting around and stayed busy writing his manuscript.

* * *

The next day, Sara delivered Choco and Latte to the dog handlers amid tears and emotion. It could well be the last time she saw them. She was thankful that Lt. Quill hadn't shown up.

After freshening her face in the restroom, she went straight to one last briefing. She intended to go through with the sting. Sara became involved from the day she purchased Talbot House. It was the pathetic reality of murder that fueled her intention to aid in the capture of the elusive madman. When life was in turmoil, Huxley's pensive blue-topaz eyes were beams of light and purpose. If not for the fear of becoming a victim herself, she would not have lost him. He might have been the greatest love of her life. It was enough to put her over the edge. She seethed inside, determined to do her part to set things right. She knew what she needed to do, and they wouldn't need to find those size sixteen rubber waders to nail the guy.

* * *

Sara had not lived in Talbot House since the completion of the refurbishing. The heating system had not been activated. Intermittent light rain fell and inside the house was as chilly as outdoors. She changed into a light leather jacket and slacks. The jacket and sweater underneath well hid the wire and microphone attached to the center front of her bra. The state-of-the-art equipment was guaranteed to pick up transmissions through walls, so her leather jacket shouldn't block voices either. She wondered if some of the deputies had already placed themselves inside the house since she had given them many sets of keys. She wondered where they might position themselves out of sight since all the rooms remained bare.

It may have been over-kill, but since the leather jacket sported pockets, she decided to carry her thin cell phone in one, a mini-recorder in the other. Everything was digital and silent, and she gave thanks for her beloved electronics.

Sara held the red and green leashes. They belonged to two loyal animals that were more human than some people; two animals she would never forget. She went to the back porch to hang the leashes on their pegs behind the inner door. They could hang there and be a part of the house forever, and that would be all right.

It was after five o'clock and starting to turn dark. No cars passed on the levee. The stillness seemed foreboding. Sara had to get through her business with Tripp. The sting operation would take place right there at Talbot House.

Leave the alarm system off, she was told. Officers will surround you, though you won't see them.

Just as she hung the leashes and turned around to re-enter the house, a man walked into the kitchen from her dining room! At that moment, Sara didn't recognize him without his cap.

Chapter 60

"Tripp," she said as she stepped inside and closed the door behind her. "You're early." The automatic door lock clicked. She turned and reset the lock to open. "How did you get in?"

"Your doors were unlocked. I called out, and nobody come." The look in his eyes was sinister. His eyeballs seemed to bulge out of their sockets.

Tripp lied. She unlocked the new deadbolts when she arrived home, but the new locks locked themselves when the doors were closed. Playing it safe until six o'clock, she hadn't yet set the locks open for the deputies. Tripp must have picked a lock! Considering she had disarmed the alarm system when she came inside, had he come in during the few minutes she took to change her clothes? "And you just decided to walk in?" she asked, trying to sound jovial.

A light rain began again and speckled the windows. The wind whipped up and whistled intermittently under the eaves.

"Mrs. T let me come in sometimes when I worked here."

"Esmerelda doesn't live here anymore," Sara said, trying not to sound angry but needing to get her point across.

Tripp's foul body odor filled the kitchen. Whatever he had been doing raised a sweat. Fresh perspiration marked the underarms of his shirt. He wore no cap and swiped his face with a sleeve, but his skin still glowed with sweat. He had something strange hanging around his neck. "So where did you park?" she asked, giving her time to figure out what he wore. The mechanism was Army green and old, hanging on leather straps, though it looked like the whole apparatus could be mounted over the top of his head.

"Down the levee some. In an orchard a ways from here."

"You could have driven onto my property, Tripp."

"I can see good with these," he said, patting the apparatus as if it were a pet. "They're my second sight."

"So why are you wearing night vision goggles?"

"So I can see what I'm doing in the dark. I can see people coming and hide so they can't find me." He smiled wickedly, but giggled, like a mischievous child at play.

Of all the luck, it was another New Moon night. She was thankful it wasn't yet totally dark. "Do you have eye problems, Tripp? Can't see well in the dark?"

"I been trompin' around your field," he said. He raised a foot to show that he was in his socks. "Left my muddy boots and coat outside. One of your dogs is dead out there. Did you know that?"

"One of my...." Sara's senses jumped to high alert. She really had to call upon her acting skills now. "Oh, no, I didn't know."

"I found your shovel in the basement, thought I'd dig a hole to bury it behind the garage. But I thought I better check with you first on where you want that dog put down."

Sara stood face to face with a man who had to be one of the most damnable creatures alive. This was what the officers needed to hear. This was what she agreed to do, but she couldn't ask Tripp to stop talking. In case authorities weren't yet listening, she would have to drag it out, sympathize with Tripp and keep him from going over the edge.

She shivered purposely and put her hands into the pockets of her leather jacket and turned a little away from Tripp. But not so far that she couldn't keep an eye on him. She felt around the phone until she found the button for 911 and pushed it and pressed the heel of her hand hard over the hearing end so Tripp wouldn't hear any voices coming through. "Tripp Unwyn," she said, feigning sadness. "I had heard you are always helpful. Did you find my other dog? Could it be dead out in the field too?" She spoke only to cover the sound of the operator answering the phone. They needed to know that Tripp was in the house and that plans for the sting had to be drastically altered. The 911 Dispatcher would notify the deputies already involved.

Surely now officers would be creeping up to the house if they heard voices coming from inside. Hopefully, they began to monitor the wire she wore as soon as she arrived home.

Being alone with Tripp could end up being one of the most dangerous moments of her life. She had mentally played the scene over and over, but nothing prepared her for the fright she now felt, or how to disguise it.

Tripp's eyes pleaded. He held the look and posture of a boy who knew he would be scolded if he didn't act right. But it was Tripp, the man, who had agreed to help with the furniture and landscape so he could be alone with her.

Moving furniture may not have been the wisest ploy, but it was the only one Sara had. Numerous boxes stood stacked in the kitchen, waiting to be unpacked. A new oak breakfast table and chairs sat in the middle of the room.

He smiled suddenly, his demeanor flip-flopping. "Nope, didn't see your other dog." He swung his body onto a chair. His head was shaved right down to the skin, and he had chaffed it in spots with the razor.

Police reports of all the burial sites had said that no human hairs other than those of the victims were found.

Tripp's eyes widened even more as he came up out of the chair suddenly. "Maybe we should go out there and look for it."

No way would Sara go out into the field under cover of darkness, especially if the officers had not arrived. "Well," she said calmly. "Since you've got night vision, why don't we get our work done before we get too tired? If the other dog hasn't shown up by the time we're finished, we'll go look."

Again, his demeanor somersaulted as he nodded like a boy eager to please his mom. Then Sara remembered that she had never heard anything about his mother. Sensing at that moment that she would be appealing to the boy in him, she asked, "Both your mom and dad are gone, Tripp?"

"Yep," he said, not looking up. "She disappeared when I was fourteen, I think it was." He looked up finally, but toward the window. "Just up and gone some place."

"They didn't get along? Your mom and dad?"

"They did sometimes," Tripp said. "When they called me Tripper, I knew everything was all right."

"And when they called you 'Tripp'?"

"Then my momma would be bangin' my dad over the head with the soup ladle." Tripp looked her in the eyes and his begged. "I felt so sorry for my dad. He was sickly and all and workin' so hard, and momma said they shoulda' had more than they did." Tripp's head drooped, and he withdrew some place inside himself, staring at the tabletop with his lower lip slightly protruding like a little boy scolded at the dinner table.

Isidoro's computerized landscape renderings lay spread on the tabletop. "Let's start with these," she said, trying to sound cheerful and hoping to make him feel needed. "I'll make us something to drink."

"I don't want none of that juice."

Since she had not moved back to Talbot House, no juice was stored in the fridge. The thought of serving juice out of a pitcher gave her the creeps. After being drugged, she had only made a fresh glassful each time she wanted some and dumped out what she didn't finish.

A thought came to her in a frightening rush and sent chills over her body. How did Tripp know about her juice? She held to the edge of the counter for support as the realization of Tripp's innocent admission opened the door to the twisted depths of his psyche. She had to get hold of her thoughts. She put a hand to her chest and was reminded that she wore the wire.

Sara prepared the filter and coffee grounds and then clicked on the coffee maker. Tripp watched her like a predator, not the least bit interested in the landscape drawings. "Look, Tripp," she said, pointing along the edges of the property. "What kind of border should I plant around the periphery?"

Tripp smiled and rubbed his chin. "Right perty and fragrant if you plant a flowering hedge. Would cover up foul smells coming up outa the ground."

"Foul smells?" she asked, thinking how cadaver dogs detect the odors of decaying flesh. "What would cause foul smells?"

He had to think a moment. Finally, he said, "Well, fertilizers and all that, you know. A lotta dead fish in them fertilizers." He watched her reactions to everything he said. "Would take a lot of digging, but I could do it. I dug a lot for Mrs. T."

"You dug for ET?" Sara asked, humoring him. "Always dug deep?"

"Yeah," he said as he ran a finger around the property border on the blueprints. "Back here by the canal, that ground's softened by the water nearby. Even those cows couldn't hard-pack it."

"You ever dig back there, Tripper? Dig up any rocks?"

The boy in him seemed proud. "Oh, yeah," he said. "I got me…." Tripp, the man, shrugged, perhaps realizing he almost said something he shouldn't. "I moved all those rocks for Mrs. T. Piled 'em in the backfield. Some real handiwork I did back there." He rubbed his fingertips over the area in the drawing. His expression took on a reminiscent glow.

Tripp seemed lost in reverie. It wouldn't be healthy to let his mind wander onto things he had done that gave him a feeling of power. Sara remembered the mini-recorder, again feigned being cold, and stuck her hand into her pocket and clicked it on. She glanced over to check on how the coffee was coming along. Non-chalant gestures, all the while, she wondered if she shouldn't sit down to keep her shaking legs from giving out.

Chapter 61

"What about right here, between the garage and the back door?" Sara asked, stretching across the blueprints. "Is this a good place for a garden?"

"The garage blocks the sun," Tripp said. "Nice and shady in that spot, though. Cool damp dirt, full of earthworms and other hungry things. My daddy and me used to dig up earthworms to go fishing." He grinned fiendishly and tapped the drawing.

"Then where would you sugg—?"

"Ain't that where they found ol' man Talbot?" he asked while watching her reaction. "Ain't that where that workshop stood?"

"Sure is."

"Ground was hard-packed in that spot. I helped those construction guys, I did," he said, like a proud child. "Helped 'em trench the footings."

"I didn't know you helped."

"While they were trenching, somebody dug a deep hole just inside that front footing, just to soften the ground so when that old man was planted, all they had to do was scrape back those shiny rocks and clear out the soft dirt underneath." He smiled, more for himself as he stared into the air. "Someone done backed a truck up to where that floor was gonna be poured. Covered that ol' fool with his fool's gold rocks."

"That's what they say."

Only the person who committed the heinous act would know about the dirt in one spot having been pre-softened. Or the reason being simply to back up a truck and discard a body right inside the wall closest to the end of the driveway. "So what would that person do with the dirt they took out of the hole?" she asked.

Tripp shrugged. "Probably used it in some flower beds somewhere." He shifted in the chair. "I didn't need to drive in tonight, though," he said as he glanced quickly into her eyes, looked away, and then turned back. "I got these." He tapped the goggles.

Everything Tripp said had a double meaning, and Sara understood both. She innocently glanced at her watch. Hopefully, every word they spoke was being monitored, but she still felt alone. How did she ever convince herself she could be as calm as Jessica Fletcher? This was not a TV rehearsal that could be stopped and re-scripted.

She went to the sink and rinsed her hands and glanced out the kitchen window to the north. The surveillance van would be parked only a quarter mile away behind the façade of eucalyptus trees. She saw nothing. Her reflection against the rain-speckled pane reminded that the darkest shades of the moonless night had overtaken them. She wouldn't be able to see a reflection off the van or windshield unless another vehicle happened by.

Sara could only hope that officers were already in place around the house instead of waiting until six o'clock. She hadn't had a chance to unlock all the doors for easier access. Though they had keys, having to use them could hinder a quick entry. She just might have to go out into the dark with this man, but not before getting him to admit to something substantial.

When she turned around, Tripp stared at her with that hard gleam in his eyes, but he did seem less threatening sitting down. She had to keep up the momentum. "Coffee smell is always appetizing."

He frowned, glanced at the coffee maker and back to her but said nothing.

She poured and sat a mug in front of him. She didn't plan to let him come anywhere near her cup. He wrapped his fingers around his mug, and for the first time, Sara paid attention to his huge hands up close. He had fingers strong enough to snap a hyoid bone with or without an accompanying fit of rage. The backs of his fingers and hands were shaved, all the way up under his long sleeved shirt. She had always seen traces of hair on the back of his hands and fingers. Shaving meant no stray hairs would be left behind.

Sara stepped to the refrigerator and brought out a plastic store-bought platter of walnut brownies. "Want some?"

"Brownies?" he asked, excited like a good little boy. "For me?"

She pulled the landscape drawings aside and placed the tray in front of him. Then she saw it. The end of the plastic wrap hung loose. Someone had already eaten a brownie. Tripp had already snooped in her fridge and eaten one. While she changed her clothes?

He giggled and leaned over the table, ripped the wrapper off, and grabbed one.

Click-click.

Tripp's demeanor switched as fast as he could pick a lock or click it closed, keeping the outside out and the inside in. "Did I do good, Mommy?" he asked, sounding like a child. "I dug deep today."

Mommy? He was remembering his mother? What exactly had he dug today?

He held the small cake with both hands and brought it to his mouth with both hands, like a child might, and poked nearly the entire thing inside. He smacked his lips and repeatedly said, "Um-m-m," and chewed noisily, finishing it off. Then he reached for another like a spoiled child. Or one used to being bribed.

Sara couldn't help staring. The energy of Tripp's self-absorption filled the room and made her nauseous. Still, she picked up a brownie and bit into it as he watched.

The only way to get him to talk might be to appeal to both the boy and the man, to try to appease either, as if she understood and also wanted to play. "That hole behind the garage a few weeks ago wasn't deep enough to bury the cat," she said as she managed a meager smile, treating it as if it were all a joke.

"Momma always told me to aerate the soil," he said through a mouthful. "Get it ready for planting."

After he had eaten three brownies, he settled back into his chair and sucked on his teeth. His facial expression alone told her that at that moment he had shifted mental gears.

Click-click.

The shift proved out when he took a sip of the black coffee and said, "I have a lot of work to do tonight." The expression in his eyes had changed back to sinister. He leaned on his elbows as if at a bar, telling tall tales through an alcoholic haze. "But you're awful smart about that hole."

"You're real good with gardening and shovels and getting things into the ground, aren't you?"

"Had me a lot of practice." His breathing seemed shallow. All the talk about putting things into the ground excited him. "But some things take diggin' real deep."

How long could the man in him keep the naughty boy contained? Or was the boy the one who kept the man in check? Sara sensed the two about to join. Explosively.

Click-click.

"Momma taught me real good," Tripper, the boy, said. "But the desert was awful hard."

"So that's why you chose softer soils near streams and rivers? That's pretty smart."

"You're smart about a lot of things too." Tripper's attitude was playfully retaliatory.

"Tell me something," she said, playing into his twisted rationale. "What made you start on this career, burying bodies? Not everybody chooses to do what you've done."

Tripper pulled his chin back. "It might have been my momma. Or maybe it was my daddy." He seemed confused.

"Tell me about your daddy. Were you two real close?"

"Was." His lower lip protruded. "Till he killed my dog."

"Your own father, Tripper?"

The boy sagged into the chair. "Yeah, I found me a cute little mutt that nobody wanted. My daddy, he always told me what to do because he was sickly and wanted me to carry on after him. He didn't want no dog, said I spent too much time playing with it and not enough working like he taught me." Tripper began to whine. "My dog bit me once while we were playing. Drew out my blood and my momma said blood shouldn't come out no time. A person could bleed all over the place, and my dog made me bleed. My daddy got mad cause I couldn't get all the stains up. One day I found my dog dead. My daddy did it." Tripper clenched and unclenched his fists. For a few seconds, he put his fists to his temples and stared at the tabletop and then looked up even more wild-eyed. "He bashed my dog's head in."

Sara gasped. "That was so cruel."

"Yeah, it was. So I fooled my daddy," Tripper said, giggling wickedly. "He was sickly like I told you. I kept my dead dog till it dried up to skin and bone." He giggled again. "Had trouble hiding the smell, but I did it."

"You kept your dead dog? You loved it that much?"

"I did. And when my daddy died, I crept into the cemetery after they dug the hole for his coffin to be placed in the next day." He had hunched over and used his hands to show how he snuck into the cemetery. "I buried my dog in the bottom of that hole, so my daddy could get paid back for what he done."

Now Sara understood. It was Tripper, the child, who killed and who liked to boast. Tripp, the adult, was who kept the lid screwed on, like a spring coiled tight, about to release.

"How do you figure you paid him back, Tripper?"

Tripper warmed to the nickname and straightened in his chair and stuck his chin out. "Cause now he has to spend eternity with my dog that he killed." He threw back his head to laugh, but no sound came out. "Then I took me a rock from the ground by his grave. That hard rock would never die, and it reminded me how long my daddy had to spend with my dog."

Sara quickly put together the psychology of it all. Surely now, Tripper killed animals to bury with his victims, just as he buried his dog with his father. But how and why did he learn to kill in the first place? She needed to be careful how she phrased things. "It's cruel that your dad killed your pet. So now when people hurt you, you make sure that they spend eternity with an animal. Is that right?"

He seemed pleased that she understood and looked into her eyes and smiled warmly. "You got that right."

"You're one smart young man, aren't you?"

"Always was. But my momma and daddy couldn't see it."

Sara had never been a mom, but one of Tripp's parents should have helped him. "Wasn't your momma there to protect you?"

"Couldn't have been," Tripper said. "She already went away." He smiled again, and each time he did, it seemed he expressed a different pleasure with each memory. "Had a rock for her too."

Chapter 62

Hair stood up on the back of Sara's neck. She choked on her coffee and then smiled weakly. "Never could drink real hot coffee," she said, lying, and setting her cup down. "A rock for your mom? Where did you plant her?"

Not a sound came from outside, and Sara wondered if she had any protection at all.

Tripper squirmed in his chair. "I started collecting rocks when my momma went away," he said. "Got lots of em after that."

Sara looked sympathetically into his eyes. "Where's Momma planted, Tripper?"

He thought a moment and couldn't seem to come up with an answer. Then he said, "Well, under one of them boulders, I know that."

How many more were under boulders? "Is she nearby, so you can visit her from time to time?"

Click-click.

"Visit," Tripp said, suddenly irritated. "I got them rocks to remember by." He thought a little longer, and then said, "We're from Arizona."

"What makes you think of home, Tripper?" Sara wished to keep the talkative boy present. "Is that where Momma is?"

"They got nice boulders there. Momma had her own rock collection before that."

She had to calm her breath. She coughed, faking a cold coming on. She needed more information. "So your momma is in the shadow box too?"

"Hell no. My daddy throwed away my collection when he got mad about my dog. Who-e-e! Mad like a hornet," Tripp said. "Threw away my big rock collection. Part of it was Momma's collection too. Anyway, I just started me a new bunch. Don't have near as many as Momma and I had together."

He was Tripp at that moment, and he wasn't talking about gardening. "How did your momma turn on you, Tripper?"

Click-click.

He pouted. "Like I told you. She used to beat my daddy with them metal ladles and spoons. She promised me she wouldn't do it no more. Time and again she promised." He sighed like he was tired. "She always lied to me. I promised to dig all those holes for her plantin' if she would quit hittin' my daddy, but she lied." He looked into her eyes quickly, again like an animated child telling a ghost story. "One day my daddy said he wished she was dead. I loved my daddy back then and felt sorry for his head being beat on all the time." He stopped talking, again lost in thought. Then he said, "I kept my momma's rock till my daddy throwed everything away."

Tripper responded well to childish things. Sara tried to cajole the boy by leaning sideways and looking at him, then leaning the other way and doing the same, like she was playing. She remembered one particular rock from Tripp's collection, the rock that sparked the connection to all the crimes. "How did Orson Talbot turn on you, Tripper? Did he lie to you?"

Sara sat down again at the opposite end of the table and glanced into her open pocket to make sure her phone was still on. It was and, hopefully, someone at 911 was listening.

Click-click.

"That old man was rich," Tripp said. "I worked hard for him. He wouldn't give me one tiny gold nugget. He said I'd go sell it and drink in a bar."

"Do you drink a lot?"

"Used to." He threw back his shoulders. "But I need my wits about me for the work I do now."

He was not drinking anymore in order to keep the lid on the jar from flying off. He was both a boy and a man, the latter remaining strong enough to hide the misdeeds of a very confused child.

"What about Esmerelda?" Sara asked. "She's always good to you."

"Yeah, like my momma."

"You know that woman would never harm anyone."

Tripp shrugged. "I couldn't hurt her unless she hurt me first. I was always watching out for that." He looked at her sideways. "I been watching you too."

Sara hoped he couldn't see the shock in her reaction. "You watched me, Tripp?" Then acting as if it was all fun, she smiled and asked: "When?"

"I had to know who moved into this house. Had to know if they was gonna destroy my planting." He straightened his shoulders. "I used to come around this house way in the dark of night, just trying to figure out the best way to handle the situation, if it ever come up." He looked her straight into the eyes. "You have no idea how many times I been inside your house."

Sara thought she might faint. Her suspicions were confirmed. The footsteps, the shovel marks, Tripp made them all! And to think Esmerelda's life had also been in jeopardy all those years.

Sara acted nicely, trying to seem like one of Tripp's little friends. If he ever had any. "So tell me," she said as if enjoying the mystique. She even snickered. "How did you find Orson in Placerville to bring him back and plant him?"

Tripp chuckled and doubled up a huge fist and pounded it lightly again and again against the edge of the table. "I planted him all right."

The wind continued to whip the rain against the windows.

Sara felt herself slipping deeper into Tripp's insanity. The only thing that kept her holding on was that she knew she was playing a role. " How'd you pull that off?"

"Was easy." He slipped down in his chair and spread his legs under the table. "He wouldn't give me one perty little gold rock. Not one teeny.... I just followed him till he got to his campsite. Took care of him right away. Brought him back and planted him on purpose under those shiny rocks, all in the same night."

Sara clasped her hands tight under the table. "Well, you're strong, Tripp. Only a strong person could do that."

"That's right. People don't know how strong I am till they make me prove it."

"So you took one of Orson's fool's gold rocks for your collection after you planted him, right?"

"I got me a mighty fine collection. One from every—" Tripp jumped up and knocked over his chair trying to get to the window.

Sara had heard the noise too. "That must be the other dog," she said quickly. "I told you it would be back." She was both relieved to hear the noise and frightened that Tripp might have recognized what made the sound.

"Don't open the door," he said. "I don't want no dog in here."

Somehow, Sara had to keep Tripp's mental state from jumping the track, had to keep him from locking up. He needed to admit to much more. "Your history is fascinating," she said, leaving her chair and up-righting his. "Tell me how you came to have such a huge collection."

Tripp looked out the kitchen window. Finally, he turned slowly, and came back to the table and sat down, but seemed wary. He sipped his coffee, and that helped him relax. His expression changed to that of an old sage preparing to orate the tales of his life experiences. That killer loved his deeds.

Chapter 63

"I love your nice rock collection," Sara said. "Remember when we were in your cabin? You have them all nice in a shadow box."

Tripp rubbed his chin thoughtfully. "Some of the most important people who turned on me is in there."

"How many would you say you've collected?" She took another sip of coffee.

"Hell, I don't know," he said, twisting around in the seat and placing an elbow casually on the back of his chair. "I lost track."

"Where are they all from? I only saw them a moment, but they were all different types of rocks." She tried to remember the shadow box and mentally count them.

"Can't say. I collected everywhere from… from Loomis up north to, maybe, San Jose down south." He looked at her as if asking a question, waiting for approval or recognition.

"You really get around," Sara said. She tried to smile at him like a friend might. But the conversation wasn't saying much. Just for a moment, Sara wondered if she would be able to pull off the ruse. "So you've planted people in all those locations?"

Tripp studied her as if he might have figured out what she was up to. "I wanna plant your dog now," he said, pulling himself out of his chair. "The rain's let up."

Sara stood. "After we finish our work."

He turned so quickly that she expected he might grab her arm. She passed him and walked into the dining room but didn't hear him follow her. She heard a click and looked back into the kitchen as he jumped through the doorway grinning fiendishly. What a child! He then simply followed her to the sitting room where boxes of household goods sat waiting.

A king-sized mattress, still in its wrapper, leaned against the wall. The platform bed frame leaned against another. A dresser and bureau stood nearby among more boxes.

While Tripp studied the mess, Sara walked toward the window, glanced out the south side and saw nothing but more rain streaks. She felt even more alone. Surely, they wouldn't desert her. Perhaps they had not rushed the house because they needed to hear something more convincing. Rushed the house? That had never been part of the plan, and the plan had surely changed since Tripp showed up early. She, and hopefully the officers, was playing it by ear.

Sara kept an eye on Tripp by watching his reflection in the darkened window. He walked to the dresser, pulled out the top drawer and stuck his hand in, like rummaging for something. Then he slammed it hard. The sudden pop startled her, and she turned around. Tripp's expression was again wretched. She avoided looking into his eyes. His murderous eyes!

"I liked you, Sara. I liked lots of people, and they turned on me. Don't know why you did."

"I haven't turned on you, Tripper," she said. "We're friends. You're here helping, and I'll pay you better than most people would because you're worth it." She heard her lie and realized she would say anything to get through the evening.

His expression changed to pleasantness again. "Well, show me which rooms you want these things put into."

At least the back staircase was no longer enclosed. She could climb the stairs and not be trapped between walls. If they went upstairs, maybe the officers could get into the first floor and hide. To occupy his hands, she pointed and said, "Bring that box, please, and that smaller one over there." She flipped on the light and walked swiftly up the stairs. Tripp simply followed. She turned on more lights whenever she came to a switch. Once in the empty master bedroom, Sara feared Tripp might try to block the doorway if he became unmanageable.

"Where'd you want these?" he asked.

"In the corner's fine," she said, pointing again. She went to stand at a window. "Tell me, Tripp, how many people have you planted?" She had to remember to always smile like a good friend sharing secrets.

He pulled back his chin and stared at her. Finally, he said, "Maybe thirty or forty." He shrugged hard like he didn't really care. "Hell, I lost track, I told you."

"You don't have that many rocks in your shadow box."

"Oh, no. Them's the ones in my flower beds. The shadow box was for special people. My daddy's in there."

"You have a dozen or more in your shadow box. But you've got way more than thirty or forty in your flower beds, all laid out nice and decorative."

"Then I guess that's how many I done planted." He curled up the corner of his mouth and shrugged again.

"Were they girlfriends? Drinking buddies, maybe?"

"Almost forgot my roommates. My drinking buddies. One keeled over on his own. The other's in the box."

"Why did you plant him?"

Again, Tripp rubbed his chin. "If I recollect, they asked my roommates about my whereabouts when ol' Talbot never turned up. My roomies told the cops I was drunk that whole weekend. Hell, they didn't know. They was drunk. After the first guy died, the other told me he was having second thoughts and wanted to tell the truth. He turned on me, Sara. He turned on me."

"So, you added another rock to your collection."

He snickered. "They ain't found him yet, neither." His smiled lingered. "Never will."

Sara's stomach tightened nervously again, but she couldn't quit. "Why not?"

"Cause he's under a big rock," Tripp said, laughing. "A boulder. Didn't have to dig much. He was tiny, like my momma. Bunched him up into a ball in that hole, like my momma, and rolled a huge boulder over him." He gestured with both arms, describing a boulder that had to be at least five feet in diameter. Tripp would know how to roll something that large. "Heard his bones pop and crackle when that ton o' rock rolled on him." He laughed hideously.

Sara held to her façade. "Where do you find boulders like that?"

"Farther down from here," he said, snickering again. "Niles Canyon, along a creek." He walked to a window along the back wall and looked out.

"Does your momma have a boulder like that?"

"Hey, they got boulders in that dry wash at Cave Creek. We're from Arizona. I told you that."

Rain had distorted any view through the windows, not that they saw anything. She was at least thankful for the moonless night but hoped the officers were positioned close against the house so Tripp couldn't see them when he looked downward.

"Can you remember where you did all your planting?"

"Who wants to know?" He smiled again, that same hideous smile that made her skin crawl.

"I was just wondering. Must be an interesting thing, planting someone." She smiled and pointed to the north wall. "That's where I want the platform bed to go."

Tripp grabbed her arm. "I ain't here to be no interior decorator," he said. "You turned on me, Sara, just like everybody else. I come to teach you about planting."

She tried to jerk her arm loose. "I'm not your momma or your daddy, Tripp. I've never hurt you." His vice grip made her arm tingle and start to go numb.

"I tried to be nice to you, and you didn't like it."

She relaxed, but only to help him do the same. "Tripp, I'm not used to attention from people I don't know." She smiled. "You move a little too fast for me."

"Not as fast as you're gonna see now. You got a right perty neck. I can do you without putting you to sleep first 'cause you ain't got no guy with you now."

Before he could say or do anything more, Sara painfully ripped her arm from his grip, took two steps away and turned back to face him. "There's no need to hurt anybody."

Why hadn't the officers come inside? Surely, they could hear Tripp's threatening demeanor. She was sure she heard them at the locks earlier. Then she realized that Tripp had been in the house a while before he showed himself. He might have set the deadbolts while she changed clothes in the bedroom. Surely, he had reset the deadbolt when he hung back in the kitchen. She swallowed hard.

"Well, you're just too late with your niceties. Left me too long to figure a way to handle you."

Sara gestured toward the doorway. "Maybe you should leave now, Tripp. I don't want to see you again till you understand I'm a friend."

He took a step toward her. "You can't change my mind. I been walking your backfield, deciding what I gotta do."

Another click came from downstairs, but Tripp showed no recognition of it as he rushed toward her.

"Stop where you are!"

He came at her gurgling with both arms in the air. She ducked and fled through the nearest doorway, into the new dressing room. She slammed the door behind her and ran into the master bath. She would have fled from there into the hallway and down the steps, but Tripp appeared in the hallway like a fiendish ghoul ready to pounce.

Click-click.

He threw back his head in a victory laugh that suddenly changed to a giggle. He was Tripper, the boy, and ready to kill.

Chapter 64

"You can't get away," Tripper said, teasing from out in the hallway.

Sara's legs felt like logs. "Stop right there!" she said, putting up her hand.

Tripper moved slowly toward her, gurgling, his hands in the air making clutching motions. He didn't pounce. Just took one slow step at a time, like a child imitating a movie monster. She backed up slowly. He was in the bathroom now, making ominous threatening sounds deep in his throat. "I gotcha!" he said, low and menacing.

Sara backed against the closed dressing room door. She opened it and stood, enticing him further. Tripper kept coming. When he was as close as she could allow, she swiftly pulled the door closed behind her. He mumbled loudly as if confused, tried the knob, grunted, and tried again. Sara ran out of the bedroom. Just as she passed the hallway door to the bathroom, Tripper, jumped out wearing the night vision goggles. She screamed and ran toward the front of the house. Tripp closed in fast.

She grabbed the banister railing on the front staircase and made it down to the landing just as Tripper appeared at the top. She started down the rest of the stairs, and the weakened banister gave way. She screamed as she flew off the nine-foot height, but managed to grab hold of the restraining rope the contractor had installed. It broke her fall, but she still smashed hard onto the floor. She sat, stunned, and looked up to see a goggle-eyed monster come sailing through the air from high above.

Sara screamed and rolled away before Tripper could land on her. He grabbed her hair pulling her back, straddled her, and thumped her head hard against the floor. She lay stunned as the vibration rolled through her brain. She fought to hold onto consciousness.

"I gotcha!" he said, through clenched teeth. His hands were tight around her throat. Tripper, the boy, gurgled with delight. At that moment he was both the man, and the boy and they were in deadly conflict.

She choked, couldn't get air, and it made her mad and gave her strength. She ripped the goggles off his head. Blood spurted as an edge cut into his scalp.

Tripper groaned, swiped at his head, and strained to see his hands in the dim light filtering toward the front of the house. "Awk! Blood! Momma said can't be no blood."

Locks clicked. Cool air invaded the house. Tripp looked around distracted, as if momentarily he had no idea where he was.

Sara screamed again and fought with all her strength. It meant her life. Tripp tried to keep her pinned with one hand while the other swiped at the top of his head. More noises distracted him, and he loosened his grip. She reached to scratch his face. He pulled away just far enough so she could kick him backwards. She twisted over onto her knees and lunged like an Olympic sprinter taking off at the gun, making it across the hallway and into the parlor, running headlong into someone inside the darkened room. Instinctively, she brought up her fists and began to thrash.

"Sheriff's Department!" the man said, firmly grasping her wrists. "Whoa, there."

Someone tripped the circuit breaker. All the interior lights and exterior flood lamps came on. Voices barked orders. Sara spun around and saw Tripp, with bloody hands, climbing to his feet as an officer made a flying tackle. Tripp grunted hard. The sickening sound of one body slamming into another and then both hitting to the floor made her cringe.

Uniformed officers filled the rooms, so many that some could only stand and watch as Tripp was taken down. He seemed stronger than the numerous officers combined. He screamed, high-pitched, like a frightened child. "I'm sorry, Momma… sorry!"

Johanna and Isidoro's faces bobbed in the fracas.

"Cuff him!" someone said.

Tripp managed to get free until someone tackled him again at the knees. He went down hard hitting his head against the wall. Only then could they keep him on the floor. They cuffed his hands behind his back, but he kicked viciously.

"Hogtie him!" another said.

An officer produced chains and Tripp was bound at the ankles with his legs bent backwards. The leg chains were secured to his hand restraints behind him. Four officers carried him outside like a dressed carcass headed for the barbeque pit. Tripp looked at Sara as they passed. She had not meant to look into his eyes ever again. Now, just for that moment, she felt pangs of pity, deep pity, for the boy.

* * *

Occasional drops of rain fell. Some of the officers wore wet rain slickers, a sign that many had waited outside.

"Sit here," an officer said, offering a seat in his car.

Sara clutched the front of her torn blouse. "Can't… can't sit." Despite the cool air, she felt hot. "Why the hell did you guys wait so long to come inside?" she asked through clenched teeth.

313

"Ma'am," the officer said. "Only eight to ten seconds passed between you falling off the banister and us taking him down."

"Seconds?" Sara felt dumbfounded. "It seemed like a lifetime."

"Hey, great tackle, Johanna," someone said.

Sara spun around. The voice was Isidoro who congratulated Johanna with a warm handshake and a pat on the back. That was worth watching.

Johanna's always-crisp uniform pants were torn at the knees. She nodded to Isidoro, barking out more orders. She needed to leave well enough alone.

Patrol cars had been parked along the levee, the Sacramento police among them. Several came down the driveway as gravel crunched. Soon as they had Tripp secured in a car, most of the officers departed. Several deputies and the forensic staff stayed behind to complete their reports. The rain stopped.

Sara sighed angrily. "Seems like my not accepting his advances really ticked him off."

Johanna thumbed to the backfield. "It's more than that. If those graves hadn't turned up, no sense in taking you out and possibly giving himself away."

"It was Talbot's remains that told him he had to do something about you," Isidoro said.

"Yeah, and by then he panicked, meant to do you no matter what." Johanna's mouth turned up at a corner. She shrugged. "Then you invited him in."

Sara shook her head, trying to dispel the truth of it all. "I need to change my clothes," she said, as her hands continued to shake. Spots of Tripp's blood speckled her jacket and blouse.

"Wait," Isidoro said. He smiled at Johanna. "You take her."

"You can have the honor," Johanna said.

"Let's both go," he said.

Sara yelped when Isidoro took hold of her elbow to direct her toward the garage. Both she and Johanna limped.

Flashlight beams radiated from the backfield.

"What now?" Sara asked. "This ankle isn't going to let me walk far."

"Sara," Johanna said. "I hope you don't hate any of us for putting you through this."

"Would you stop apologizing?" Isidoro asked. "Just tell her." They sounded like a married couple.

"Tell me what?"

They came to the back corner of the garage. Johanna took her shoulder. "This isn't gonna be nice, but you need to see what Isidoro found."

They rounded the corner flashing their lights.

"Stay back," an officer said as he stretched yellow Sheriff's banner from the garage to some stakes another officer stuck into the ground out in the field. Two officers stood ready to begin marking, photographing, and collecting evidence.

"Not again!" Sara's knees almost gave out. Johanna kept hold of her arm. A shovel stood against the back garage wall. Weeds and a thick layer of topsoil lay rolled back in strips, much like a person would lay sod on fresh soil when planting a new yard. A hole, big enough and deep enough to put someone into, waited. A small dead dog lay nearby.

"He could have been back here at the time you arrived home," Isidoro said. "No way you could have known."

That meant the officers had not arrived until after Tripp was inside the house. Sara felt faint.

Johanna flashed her light around. Rain had already washed away much of the scattered soil from the hole. "All he'd have to do is roll those hungry weeds back over that grave and let 'em flourish in the rain."

Chapter 65

Sara accompanied officers to Sheriff's Headquarters to attend a debriefing. It had to be done immediately. Timing was important for memory and talking things through would be good therapy for her. They gave her contact information for the department psychologist if she needed follow-up. After signing over the tape from her recorder into evidence and on her way out, she caught Johanna leaving to resume patrol.

"I-I'm sorry, Johanna. I couldn't get him to tell where all the bodies were."

Johanna chuckled and looked at her sideways. "You got enough out of him to send him to the needle. They'll keep him alive, maybe till we can turn up the bodies for some of those rocks he's collected."

Sara swallowed hard. "Who'll tell Esmerelda now?"

Johanna started again for the door. "She already knows."

Sara glanced at her watch. It was after midnight. "Already?"

Johanna stopped again and turned. "Detectives went to secure Tripp's cabin and work area till we can follow up on the search warrant." She sighed and sounded weary. "Thanksgiving will delay lots of paperwork, you know."

Esmerelda wouldn't get much sleep now. Sara headed straight over. The hour drive from Sacramento to River Hospice stretched to nearly two and seemed endless. The insistent rains and moonless night slowed her down. The heater was on, the radio off.

All the lights were on in Esmerelda's house. Sara drove down the hill onto the hospice property and saw a nondescript sedan parked behind the edge of the patient building, pointed in the direction of the cabins. Sara made out movements of two people inside.

She knocked lightly on Esmerelda's door and then let herself in. Poor Esmerelda had been weeping. Minus her immaculate makeup, her eyes sagged, and swollen eyelids hung like eaves on an old house. She fumbled nervously with the satin sash on her bathrobe. They rushed into each other's arms.

"I'm so sorry for you," Esmerelda said. "So sorry what you went through." That stoic woman wasn't even thinking about herself and her loss.

Sara couldn't hold back tears. "We got him," she said through clenched teeth.

"You're limping."

"I'll get over it."

They sat and talked about events from the time Sara knew who the killer might be. Esmerelda needed to hear every detail, plus why she wasn't told about Tripp earlier.

"The guys in the car?" Sara asked.

"Guards. They put a lock-out knob on Tripp's door," Esmerelda said. "They wanted to string that yellow tape everywhere. I told them I would be having some dignitaries over for dinner tomorrow—well, that's today—so they sent two guards instead." Esmerelda rolled her eyes. "I want to take them a fresh thermos and something to munch." She smiled tentatively, which only exemplified her nervous state of mind. "Today I celebrate a special Thanksgiving. They'll release Orson's remains soon, and his spirit and I will carry on. I'm removing all evidence that Tripp ever crossed our lives."

Esmerelda shouldn't be left alone. Sara left a message on Pierce's answering machine that she would stay the night at River Hospice. She would be there in time to help him with their Thanksgiving meal.

Sara rose before dawn from little more than an hour of fitful sleep. In the darkness of Esmerelda's spare bedroom, she made yet another pre-dawn call to Linette and Buck to let them know what happened before they heard it exaggerated through the grapevine. Both were on extension phones and screamed about why she had agreed to participate in such a dangerous scheme. Yet, they were jubilant and thankful she had not been hurt and about having caught the maniac. They wanted to drive over if she needed them. "I'll be fine now," she said. They would read the details in the newspapers and get together as soon as possible. Sara heard Buck say to Linette as he hung up the phone, "That's not the same Sara we grew up with."

* * *

Sara had not meant to do anything special on Thanksgiving Day, just watch the celebrations on TV and zone out while preparing the holiday meal.

Pierce continued to write. She did most of the cooking, thankful for his preoccupation. Still numb, her ankle had swelled, and a huge blue bruise covered her upper arm and elbow. She intended not to talk on the phone, seeking solace through distraction. Her cell phone rang anyway, and she well knew the number that appeared. "What's up Johanna? Don't you get a day off?"

"Ha! Don't want it with this case. We've waited too long to nail that deranged loony."

"How's that going?" Sara clicked the mute button on the remote for Pierce's new kitchen TV.

"Hey, this guy's so slippery," Johanna said. "He could pick locks with his fingernails, if he'd let 'em grow. We've got him really tucked away," She sounded tired.

"Is Tripp talking?" Not until that moment did Sara wonder if Tripp was actually the confused boy she recognized, or if it was all an act.

"A psychiatrist saw him. They wanna wait till he calms down. He's on suicide watch."

"Oh, no. Does that mean Tripp will get out of this with an insanity plea?" Sara asked. "Assigned to a hospital and get out in two years?"

"That's not gonna happen," Johanna said. "He's too much of a danger to society. Besides, detectives got a solid case of pre-meditation going."

"You know why he wore night-vision goggles, don't you?"

"No, hadn't put that together. Why?"

"It's on the tape. So he could see in the dark." Sara obsessed over trying to piece things together. "Johanna, I think he did away with his victims on New Moon nights."

"On what?"

"When there's a new moon, it's pitch black out. That's why it's called *the dark of the moon*. Same when he drugged Pierce and me. A new moon yesterday evening too."

"You're saying that on a New Moon night, he'd have less chance of being seen?"

"Exactly, but he could see through night-vision goggles." Sara had more to say. "If you hear the tape, it sounds like he also helped his mom kill people. That's where he learned about collecting rocks. She was a killer, too, and had her own collection."

Johanna's silence on the other end meant she was mentally putting the pieces together. "Sara, you gave us clues that broke the case. Guess we oughta' start by checking to see if any of these others went missing on a New Moon night. Dunno if we can get Tripp to admit to that."

"You know? Him using the goggles says he premeditated everything."

"Hey," Johanna said, sounding more upbeat. "I called to remind you to see a doctor about your injuries. You need to get yourself to Sacramento. It's all set up in Emergency. County's paying for it. You can even go today."

"Thank you. I appreciate it," Sara said, but she didn't feel she a needed a doctor.

"You at least need to have your head checked," Johanna said. "He knocked you hard against the floor. You could have a concussion."

"I'll go if I don't feel better after Thanksgiving," she said. "Oh, one more thing."

"Yeah?"

"That femur I saw on the gravel bar in Snodgrass Slough. Tripp buried his victims close to water. What if that was one of his?"

"I don't know, Sara. Anything's possible. With the number of rocks you say he collected, many remains may never be found."

* * *

Sara had prepared too much food. Turkey meat was too rich for Pierce's digestive system. Instead, they roasted the biggest chicken they could find. Over dinner, Pierce said, "I hope Jade's home for good this time. Daphine needs to know something other than a broken family."

"She's not seeing Fredrik anymore?" Sara asked.

"She'll never have a lasting relationship unless she can get past her hurtful memories."

Sara knew what that meant. She, too, hadn't had a relationship in decades. Hers with Huxley could have been a meaningful one, but he had not been curious enough to return her call. She had been too impulsive with the realization that she could be in jeopardy. Her fear had hit hard and fast at a most inopportune time. She shook her head, didn't want to think about it. "Maybe Jade can help mend the past."

Daphine had previously admitted to keeping the two-bedroom place because that's where Jade grew up. "She can't afford that house," Pierce said. "Her landlord in Locke doubled the store rent. She was ready to abandon the house for a studio apartment in order to keep the store. Then Jade showed up."

Chapter 66

Sara spent the Friday after Thanksgiving reading and editing portions of Pierce's exciting manuscript. She worked nonstop. The phone rang early that evening. She sighed, tempted to let voice mail pick it up. She didn't know how she would spend the rest of the long weekend, but it wouldn't be chatting on the phone.

Again, she recognized the number displayed. "Esmerelda," she said. "How are you holding together?"

"I'm just fine." She really did sound that way. "I know you two had turkey yesterday, but how about coming over and helping me wade through my leftovers."

"We had chicken. I'm stuffed, really. Haven't eaten like that in years."

"Oh, please come. All the guests are gone and, well, I could use your company."

Esmerelda had never asked for much. She was a giver that kept giving even when she hurt. Now she asked for a simple thing like company. "When's dinner?"

"Come now. Come as you are. And wait till you see what's going on over here."

When Sara pulled onto the hospice property, Esmerelda's words rang in her ears. Numerous cars and vans had parked haphazardly. Men and women with badges scurried everywhere. A backhoe worked. The lawns, walkways, and drives were an oozing mess of mud. Yellow banner cordoned off flowerbeds around each structure, with the flowers and small boulders already dug out. Officers with cameras went in and out of Tripp's duplex. Because of the way one of the forensic vans had parked, Sara saw in through the rear doors where a growing heap of sealed brown bags was stacked. Two people came around the backside of the far cottages, one with a sniffer dog, and the other with a metal detector. The entire property crawled with activity like a plague of ravenous grasshoppers. The beauty that Tripp took years to create and maintain was gone.

The hospice's Mexican laborers stood and gawked. Then Sara saw something that almost made her chuckle. Fredrik stood watching through the window in the hospice doorway.

Esmerelda came down her stairs. She wore her denim and boots. "It's time for a new face," she said.

"A backhoe? They don't think bodies are buried here, do they?"

"No, it was my idea. The investigators think you're right. They told me this was probably where Tripp unloaded any dirt left over from burying people. The dirt, his flowers, everything, I want it all removed. Digging helps the investigation anyway. They might find more rocks related to other burials." She kept looking around like the activity excited her immensely.

Sara remembered Tripp's sudden appearances several times when she arrived to load the dog cages. "Esmerelda, this may sound strange, but you should find out why Tripp always appeared from behind your garage."

Esmerelda didn't seem to understand. "Okay, but let's go indoors before it starts raining again. She kept looking around.

Sara was hungry after all. She had not tasted turkey prepared by Esmerelda. She felt able to enjoy a small meal. She opened the refrigerator expecting to see a half-eaten turkey with piles of containers with all the trimmings and saw nothing. Not even a sliver of pie sat under cover on the counter. "Oh," she said, looking up, embarrassed. "Dinner is over at the facility. I should have known."

"I'm on my way to get it."

"I'll go with you."

"Nonsense. Make some juice or get the drinks ready. Ice, whatever." She disappeared out the door before Sara could object.

Sara looked in the refrigerator for juice mixings and saw nothing, not even sodas, not even inside the freezer. Esmerelda was surely confused by the excitement outside.

Sara looked up and realized that she was standing at the same window, looking out over the same levee, and remembered seeing a sedan slow down and turn into the property. She had made juice on that occasion. She remembered carrying it out to the deck and nearly running into the arms of the man with the wildest blue-topaz eyes.

Come as you are, Esmerelda had said over the phone back then. That evening she danced in sneakers. *Come as you are*, Esmerelda had said but an hour ago. Now she wore boots, but there would be no dancing, not for a long, long time. Sara put her hand over the cell phone attached to her waistband and stared into the sink. "No juice today," she said. "No Huxley either." Her voice cracked. She sighed and wondered how she might call him. She felt like such a fool.

Suddenly, she yanked the phone from her waistband and punched in Huxley's number. The only way she would be a fool is if she couldn't apologize. Surprisingly, for being as busy as he always was. his phone was turned off, but then it was a holiday weekend. Her call transferred to voice mail. She wasn't prepared for that. Now she had to leave her message into empty space.

"Huxley," she said, faltering. Once she said his name, she had to continue. "I made a big mistake. I'm sure I did. If you knew the whole story, you'd understand, but I don't expect to hear from you again. I just want to apologize for any hurt I may have caused you." She thumped the phone to end the call and stood perspiring and feeling clammy. The call had to be made. She owed him that much. She simply stood, looking out the window through bleary eyes.

The door opened and closed again. Spry old Esmerelda had made a quick trip. Sara heard footsteps behind her and quickly wiped her eyes.

"Sara," a male voice said as if needing to be cautious. "Can we try again?"

Sara gasped, spun around, and saw his pleading sad eyes and sallow worried look. She threw herself into Huxley's arms. "Yes!" she said, breathlessly, as her body melted against him.

He wrapped both arms around her. They kissed, one long endearing kiss, to seal the moment forever. Tears ran down her cheeks and wet his face as well.

He held her as tight as breathing would allow. "I couldn't call you back," he said, whispering like he was sorry. "Thought maybe you only wanted a casual relationship, and I didn't want to be anyone's toy."

"Then how did you—?"

"I called Esme yesterday morning to wish her Happy Thanksgiving before I left for Oregon. She asked about you and me. I sort of told her it wasn't working with us."

"But you didn't go home to be with your family."

He pulled back to see her face. "I couldn't, not after hearing what you'd been through."

"I'm so sorry. I was—"

"You were scared, didn't know much about me. It was Esme who pieced it together." They still clung together. "You remember what I said that night about not letting you get away?"

"I remember every moment, every word, and every sorrow since," she said. "You said 'I'm not letting you get away now' and that spooked me so badly."

He gently clutched the hair at the back of her head. "I didn't mean to frighten you." He drew in a breath and stared deep into her eyes. "I'm not letting you get away this time, Sara. I don't care what it takes." They clung tighter still, couldn't get enough of each other.

"We'll have lots of time now," she said into his shoulder again.

"I knew from the day I first saw you in Sacramento. You're the one." His voice quivered, choked with hope and relief. "And then it ended so abruptly that night."

She pulled back and studied his face. Tears ran from his eyes, and he wasn't ashamed. She kissed his eyes and tasted his tears. Huxley was serious, the way she wanted things to be between them.

The front door opened and closed.

"Here, you two," Esmerelda said. They pulled apart slightly. Esmerelda offered bags of food in plastic containers. "This'll hold you over for a while. Hide somewhere and don't come out till the dust settles."

Sara needed to express her heartfelt thanks. "Esmerelda…."

"Go, girl," Esmerelda said, nodding toward the door. "Get outa' here."

Chapter 67

After more than a week of intense teamwork, Talbot House stood poised to admit the world. The new banister spindles arrived in the nick of time. The railing that gave way when Sara fell merely pulled out of the wall. It was easily secured.

Huxley had stayed. "I'm as much a part of this as you are," he said when Sara playfully accused him of wanting to be the boss. Their love and lovemaking nourished them.

He looked better than ever. His dark blue slacks and sports jacket set off a blue-green shirt left open at the throat. He looked Gucci all the way down to his shoes, but Sara wasn't sure about the loafers without socks, especially in cool weather. She wore stilettos and a red midi-length silk dress that Esmerelda helped pick out during one of their shopping sprees.

Esmerelda's chandeliers sparkled like stars from heaven. In the parlor, the tall Christmas tree, weighted down under myriad decorations, competed for attention. Pine branches scented the air throughout the floors. Decorated professionally, the house stood readied for the first OTF social. It hadn't rained for a week. The strong late afternoon sun beamed through the bird and floral stained glass windows and made them twinkle.

Beni Noa, wearing a beautiful new Aloha shirt and black slacks, kept the fireplace burning in the sitting room. Pierce came early with Daphine. He stoked the fireplace with Beni, glad to be helpful with the party in any way possible. He had an abundance of determination and mixed well in crowds. Sara wasn't concerned about him feeling left out.

"Our two detective board members are out by the gazebo," Huxley said.

"And Esmerelda's attorney… uh, our attorney, just went to freshen her face," Sara said.

Out at the gazebo, the blue, white, and gold OTF logo flag waved below the *Stars and Stripes* and the *California Bear*.

A three-piece chamber ensemble entertained from the windowed alcove of the sitting room. Comfortable chairs waited everywhere. Tantalizing odors of Zoki's oriental foods drifted through the house. Tiny eating tables and chairs waited throughout the first floor. With his food, people could eat a casual but full dinner while they sat, stood, or wandered the grounds. Guests could walk through the rooms anywhere they wished, from the basement to the attic. The kitchen, dining room, and master bedroom were the only rooms containing permanent furniture, and sparse at that.

Sara was sure that Huxley instigated Daphine's offer for a silent auction of some of her numerous art pieces.

"It's awful what Jade did to her," he said.

Daphine neurotically made last minute switches of some art pieces from one room to another. She motioned for Pierce to stand back and check that each picture hung evenly. Her attire was fairly casual; a dressy floral capri pants with a matching top. Something about the way Daphine presented herself labeled her as an artist secure in her image.

"Jade came home only to convince herself that she did the right thing by staying in China," Sara said. "The least she could have done was send a complimentary wedding announcement before the big event."

Huxley shook his head. "And not come home after the fact and leave again without so much as a hug and a kiss."

Sara hurt for Daphine, who once again, smothered her feelings behind the busyness of her creativity.

Framed art pieces hung throughout the first floor. Tiny tables standing beneath each held bid sheets, free self-adhesive OTF logo decals, and OTF mission statements.

"Daphine's magnificent art should have been known around the world by now," Sara said. "She lacked the funds to promote herself."

Sara's cell phone rang. Her business manager sounded overly excited. "Why haven't you sent back the contract?" he asked. He was home-based in New York, the better of two referrals her Caribbean bank manager recommended. He had flown to Puerto Rico to meet her.

"Contract? What contract?"

"Sara, the company's buying your two kids' games. They also want to sign you on as a game designer."

"Me? Oh my… oh my!" She took Huxley's hand to steady herself.

"Soon as you send that contract back," her manager said, "there'll be a whopping check coming your way."

"Already?" Sara asked. "I'm in the middle of a big event."

"I can hear some of it in the background."

"Been planning this for weeks. Haven't opened my mail in days." She promised to get back to him on Monday morning. She and Huxley stepped into her office where she found the envelope and laid it on the top of the pile. "Tomorrow," she said.

"After we take a while getting out of bed," Huxley said, drawing her close. They kissed sweetly.

Sara went to check the posters mounted in a strategic location at the front entry. One poster showed the new signpost that would be installed out where the workshop once stood. It would be a large framed ceramic tile composition of the drawing that Daphine made of a man's hands holding a pan containing gold nuggets, with the initials OTF and the wording spelled out. The other poster announced future charitable events. Among them, Beni Noa's Hawaiian luau and Polynesian review, to be held outside around the gazebo in the springtime.

Guests began arriving. They wandered the rooms, examined the house, and ogled the art. The next time Sara took notice, the house had filled with people. They lined up to enter bids that would benefit both Daphine and the foundation.

Esmerelda hid her despondency with a plate heaped with delicacies. She was one of the few Caucasian women who could wear a Chinese dress stylishly. Maybe it was Orson's elegant gold jewelry, too, that she finally brought out of her safe deposit box that made her look expensive. "Look at this," she said. "That Zoki can cook."

Buck and Linette found her. "We hear things with Tripp are adding up," Linette said. She handed Sara a news clipping. Sara opened it as the others read over her shoulder.

One of the ways the Delta people thanked an anonymous donor was by making the donation headline news. The principal of the Rio Vista High School was shown in a photo with stacks of books about the Delta. The article reported that all Delta schools along the river, from Rio Vista to Clarksburg, received the same anonymous gifts. Sara smiled. The article would become part of a scrapbook.

"I told the investigators to dig behind the garage, Sara, like you suggested," Esmerelda said.

"And?"

"They found two small dead dogs wrapped in black plastic sheeting, the kind of sheeting used in that San Jose case." Esmerelda kept eating and spoke between mouthfuls. "When the sniffer dogs refused to go near the area, detectives noticed a chemical odor. Tripp kept other creatures from digging by spraying with animal repellant."

"Everything he's done points to premeditation," Huxley said.

"They also found my missing jewelry pieces inside Tripp's filthy pillowcase, which he evidently slept with every night since he stole them."

Sara remembered Tripp's immaculate front room, but also the horrific disarray in the back room; a dichotomy, like his mind.

"Would you look who just walked in," Sara said. "Caren Olof?"

They craned their necks. "Oh, yes," Huxley said. "Norwood and Caren York." He went to handle the first greeting.

"He knows the Police Commissioner?" Sara asked. "And invited him?"

Esmerelda smiled like a cat. "Look over there," she said, pointing slowly with her chin. "That's Representative Poole, Stan Poole, and Nelda."

Sara mingled, made sure she greeted every single person, even though she, the little nobody from thirty years before, could barely keep steady as her legs wobbled. Esmerelda's suggestion of laying out nametags if guests wished to identify themselves was helpful.

Of course, important people would be interested in her foundation, especially now that she and Huxley had teamed together. Sara met two others that mentioned their own family losses in Vietnam and how they were affiliated with Huxley. Other guests included dignitaries and philanthropists affiliated with Esmerelda's hospice. The house came alive with boisterous, charitable, wall-to-wall people.

Sara and Caren exchanged friendly conversation. Then Caren joyfully made her way around the room, easily conversing with friends she knew, which seemed nearly everyone. Sara had to guess at social niceties and protocol and walked up to the guests she did not know and struggled to make conversation.

Daphine came down the showcase steps. "I just love your playroom," she said.

"You've been up in the attic again?" Sara asked.

"So much north light."

Painters needed bright north light. An idea raced through her mind and Sara could barely control her thoughts. "It's yours, Daph," she said happily as Huxley joined them.

"What are you saying?"

"North light, Daph. You can have the space, the whole attic, if you want to set up a new studio."

Daphine's mouth popped open and shut as she tried to speak. Nothing came out. She looked at Huxley and back again, finally throwing up her hands. "I can't live that far away from my studio. Gotta be able to get up in the middle of the night, if that's when creativity hits. Too far away, but thanks."

Huxley had caught on, squeezed Sara's hand, and waited. Sara went on. "It wouldn't be if you lived here."

Daphine looked confused and shook her head. Questions filled her eyes. "Here?" she asked, and it came out in a squeak. "You mean I'd get to meet the ghost?" She joked, her way of covering nervousness and then said nothing more. Daphine kept staring at Huxley and then tried to subdue a gasp.

Sara guessed that Daphine remembered Huxley's advise about not wasting opportunities. "Pick a bedroom," Sara said, pointing upwards.

Daphine turned slowly and went to climb the staircase. Halfway up, she turned and looked back, seeming in disbelief.

Chapter 68

Johanna and Isidoro walked in through the kitchen door. "You two staying for the announcements?" Sara asked.

Isidoro checked his radio. "If we don't get called. He went in to join the party.

"Glad you're here," Sara said, walking Johanna back out to the porch to show her Choco and Latte's red and green leashes hanging on the pegs.

"I thought we had those in evidence." Johanna looked puzzled.

"I bought new ones. You remember when you confiscated the first ones?"

"'Course."

"You wrote on the bag: *Choco – Red, Latte – Green.*"

"I guess so, if that's what I found at the time."

"Johanna, only a person familiar with the dogs knew which color to attach to each pup."

Johanna rolled her eyes and whipped out her notepad. "That psycho's circuits aren't as shorted out as everyone thinks." She shifted her stance. "You been reading the papers?"

"Haven't had time."

"They found your weapon in Tripp's toolbox. A big stash of old Rohypnol tablets too."

Zoki's caterers carried empty chafing dishes and pans past them and out to his van. "The next round is dessert," he said.

Soon, the sun set, drenching everything in moonlight from the Full Moon having appeared three nights prior.

Isidoro found them again. "I meant to tell you. They found some shale in Tripp's collection. Far as forensics can determine, it came from one of the Rio Vista gas fields when they dug new wells."

"Rio Vista?" Sara asked. Chills ran over her body. "Remember Iana Underhill?"

"There's a big dump site for gas well rocks," Johanna said. "Just north of the Rio Vista Bridge on their side." Accumulated rocks left from drillings were deposited along the riverbank. It helped fortify the levees when they became soft in spots and eroded from the river tides.

"The Rio Vista P.D. starts searching down there next week," Isidoro said. "They're bringing in a dog. Eldon's Crane and Rigging volunteered heavy equipment."

The guests had eaten their fill and settled into dessert. It was time to make the announcements. "I knew we'd have a crowd," Huxley said as they stood in the pantry at the electricity breaker box. He clicked on the exterior floodlights.

"We only mailed fifty invitations," Sara said, teasing with her eyes. "Wonder who could have invited all the others."

Huxley cleared his throat. "Must have been Esmerelda."

Sara looked down the length of the rooms. The wide, ceiling-to-floor pocket doors between the dining and sitting room, and the sitting room and the front parlor, stood wide open, creating the effect of one long large room. Small easels with signs and other objects stood covered on the dining room table. Beni had set up his karaoke machine to serve as a microphone.

News media crews showed up. Sara took the microphone and thanked everyone for coming. She shook badly and decided to cut her welcome presentation short. She would need more self-confidence, and fast, if she hoped to function in the public eye. She passed the microphone to Huxley.

He gave a brief greeting then said, "Our new Police Commissioner, Norwood York, will say a few words."

Caren slipped through the crowd and came to take hold of Sara's hand and interlaced their fingers at their sides. Sara felt overwhelmed.

Norwood's talk was mostly to extend his thanks for the establishment of the Orson Talbot Foundation and its purpose. He spoke of Esmerelda and Orson and motioned to Esmerelda to stand beside him. Norwood was a passionate speaker.

Caren stepped up beside her husband and handed him an envelope, which he opened. "This," he said, waving a check high in the air, "is a donation to the Orson Talbot Foundation from the Sacramento group, *Every Child Counts.*"

After accepting the check, Sara felt vindicated and stood stoically beside Esmerelda and Norwood. Shyness has nothing to do with her mood at that moment.

As guests floated in and out of the rooms trying to hear, Huxley spoke some about his trips to Vietnam. Many became emotional when he talked about the MIA recently located. He talked about how his group decided to join Sara and her foundation to find missing local people. Then it was time for the unveilings.

Suddenly, people stepped aside at the sitting room entrance. Sara looked to see who might enter and gasped. Upton Zeno, the County Sheriff himself, in full uniform, squeezed in.

Sara could no longer allow herself to be nervous and hesitant. Her commitments were being validated. "The first thing we want to show you—everyone—is this," she said as Huxley pulled the cover off the first item to be exhibited. A large drawing showed the rear acreage complete with swimming pool, pavilion, bathhouses, gardens, and parking lot south of the garage. "Our pool will be available for swimming lessons for Delta youth," Sara said. "In fact, I hope all of you will consider these grounds for your festivities. Proceeds will benefit both your organization and the Orson Talbot Foundation."

Sara called attention to Isidoro, who designed the drawings. He would maintain the grounds. She called attention to Beni Noa, who had almost single-handedly built the gazebo out front. He would continue to oversee building the rear structures.

Huxley made the last presentation. He wasted no time and pulled the cover off a large black shatter-resistant case, opened it, and carefully pulled out the item and lifted it for all to see.

"The Orson Talbot Foundation has acquired one of these," he said. "It's a thermal imager." Quite a few didn't understand what that meant, but Norwood did. The Sacramento Police Department already had a couple. Upton Zeno crowded in closer, almost drooling. Huxley said "I recently learned that the Department of Defense's Drug Program denied a request to the Sacramento Sheriff's Department, so they're working on a grant to try to purchase one of these. In fact, Rio Vista is the only town in Solano County south of here to have one."

Many in the crowd remained mystified. Upton shifted from one foot to the other.

Huxley continued. "This device is so sensitive it can pick up heat transferred from a hand to another object. It can sense the heat left by footprints and car tires." He paused only a couple of seconds. "It can pinpoint graves."

A collective gasp rolled through the rooms. Finally, Upton stepped forward and held out his hands. "Can I just hold it?" he asked.

"Sure, go ahead," Huxley said, loud enough for all to hear. He looked around the room, and everyone seemed suspended in anticipation. "There's another one here," he said, pointing to one unopened container. "That one's for your department."

The crowd screamed and clapped. Someone slapped Upton on the back. He nervously returned the imager to avoid dropping it. Norwood came to shake Upton's hand. He wrapped his arm around Sara's shoulders. "It's been a better place, this Delta," he said. "After this hometown girl came home."

The crowd began to thin. Caren herself carried out one of the two large paintings she won in the auction. Without a doubt, she got the best of the lot, if Sara was to pick. Almost three-dozen works of art were purchased.

Esmerelda helped send Zoki out the door, conning him out of his leftovers. She joined them in the parlor, where they congregated around the magnificent Christmas tree. "I'll have to get busy painting again to replace all the pieces we just sold," Daphine said. "Wow."

"I'm glad you decided not to offer the Peregrine Falcons," Pierce said.

"You're off to Asia again," Esmerelda said to Huxley. "I wish I could go. I'm still strong. I don't know why they keep turning me down."

Gravel crunched. Fredrik, who had been by earlier in the evening and left again, returned to retrieve Esmerelda. Now he, too, would get to sample Zoki's delights, albeit reheated.

As Daphine packed her things to leave, she said, "Thousands, you guys. Did you know that? Tens of thousands."

"Tens?" Huxley asked.

"Look at this." She produced a pouch of checks people wrote to pay for the art. "Some of these are outright donations to OTF." She handed the pouch to Sara. "Some are made out in my name. We can settle up later." Before she and Pierce walked out the door, she turned, pointed upward, and said, "The front bedroom, the one overlooking the river. I'll take that one."

* * *

At once, the house was empty and eerily quiet. Sara turned her back on the mess. The cleaning crew would come by the next afternoon. She and Huxley grabbed drinks and climbed the showcase steps with arms wrapped around each other. They showered and then lay down to talk. They always talked.

"Maybe once Daph gets on her feet, she can visit China," Sara said.

"I hope so," he said. "In the least, Daphine going there might get through to Jade that her mother loves her."

"Hux," Sara said. "I'm surprised Esmerelda hasn't gone with you to Vietnam."

"They won't fund her," Huxley said as he stretched and yawned. "She's considered too elderly to make the trip."

"What? I saw the photos on the website. Some of your guys are ancient."

"But they're ex-military, been returning there for years." He scooted closer to her on the bed.

"Didn't you once say that trail was now wide enough for a Humvee?"

Huxley eyed her. "They won't fund her, Sara. She's too elderly, never been through a trek like that, and they won't be responsible for her health."

Sara leaned against him, and they kissed briefly. "Her health? Sweetheart, what about her mental health? If Betty's remains are never found, at least Esmerelda will die closer to peace knowing she walked where her daughter last walked."

Epilogue

"Family is everything," Huxley said.

"Turn here," Sara said. "I'll show you where they're buried."

They were on their way back from the doctor's office in Sacramento, a visit Sara dreaded. She was nauseous and thankful that Huxley drove.

Strong Delta winds blew. They stood at the foot of the graves. He zippered his jacket and went to stand beside a tree, to give her time alone. The tree had been a sapling the year her family died.

Sara cleaned twigs off the graves and threw them under the nearby bushes. She paused in front of her parents' headstone. Try as she might, she could only see them now as skeletons. She sighed heavily. "I hope you two made amends at the gate," she said softly. "And that St. Peter saw fit to let you in." She stooped down in the wet grass in front of their headstone and poked the spikes of a Christmas wreath into the ground. Her arms ached doing so.

She stepped in front of Starla's headstone, stooped down, and planted another wreath. For the first time, she saw Starla as a skeleton in a faded pink dress; the white bows dingy, the fuzzy bunny now a limp rag. She closed her eyes and shook to dispel the scene. Tears came as she remembered Starla singing to her from the front seat of the car: '*When you feel there is no one to guide you... look for a star.'* She willed herself to see Starla like she needed to remember, lying peacefully and whole in her sweet pink dress with clean white bows and the fuzzy bunny tucked under her arm.

Sara rubbed her arms against the cold and felt the pain. The barrage of inoculations made her stomach queasy. She glanced over at Huxley. His love for her showed in his magnificent eyes. They could finally get on with the rest of their lives. He joined her and stooped down beside her.

"Sis, I'm going with Huxley to Oregon for Christmas," she said, talking to Starla's headstone. "And guess what? *I'm* sponsoring Esmerelda, and she and I will go with Huxley to Vietnam in the spring."

* * *

We hope you enjoyed reading *River Bones*. If you have a moment, please leave us a review - even if it's a short one. We want to hear from you.

The story continues in *The Howling Cliffs*.

Want to get notified when one of Creativia's books is free to download? Join our spam-free newsletter at www.creativia.org.

Best regards,
Mary Deal and the Creativia Team

About the Author

Mary Deal is an Amazon bestselling, award-winning, multi-genre author of suspense/thrillers, a short story collection, writers' references, and self-help. She is a Pushcart Prize nominee, Artist and Photographer, and former newspaper columnist and magazine editor.

Mary's first feature screenplay, *Sea Storm*, and *Chin Face*, a short story, was nominated into the Semi-Finals in a *Moondance International Film Festival* competition.

One of Mary's many short stories, *The Last Thing I Do*, appeared in the anthology, *Freckles to Wrinkles*, by *Silver Boomer Books*, and was nominated for the coveted *Pushcart Prize*.

She has traveled a great deal and has a lifetime of diverse experiences, all of which remain as fodder for her fiction. A native of California's Sacramento River Delta, where some of her stories are set, she has also lived in England, the Caribbean, the Hawaiian Islands, and now resides in Scottsdale, Arizona. In addition to originals and art prints, her paintings and photography are also used to create gorgeous personal and household products.

Books by the Author

River Bones (Sara Mason Mysteries 1)
The Howling Cliffs (Sara Mason Mysteries 2)
Down To The Needle
The Ka
Legacy of the Tropics
Off Center In The Attic
Sea Cliff: A Love Story

Find Her Online

Her Website: https://www.marydeal.com
Amazon Author Page: http://tinyurl.com/y9ca5u8t
Barnes & Noble: http://tinyurl.com/o7keqf7
FaceBook: http://www.facebook.com/mdeal
Facebook Author Page:
https://www.facebook.com/MaryDealBooks
Facebook 4 & 5 STAR Book Reviews:
https://www.facebook.com/groups/powerwriters
Twitter: http://twitter.com/Mary_Deal
Linked In: http://www.linkedin.com/in/marydeal
Goodreads: https://www.goodreads.com/MaryDeal
Cold Coffee Press: www.coldcoffeepress.com/mary-deal-books/
Instagram: https:www.instagram.com/mary.l.deal

Her Art Galleries

Mary Deal Fine Art
http://www.marydealfineart.com
Island Image Gallery
http://www.islandimagegallery.com
Mary Deal Fine Art and Photography
https://www.facebook.com/MDealArt
Pinterest
https://www.pinterest.com/1deal

Lightning Source UK Ltd.
Milton Keynes UK
UKHW022232091121
393700UK00003B/315